Dark
Before
Dawn

Book Three *of the*
ARCHANGEL PROPHECIES

MONICA McGURK

RIVER GROVE
BOOKS

This book is a work of fiction. Names, characters, businesses, organizations, places, events, and incidents are either a product of the author's imagination or are used fictitiously. Any resemblance to actual persons, living or dead, events, or locales is entirely coincidental.

Published by River Grove Books
Austin, TX
www.rivergrovebooks.com

Distributed by River Grove Books

Design and composition by Greenleaf Book Group
Cover design by Greenleaf Book Group and Kim Lance
Cover images: [girl] ©Thinkstock/disqis; [oil rig] ©Thinkstock/DanielAzocar; [fire wing] ©Thinkstock/-M-I-S-H-A-; [hair] ©Thinkstock/whiteisthecolor;

Cataloging-in-Publication data is available.

Print ISBN: 978-1-63299-085-3

eBook ISBN: 978-1-63299-086-0

First Edition

To those who fought but did not survive—

may you be remembered.

AUTHOR'S NOTE

Though this book is written in the fantasy genre, many of the topics it discusses are serious and real. While I have made every attempt to depict them in a way that is respectful and age appropriate, I would strongly advise discussing the contents of this book with your teen and having a meaningful conversation about ways to keep oneself and one's community safe from Domestic Minor Sex Trafficking (DMST).

If you are a teacher and wish to take the fight against DMST into your middle school or high school classroom, please visit my website, monicamcgurk.com, to access free curricular resources to integrate *The Archangel Prophecies*, DMST, and modern-day slavery into your language arts, social studies, or other curricular plans.

PROLOGUE

They'd left the window open. The gauzy, Swiss-dotted curtain billowed and danced on the spring breeze that filtered through the screen.

It was twilight, the fireflies just starting to flash and flicker in the deepening navy of the Atlanta sky. The baby—still on the seemingly endless cycle of sleeping and eating that cut up the day into three-hour increments—had been put down for her evening nap, giving her mother a precious few hours in which to nap herself. Her mother was just down the hall, the baby monitor transmitting each rustle of blanket and each little coo.

The curtains billowed again. But this time, a wisp of shimmering smoke rode in with the breeze. Another, then another. They buffeted the delicate fabric of the curtain, writhing and twisting together, as a fourth delicate filament ghosted in to join them. Then the four danced together, merging in a flash of brilliant light that for a split second illuminated the darkness that was seeping into the room with the setting of the sun.

The pulsating mass floated over to the head of the crib, a slight electric tang filling the air as it settled and began to flicker.

And then, one by one, the smoky shapes separated out and took up their forms. Bone. Flesh. Wings.

Muscle-bound and armor-plated, the four angels stood before the crib and peered in. They had hard-planed faces chiseled by worry and war, but as they gazed on the sleeping babe, their soft eyes melted.

One, an older man, shook out his wings, releasing a soft rush of wind. The blond angel at the head of the crib shot him a dirty look, then looked pointedly at the baby monitor. The offending angel—Arthur—rolled his eyes and extended his wings again, unfurling them just to make his point before turning the knob on the monitor to "off."

"Really, Michael. Mona's not going to notice a thing," Arthur argued. "She's exhausted. She's so afraid of missing something; keeps saying she wants to take advantage of every moment. I just sent her and Hope both to catch some sleep. Rocked Rorie to sleep myself."

The archangel Michael ignored him, turning back to the crib.

"Aurora," he breathed, leaning over the railing to get a better look at the child. "Our Rorie."

As Arthur—Mona's confidant, now more than ever—had explained to the other angels, Mona had gone through agonies in choosing her baby's name. She had wanted something to honor her late husband, Don, but hadn't wanted it to be obvious. The play on words she'd come up with—Aurora, meaning dawn—was clever, just like Mona. Michael wondered if the allusion to the goddess who renewed herself daily, a symbol of hope and of life's eternal wheel, was deliberate, too.

Aurora was tiny, and apparently feisty, having wriggled out of her swaddling to splay herself out across the mattress, defying

Arthur's plans for her nap. Her skin was so delicate that it was nearly transparent. Michael reached out a finger to follow the tiny trail of veins that stretched like lace across her open palm.

In her sleep, she grasped his finger, refusing to give it up.

"She's got a kung fu grip." Michael chuckled, wiggling his finger.

The lone female angel, Gabrielle, moved to Michael's side and tucked her arm into his.

"She's beautiful, Michael. Truly beautiful." Her brows knit together as she looked at the baby, as if she was puzzling over something.

"I just wish Mona would have changed her mind and allowed for a real christening," Raph, the last angel in the group, added gruffly. "Then we wouldn't have to waste our time and abandon our posts like this."

"She'd see it as giving in to Don's old religious whims," Michael said, the vein in his forehead pulsing slightly at Raph's reproach. "Besides, there's no need. We're here now. We'll be her witnesses. Heaven can spare us for the few minutes it will take."

"Real-life fairy godmothers," Arthur chimed in, grinning as he tried to lighten the mood.

Michael smiled despite himself. "Something like that."

He gently pulled his finger from Rorie's fist. "Everyone, it's time."

They took their places around the girl, each warrior angel taking one side of the crib, Michael, their captain, retaining his place at the head. Arthur shifted on his feet.

"It doesn't seem right, doing this without Enoch. Or Hope." He looked pointedly at Michael.

"Enoch isn't a soldier," Michael responded, his eyes never moving from where they watched the slight rise and fall of Rorie's breathing, "and the time may come when we will have to fight for her. It wouldn't do to make pledges we cannot keep. And as for

Hope—" His voice broke with emotion as he spoke her name. "It's too soon. She cannot know of us. Not yet."

"I don't know why you don't tell her, Michael," Arthur argued softly. "About the choice God offered to her. You say nothing, letting her wonder if you have risen or not, letting her believe you have left her alone. Why?"

Michael's jaw stiffened. "We'll not speak of it."

"But why?" Arthur asked. "You know she still spends all of her spare time looking for you. Her bedroom walls are covered with things she's printed off from her Internet searches, dribs and drabs that she's hoping add up to proof that you are resurrected. She's suffering, and you let her."

"Do you think it's fair, Michael, to keep her choice from her?" Gabrielle added, carefully appraising Michael's reaction. She did not wish to goad him, and in all honesty, she thought the idea of the girl and Michael being joined together absurd. But the sooner the ridiculous offer was seen and rejected for what it was—an impossibility—the better.

The muscle in Michael's jaw tensed. He stood up, stretching his wings wide. Even in the half-light of dusk, they glinted and sparkled, majestic.

"It's too soon to thrust such a choice upon her. I will tell her when the time is right. For now, it is just us four. Now." He wrapped the crib rail in his massive hand, the scarred and bruised flesh a contrast against the bright, carefully turned pine. "Let us begin."

A sense of gravity came upon them as they considered what they were about to do.

"I'll start," Arthur said.

The angels closed their eyes as if by silent agreement, and Arthur reached a gigantic hand over the baby's head in blessing.

"Daughter of God, we gather here as witnesses and to pledge

you to Him. In His name, I offer you the gift of laughter to sustain you on your journey."

He withdrew his hand from the baby, and Gabrielle's took its place.

"I offer you the gift of insight," she intoned, the corners of her mouth drawing down as she voiced the words. "May it guide you to wisdom in His path."

"I offer you the gift of strength, to sustain you in times of physical and emotional duress," Raph mumbled under his breath, the words rushed as if he were anxious to get it over with. "Don't think I'm going to like Hope, or any humans now, just because of a baby," he hastened to add, his hand hesitating before reaching down to caress the crown of Rorie's head.

Michael arched a brow, silencing Raph. "Heaven forbid," he answered.

Raph snatched his hand back, chastened.

It was Michael's turn. He let the uncomfortable silence settle around him as the angels shuffled anxiously, waiting for him to say his part. Then, slowly, he stretched his muscular, scarred arm above the baby.

"I offer you bravery. May you have no need for it."

He raised he eyes and looked sternly at each of his comrades in turn. "Together, we pledge to come to your aid, to protect you in your need, to be your sword and your shield. In the name of Heaven, I swear it."

"I swear it," Gabrielle breathed, her shoulders sagging with resignation as the promise was drawn from her.

"I swear it," Arthur added, his normally twinkling eyes suddenly grave.

There was a long pause. Michael looked at Raph, barely containing his impatience.

"I swear it," Raph muttered, and the tension in Michael's face finally dissipated.

"Now it is done. We are bound to her." Michael turned to the other angels. "I know you do this for me, and for no other reason. I thank you."

"Look, she's awake," Gabrielle whispered.

Everyone turned back to the crib. Rorie's eyes were wide open, a startling blue that was nearly violet. Her tiny arms flailed as she stretched, unable to control the movements of her body. Arthur leaned over to draw the baby up in his arms.

"Hello, baby girl. You're safe here, with us." He held Rorie against his massive chest, the baby's wee chin propped against his armored shoulder. "She's such a good baby," he explained to nobody in particular. "She barely ever cries."

Michael watched, his eyes glued intently on the tiny bundle.

Gabrielle winced. She had seen that longing look on his face before as he'd hidden in the shadows, watching Hope holding her baby sister in much the same way. She knew that he was imagining a future—a future with Hope. She shook her head. Why he was torturing himself with the unseemly idea of becoming human? There was so much else at stake in the world.

"We should leave," Gabrielle insisted, moving across the room to remove the baby from Arthur's arms. "You should be back at the Gates to oversee the changing of the guard," she said pointedly to Michael. "And we should be there to review the troops."

"The Fallen have been quiet for some time," Michael protested, his eyes lingering on Rorie. He looked up to see the stony faces staring at him, resentful. Only Arthur's face held a sheepish trace of understanding. "But yes, of course, you are right," Michael whispered, clearing his throat.

Gabrielle buried her nose in Rorie's fine, wispy hair, breathing in her sweet baby smell and avoiding Michael's gaze. Her scent was intoxicating, Gabrielle had to admit. But they had better things to do than moon over a helpless human. She laid the baby down, turning away from the crib without another look.

"Don't forget where your real duties lie, Michael. The Fallen may have been beaten back for the moment, but they could storm the Gates again at any time. Whatever promises we make here, our first responsibility lies in Heaven. And with God's chosen ones— not yours."

Michael's eyes flashed, the cerulean deepening to near-black.

"I am aware of my obligations—as well as my debts," he snapped, fixing Gabrielle with a cold stare. He let his eyes drift to Raph, who stood scowling in defiance, hands curled. "They are mine to bear. Not yours. And I will choose when and how I fulfill them." He turned back to the babe, his face softening. "Goodbye, Rorie," he whispered, backing away from the crib. "You'll keep us posted, won't you, Arthur?"

Arthur nodded. "Of course. Just like always. It will be easier now that Mona has decided to move into a more secure home. It will be strange for Hope, I'm sure, being behind a fence and gate, but with me living in their carriage house, I'll be sure they're kept safe, whether it's from traffickers or the Fallen. I'll be there to watch over them."

Michael turned to face him, his face somber. "Thank you," he said simply, his voice cracking with emotion.

Arthur clasped Michael's shoulder, warrior to warrior, brother to brother, the understanding between them so deep that there was no need for words. With a shimmer, Arthur put away his wings, turning back into his human guise before slipping out of the room.

Wordlessly, the other angels began their own metamorphoses. From flesh and bone to shadow and air they shifted, swirling about the crib for a final look at the special little girl they had promised to watch over; the special little girl whose father had been sacrificed for the fulfillment of an angelic prophecy not even a year ago. As they took their leave, they swallowed their resentment out of respect for Michael's role as commander of the heavenly army, and out of respect for Hope, for whom, they knew, Michael had done this. The battle against the Fallen had not yet been won, Michael knew, and if he couldn't yet be with Hope, he could at least be sure to protect her and those she loved.

Each angel had his own thoughts as they left the baby. That it was unfair being pressed into service in this way. That it would never come to pass that they would need to defend her, anyway, making it an empty promise, a gesture. That the babe seemed so sweet and helpless, yet strangely wise with her big, serious eyes.

And the wistful thought that Gabrielle kept brooding upon: that Hope, herself, looked so natural with a child in her arms; that she would be so beautiful with a child of her own. Something that might not ever happen if Michael continued to let her cling to his memory. It wasn't suitable for an angel of his stature; as much as Gabrielle admired Hope's grit, she was, at the end of it all, just a human. Perhaps it was best for Michael to harden himself to his feelings for her. Perhaps she should remind him of that, one day.

They kept these feelings and thoughts to themselves as they floated away from the crib and out the window.

And so they were too preoccupied to notice that there was another presence hovering in the shadowy corner of the nursery.

The presence waited for them to be gone before moving from the dark corners of the room and faintly materializing itself beside the crib. It was an angel, too, but of a different kind.

"They brought you gifts," the angel sneered, "but they didn't invite me to their party. God has claimed you, now, and I suppose they think that will keep you safe. But I have brought you my own gift. I will bestow upon you the gift of endurance."

His lips twisted into a strange smile as he held his hand over the child, his image flickering, too weak to remain substantial.

"May you have endurance to bear your suffering well. For suffer you shall. May you be able to bear the pain of doubt. Of rejection. Of loneliness. Of fear. Of pain so excruciating, it makes you grind and crack your teeth and cry out for the release of death."

He paused, closing his eyes to imagine all the pain he could inflict upon this babe, so innocent.

He knew pain. After millennia of rejecting the One on High, he was crazed by it, hollowed out in his very soul from enduring the constancy of it.

Yes, he smiled to himself. He knew pain.

"May you endure all these things and yet not pass unto your death. May you be forced to carry on in the grip of loss so profound it would break the hearts of other mortals and send them early to their graves."

He let his eyes flutter open and rest upon the tiny girl, who stared up at him, wide-eyed, unmoved by his speech. He reached down and touched her cheek with his rough hand, which was so translucent it seemed to be absorbed into her very skin.

"You will be the instrument of my vengeance upon Michael and Hope," he whispered, eyes glittering in the dark. "Eventually, I will have my way."

The doorknob turned.

In a flash, the angel vanished.

Mona, the baby's mother, walked into the room. She paused just inside the doorway, tilting her head and sniffing the air. The curtain fluttered, the chill of the evening air seeping into the room. Mona pulled her fuzzy, worn bathrobe closer about her before striding over and firmly closing the window sash, shutting out the cold. She sniffed the air again, alert to any danger, real or imagined.

"I'll have to check the gas," she said to herself before walking to the crib and swooping her baby daughter up in her arms. "For an instant, I thought it smelled like sulfur."

one

HOPE

Even though we'd moved to the mansion in Buckhead in time for my junior year of high school, I'd never really felt at home in it. I could rationalize why we'd made the move—for safety, Mom had reasoned, after the mysterious murder of my father. His death may have been part of the general mayhem of rioting that had swept the world only a few years ago, or it may have been a targeted killing in retaliation for my disruption of a human trafficking ring.

But whichever it was, I knew there was another reason for us all to be kept behind lock and key, one of which my mother was unaware: I had interfered with the Fallen Angels in their fight to regain Heaven. No doubt, they hadn't forgiven me, and there was an ever-present risk that they might hunt me down for revenge.

Never mind that many of them had reentered Heaven peacefully because of what I had done. What Michael—the archangel I'd fallen in love with—had done. Our search for the Key to Heaven had ended with us realizing that his death was the sacrifice that would earn forgiveness for all the Fallen Angels, allowing any of them to return to Heaven and to a relationship with God.

Michael.

A wave of loneliness engulfed me as I continued to pack my workout bag for Krav Maga class that evening. I'd only recently removed the layers of newspaper articles and Internet printouts that had papered over my bedroom walls, the detritus of my search for evidence that Michael had been resurrected after all and was back to his earthly work defending the people of God. But I had really never stopped searching for proof. And though the papers were gone, their faint outlines, bleached into the wall by the sun, reminded me every day of what I had forfeited.

Over the past two years, however, I had gradually accepted that he was lost to me. My search, now, was one of habit. My loneliness was an ever-present friend, something comfortable and familiar that I now recognized as an immutable fact of life, just as real and unchanging as the stars in the sky or the chill of a December evening. I came to welcome, even seek out, my solitude, like the cold underside of a pillow when I lay in bed, gripped by fever and insomnia. It was as much a part of me as the Mark etched across the back of my neck, delicate as lace, branding me as the Bearer of the Key in the ancient prophecy that I had played a part in. Only my family and the few people who knew the story of my disappearance—even if they didn't know the full truth of the time I had spent on the run with Michael—were let into my circle.

Nobody was surprised that I had struggled to adjust after everything that had happened to me. They couldn't exactly relate to the vicissitudes of my emotions—caution swinging to confidence, frenzied activity ceding to paralysis, the desire for isolation giving way to a yearning for connection—or to what provoked them. But my tiny makeshift family—my mother and Arthur, the family friend who'd moved into our carriage house, who'd woven himself into the fabric of our family over the past two years—had recognized that while academically I would manage just fine, socially I was not quite ready to be plunged into the teeming cauldron of campus life. My mother had swiftly agreed to my request for a gap year, and so I found myself living at home, staring at the shadow- and sun-dappled walls of my bedroom in early evening, alone again.

A knock at the front door interrupted my reminiscing. I hadn't heard anyone buzzed up to the house from the gate—Arthur was usually a stickler for following the rules, careful about our privacy and safety. I glanced at the clock: it was getting late. My mother wouldn't be home for another hour, bringing Rorie from her music class. I could feel the frown knotting my face into a map of worry as I worked my way downstairs to the front door, dragging my gear behind me.

I swung it open wide, peering out to see just exactly who it was that Arthur had cleared to come up the drive.

"Hello, Hope."

I heard his voice—a rich, throaty, familiar growl—before I saw him.

His lean body was wrapped in a gray tank top, a chambray shirt, and worn desert fatigue cargo pants that clung to every muscle. His golden skin glowed, the aftermath of time spent in some exotic location, or perhaps evidence of the heavenly fire that lit him from within. My eyes raced over the length of him, years of worry and fear driving me to confirm, now that he stood before me, that he was whole, that he was indeed real.

Michael.

His blue eyes flashed with amusement as I stared at him.

"Aren't you going to say something?" he asked, as if it were perfectly natural that after over two years of nothing—no communication, no sightings, nothing at all—he just turned up on my doorstep unannounced. A shiver of fear, a frisson of doubt, crept up my spine.

I hung back in the doorway.

"How do I know it's really you?" I whispered.

He gripped his tank top, yanking it down to bare his chest. There, over his heart, was the imprint of a hand. My hand. It was a scar I'd left one windswept morning on a faraway Irish isle, when we'd finally opened up to each other, proof that by absorbing his energy and breaking down his defenses, I could mark him as my own, just as he had claimed me.

I shook my head, refusing to believe. "Anybody could do that. Any angel could disguise himself as you."

He cocked his head, fixing me with an appraising look. "Could any angel do this?"

He held out his hand, palm outstretched, waiting for me to take it. Cautiously, I reached out to touch him. The surge of heat between us was familiar, something I'd dreamt about for hundreds of nights since Michael had been lost to me. I closed my eyes as he wound his fingers around mine.

"Here," he whispered, pulling me closer. I opened my eyes to watch as he unwound our fingers and placed my splayed hand over his heart, my hand perfectly matching the imprint burned on his skin.

A rush of memories and thoughts came coursing to me, unbidden. I felt the anger and frustration, his fear that I was hiding something from him while we waited in Ireland, searching together for the Key. Over and over again—under a star-washed sky in Istanbul, in the cramped Irish lighthouse, in the spare hotel room in France—the memories of his longing for me washed over me. I felt his sadness and disappointment when he realized I'd distrusted him so much that I'd unwittingly betrayed him to my own Guardian Angel—putting him on a collision course with the Fallen who were hunting him down. I felt the shock of pain as the rock—the same rock that had felled Abel—crushed his skull, wielded by Lucas, the leader of the Fallen. I felt the cold stones under his shoulder blades as he lay on the floor of the chapel in France, the life ebbing out of him.

I jerked my hand away, unable to relive the despair and helplessness that had engulfed me as I had watched him die before my eyes. But now the thing I'd hoped for, had waited for—the thing I'd finally given up on—had happened.

Michael had come back to me.

I stared at him, tongue-tied, my face flushed under his watchful gaze. Underneath the shock, a cold, hard pit was forming in my stomach.

"Oh," he said. "Before I forget, there's someone I want you to meet. Well, not exactly meet. You'll see." He whistled, and I heard a joyous bark. A large yellow dog came streaking across the yard. It leaped up the steps to sit obediently at Michael's feet. The dog's long tongue lolled outside his mouth, the look on his face almost a grin. He barked again, looking at me expectantly.

I stooped to my knees. "Is this—?"

Michael laughed. "The very same. We went back to Istanbul and found your stray. Only he's not a stray now. Hope, say hello to Ollie."

I held out my hand, and Ollie wiggled up to me, demanding to be petted. I scratched behind his ears, dumbfounded. My dog. Michael. It was too much to take in. Reluctantly, I stood up, leaving Ollie to wait for more attention.

"How'd you get in here?" I finally managed to spit out, forcing my heart to shutter itself before any of the joy, or the pain, could leak through to the surface. "No, wait, forget I asked that. Of course, I'm being stupid. You're an archangel. You can get in here however and whenever you want."

And then my nostrils flared as I let one emotion filter itself to the top of the queue: anger. "You just chose to not do so for over two years."

He flinched, ever so slightly. "I checked in at the gate, just like anybody else. Arthur let me in."

"Why would Arthur let you in?" I said, my confusion momentarily overriding my anger. "He doesn't know who you are. There's no way he'd let a total stranger wander unescorted up the drive. Wait a minute—how do you even know who Arthur is?"

Michael shuffled uncomfortably under my withering glare. "I may have met him before."

I stared at him in disbelief.

"Are you telling me what I think you're telling me? Is he one of you?"

He nodded. "We, um. We go way back. He's been watching over you for me while I've been gone."

"While you've been gone? That's what you call it? You planted one of your angel goons to keep tabs on me so you could go off and do whatever the hell it is you've been doing? That's great, Michael. Just great."

I let my anger have its way, drawing strength from the intensity of it. I realized, of course, that there would have been no way for me to know Arthur was an angel—no way for anybody to ever detect an angel in their midst—unless he wanted me to know. But still, it stung to know that the friendship Arthur exhibited toward us all— indeed, his place within our odd, broken family—had been a part of Michael's plan. I could feel hot tears threatening to brim over.

I pushed past him. "I have to go to my exercise class," I shot over my shoulder, picking up the pace as he trailed behind me.

"Hope, please, you don't understand. Give me a chance to explain."

His strong hand clamped down on my arm. A burst of warmth shot through me, my body betraying me to the thrill of his touch. Angry with my body, angry with him, I let my instincts take over and jabbed him hard in the solar plexus with one of my Krav Maga moves. I felt the hard muscles pop as I connected with my elbow, heard the sharp intake of his breath. He let go of my arm and dropped to the pavement.

Without another glance back, I threw open the door of the SUV and tossed in my bag, climbing up behind it into the driver's seat. Without another glance, I turned the key and floored it to back out of the driveway, my only object to get as far away from him as possible.

I felt a thump and heard the sound of something hitting steel. I darted a panicked look at my rear view mirror.

"Hope, please," Michael begged, looming larger than life behind me. Irritation surged through my veins.

"Get in the car," I ordered. Without hesitating, he opened the door for Ollie, who clambered into the backseat, and then he climbed in beside me. He'd barely made it into the car before I hit the gas, screaming down the driveway.

We dropped Ollie off at the gatehouse, where I glared at Arthur. "Keep an eye on Ollie for me. Give him some cheese or something," I spat, daring him to say a word.

He let us out, and I drove without thinking, blinking away the angry tears that kept threatening to overwhelm me. A rush of questions attacked my fragile psyche, the defenses I'd so carefully constructed over the last two years crumbling under the assault.

For how long had Michael been resurrected? Exactly when had he arranged for Arthur to guard my family and me? Why hadn't he told me he was alive? What was he doing on my front steps? And why? Why now, after two years, had he finally shown up?

But I couldn't bring myself to ask Michael any of these questions. I couldn't even stand to look at him in the seat next to me. Instead, my anger and fear—fear that he'd abandoned me because he had never really loved me—simmered and roiled inside me, making me sick to my stomach.

I pulled into a quiet parking lot. I looked up from where I was hunched over the steering wheel, crying, and realized I'd wound my way through the vaunted Atlanta traffic to the only real sanctuary I'd ever known: the quiet cemetery that held my father's grave.

Abandoning the car, I ran through the wrought iron gates and stumbled over the spotty grass, dotted with lumps of red Georgia clay and knotted with exposed tree roots, to seek his headstone. But Michael was waiting for me under the leafy expanse of a great oak tree. He'd used his angelic powers to beat me to the grave.

I took a deep breath and wiped my face with the back of my hand.

"Do you know what you did to me?" I challenged him, daring him to argue with me. "Do you know what happened after you left me here to fend for myself?"

Michael dropped his head in silent acknowledgment of my need to speak. Did he have any idea how much I had hurt? Was still hurting?

"I waited. You didn't come," I said. My voice had an angry edge to it, surprising even me. "I thought you would rise again. I escaped from the chapel where you died. I made my way back home. I waited for three days. Three days came and went. But you didn't come."

My voice was trembling, the pain feeling fresh.

"So then I counted for seven days, like the Creation. And then for forty days and nights, and just about any other biblical number I could come up with. But you didn't come back for me.

"My dad died. He was killed, Michael, because of what we did," I added, my voice breaking as I gestured at the cold granite headstone before us. "You knew that. You knew. And still you didn't come."

I stopped there, unable to say more, knowing the misery and accusation in my voice was clear enough.

He shoved his hands deep inside his pockets. But his sapphire eyes never looked away.

"I'm so sorry, Hope. So, so sorry about your father. I never intended, never thought, that anything like that would happen. My whole reason for disguising myself as him in Las Vegas was to protect him. You know that."

"It didn't work."

He nodded solemnly, letting my resentment wash over him, absorbing it with kindness.

"I'm sorry." His simple apology deflated my fury, leaving me to feel the emptiness that had been my constant companion for these long two years.

"I blamed myself, you know," I said. "And what was worse was that every day, I had to look my mother in the eye knowing that it was my fault my father had died, knowing that even if I didn't mean to do it, it was me who'd snuffed the light out of her eyes. The guilt was eating me alive. I nearly went crazy. I was obsessed with trying to find you—paranoid—the walls of my bedroom were plastered over with pages and pages of news stories that I'd searched again and again, just for some sign that you were out there. I waited and waited and waited for you. And now, just when I've taken every-thing down, just when I'd accepted that you were never coming back and put it all behind me; when I'd started to adjust to the idea of life without you, you choose to show up."

"I never left you. Not really. And I always ensured you were safe."

"This isn't about me being safe! I never cared about that."

"You should have."

"Stop telling me how I'm supposed to feel!"

"I'm sorry."

I was on a roll now, barely able to register his contrition as I vented all the anger and shame I'd pent up.

"'Sorry' doesn't explain why you didn't come back. Tell me: if you were resurrected, why didn't you come back right away? Was I not good enough for you?" My voice rose, carrying through the tall pines and shady oaks, over the crumbling angels and crucifixes that dotted the graveyard. "Was I too plain, too common for the King of Heaven or whatever it is they call you now?"

He rubbed his hand over his face, unable to speak for a moment. I watched his Adam's apple bob in his throat, fixing my stare on it to avoid getting caught up in his blue eyes. Then I dropped my gaze to the clay beneath my feet. I needed to have a clear head to get the answers I deserved.

"It was you, wasn't it? Here, in the cemetery. On the day we buried my dad."

I looked up to see his answer. He nodded, eyeing me warily.

"How long had you been here? I mean, here on Earth. Alive. Watching. How long had you been resurrected by that point?"

He cleared his throat. "Not long." He stood awkwardly, uncomfortable under my critical eye. "I remember you had cut your hair," he whispered. "You've kept it short."

My fingers moved awkwardly to the hair at the nape of my neck. I remembered the day when, desperate to feel anything, I had hacked my hair away, leaving it in clumps on the floor so that my Mark was visible to all. I flushed, wondering if it was only habit, now, to wear my hair cropped, or if it still meant something.

I pushed the unwelcome thought from my mind, crossing my arms to square off against Michael.

"Explain yourself."

"Here? Now?" He leaned into his questions, incredulous, looking around at the empty graveyard.

"Whatever you have to say, I want you to say it here. In front of my dad."

He clamped his lips closed into a tight, hard line.

"I don't remember you being this . . ."

"This pushy?" I finished for him.

His face softened. "I was going to say prickly."

I scuffed my toe in the dirt, trying to stifle the grin that was threatening to steal across my face. "Don't think you can sweet-talk me. Answer me."

The light spring breeze skittered through the leaves, their gentle rustle filling the graveyard like a lover's longing sigh before fading away.

"You shouldn't have doubted yourself," Michael began, his voice low and steady. "You were right. I did rise. But when I did, all Hell was breaking loose. Literally. I had to take my place as the leader of the Host to fight off the armies of the Fallen until I knew Heaven was safe. It was my duty. So I couldn't come. Not for a while, anyway."

I looked at him skeptically. Memories of my feverish dreams of bloodshed and war, proof that he was telling me the truth, warred with the defenses I had built up to protect myself against the pain of loving him.

His eyes softened, their blue sparkling like the seas, and I melted just a little.

"The Fallen misunderstood the Prophecy. They thought they could storm Heaven once I was gone. But they were wrong." His voice rang out, betraying the slightest hint of pride. "Only the ones seeking real forgiveness managed to cross over. You should have seen it, Hope—the look in their eyes when they realized they'd gained their freedom, after centuries of pain. At long last they had release, and grace. And that was thanks to you."

He cleared the space between us, reaching out his hand. I looked at it carefully before taking it. Then I turned it over and pushed up his sleeve. There, against the pale skin, was the jagged scar where broken bone had once pierced his arm, evidence of the brutal beating he'd received at the hands of the Fallen after they'd trapped us with the Key.

I ran my finger along the scar on his arm, let my hands wander to his face, brushing away the golden blond hair that had fallen onto his forehead. The scar tissue I felt under my fingertips was rough and real on his head. I felt a slight impression in the place where Lucas, the leader of The Fallen, had crushed his skull with the Key, the same rock Cain had used to slay Abel.

There were other wounds, wounds I knew Michael would have received in more recent service to God: protecting the persecuted, refugees or political prisoners or who knew whom from the vagaries of fate here on Earth. They would fade quickly, I knew, but they stood in witness to his continuing role as the protector of mankind.

I brushed against the angry welt on his neck, the fresh cut above his eye that was just beginning to scab over, and he winced.

"The battle was a fierce one," he said, remembering, his eyes glinting as he imagined the violence again. "They were so many that the skies turned black as they swarmed upon our gates. The stench of sulfur was suffocating, the air split by their shrill battle cries. My army stood its ground, repulsing their charges, holding the line under wave after wave of attacks. Day turned to night, the Fallen growing more desperate as they failed to reach their goal. And still they kept coming; still their fiery swords shrieked as they swooped through the air, clashing on armor with a sound like thunder; still the days turned.

"They'd never dared to storm Heaven's gates before. And they'd never fought as wildly. But ultimately we prevailed. Many good angels fell to make it so."

I sucked my breath in. "Raph? Did he—?"

Michael shook his head. "God was with him, as he was with Gabrielle, and they were unharmed.

"In the end, we couldn't quell the horde until Lucas himself was struck down, still clutching that damned rock in his hand like a talisman and swearing he would have his blood payment. The damn fool could have had Heaven, but he threw it away out of pride. Just like the first time."

He pressed his lips together in grim satisfaction as he recalled the scene, and I knew that it had been his hand that had sent Lucas to his end.

His story made sense. And yet . . . I'd watched the violence that had swept the Earth as the Fallen had unleashed their jubilation upon the world, thinking that they had finally beaten Michael and could take Heaven by force. I had watched, terrified, as it ebbed and flowed. But finally the violence had petered out, and nothing else had happened. I'd thought surely that meant the uprising had been quelled. Surely Michael was victorious and could come to me.

And yet he hadn't, until now.

"How long ago was this?" I asked him suspiciously.

He stilled my hand, gripping my fingers in his.

"Time in Heaven is different than time on Earth, Hope. There is no rhyme or reason to it. I'm sorry to have made you wait so long."

A wave of insecurity overwhelmed me, a feeling of rejection I'd been trying to ignore ever since he'd pushed me away in the tiny hotel room in Puy-en-Velay. I dropped his hand and stared at the gentle mound that marked my father's burying place. My voice faltered. I hated myself for feeling the way I did; hated that I had to ask the question, but I had to know where we stood.

"I was so afraid you didn't want me. That I was just an inconvenience. A necessary part of the Prophecy. And now that the Prophecy is over, you don't need me anymore."

I heard him suck in his breath.

"Ah, Hope. How can you even think that?"

"That night, in the hotel in France—"

He groaned. "I wasn't rejecting you, Hope. That was for your own good."

I stubbornly stared at the ground, too embarrassed and humiliated to look him in the eye. He tilted my chin up, ever so gently, and my vision blurred as he forced me to return his gaze.

We stood there, silent in the gloaming, and somehow I knew I wasn't going to make it to Krav Maga tonight.

"Do you remember how angry you were with me after Las Vegas?" he asked.

I nodded, not sure where he was going with this. Las Vegas was a bitter memory—a time where the flame that glowed within Michael had overpowered both him and me in a fit of emotion, burning my body and marking me with scars that only faded once the light had gone from his eyes. It was our time in Las Vegas that had sowed the doubt and distrust that had led me to hide things from Michael, which ultimately led to Michael's death.

"Do you remember what you said?" he prompted me patiently.

I had said a lot of things. I just shook my head, no, allowing him to continue.

"You hated me for leaving you with just a memory, a memory of a kiss that you thought you'd never experience again. That was just a kiss, Hope. How could I, knowing that I was about to die, do so much more? And do it in sadness when making love to you should have been a moment of joy? I couldn't do that to you. I just couldn't. It wouldn't have been fair, especially when I didn't know how it was all going to turn out."

I wanted to believe him.

"Hope," he breathed, "I had to stop because I love you. None of this would have mattered if I didn't love you. You understand that, don't you? None of it. My death was meaningless without you. It only became a sacrifice when I had something to lose."

I began to cry, silent tears shaking my body. The memory of us huddled together on the cold stone floor of the chapel came rushing back to me.

"I felt the life seep out of you. I couldn't stop it. And it was my fault." The words came out in broken bursts. Betrayed. I had betrayed him.

"Hope, look at me. It wasn't your fault. It was meant to happen."

I shook my head; my guilt was a cancer eating me alive, and I needed to put it out there.

"I betrayed you," I said. "Gabrielle told me I would do it. That day on Skellig Michael. I didn't believe her, but in the end, she was right. I gave the Key to Lucas, Michael. I fulfilled the Prophecy. You died because of me!"

I was shaking so violently now that I didn't know if I would ever be able to stop. I was waiting for his rejection. Waiting for the tiny splinter of belief that had embedded itself in my heart to leave me to bleed and fester.

"Hope." His voice was gentle, a balm to my soul. "You misunderstood Gabrielle. Giving the rock to Lucas wasn't your betrayal."

He paused. "What hurt was that you kept things from me—most importantly, that your Guardian Angel was still with you. I knew that circumstances made our . . . situation . . . complicated. Uncertain. But I thought that you still knew we were on the same team. That we were like a rope, the individual fibers of our souls woven and coiled tight, stronger together than we were on our own. But there was rot at the center of the rope, Hope. Distrust. That was the betrayal. Nothing more and nothing less."

A fresh surge of shame overtook me as I remembered how I'd confided in Henri, my Guardian Angel, while I'd let Michael think Henri had abandoned me. It had turned out that Henri had been spying for the Fallen all along, playing me for all it was worth.

I dropped my gaze to the floor, Michael's gentle rebuke too much for me to bear. But again he nudged my chin up, forcing me to look at him.

"I don't like it, but I can understand it," he said. "And I forgive you. I forgave you a long time ago."

I gulped hard and nodded quickly, dashing another tear from my cheek. He might have forgiven me, but it would take me a bit longer to forgive myself.

"As for the rest, it was meant to be. You couldn't have stopped it, Carmichael—nor should you have even tried," he said, slipping effortlessly into his casual nickname for me. "It was meant to happen. And whether you want to admit it or not, by being part of the story, by helping it come to pass, you saved the world." He spoke the words almost reverentially, pulling me into his embrace and pressing his lips to the top of my head.

"It has not gone unnoticed," he whispered against my hair.

"What do you mean?" I asked, taking a shuddering breath to stop my tears. I looked up into his eyes. They shone with excitement. He drew my fingertips to his lips and kissed them, sending a shiver down my spine.

"Look," he said, turning my palm over in his hand. "You can still withstand my heat. Just like I never left. Like we were meant to be." He kissed the heart of my palm, and then, distracted, he murmured against my skin: "The Heavenly courts have granted us an opportunity. A choice."

I frowned. "I haven't liked the choices Heaven has presented me with so far."

He laughed, a hearty guffaw that shook the silence of the cemetery. Then he clasped my hand, pulling me in even closer. I let my body sink into his, letting my armor melt away as I molded myself to him. His familiar scent—leather and hay, honey and sunshine—flooded my senses, confirming once again that I wasn't dreaming. This was real.

"Hope, God has made us an offer. He's given us the chance to be together. Forever."

I held my breath. Forever? I looked up into his eyes, confused. "How?"

He smiled. "Here's one of your choices: I can become human and join you here on Earth. I can be Michael Boyd forever."

I frowned. "Not forever. If you become human, you'll die."

"Eventually," he acknowledged with a nod of the head. "But if we're lucky, not until after living a very full life. Together."

I rolled that around in my head. "What are my other choices?"

"Only one other: you can join me in Heaven and become an angel."

He paused, tilting his head to look at me thoughtfully as he gauged my reaction.

"I've learned too much about prophecies and promises to

believe that this is a straightforward offer," I answered, not bothering to quell the bitterness in my speech. "If I join you, I have to say
goodbye to my family, don't I?"

He didn't answer at first. "There is precedent," he acknowledged.
"Enoch, for example." Suddenly, he grinned. "He sends his regards,
by the way. He's very sorry about the mix-up with Lucas, you know.
He feels just terrible."

I knit my brows together. "You make it sound as if he were late
for dinner or something."

He chuckled. "I don't mean to downplay it. It's hard to put into
words just how remorseful he feels. He always had a soft spot
for you."

I thought about Enoch for a moment. "Enoch's allowed to pose
as a human. So even though you and all the other archangels are
allowed to pose as humans, I will not be?" I challenged.

He shook his head. "We don't do it to maintain dual lives," he
countered softly. "Only in the pursuit of our heavenly mission.
You would be expected to do the same, giving up your particular
human ties to embrace your duty to humanity as a whole."

"My particular human ties," I echoed, the very thought of abandoning my family plunging like an icy shard into the center of my
heart. "And I can't just wait them out?"

"You mean, live with them as a human until they have slipped
their mortal bonds? No," he answered. "No, it doesn't work like
that."

"Michael," I whispered. "What have you been doing? While
you've been waiting, what have you been doing?"

He shrugged. "I've been protecting the chosen ones. Me and
Gabrielle."

I raised an eyebrow. Michael's missions had always been solo
ones in the past.

He kicked his boot into the dirt, looking sheepish. "Even after I rose, I never fully recovered all my abilities." A fresh wave of shame washed over me. We both knew that the loss of Michael's intuition was my fault. I had sucked it away from him, absorbing it myself. "I needed a guide to help me find my way. Gabrielle was the only one willing to do it. Once we're together, though, I won't need her. I'll have you."

My spine stiffened in protest. I stared at the line of trees surrounding the graveyard and forced myself to engage in the debate he was hoping to avoid.

"You're assuming I'll go with you," I said. "You could come to me. We have that option."

He paused. "I am not entirely confident that my duties would be borne well by the others."

I nodded. "Raph didn't like you choosing a mere human."

"No. He didn't. Nor, honestly, does Gabrielle, though her reasons are different."

I let his words roll around in my head. After all this time, after everything I'd done to prove myself, I still hadn't won them over. I felt defeated. Exhausted.

"So the choice we've been offered was—and is—a false one. I have to give up everything for us to be together."

He didn't dispute nor confirm my conclusion. The wind whispered through the pines again. It was a lonely sound.

"You see why I couldn't ask it of you. Why I had to keep it to myself, to protect you until you'd recovered from your father's death. But now, I know you're ready. We can be God's sword and shield, protecting God's people from the Fallen who refuse to accept their chance for salvation, even now." He paused for a moment. "And the people need protection. Lucas has been defeated, but his exile is only temporary. He'll be back. Far sooner than I'd like, I'm sure."

I couldn't even think about this last possibility yet. I felt exposed, raw. After the years of waiting, it was heady to have him here with me. I was drunk with possibility, every nerve ending on fire. But I hadn't expected to be confronted with such a momentous decision. It was too much, too fast.

And it was unfair.

I turned back to face him.

"It was my choice to make," I said. "Not yours."

His blue eyes widened at the unspoken accusation. But I was just getting started.

"It wasn't for you to decide whether it was the right or wrong time to tell me what I'd been offered. You had no right to make that decision for me. No matter what I was going through, I deserved to know the truth, not be left twisting in the wind, wondering what had happened to you. And now you think you can just waltz in here and say, 'Hey there! Just kidding! I really didn't die, you know, I've been here all along! Sorry you suffered all those years, agonizing over whether or not I was dead or alive, believing you had been to blame! I'm here now!' And you think we can just pick up where we left off?"

I closed the distance between us, pushing my finger up against his chest.

"It doesn't work that way, Michael. I have a life, now. It may have taken me a while, but I'm getting ready to go to college. My sister is just a toddler. You want me to leave her now? It would be like tearing my own heart out. And my mother?" My words caught in my throat, harsh and broken with emotion. I turned away from him, too angry and confused to withstand his gaze.

I knew that the alternative—Michael becoming human—was impossible. It meant leaving the world without its protector, and Heaven without its captain. With the Fallen still out there, our entire world was in a very precarious situation, one whose balance could shift in the blink of an eye. I remembered him watching the television set in the hotel room in Las Vegas, seeing the helplessness of the people he could not save. I remembered his pain as he relived the ancient slaughter in Aya Sofya. I remembered the hollowed-out, haunted, guilty look in his eyes.

If I asked him to become human, he would look at me with those eyes, and he would blame me. Say what he would, it would never be the same between us at all. And that, I couldn't live with.

I thought all these things in an instant; I thought and felt them like a wound. There was too much there to unbundle, too many hurts and fears to number.

"Look at me," he insisted, the low tones of his voice coaxing, pulling me in. Despite myself, I turned around, dragging my gaze along the uneven ground of the cemetery until I was staring at the tips of his work boots.

I felt angry, but it was anger directed at myself, because I knew that if he asked me to go away with him again, I wouldn't be able to stand my ground. I was frustrated that with a few tender words, he could make me feel like that lost teenage girl, longing for his love, that I'd been just two years ago. How easy it was to bring back all those feelings that I thought I'd outgrown.

I thrust that girl into the recesses of my memory, resisting the temptation posed by Michael's warm touch.

"I can't," was all I managed to say. "Don't ask me to decide yet. You can't come back after all this time and expect things to be the same. You just can't. It's not fair to me."

He pulled me closer and kissed away a tear.

Ah, Carmichael, he began, as I felt his spirit entwine with mine, sending forth his energy. *I'm so stupid. Of course I can't.*

What felt like a sigh escaped from him, its whispering concession soothing my anger and pain. And then his energy began to retreat, but not before embracing each of my hurts one last time. He was leaving me, and already the empty spaces left inside of me ached. I shivered against his body, yearning for the heat of his soul, as he brought my knuckles up to brush them with his lips.

Then he pushed my hand away and stood back, appraising me. He reached up to brush my tears away, light like a butterfly's wing, before tilting my chin up. His eyes, deep like sapphires, gazed at me sheepishly.

"I'm sorry. So, so sorry. I've never done this before. I'm not very good at it."

"Obviously," I conceded grudgingly.

"Can we start over?" he appealed, tilting his head. "I'd like the chance to earn your trust again, Hope. To win your forgiveness."

My face burned red. "I didn't mean—"

He interrupted me before I could finish. "You don't have to explain yourself. You don't have to defend your feelings to me or anybody else. But I'm not going to accept that our story is over. I want us to start a new chapter. Beginning today."

I looked at him warily. "What are you proposing?"

His grin widened and he arched one brow. "I believe you humans call it wooing."

My cheeks flamed even hotter. "You want to . . . woo me?"

"Is that a problem?"

I stared at him. This impossibly perfect creature, golden haired with eyes like flame, wanted to win me back? A tumult of emotions warred inside of me.

"In the twenty-first century, we call it dating," I finally answered, with the safety of sarcasm.

He laughed. "Duly noted. So, what do you think? Will you give me a shot? Do we have a deal?"

I looked at him skeptically. "I'm not promising you anything, Michael. I may never agree to go away with you. Or for you to join me here on Earth. Just so we're clear."

"All I'm asking for is a fair chance."

"What, exactly, would be the terms of our, er, dating relationship?" I chewed on the inside of my cheek, shifting on my feet as I eyed him.

"I'll have to be gone a lot, of course."

"To keep up with your duties."

He nodded, conceding my point. "Is that acceptable to you?"

I shrugged, heart in my throat.

"I would understand if you wished the freedom to see others," he continued, but I cut him off with a quick shake of my head.

"I don't need to see anyone else," I mumbled, dropping my eyes to the dirt. It was an easy promise. I would never admit to him that there hadn't been anyone else yet. There had been no point, it had seemed.

He tugged at my chin, drawing my gaze up to meet his. "I'm glad."

A wave of heat swept through my body, threatening to wipe out any reason. I swayed, unsteady on my feet. But finally, I cleared my throat and looked him straight in the eye.

"We'd better get you back home, then," I said, "so that I can introduce you to everybody all over again."

two

LUCAS

Hell is not a place of fire and brimstone, as the hoary imaginations of terrified Bible thumpers would have it.

No, Hell is a place of dislocation. Of separation. Of isolation.

Hell is a place of waiting. Waiting and waiting and waiting, with nothing to distract oneself from rehearsing in one's mind, again and again, the complaints one has hoarded over centuries of dispossession—the newest of these insults still fresh—nor the gnawing, incessant need for revenge that preoccupies one's thoughts.

I am waiting for my banishment from corporeal form to be over, for only then will I be able to rejoin that wretched race called human and exact my own punishment on Michael and that—that *thing*, that *girl*—of which he has become so enamored. It will take some time, as it always does. This time will take longer than the others because in their twisted calculus of right and wrong, the audacity of my crimes—daring to take the life of an archangel, storming Heaven's Gate—deserves it.

At least I'm not being blamed for Hope's father's death. Though I would have been within my rights to punish him—after all, if it weren't for his training, I could have easily defeated Hope—I had a greater goal in mind, and I had no involvement. That the trafficking syndicate targeted him shouldn't have surprised me, but I must admit, I was a little wistful when I learned of his death. Without even knowing it, he had proven to be a wily foe.

But I digress. There is no atonement for what I have done, of course. My banishment is really just the equivalent of a cosmic time-out. If I am honest with myself, my isolation here, in this vast, icy, empty void, is not that different from the decades and centuries and millennia that have preceded this moment.

Here, though, there are no vile humans with whom I can entertain myself while I live out my sentence of exile. Instead, I'm stuck with their forms of entertainment. It's God's sense of justice: I can only access those limited distractions the human mind is capable of inventing. I play Candy Crush and Farmville. I sing showtunes to myself: after all that time on Earth, I developed a weakness for the stylings of Stephen Sondheim and Cole Porter, though if I ever run into Stephen Schwartz, I'll run a pitchfork through him as punishment for inflicting that whiny, insipid *Wicked* upon us all. I guess the answers on *Jeopardy*, though really, that Alex Trebek is no match for me. After all, I've lived through everything he ever asks about.

And of course, if I concentrate, I can project my spirit out into the earthly world. The projection is too weak to do anything, and I can only do it for a brief period of time—for example, time enough to offer my twisted blessing to a newborn child. Otherwise, I simply watch.

I watch and I wait for my moment to strike.

It is sort of sick, I suppose, how drawn I am to watch the humans live out their puny lives. But what can I say? Each passing day proves me right. They are not fit to hold God's love and attention.

Michael knows where I am. And he knows it is only a matter of time before I return to demand recompense, to hold him accountable for his love of wretched mankind.

He would never admit it, certainly not to me, but I think he understands why I do what I've done.

Before, we were brothers in arms. He was God's sword—majestic, merciful to the just, harrowing to those who defied God's will and threatened His people. But I—I was God's shield. If Michael cut down the threats to God's rule, I shielded God from insult and threats—and, most importantly, from breaches from within. I searched His rules and His logic for loopholes and risks and contingencies, ensuring that the world He created made sense. Like the chambers of a nautilus, the delicate spine of a perfectly formed snowflake, or the feathery veins carrying life-giving water through the lush leaves of a bower: orderly, perfect, complete. One only had to look at it to know that it was right.

And then He had to ruin it by His fascination with those damned imperfect humans.

He wouldn't listen to reason. He couldn't see how they weakened His glory with their continual failures, their disappointing relapses. They were a blotch upon His creation. But instead of acknowledging it and dealing with it as He should, He made excuses and gave them chances, time and time again.

And Michael was right there at His side, encouraging Him. Enabling Him.

It was illogical. It was a blight upon His perfect world. Is it any surprise that I was sympathetic to Lucifer when he challenged God's judgment and demanded that God step aside?

How ironic, then, that He—who was so quick to forgive mankind's follies—cast us unceremoniously out of Heaven, inflicting the endless pain of His displeasure upon us for all eternity. And again, Michael, my former comrade, was right at God's side. In fact, he was the one who expelled us, his army of faithful angels refusing to listen until we had fallen far, far away, leaving Michael to turn the key with a resounding, hollow *click* behind us.

And now he dares to offer *her* the role of God's shield? As if I never existed? As if she could ever play the role that once I played? I do not envy them their human emotions. But to reward her with what was once mine, to besmirch it with the insipid entanglement they call love, is unacceptable.

If he saw her as I saw her, perhaps he might think differently. But he cannot. His thinking is clouded by the slurry of human hormones and emotions that clogs his brain when he chooses to take that form. Besides, he did not have the direct access to her thoughts that her turncoat Guardian Angel gave me. Michael thinks she was part of the Fallen's redemption? Ha. She fought it at every turn. She would have given anything, anything at all, to prevent his death.

That is not bravery. Nor is it sacrifice.

She is just another weak human, thrust upon the stage of heavenly greatness by an accident. Her elevation is just another in a string of mistakes made by a God who refuses to admit He was wrong.

God is not ignorant of the facts of humanity's behavior. He just refuses to acknowledge that those facts signify any unpleasant truth about His creation.

Why would I want forgiveness on those terms? Why should I admit I am wrong, when He cannot do the same?

Besides, I am *not* wrong. Humanity is an abomination.

Ah. Even now, God smites me with pain for daring to speak the truth. I am His angelic pincushion. Loving God, indeed. He doesn't realize I cherish the pain, I jealously hoard it unto my heart—proof, in the end, that I am right.

Those Fallen who embraced their chance to return to Heaven— they are nothing, nothing compared to the legions that wait out their *real* salvation. They will continue to wait faithfully for the day when God must admit that we were right—that His perfection is marred by mankind, and that, therefore, they must go. And when I return, I will lead them, on behalf of my Master, once again.

But what is more: I will wake Michael up to the truth about humans. I will show him how easy it is to lure humans to prey upon one another, betraying their very nature. I will show him how easy it is to break them down, stripping away the very things that make them human and revealing them as the base animals they really are. I will make Hope pay for her presumption in the worst possible way—by striking at her family. I will show him how even his precious Hope, if pushed far enough, will choose vengeance over mercy.

And when she does, they will see, through my eyes, just how corrupt the hearts and flesh of men can be.

They will be as desolate as any of the prophets set to wander the desert. They will be as desolate as this place in which I wait. They will be as desolate as my soul, and they will know the truth.

And when they do, God will have to acknowledge that I am right.

Just watch.

three

HOPE

Ten years later . . .

We heard the door swing open, the buzzing of our alarm system giving us warning that someone was penetrating the security of our Buckhead home. Ollie began dancing around in a frenzy of barking, his lopsided gait betraying his age. He was a year older than Rorie—an old dog now at thirteen, but still insistent upon playing guard.

"Anybody home?" Michael's voice bellowed from the front of the house, bouncing off the marble and stone hallway. My heart thumped in recognition, ready to welcome him home.

"Back here!" my mother called out to him, smiling knowingly at me as she deactivated the alarm. It had been six months since we'd last seen Michael, and she had been counting the days, just as I had, until his return from what we referred to as his latest "tour of duty." Over time, my mother had come to accept the explanation for his regular absences. His "career" as a military contractor was the perfect cover, giving him wide berth to be gone for long stretches of time, explaining his familiarity with the far-flung troubled reaches of the world that were his haunts, and letting him avoid any deep inquiry on the basis of "national security."

My mother had eventually just given up probing for more and accepted his excuses, mostly due to the fact that she had grown to genuinely like Michael. She'd grown in lots of ways over the years, barely recognizable now as the polished corporate executive she'd been only thirteen years earlier. Her uniform of black suits had been banished, and she'd let the hints of red that streaked her long, mahogany hair run riot along with her curls, which she no longer bothered to straighten or pull back. Her hair cascaded around her pale face, its bounty threatening to overwhelm her delicate frame. She'd softened, if not mellowed. Her grief over losing my father, and over the time they'd wasted apart, had long ago been set aside so that she could focus her energies on raising my now twelve-year-old sister, keeping her intellect sharp with the occasional consulting gig and a portfolio of board appointments.

That mellowness had been hard won. I remembered the months leading up to Rorie's birth. After I'd finally emerged from the fog of my own grief, I'd looked at my mother; really looked at her more than I had in a long time. Her face had become lined, deeply etched by sorrow. Her thick mane of dark hair was shot through with even more silver, and she'd stirred her coffee listlessly with a spoon, unable to bring herself to eat anything substantial. She'd seemed so fragile, then, like a dry leaf that has seen the prime of summer and been left an empty husk. I tucked her in at night, looking in on her after she'd fallen asleep, and invariably I'd find her hands clutching the old photograph of her and my father on their wedding day.

It had taken Rorie's birth to wake my mother from her slumber, the new baby forcing her to pick up her life again, to live it, to embrace the tiny wonder she had borne and to embrace along with it the mundane things that made our world a beautiful one: the feeling of satisfaction of snapping up the red flag on our mailbox to send out a handwritten note on creamy, crisp stationery; the smell of gardenias wafting in from the garden; the soapy bubbles up to our elbows as we stood, side by side, washing dishes to keep our home tidy and cheerful. The little moments we had together, as a family, were what had drawn my mother back.

Michael strode into the room, a whiff of honey and hay preceding him, and took us all in. My mother, dressed in yoga pants and a billowy top that was splattered with clay from her pottery studio. Arthur, a permanent presence in our lives, his body a wall of muscle shielding my mother from any intrusions. My best friend Tabby, the outward rebelliousness of her high school years tempered now that she had followed her father's footsteps to become a minister herself, her funky cat-eye tortoiseshell glasses the only nod to her insistent individuality. Ollie—our stray, adopted from Istanbul—danced at his feet, barking his welcome and demanding attention from the only person besides me whom he would recognize as master.

And then there was me. Michael's azure eyes sparkled as they came to rest on my face, his grin widening.

"No suit. Home on a weekday? You didn't get yourself fired, Carmichael? Decide to hang it up and do yoga like Mona?" There was a note of hopefulness underlying his jest as his gaze ran over me.

I laughed. It was the same every time we came together: he searched me for wholeness, making sure that I hadn't somehow been hurt in his absence. But I was a different person now than the confused teen he'd come back to ten years ago. Confident. Poised. Living in the present. While I desperately missed him while he was away, I had my own, full life: a profession at which I excelled, and a close circle of friends and family. My cropped hair had grown out into a sleek, sophisticated bob, hiding the tattoo-like Mark on the back of my neck lest it become a distraction to the juries in front of whom I argued my cases. The Mark itself, and all that had come with it? To me, now, it was a representation of strength, of all I had come through to get to this point in my life.

"Even public defenders and prosecutors can take a day off now and then," I said. "It was too beautiful a day to sit in a stuffy office, especially since I knew Rorie had the day off from school. But don't worry." I reached down to where my overflowing briefcase rested next to me, patting it with my manicured fingertips. "I've got plenty of case files here with me."

"That's not what I meant," he said, his eyebrows drawing together slightly. "You know I think you work too hard as it is."

Something about his tone startled me. Me "working too hard" was an old complaint, and one that I knew had to do with his desire for me to loosen, not tighten, my earthly bonds so that the choice that faced me would be easier. But this time, there seemed to be an edge to it.

I pushed aside the niggling of my intuition and let my gaze race over his body, tallying his every scratch and wound, knowing that before they faded he would recount for me the battles against evil each mark represented. I realized that I'd been holding my breath, waiting for this moment.

"You're a sight for sore eyes," he whispered gruffly, his face softening as he pushed aside whatever it was that was making him so tense.

I let out my breath in a shaky laugh.

"We could say the same, except you're a bit stinky, if I do say so," Arthur interjected, his face a mask of mock disgust. "Where've you been that you've had no water for a shower?"

Michael laughed and shrugged, running a hand through his hair so that it stood up on end, the moment of tension between us gone.

"I'm sorry. I guess I was a little eager to get here. I came straight from the airfield."

"Never mind that," my mother interjected, rising from her comfy rocker. "You've had a long trip, that's for certain. Sit down and I'll make you up a plate of something to eat." She walked over to where he stood, towering over her, and gave him a little squeeze. "I insist. Go sit down next to Hope."

He looked after my mother with affection as she walked with purpose to the kitchen. He threw himself into the chair she'd abandoned, letting his lanky body stretch out next to mine. Ollie stationed himself right next to the chair; Michael began absent-mindedly scratching his ears. He was still dressed in desert camouflage, and the cotton fabric clung to his thighs. He caught me staring at him and arched a brow.

My cheeks flushed. He shot me a wicked grin and thankfully launched into conversation.

"Mona in the kitchen. Shocking. Can she actually cook now?"

Arthur laughed. "Don't worry, she'll probably just arrange some fruit and cheese on a plate. No risk of food poisoning. It's hard to imagine that she used to arrange some of the biggest mergers and acquisitions in the world. But those days are gone. I'm telling you, man, she's a different woman. Yoga, pottery . . . she's even the vice president of the PTA at Rorie's school."

"Much to the horror of everyone else on the PTA. Last meeting she proposed they not require a consensus majority rules vote on every piece of PTA business. You'd think she'd proposed they go club baby seals to death or something," I added, remembering the rash of horrified Facebook postings and letters to the editor her suggestion had unleashed.

"She even inflicted PowerPoint upon them," Tabby added with faux gravity.

"Troublemakers all, you Carmichael women," Michael intoned with mock seriousness. "I include you in that group, my good doctor," he added for Tabby's benefit. "How fares your congregation?"

She peered at him over the rim of her glasses.

"They're fine, thank you. Preparing for a visit to the federal prison to minister to the inmates." She pursed her lips. "Mona won't let Rorie come with me. She thinks it's too dangerous."

Michael shrugged. "I happen to agree with her. I suppose she went full nuclear on you when you raised the idea?"

Tabby winced at the memory. I laughed.

"She's mellowed with age, but not that much. She can still wield the hairy eyeball at will. And she's still protective of her baby, that's for sure."

"That's good. There's time enough for Rorie to encounter all the evil in the world. What is she now—twelve?" He didn't wait for anyone to answer. "Let her enjoy her innocence while she can."

He let his eyes linger on my face and reached out his hand. I gripped it in mine, our fingers intertwining, letting the jolt of heat that still ran between us flood my senses.

Michael sank deeper into the cushions of his chair. "Ah, it's good to be home," he muttered to no one in particular, letting his eyes flutter shut for just a moment.

My heart swelled to hear him call this place—us—home. And it *was* home—my downtown apartment still felt like an outpost to me. But I knew that for him, this place would never be more than a temporary hearth, nothing but a way station on the way to our union in Heaven—for him, my choice was a foregone conclusion.

I looked around at my family and felt the twinge of anxiety I always experienced when I thought about leaving them.

My mother came back in, bearing a tray of fruit, cheese, and crackers, distracting me.

"What did I tell you?" Arthur muttered to Michael.

"What was that?" my mother demanded.

"Nothing," we all chimed in, laughing.

"This looks great, Mona, thank you," Michael said with real appreciation. I marveled sometimes at how well he played his role as human. I knew it was physically draining, but he hid it well.

"Mom?" a childish voice called from somewhere. A barrage of words tumbled out, faster and faster, closer and closer. "Mom? Can Macey and I go to the pool? All my friends are going to be there this afternoon. I know you said you wanted me home today, but—" A lone figure emerged on the stairs and paused.

"Michael!"

The tiny, fierce bundle of energy flung herself down the rest of the stairs, hurtling into Michael's arms.

Rorie.

She had my mother's build—petite and compact with muscled strength—and so far, she had somehow avoided the awkwardness that typically comes from the growth spurts and hormones of impending teen-dom. While her love of fashion and makeup and countless hours of watching video bloggers meant she could emerge from the cocoon of her room in any number of guises, she was just a child today, dressed in a T-shirt and shorts, her blond hair, so carefully highlighted to add a sunny glow, pulled back simply into a bun so that the warmth and intelligence of her violet eyes shone. She disentangled herself impatiently from the enveloping hug with which she'd greeted Michael and began peppering him with questions.

"Nobody told me you were coming today! When did you get here? Why didn't anybody come and get me?" She paused to shoot me a wounded, pouting look, but her imaginary hurt passed as quickly as it came, and she turned her attention back to Michael.

"I missed you so much." She began patting the many pockets of his cargo pants. "What did you bring me?"

Michael laughed. "Glad to know you're the same girl I remember, looking for your presents before I even have a chance to catch my breath. But what's this?"

He gently poked at her face, pulling away a finger and holding it up for a theatrical inspection in the light before wrinkling his nose. "Mascara? Lip gloss?"

She swatted his hand away playfully and laughed.

"All the girls in seventh grade wear makeup. It's just a little bit. Besides, you're just trying to distract me. You haven't answered my question yet."

He sighed the sigh of a long-suffering parent. And indeed, I knew that he often felt like a surrogate father to Rorie. They had always had a special connection.

"I may have something here for you. Let me see." Rorie squealed as he began making a big show of searching his pockets. Finally, he pulled out a big wad of tissue paper that had been painstakingly wrapped and taped to secure its contents.

"Ah, yes, here it is. Now, this is very delicate, Rorie. You'll have to unwrap it carefully."

Rorie ignored him, eagerly tearing into the paper, little scraps of tissue spilling onto the floor for Ollie to sniff through as she dug into the heart of the bundle. She fished out a polished sliver of iridescent stone. With nimble fingers, she drew out a long, silk thread and let the stone dangle in the light. It was a pendant, sparkling with the colors of the rainbow, mere millimeters thick.

"My goodness, that is something else," my mother declared.

"It's called iris agate, from the chalcedony family. I got it in

Israel. The jeweler had to carve it off from the larger stone. See, it's almost translucent."

Tabitha's brow crumpled in concentration. "Chalcedony. As in the reference to the foundations of New Jerusalem in Revelation?"

Michael shrugged, never taking his eyes off of Rorie, who was fascinated by the play of light on the stone.

"I bought it because the rainbow reminded me of Rorie and her name. Nothing more."

"I love it!" Rorie trilled, throwing her arms around Michael and burying her face in his neck.

"I hoped you would," he said, laughing. He drew her up. "Here, let me put it around your neck." Carefully, he looped the silk cord over her head. She fiddled with the agate, arranging it just so.

"It's perfect!" She threw her arms around him again and pecked his forehead with birdlike kisses.

Suddenly, she drew herself up, squishing her face into an expression of disgust. "You're smelly."

Michael roared with laughter. "So I am. Occupational hazard. I promise, I'll go clean up for my best girl." He tousled her hair and she wriggled away, smoothing her hair down.

"You better. Hope won't kiss you if you don't smell nice." She stuck her tongue out at me. "Mom, is the pool okay?"

"Yes, of course. I'll bring you there myself."

She shifted nervously, chewing a bit of hair. "You'll just drop me off, right? All my friends will be there."

"And you don't want to be embarrassed by me?" my mother said pointedly, raising one sharp brow.

"You'd never embarrass me, Mom. I just don't need to be babysat."

"We'll see." My mother crossed her arms, her signal that now was not the time to have this particular debate.

"I'll go call Macey and tell her. See you later!" She bounded out of the room, confident she would get her way. Mona looked after her, her gaze troubled.

"She's growing up too fast."

"How is she adjusting to middle school?" Michael prompted.

"Well enough," my mother replied. "But most of her friends have older siblings. They seem so much worldlier than she is. She is so innocent. I worry she'll be—"

"Mom," I interrupted, "you know she's got a good head on her shoulders. She'll be fine."

"I know. Don't get me wrong—she hasn't done anything bad, and she's still getting good grades. And her friends are good kids. But she is just so different than how I remember you at that age, Hope. I mean, based on the little that I got to see of you, then," she added, slightly flustered at the old memories of the estrangement that had been forced on us by the determined isolation with which my father had raised me. "She reads all those fashion magazines. She seems so concerned with being pretty and popular. I just worry that she'll lose sight of what really matters in the process."

"Well, she doesn't have to work at being either of those things. She is the center of her little group, that is for sure," I noted dryly. It was true. Rorie was almost completely unlike me at that age. She was normal. Which was, all things considered, a happy thing.

My mother sighed. "She's just different than you were. It's not good or bad, I know. Just different. And harder for me to relate to. Anyway"—she shrugged—"she's not getting rid of me so easily. Embarrassing or not, I'll be at that pool."

"Who's her friend, Macey?" Michael wondered. "I've never heard her mention that name before." Rorie had been with the same pack of girls since pre-K, so it was noticeable when a new face joined their crowd.

Arthur smiled. "The latest stray Rorie has taken under her wing. She's the daughter of one of our neighbors. They began fostering her a few weeks ago and enrolled her in Rorie's school. Rorie has taken a shine to her."

"Fostering? So she's had a tough life?" Michael probed, sitting up in his chair with interest.

Arthur nodded. "Single mother who's an addict, in court-ordered rehab now. Apparently the mom had a boyfriend who beat her up regularly. Her last trip to the hospital at least got her some help. Macey's father has been in and out of jail for years and can't be found, which is probably for the best right now. Not that Rorie knows any of these details. She just knows the kid's had a rough life and is spooked. Jumps at her own shadow. Rorie feels sorry for her, I think."

"I just hope she knows she can't make a project of her," my mother fretted. "This child is not a bird with a broken wing. She can't be fixed. And she can't be shielded from the pettiness of the girls if they don't want her in their group."

"Mom, I thought you'd be proud of Rorie for being so kind-hearted," I said, surprised at my mother's stance.

"She thinks she's invincible. That she can get people to follow her no matter what."

"Maybe she can," I prodded. "After all, she's your daughter."

My mother smiled. "Maybe. But she's young to be exposed to some of what happened to Macey. And girls this age can be mean. Macey definitely doesn't fit in. You'll see what I mean later when you meet her. I just don't want Rorie's heart broken if it doesn't work out the way she hopes."

"Honestly, Mona," Tabby began, pushing her glasses up on top of her head and leaning in to challenge my mother. "I think it's good for her to see the real world and how ugly it can be; to learn to stand up for those who are weaker than she is. You've kept her tucked away in this gilded cage her whole life. She needs to know what's out there."

"Can you blame me?" my mother challenged. Her fists were bunched into tiny balls, and I knew she was reweighing every choice she had made in raising Rorie, reliving the careful calculus she'd wrought—the value of Rorie's spirit and freedom weighed against her safety. I felt a pang for her, for how vulnerable motherhood had made her. It was the same for mothers everywhere, I knew, but this was my mother. I had inflicted enough pain on her myself over the years. Everything that had happened because of me—my disappearances, my father's murder—all of it had stoked her fear for Rorie. She didn't want to be overprotective, like my father had been, but she couldn't help it.

"She's got good role models in the three of you." Arthur jumped in, enveloping my mother's shoulders in a massive squeeze as he tried to defuse the situation. "Three strong, independent women. She couldn't ask for more."

Michael reached out and gripped my hand in his as he echoed Arthur's words.

"No, she really couldn't."

"I suppose you're right," my mother assented, but worry still stalked her eyes.

"Do you want me to go with you to the pool, Mona?" Tabby asked, contrite at having upset my mother. "I'm guessing Michael and Hope might have other plans." She smirked, trying to lighten the mood.

My mother smiled. "Thank you, Tabby. I could use some backup."

"Say no more." Tabby stood up, stretching. "I'll run home now to get my suit and meet you there."

"I've got some errands to run, Mona—unless you want me to drive you?" Arthur offered.

"Like old times? No thanks, Arthur. I think I can get the girls to the pool myself."

He gave her shoulder a little squeeze. "Just call me if you need me. I'll be in the carriage house later on."

And suddenly, just like that, Michael and I were alone, with only Ollie—who kept nudging our clasped hands in hopes of some belly scratching—to keep us company.

We laughed at Ollie and shooed him away. "Go find Mona," Michael commanded. The dog tilted his head quizzically, as if he was hoping he'd misunderstood, and then he trotted off in search of my mother, his lopsided gait telling his age.

When he was gone, Michael and I eyed each other with an air of nervous anticipation. After all these years, the pull of his body on mine had only gotten stronger, like the moon pulling in the tides. I wondered idly if the fact that we hadn't allowed ourselves to consummate our physical relationship served to heighten this attraction, keeping us in a state of perpetual tension, but I didn't really care. I just wanted to give myself over to the sensation of him here, before me, now.

"How long has it been?" Michael asked me, rubbing his thumb along the top of my hand.

I closed my eyes, enjoying the shivers of heat that trailed after his touch.

"Six months, Michael. You've been gone for six months."

He squeezed my hand.

"I'm sorry. Maybe this contractor story was a bad idea. I'm always afraid to come back too soon and raise your mother's suspicions."

I opened my eyes and smiled brightly at him. His eyes had

turned a cloudy gray, the color they always took when he was worried about me.

"It's for the best. No matter what we did, it was going to be a
weird situation."

"'A weird situation.' Is that what we're calling it now?" he teased.

"I think that is the official term for it. Yes."

He tilted his head, studying me. I flushed, wondering exactly
what he was thinking. His eyes flickered abruptly.

"Come swing on the porch with me," he said, his mouth compressed into a thin line as he pulled me to my feet.

We walked hand in hand to the open-air wrap-around porch,
me trailing behind him, confused at the sudden change in his
mood. The scent of magnolias and roses wafted to us on the breeze.
He pulled me down onto the swing cushions, nestling me close to
his side. His warmth instantly relaxed me as I rested my head on
his shoulder.

Perhaps I had misread him. I let a slow sigh escape me.

"Better?" he asked.

I nodded, nestling closer. He kissed the top of my head and
wrapped his big hand around mine. He was letting himself age
along with me, to keep up appearances, and up close, I could see
the faintest of smile lines beginning to mark his skin.

"I've missed you," he stated flatly, kicking his foot against the
floorboards to start the swing rocking. As I melded my body to his,
I felt the tension in his muscles.

There was something he was keeping from me; I was sure of
it now.

"I've missed you, too," I said. "Where were you this time?"

"North Korea. Malaysia. All over Africa, of course. There is
plenty of evil in the world to keep me busy. Too busy."

I turned his hand over to inspect the mark I'd spied on his wrist.

It looked as if his skin had been rent and was halfway through binding itself up.

"You still heal too slowly because of me."

"I heal. That's what counts," he reassured me. "It will be gone by tomorrow. Just like all the others."

I pressed my lips together, unsatisfied with his answer and more than a little guilty. I still didn't like that our first physical encounter, years ago in that Las Vegas hotel, had not only permanently transferred a bit of Michael's intuition to me, but had also drained him of some of his other angelic powers, like his ability to rapidly regenerate from injury. It also made him more dependent on others as he fulfilled his duties as the Protector of Heaven and the Faithful here on Earth, and the situation he'd described to me years before, where he'd worked in a team with his fellow archangel Gabrielle, had become permanent.

Thinking of her, I frowned. Over the years, Gabrielle had frequently accompanied Michael on his visits to Atlanta. She'd been nothing but polite, but I'd gotten the sense that she merely tolerated me, grudgingly accepting the central role I had in Michael's world. She'd also been conspicuously absent the last three times he'd come to visit.

"Did Gabrielle not come with you this time?"

He nodded.

"She's here. But she was gracious enough to give me some time alone with you."

I blushed. What did she think we would do with that time?

"So," he said, nudging me. "How is the world of criminal law?"

I smiled. I was relatively new in the County Attorney's office, but I was passionate about the work we did prosecuting felonies, bringing people who thought they were untouchable to justice in the name of all the innocents whose lives had been warped and destroyed by misused power. And I was good at it. Perhaps not surprisingly, I'd inherited my mother's sharp, logical mind. To put it to work solving the puzzles of criminality each case presented was a joy, the search for that last missing piece—sometimes just a wisp of an insight, an indescribable gut feeling—was addictive. I didn't have a fancy office—in fact I was shoved into what looked more like a closet than anything else—but I made a difference. I was proud of my work.

"Andrew said he thought I had potential for the DA's office. Maybe the next job opening, even. He said he'd help me."

Michael squeezed my hand. "That's great, Hope. Really great. They're really going to miss you when you're gone."

I felt myself stiffen, involuntarily, next to him. "I know, but just think of it," I said. "The cases I'd get to work on at the state level would be amazing—they'd be precedent setting."

"That's not what I meant, Hope, and you know it."

It was inevitable; it had been hanging between us for ten years. He always pressed the question on me at some point during his visits: when would I make my choice?

But he'd never brought it up this soon before, or this insistently.

I sighed and pushed myself away from him so that I could look him in the eye.

"Do you really want to have this conversation now?"

He raised an eyebrow. "I always want to have this conversation. I thought you realized that by now."

"Michael, I'm not ready to decide. I told you last time, it's too soon."

"It's been ten years, Hope. And for me, it's been even longer. Remember, I waited for another two years before I came to you."

"How could I forget?" I snapped at him. "You let me think you were either truly dead or had abandoned me. Trust me, I remember that time all too well."

His eyes narrowed slightly at the accusation, but he forced himself to let it slide. "I just don't understand. Why don't you want to be together? Seeing you in bits and pieces of time . . . it's just not right. It's not how it was meant for us to be. We're meant to be together. Every moment you delay, well—"

"Well, what?" I asked sharply.

"It pulls me here. To you. Which means I'm pulled away from my *duties*."

All the air seemed to rush out of my lungs. Was he really accusing me, and my lingering reluctance to choose, of putting the world at risk? He'd used all sorts of logic on me in the past, but he had never stooped so low as to accuse me of distracting him from his duties.

Was I?

"Please, let's not fight," I said to him.

"Then talk to me, Hope. Tell me what you're thinking. Don't you want to be like this forever?"

He pulled my fingers up to his mouth and kissed my knuckles. I shuddered, little tendrils of warmth twining themselves up my arm.

"And this?" He shifted me up onto his lap and I wrapped my legs around his hips. His hands reached back to caress the small of my back. There was no space between us now; through the thin cotton of my shirt, I could feel his heat.

He pressed my hand to his chest. Under my palm, I could feel his heart beating wildly.

"Why can't you bring yourself to choose me? Either way?"

His words seared themselves into my brain, accusing. I shoved myself away, taking refuge in the far corner of the swing.

"You wouldn't understand," I said coldly. I wasn't ready to explain how I felt. I could hardly explain it to myself.

"Fine." I had wounded him, and his lips compressed into a grim line as he stood up from the swing. The chains creaked as it began to sway, unbalanced. He ran a hand through his hair, making it stand up on end.

"I'll go clean up and leave you to yourself until dinner," he said, crossing his arms. "I'm warning you, Hope. We have to talk about this. You can't keep putting it off forever. Whatever reasons you're keeping from me can't be anything worse than what we've already gone through. So do whatever you have to do, but you'd better be prepared to talk when I come back."

He didn't wait for me to respond, but stormed off. A minute later, the sound of the door slamming behind him echoed through the house.

I cursed myself. Why did this have to be so hard? And why, after all this time, was he putting so much pressure on me now?

I pushed my foot off the floor, setting the swing in motion, and huddled in the corner, chewing my lip. Why couldn't he see that nothing had really changed? Ten years had passed, true. But ten years hadn't brought an end to the risks posed by the Fallen, and I couldn't expose the world—including my own family—to the consequences of selfishly choosing to make Michael human.

And those ten years also hadn't made the pain of saying good-bye to my family any less. If anything had changed, in fact, it was that now I had a life of my own—a life that was more than just being my mother's daughter. A life that made a difference to others. A career I loved, that I was good at.

Could I give it all up for love? To be what—Michael's sidekick? A junior angel? What—and who—would I really be if I took Michael up on God's offer?

But how could I live if I lost him forever?

My head was beginning to pound with the stress of it all. I knew from the look on Michael's face that my time was running out. He had been patient, letting me have the experience of college and law school, letting me see Rorie grow up.

Letting me. I chuckled to myself, chiding my errant thought. He didn't let me do anything. It was my choice.

And it was an impossible choice. But I knew that not choosing was, itself, a decision.

Dinner was an awkward affair. My mother had not wanted to do anything fancy after everyone got back from the pool, so she'd just ordered in pizzas. Gabrielle had come along with Michael. They both sniffed at the food, probably longing for the simplicity of their manna. Michael was distant, and Gabrielle, as she often did, remained silent, shooting me meaningful looks. Tabby, herself, watched the few words that passed between us with the intensity of an anthropologist observing a strange, foreign tribe, trying to learn its language and customs for the first time.

My mother, noticing everything, arched her brows and looked at me pointedly. I shook my head slightly, silently pleading with her to leave us alone. Only Rorie, chattering away while she ate, seemed oblivious to the tension in the room.

I tried to ignore what was going on by focusing my attention on Rorie's friend, Macey, who had joined us for dinner. It wasn't the first time I had seen her, but always, my impression was the same: she was a sad little mouse, indeed. She was bigger than Rorie, and she seemed self-conscious about it, hunching her shoulders in and letting her head drop as if she wanted to shrink herself down to nothing. She sat like a lump on the bench next to Rorie, watching Rorie speak, barely mustering a muttered "yes" or "uh-huh" as Rorie raced along in her monologue about her latest shopping purchases and trip to the mall. Her coarse, broken hair, still wet from the pool, fell in pieces into her face, covering her eyes. Through the cotton of her swim cover-up, I could see the little buds of breasts and a round tummy. She was awkward, growing into her body. My heart went out to her.

Rorie paused, taking a big breath before launching into the next part of her story, and beamed at Macey, happy to be the center of attention. Macey darted her a grateful smile and then looked down sheepishly at her hands. She rushed to pick up her glass of milk, and in her rush she knocked over the glass, sending milk flying all over the table.

"Oh, no!" My mother's arm darted out to sop up the mess with a napkin, and Macey flinched, shrinking back into herself and shielding her face with her hands.

My mother froze, dropping the napkin. We all watched as, slowly, she drew herself down to Macey's side and gently pulled Macey's hands away from her face.

"Macey," she said softly. "Macey. Look at me." She put her finger under Macey's chin and drew her face up to meet her gaze. "It's okay. It's just some spilled milk. It happens all the time."

Macey blinked away some tears.

"We'll clean it up and get you another glass. No problem. Okay?"

Macey nodded, wiping her face with her sleeve, and I watched my mother give her hand a little squeeze.

Rorie looked uncertain, confused about what she would do. "I know," she said with false brightness. "Why don't we clean up and then you and I can go in the other room and have dessert? We can make sundaes and eat them in front of the TV."

Tabby cleared her throat. "We'll clean up for you girls. Why don't you run along, and we'll bring you your sundaes in a few minutes?"

Rorie shot her a grateful look.

"C'mon, Macey. Maybe we can do our nails later, too." She dragged Macey up from the bench, pulling her behind her through the kitchen to the family room. Macey waddled after her, grateful to be trailing in her shadow.

When the doors swung shut, we all let out our breaths.

"That was rough," Michael said, shaking his head. "Just think what she must have gone through. I'm guessing her mom wasn't the only one who got beaten in their household."

Mona picked up the napkin and began wiping at the spilled milk with big, angry strokes. "To hit a child. Who could ever do such a thing? She's afraid of her own shadow."

"It's good she has Rorie," Tabby pronounced. "Rorie will help her get her confidence back."

"Will she?" Gabrielle stood up from the table and lazily stretched out her long, lithe body before shrugging. "She might get tired of being Rorie's pet. She might soon resent being in her shadow. It is not easy, being the object of someone's pity. Not much of a life."

We all looked at her, agog. While Gabrielle was always quite direct, she was never cruel.

"How can you say such a thing?" Tabby countered. "Rorie doesn't treat her with pity. She's befriended her. Having a friend has got to be better than getting smacked around."

Gabrielle flicked her long, blond hair over her shoulder as she took her plate to the dishwasher. "You never know."

"That's one of the most cold-hearted things I've ever heard," Tabby said angrily.

Gabrielle paused, holding her dirty dish in the air, a speculative look in her eyes.

"People who grow up friendless and abused do not think the same way you do," she said. "They do not know how to be friends. Jealousy and want are below the surface at all times. Those are powerful emotions, and you would be surprised at what they drive people to do sometimes. The pet may bite the hand that feeds it."

She placed her plate in the dishwasher and gracefully closed it. As if her pronouncement had ended the debate, she floated out of the room.

Tabby fumed. My mother said nothing, quietly scooping ice cream into bowls. Michael looked around, obviously nonplussed by the conversation that had just taken place.

"I love a household of women with strong opinions," he said, trying to smooth things over. "That said, I think I'll go check on those girls."

"Here, take these with you." My mother forced two heaping bowls of hot-fudge sundae onto him.

"Yes, ma'am," he answered, backing out of the kitchen with full hands.

My mother and Tabby stared at the doors until they swung back into their quiet starting position. When my mother turned back to face the kitchen table, her brow was sharply arched.

"I do not like that woman," she announced, crossing her arms across her chest.

"That makes two of us," Tabby added. "I don't know how you can stand her, Hope, prancing around in her tight jeans and tank tops, leaving nothing to the imagination."

I felt myself flushing and began picking nervously at my napkin. "She doesn't mean anything by it. Honestly. I don't think she was trying to pick a fight."

Tabby rolled her eyes, throwing her own napkin down in her

plate. "She has some pretty strange views on friendship, by the sound of it. I'd watch my back if I were you."

"What do you mean?" I asked, confused.

Tabby snorted as she got up. "Really? Am I going to have to spell it out for you?"

"She means, how much can you really trust her around Michael, Hope?" my mother clarified in her most neutral voice.

I looked at them both, stunned, as they began cleaning up the dishes.

"You can't be serious."

"How well do you really know her, Hope?" my mother prompted me, tactfully, while she wiped a dish.

"She's been coming here for years," I protested. "She's one of Michael's best friends. He depends on her for his life in war zones."

"He can trust her," Tabby said pointedly, "but can you? You have to admit, she's gorgeous. All those months when they're out in the field together, away from you? If she wanted to, she could really get under Michael's skin."

My face was burning, mostly with the embarrassment of realizing that the thought had never crossed my mind. Of course I knew that for the majority of their time together, the angels were incorporeal. But the idea that Gabrielle could get under Michael's skin? That was certainly true, and it was clear that something was different between them since the last time I'd seen her.

I pushed away from the table and stormed out onto the porch. But out of the corner of my eye, in the shadows of the family room, I caught a glimpse of Gabrielle sidling up to Michael. I stopped short to watch. She was resting her hands upon his broad shoulder, standing just a little too close. She tilted her head toward his, whispering in his ear. He chuckled, a low sound that carried over the distance, and she tossed her glorious mane of hair, joining in whatever joke they were sharing.

I didn't need to see anything more. I slipped out to the porch, alone, and flung myself into a chair.

Did I have reason to worry? I told myself I was being silly. But a sliver of doubt had opened up in my mind.

I heard the door creak open. It was Tabby. She sat down right next to me and reached a hand out onto my knee.

"Hey. I didn't mean to upset you. I just, I don't know. I have a funny feeling about her. I always have."

"You know they don't really have to stay in their human bodies," I said. "They're just pretending. She doesn't even have to be female if she doesn't want to be."

"Did you ever ask yourself why she always shows up that way, then? Dressed the way she does? Why does she even have to be with him?"

I sank deeper into my chair. "She helps him find his way. You know he's not as good at it, since—"

She didn't let me finish. "Yeah, yeah, I know. Since you sucked away all his mojo." She leaned forward, conspiratorially. "Listen, all I'm telling you is that you'd better make sure you give him some awfully good memories to take with him after this weekend, so that he isn't prone to temptation. If you know what I mean."

My cheeks were burning, and I looked down at my hands, fumbling around in my lap.

Tabby laughed at my discomfort. "Don't be such a prude, Hope!"

"It's not that. It's . . ." I looked up at her, pleading.

She looked at me funny, and then she realized what I was trying to say. Her mouth dropped open.

"You mean to tell me that you've been together for ten years and you're not having sex? You're twenty-eight years old, Hope! You've got a hunky archangel pledging his eternal troth and lusting after you. What are you waiting for?"

She jumped to her feet and began pacing in disbelief.

"I don't know," I mumbled. "It just never seemed like the right time."

She wheeled and flung her arms wide, ever the drama queen, as she began lecturing me.

"When would be the right time? The Apocalypse? That's about the only thing left that hasn't happened to you two since you've been together. Seriously. What are you thinking?"

"I don't know," I repeated, defensively. I was regretting I had admitted anything.

"Honey," she said gently, coming down on her knees and taking my hands in hers. "Are you afraid? After the fire? Are you afraid you might get hurt again?"

I shook my head. My lurid memories of my oozing skin, scorched by second-degree burns after Michael's spirit had turned to flame, had faded with time, and I knew that the risk he posed to me was gone.

"No. That's not it. I'm pretty sure we're still in balance with each other. I can feel his heat, but it's never more than that when we kiss. It's perfectly safe, I think."

She frowned. "Then what can it possibly be? Does he not want to?"

I sighed, closing my eyes. The crumpled spot in the drywall above my headboard was a constant reminder that no, Michael had no qualms about this, and that he was indeed getting impatient. About this and other things.

"I'm just not sure I should. At least, not until I know for sure that I can be with him forever. It will just make it that much harder when—if—I have to say goodbye."

She whistled low and sat back on her heels.

"I never would have guessed. Now listen. You're my friend, and I don't want to worry you unnecessarily. But don't assume that that archangel friend of his is *your* friend. You've told me enough about angels to know some of them aren't so fond of us mere mortals. Don't let her find a way to weasel in between you two. If you want to end things with Michael, that's your call. Don't let someone else do it for you."

She patted my knee before rising and leaving me to think about what she'd said—and what I'd seen pass between Michael and Gabrielle.

I wasn't left long to myself before Michael snuck in, empty bowls in hand.

"Hey," he said softly.

"Hey back," I answered, giving him a tremulous smile.

He sighed, looking over his shoulder to where Gabrielle was pacing.

"I have to go. Gabrielle is sensing something that requires our attention."

He waited, standing awkwardly as he balanced the bowls, one in each hand.

"What I said earlier. I meant it, Hope. We can't keep going on this way."

I looked up, trying to read his eyes, but in the fading evening light I could only see them glitter, mirrors reflecting back my own doubt.

I nodded, uncertain if I could trust my voice.

"I'll come back again, as soon as I can break away." He darted another glance at Gabrielle and I realized, perhaps for the first time, how much influence she had on my access to Michael. "In the meantime," he continued, "would you like me to send Enoch to visit you?"

His suggestion startled me, but before I could even process it, relief flooded my body. Enoch. Enoch would be perfect.

"I figured he might be the only one who could understand what you're going through. The choice you have to make."

"Because he was human once, too."

"Yes. Because he was human once, too."

I blinked away a tear.

"Thank you for understanding. I wish I could—"

"Sshh," he interrupted. "Don't apologize. One way or the other, we'll get through this, too. I love you, Hope."

My heart surged, never tiring of hearing the words.

"I love you," I whispered back as he walked out the door, leaving me to wonder how I could be so crazy as to make him wait.

four

LUCAS

I saw them before they saw me. They moved like a swarm through the suburban Atlanta mall, aimless in their wandering, searching voraciously for affirmation amidst the bright lights and shiny shop windows.

They were at that age when knees and elbows seem to protrude just a little bit too much, when baby fat suddenly melts away, leaving them poised at the moment when awkwardness turns into grace. They know it, though they aren't quite sure exactly what is happening, aren't yet sure of themselves, and they try out their new power awkwardly, like newborn fawns trying to walk. They flip their hair and steal glances in the plate-glass storefronts, comparing themselves to one another to assure themselves that they are normal. No, they are better than normal—they are pretty, prettier than the girls walking beside them.

There is always one around whom the swarm swirls: one girl

who does not go through this crisis of confidence, one girl whose worth doesn't come from looking at the awkwardness of another child. There was one such child in this group of thirteen-year-olds. The others jockeyed for position around her.

I was not interested in her. Not yet, anyway.

It was the one at the fringe who caught my eye today. I had been watching for months now. Her body's lines were not the lean graceful ones of her peers. They were soft and doughy, the growth spurt for which I was sure she longed not yet having materialized. The others moved like gazelles or colts, frisky and playful; she moved deliberately, her limbs heavy, afraid of doing the wrong thing. She had tried to dress like them, but she'd missed the little things—her tank top was too short, baring a bit of pudgy tummy, baby fat that would earn her the disdain of the others. Poor thing. She tried to be like them, but she was not one of them. She was there, I thought, under the grace of the queen bee, but for the moment, the queen had forgotten about her as she giggled and gossiped with other friends, sucking hard on the straws of the smoothies and frappuccinos they carried like emblems.

This one on the edge—the hanger-on, the vulnerable one—was the one I wanted. It would be like culling her from the herd.

I watched as they circled back to the food court. They nursed their drinks, none daring to order more food. The misfit snuck furtive looks at the pizza stall.

I smiled. Even if her stomach was full, her mind still remembered what it was like to be hungry. In this food court, a false cornucopia of plenty, she was reminded of want. In the final days of my exile, before I could again take physical form, I watched her in her shiny, clean foster home, hovering in the corners, my movements just a flicker of shadow and air that she never sensed. I saw how, when she thought everyone was asleep, she snuck into the kitchen and shoved her face full of whatever she could find—handfuls of crunchy cereal, snatched straight from the box; pillowy mouthfuls of snowy white bread, eaten so fast she nearly choked on the crusts—fearful that the next day, it would all be taken away from her again.

I smiled because I knew that her memories and her fear would betray her, and she would be mine.

I nodded, and my Fallen comrades fell in around me. We were just a few; too many of us would attract attention. But as long as the girls outnumbered us, as long as we looked a little baby-faced ourselves—too young to be a *real* threat, as the anxious mothers would rationalize—as long as we spent our money here, spreading it liberally among the purveyors of the artificiality that passes for American culture, we faded into the background, passing unnoticed.

With what should I tempt her? What should be the modern-day, mall-culture equivalent of the apple that tempted Eve?

An ice cream cone. I thought that would do it.

We sidled up next to the girls, where they had perched themselves next to the fountain at the mall, a prime site for watching and for being seen. The mother of one of the girls had dutifully agreed to chaperone them at the mall. She was seated a discreet distance apart, whiling away her time on the bench by checking her phone. She darted us a glance, once, sized us up as safe teenagers, and went back to her texting. Neighborhood gossip? Berating a misbehaving child? No, wait—she was twirling an errant lock of hair around her finger, her three-inch heel dangling from her foot. The way she touched her face, the fleeting smile—I'd bet on harmless flirting with the stay-at-home dad from down the block. Whatever it was, it didn't matter. She was not like Hope and Rorie's mother: no keen eye of observation, no watchful alertness, ready to strike at any potential threat. She was fully absorbed in her phone, too caught up in her tiny world's intrigue to notice anything we did.

And so we continued insinuating ourselves into the girls' midst. We joked with them, easily, letting slip ever so casually that we'd all dropped out of school to work in the music industry.

"I bet you can sing like an angel." I smiled, knowingly, at the awkward one, watching her unbelieving expression as I offered her the cone. She stared at the perfect swirls of vanilla, concentrating hard to keep herself from blushing as she listened to what I told her. I leaned in close, so close that I could feel the heat of her burning cheeks as I whispered in her ear.

"I bet you sing like an angel because you look like one," I told her. "You're the prettiest one here."

She stammered something incomprehensible, holding the cone stiffly out as if she didn't know what to do with it. I smiled indulgently.

"Don't let it melt. I'd hate to see that creamy goodness go to waste," I said, trailing my finger over the place where the melting ice cream dripped over the edge of the cone and onto her hand. When I licked the ice cream off my finger, her mouth dropped open slightly. Even *I* wanted to groan at how over the top it was. But it seemed to be working.

I fought off the grimace that rippled across my face as the pain overwhelmed me—I mustn't scare the girl. But the pain pleased me. If God was displeased, I must be doing something right. It might be twisted reasoning, but it was the only reasoning my brain knew after millennia of punishment. I welcomed it, a comforting constant after the surprise of my early release from the incarceration that I suffered following my failed attack on Heaven's Gate.

An early release. Even as I'd reveled in the freedom, unfurling my wings to ride the wind currents with abandon, I'd wondered if it was a trick, a trap of some sort. For months I'd hung back, gathering my forces about me and grilling them for news, looking for signs, trying to discern His will. But they had nothing: no insights to help me understand the mind of my enemy, not even evidence that God's army was aware that He had released me.

And before long, the lure of revenge had proved too strong, drawing me back to meddle in the lives of these pathetic humans.

It stung my pride, to be sure, but it would be typical for God, in His hubris, to dismiss me as harmless. Or perhaps He simply needed the oppositional force of my hatred to justify His existence. It wasn't for me to decipher His ways; I'd never understood His logic. After all, it was His complete rejection of the facts about His abomination, mankind, that had gotten us into this mess to begin with. All I knew was that it was my duty to oppose His failure in the best way I could. I hoarded every jab of pain to my heart like a treasure—His displeasure my reward, the agony of it simply a signpost along the journey, an encouragement and blessing in its own way.

Even when it meant singling out a pathetic little creature like this girl for my attention, it served a higher purpose, and so I embraced it.

"My name is Luke," I continued. "What's yours?"

"Macey," she finally managed to blurt.

Some of the other girls were snickering at her, but she didn't notice them. Her attention was entirely on me. I grinned, rewarding her for telling me her name.

"I hope to see you here again, Macey."

The other girl, the queen bee, barged through the cluster of girls to grab Macey roughly by the shoulder. She shot me a venomous glare, asserting her authority, before she addressed her friend.

"Come on, Macey. We need to go."

Was the queen bee impatient? Embarrassed? Afraid?

I noticed the slight lift of her chin, the way she wrapped an arm around Macey.

No, she was none of these things. She was protective. She didn't want Macey's feelings hurt by the other girls. And she didn't want Macey's hopes to be raised, and then dashed, by me.

Or maybe, just maybe, she was incredulous that anyone but she could merit my attention.

I let a wicked grin spread across my face. Jealousy was such a fascinating emotion. A little dash of it, especially when I hadn't planned on it, always added depth to my little misadventures, for underneath jealousy I always found a tiny bit of shame. It made someone's downfall that much more rewarding to orchestrate.

"It's time to go," the queen insisted, shooting me a warning look before dragging Macey away through the sea of food court tables and chairs.

The girls fell in behind them, the queen having spoken. Macey looked back at me over her shoulder and I winked. She flushed a deeper red and looked away. But before she disappeared, I caught her looking my way once more, the expression on her face as full of longing as the nights I watched her standing before the fluorescent glow of the open refrigerator, poised on the edge of doing what she knew, rationally, she shouldn't do.

The bait was set.

This was shaping up to be more interesting than I'd anticipated.

In the meantime, I could be patient. I had waited over twelve years to get to this point, after all. And at the end of my wait, it would not be these two silly girls I would destroy. It would be Hope and Michael.

five

The final bell had rung, disgorging a swirling torrent of bodies into the wide halls of the prestigious Buckhead school. Rorie moved deliberately through the crush, the eye of her own storm, people parting to make way for her entire group of chattering girls as she scanned the streams moving about her. The banter swirled about her, but today she didn't engage, didn't even seem to care. She had a few minutes before basketball practice. A few precious minutes to make sure her girls were all in order. And today—after the incident at the mall last week—there was one girl in particular she wanted to keep an eye on.

She spotted Macey down the hall and spun out of the group, her kilted skirt twirling about her.

"Rorie, where are you going?"

Rorie looked back over her shoulder. Her friend Melissa stood at the edge of the crowd, her arms hugging her books to her chest, one eyebrow arched in silent accusation.

Rorie smiled. "I'll catch up with you at practice. I just need a minute to talk to someone."

"Someone?" Melissa demanded, tilting her head. "Don't you mean your pet, Macey?"

A snicker rippled through the girls, who had gathered themselves into a small knot to watch the exchange between Melissa and Rorie.

"Don't call her that," Rorie stated quietly. "She's my friend. You could stand to be nice to her once in a while, you know."

"What for? Honestly, Rorie, you're wasting your time."

"Was it a waste when I stopped people from gossiping about you being a bed wetter in fifth grade?" Rorie shot back.

Melissa blanched as a twitter of amusement went up around her. She clutched her books so tightly that her knuckles turned white, embarrassed into silence.

Rorie smiled a treacly sweet smile and fluttered her fingers in a wave, dismissing Melissa and with her the crowd, knowing that her own meanness would be the subject of a flurry of posts and chats and then be forgotten, washed away by the next wave of gossip.

"Love you!" she called above the noise of the busy hall, reminding them that while she was in charge, it was they, themselves, who wanted it that way. They wanted to bask in the sunshine of her approval. She had a vague but growing sense of the gravitational pull she exercised on the tiny universe of which she was the center, and a sense of responsibility to exercise that power wisely.

They called Macey Rorie's project. Sometimes it infuriated Rorie. Was she the only one of them who saw Macey as a real person, she wondered? Was she the only one who was amazed at

Macey's courage, having to make her way into a new family, a new school, while her real family disintegrated before her eyes?

Of course, the others didn't know that. None of them were supposed to know anything about it. But sometimes, Rorie knew, staying on the teachers' good sides paid off, like when she got excused from French class to work in the attendance office. Sometimes, if you worked on it, you could put yourself in the right place to hear the things that adults wanted to keep from you. Real world things. Rorie liked the important feeling she got, knowing things that the others didn't know.

"Macey!" Rorie grabbed her friend by the shoulder. Macey turned, startled, a fearful expression on her face until she realized who it was. Then she allowed herself a shy smile.

"Hi, Rorie. Don't you have practice?" Rorie noticed that Macey's free hand was hanging behind her back. Macey was hiding something.

"What's that?"

"What?" Macey said, pretending she didn't understand and blushing furiously.

"Is that your phone?" Rorie demanded. "Are you talking to that boy from the mall? Here, let me see!" Rorie, ever used to getting her way, reached around and pulled the phone from Macey's hand, holding it above her head as if taunting her.

"No, Rorie. Please . . ." Macey's whining died out as Rorie began to read, turning her back on the red-faced Macey to walk down the hall.

"You are! You're texting him. You shouldn't have given him your number, Macey. He's got to be in high school. Or at least old enough to be—"

And then, still reading the message, Rorie stopped short.

"You can't be serious." Rorie turned around to confront her

friend. "Macey, you can't meet him downtown. That's dangerous. You don't know anything about him."

"Do too!" the other girl yelped, snatching the phone back from Rorie. "I know he likes me."

"Honey, lots of people like you," Rorie soothed. "You have lots of friends."

"No, I don't," Macey insisted, shaking her head. "*You* have lots of friends. Friends who barely tolerate me. He could be *my* friend. *My* friend, Rorie." Her eyes drifted behind Rorie.

Rorie looked over her shoulder, following Macey's gaze, to see her other friends huddled by their lockers, watching and laughing, barely bothering to hide their amusement. Melissa stood slightly apart, stony-faced, still smarting from the embarrassment Rorie had just inflicted upon her.

Rorie mouthed, contrite, *I'm sorry.* Melissa drew her eyebrows together sharply, tilting her head as if weighing Rorie's apology. And then, shrugging, she turned to the other girls, gathering them up and herding them toward the locker room. Melissa shot one last glance over her shoulder from the edge of the drifting pack of girls as they left. Rorie beamed at her, mouthing back, *thank you.*

Macey muttered something under her breath as she fumbled with her phone. Rorie turned back to her.

"What? What did you say, Macey?"

She didn't look up. "I said, maybe he could even be, be my boyfriend."

Rorie sighed. She could see how badly Macey needed this. She needed to feel wanted and accepted for herself. If Rorie couldn't make that happen here, at school—at least not *yet*—the least she could do was be supportive of Macey.

But something about the situation still didn't feel right to her.

"Don't you think he's a little old for you, Macey?"

"He's not that much older," Macey countered. "Not even six years. That's nothing."

She was right, Rorie guessed. Six years wasn't that much.

Yet Rorie heard her mother's voice in her head. For adults, maybe, six years wasn't much. But at this age? Six years was a whole ocean of time and experience, the difference between taking the school bus and being behind the wheel. It was the gap between PG and R, between Disney Channel and horror movies, between mooning over holding hands and, well, other things.

Rorie felt herself blushing at the thought of it.

Rebelliously, she squashed the suspicions that her mother's cautious nature had implanted in her brain, almost as strong as the imprint of her DNA. After all, Rorie's mother had been apprehensive about Michael for a long time, too, infecting Rorie with her fear that there was something not quite as it seemed in his long absences—with his shrugging, off-handed explanations that they were "top secret"—and in his patient interest in her sister, Hope.

But Rorie had known better, deep in her heart. She'd known it from the instant she'd met Michael. He'd plopped down onto the floor next to her and taken her tiny, pale hand in his calloused, sun-worn grasp, letting himself be led into an afternoon of playing with her dolls, not even blinking an eye when she'd forced a pink-swathed Barbie onto him and chosen the grizzled GI Joe for herself. She'd known then, even if she had been too young to articulate it, that Michael was genuine.

No, Rorie wouldn't let her mother's mistrust of the world color her own views. After all, look how things had turned out with Michael and Hope. Surely it could be just as good with Macey and—what was his name?—Luke.

Rorie turned to Macey and forced a grin, wanting to cheer her

on. She wound her arm through Macey's and leaned in, conspiratorially, to talk as they began to walk toward the locker room.

"He'd better be taking you somewhere good."

Macey beamed, squeezing Rorie's arm excitedly. "Karaoke. I'm
going to sing 'Popular'—you know the one, from *Wicked*?"

Rorie wanted to groan. Macey, like every other girl in this middle school, seemed quite unable to grasp that the song was meant
ironically. Oh, well, Rorie thought.

"He'll love it," she chirped brightly. "You'll call me as soon as
you get home, right?" she urged, unable to fully quell the protective instinct that hovered near the surface. Her mind was racing
with the possibilities of what could go wrong, and what she could
do if it did—her mother's daughter, after all. She had to learn to
trust her friend more.

"I'll tell you everything," Macey gushed. "I promise."

six

HOPE

"Miss Carmichael, you have a visitor. A Mr. Angelus?"

"Mr. Who?" I blurted from behind the mounds of papers piled on my desk.

"A Mr. Enoch Angelus?" the harried receptionist repeated, looking a little scandalized from behind her proper spectacles and high-necked blouse. "He doesn't have an appointment. And he seems a little . . . different than your usual clients. Shall I ask him to get on your calendar another time?"

I hid a smile. If she tried her normal gentle persuasion to tactfully get Enoch to vacate her reception area, she'd be in for a big surprise—she'd be more likely to find herself on a dinner date to the local Hare Krishna temple than be able to get rid of him.

"No, let him in. I was expecting him. I'll just take my lunch break now."

"If you say so," she said, looking doubtful, before disappearing to retrieve my guest.

I'd been waiting on Enoch's arrival ever since Michael had left. It was a relief, then, when he burst through my office doorway in his old guise—a blind, slow moving, cane-wielding hippie once again.

"Enoch!" I moved swiftly across the room, throwing my arms around him. "I'm so glad to see you!"

"And I you, my dear. At least, in a manner of speaking."

The receptionist pursed her lips in disapproval. "Will you be going out to lunch, then?"

"Thank you, dear, but not for me," Enoch responded with a smile. He patted the pocket of his army-issue fatigue jacket. "Brought some jerky, so I'm fine."

"I packed my lunch today, too."

The receptionist hesitated, lingering awkwardly at the door.

"What is it, Elaine?"

"Er . . . it's just that Andrew asked me to remind you that he's waiting for you to write that motion on the Washington case."

I glowered back at her. The Washington case was my bugaboo, and everyone, even Elaine, knew it. Ike Washington was a functioning adult, but his IQ was low enough to legally classify him as intellectually disabled. Add to it that he had a history of being abused as a child and the equivalent of a third-grade reading ability, and I thought he qualified more for extra services than jail time. I didn't think it was right to prosecute a man like that. But as my boss kept reminding me, he picked the cases, and he had his own reasons for picking them. It was my job to prosecute them and do the best I could to win—even when I was winning against Ike Washington.

"Don't like it? Just think of yourself as playing devil's advocate," he'd said, dismissing my qualms with a wave of his hand as he flipped through the case files. "It's good practice. Everyone needs someone to argue the other side. That's all the devil's advocate is— the voice of doubt, making sure the justices have taken everything into consideration. Even the popes used to use them when they evaluated presumed holy people for sainthood." He'd thrust the file at me, and the discussion was over. I had no choice. Prosecuting Ike Washington was, in his mind, just another job to do.

"Thank you," I said tartly, skewering Elaine with a pointed look until she faded away.

"Come sit down with me," I said, dragging Enoch behind me to the small conference table in the corner, swiping the extra case books and files away to clear a space for him. I was too junior to have a window, and the space was tiny, but the maintenance staff took care with the ancient pecan paneling that graced our walls, burnishing them to a glow that seemed to scatter a diffuse light around the room. The layout and architecture, while completely inconvenient, was a lovely reminder of the graces of old Atlanta.

I settled him down and went to my desk, pulling my insulated lunch bag from a drawer. Enoch was unwrapping his jerky as I rejoined him.

"Bon appétit," he said, holding up the shriveled meat. I saluted his lunch with my own, a cup of soup in a Thermos.

My mind was racing, trying to figure out where to begin. I fought off a rising sense of anxiety as I slurped my soup. I needed to move to be able to talk about Michael's and my decision; just thinking about it made me feel like I couldn't breathe, and I knew from experience that Enoch's blind stare only made me feel more pinned down. If my body was in motion, maybe I wouldn't feel so trapped, like any choice I made was the wrong one.

As it was, I needn't have worried, for Enoch dove right into the conversation. He didn't ask me what I was thinking or what was going on between Michael and me, for which I was grateful. Instead, he launched into a story.

"Do you know, Hope, that it was Gabrielle who came to me when I was offered my own opportunity to become an angel? It was her right in her role as Messenger, I suppose. So it was she who came to me. I found her waiting at a well when I came near to draw water for my herd.

"When I realized who she was and why she was there attending me, I was surprised, of course. And troubled. Who was I to leave aside my humanity? Who was I to sit in the heavens? And I could see that the very same thoughts were warring in Gabrielle's mind. She could scarcely believe the message she'd been entrusted to deliver. And yet she spoke the words, as distasteful as they were to her, letting God's will be known."

He paused to bite off a hunk of jerky and chew.

"Gabrielle didn't want you to become an angel?" I asked. "But why?"

"Oh, she means well, our Gabrielle," he answered, dabbing at the corner of his beard. "She doesn't despise humans, like the Fallen do. Nor does she blame them for the evil in the world."

"Like Raph does," I interjected, remembering how hard it was for Raphael to set aside his disgust at mankind long enough to help Michael and protect me from the Fallen.

"Yes," Enoch nodded, waving one hand in the air as if the animosity of one of God's mightiest archangels was a trivial thing. "Like Raph. Gabrielle didn't—doesn't—feel the same way. But she does think of humanity as inferior to the angels. Beneath them, if you will. The offer of angelic immortality to a human confirmed this deeply held belief, you see; what could such an offer mean if not that it was better, after all, to be an angel? But it shook her, too, for if a human could be offered such glory, there was really very little difference between us. If we could be worthy of that, we were not such inferior creatures, after all."

I peered at him over my cup.

"Does she still think that, Enoch? Does she still think that humans are less worthy than angels?"

He brought gnarled fingers to his grizzly beard and thought about my question. "I would imagine so."

"So your ascension was hard to swallow."

"As I imagine it was hard for her to join in Michael's pledge to protect your sister."

His comment surprised me; I had never realized she was a less-than-willing participant in that vow.

"But she seems perfectly fine helping Michael with his duties protecting the innocent on Earth," I countered, confused. "Why would she object to adding one more to the list?"

"He singled Rorie out for his particular protection. It was his choice, not God's. And he did it out of his love for you, which, I imagine, Gabrielle finds to be a distraction from his duties. After all, if it weren't for you, she wouldn't have been dragged into helping him defend God's people here on Earth."

I ignored the stab of guilt at the mention of how I'd hobbled Michael's senses, forcing him to rely upon his partnership with Gabrielle to find his way. "He does love me, doesn't he, Enoch?" I sounded a little too plaintive, even to my own ears, and I looked down at the conference table, rubbing at an imagined mar in the marble as I waited for him to answer.

"My dear, if your heart does not know the truth by now, it never will. The mutterings of an old fool such as myself will make no difference. And the feelings of one disgruntled archangel are irrelevant, as well. What matters is how you feel about him, and about your future. You love him, too, yes?"

I felt my heart constrict a little, just thinking about him. It had been three weeks since he had left, and the emptiness I felt just seemed to grow.

"Of course."

I let the certainty of my answer stand on its own while Enoch and I ate in silence.

"Enoch, how could you leave them behind?" I finally asked. "Your family?"

"Ah. That was difficult, it was. But you must remember, my dear—I was an old man, much as I appear to you now. My children were grown, grandfathers themselves. My favorite wives were dead. My story had been told. If I stayed among them, it was to count out the last of my days, slowly drying up and desiccating before them. But to become spirit—to move like the wind and even the rain among them—ah, that, to me, was a gift."

"I never thought of it like that."

"Like what, dear?"

"That by becoming an angel you'd be able to be with them always. I thought of it more as abandoning my family," I confessed.

"Is that what is bothering you, then? The thought of leaving them behind?"

I nodded, trusting that he could see me through his blind eyes and dark glasses. "I don't understand why they—why God won't let me live out my life here on Earth, like you did. It doesn't seem fair."

"I don't think God bothers Himself much with precedent," he muttered wryly. "After all, He gets to set the rules. If He wants to make sure His people are protected, and that Michael isn't torn by competing loyalties, He may feel time is of the essence—that He must force your hand. In some respects, He has been extraordinarily generous, giving you as much time as He has. After all, it has been twelve years. You will accomplish nothing by railing against the terms of His offer. You just have to come to grips with your choice."

"Why now? Why, after all this time, must I rush to my decision? Why is Michael pushing me so hard?" I thought back to the hushed exchange I'd witnessed between Gabrielle and Michael. Something had subtly shifted in the constellation of stars that governed our agreement—something I couldn't put my finger on. But it was there.

"I don't know, Hope," Enoch replied gently. "But I sense that this is not the only question bothering you about your decision."

I shrugged, not sure if I could actually articulate my feelings. "Go on, then. Tell me what it is."

I hesitated. My other reason sounded supremely selfish and self-centered. But I had no one else to share it with.

"Who would I be, if I wasn't myself anymore?" I asked. "If I wasn't . . . Hope?"

"Ah. I see. Your personhood. It is important to you?"

I looked at him sharply. "How could it not be?"

"Fair enough," he assented, laughing. "What you are raising is a weighty question. And I acknowledge: your identity is not something to be taken lightly. I spoke of it, in fact, the first time we met in the desert—you remember?"

I thought back to that day when Michael and I had sought him out for information about the Prophecy. He'd talked about my name, and what it signaled about my connection to Michael.

"I remember, Enoch."

"Yes, your sense of self is important. But of whom do you speak when you speak of Hope Carmichael?"

I sighed. I hated it when he went all philosophical on me.

"You know who I am, Enoch. Do you really need to practice the Socratic method on me? I feel like I'm back in law school."

"Indulge me," he said with a slight grin. "Just tell me, who is Hope Carmichael?"

I wriggled on my chair, suddenly uncomfortable. "I'm a lawyer."

"Yes, I see that. Your fancy office and all that," he said, raising a hand to gesture dismissively at the rows and rows of shelves stuffed with books and the grand diplomas hanging crookedly on my walls. "Go on."

"I'm a Tech alum. I'm a friend. I'm a sister and a daughter."

"Of whom?"

"Oh, come on, Enoch, this is nonsense."

"I have a point in asking you these things. Believe me. Just answer the question."

"Fine." I shrugged, not knowing where he was going with this. "I'm a friend to many people, but to Tabby most of all. I'm a sister to Rorie. I'm Mona's daughter. Mona's and Don's. And I am the Bearer," I added, my fingers trailing up to the Mark on my neck. "I'm the Bearer of the Key." I deliberately left out any reference to Michael.

"Good," Enoch said, giving me a satisfied smile. "You see it, don't you?"

I stared at the shiny lenses of his sunglasses, not understanding.

He patted my hand. "What you have done is define yourself in relationship to other people. When you think about it this way, you do not exist as an entity unto yourself, Hope. Even your profession—it couldn't exist except in relation to your clients." He gestured at the heavy chair of carved cherrywood that was poised, empty, in front of my desk. "Without someone to sit in that seat, you are not really a lawyer. Everything requires relationship. And your role as the Bearer is no different. It connects you to all of the angels, but to the Fallen—and to Michael—in particular.

"This means that by choosing to be with Michael—by becoming

an angel, like him—you would not be subjugating your identity to his. You would just be embracing and bringing to the forefront this other aspect of your identity: the aspect of your relationship to him."

I stared at the empty lunchbox on the table in front of me. "You make it sound so simple."

"It is simple, if you can accept that you will always be defined in a context, not as an absolute. It is that way for all of us, Hope. Why should it be any different for you?"

What he was saying sounded logical. So why did it feel so difficult?

"I still think of myself as that old desert dweller, Hope. I still think of myself as a husband, a father, a grandfather, as well you know. But I am an angel, too, and in the fullness of time, that part of my story demanded to be told. Telling it does not negate what came before. And—and this is the most important—it does not change the essence of who you are. The core of you is eternal, and it remains the same regardless of the role you happen to be playing at any given time. That is how it is for me. And it would be the same for you."

"No. It would be different."

"Why do you think so?"

I stared at the worn wood that made up our office. The chrome and plastic signs of modernity were intruding on it everywhere— the computer screen on my desk, the speaker phone on the conference table.

"You lived in a time," I began, "when man accepted as reality that there was some dialogue between Earth and Heaven. People back then knew about angels. Your family knew what had happened to you. They watched you ascend into Heaven. Mine won't have that luxury. Mine will be left wondering what happened to me." Just saying the words made the sharp pain they would feel come into sharp focus.

"Knowing did not diminish my family's loss, Hope," he chided me gently, reaching across the table to pat my hand. "Other than giving them certainty. You could give them that, too, you know. You could tell your family where you were going."

I could see it in my mind's eye: my fumbling attempt to explain the unreality of my life to my mother, whose whole life was premised on logic and order; the unraveling of her worldview, and her, as she realized that the tragedies of her life—the great mysteries—were not mysteries at all, that I had been an actor in them, causing the losses and the pain.

No. Even if the offer allowed for the possibility—which I knew, based on how Michael had explained it to me long ago and many times since, it didn't—I couldn't tell my mother the truth. Nor could I keep up a pretense of a human life, far away, punctuated by visits. The compromise that had allowed Michael to see me over the last twelve years while I made up my mind would not be an option for me. Heaven was forcing me to make a choice.

Enoch's blind eyes seemed to watch me from behind his sunglasses.

"So you must have complete separation," he said. "And in the scenario you envision, you feel it is a choice of your happiness versus theirs?"

I nodded.

"I see. Then, indeed, you do have a dilemma. But that Mark upon your neck—the Prophecy of which you are part—has always posed difficult choices to you, hasn't it?"

I seized upon his statement to ask him something that had been occupying my thinking more and more lately.

"Enoch, why didn't more of the Fallen take their opportunity for forgiveness? Why did they insist on trying to overthrow Heaven when all they had to do was accept the grace being offered to them?"

He crumpled up the spent wrapper of his jerky and threw it on the table. "Ah. That is an excellent question. I don't know if I have the answers for you, Hope."

"But what do you think?" I prompted.

His gnarled hands gripped the top of his cane as he considered my question.

"Maybe their minds were too addled to understand what they were being offered. They suffered from millennia of pain, the punishment of separation from God. You saw how that affected Michael, even in a short period of time. Imagine what hundreds and thousands of years of that would do to someone."

I shook my head. "Then none of them would have understood. None of them would have crossed over. But many of them did. It has to be more than that."

Enoch nodded. "You are right. It was more than that. It is the same as it is for mankind. Even though forgiveness has been offered, the Fallen have to accept their redemption. They have to ultimately believe themselves forgiven, even though they know very well that they do not deserve it in any sense of the word. If they cannot believe it, if they therefore cannot forgive themselves enough to accept this grace, they will find the doors of Heaven closed to them forever. And to believe themselves forgiven, they must first admit that they were wrong: wrong to rebel against God, and wrong in their rejection of mankind. You realize their aim, do you not?"

"What do you mean?"

"The Fallen do not torture mankind, tempting them to sin, out of idle boredom. Their goal is to alienate God and man. The holdouts refuse to admit that Christ's redemption of man will stand for all time, even after Christ told them himself that it would."

"1 Peter 18–20," I said, recognizing his reference to Jesus speaking to the imprisoned spirits—or, as we knew them, the Fallen Angels.

"That's right. They still think they can prove to God that His creation is flawed. Irredeemable. They want to get Him to change His mind; they've always thought that they can provoke mankind into such horrible acts that God will have no choice to but acknowledge their point of view. Those who refuse their own redemption—the forgiveness hard won by you and Michael—still cling to this fantasy. And as long as they do, the Prophecy may forever remain unfulfilled. Lucas being the prime example."

His mention of Lucas jolted me.

"What do you think happened to him, Enoch? What has he been doing all this time?" I whispered, almost afraid that speaking of him aloud would somehow invoke him or summon his presence.

"Michael's defeat of him only merited us a temporary spell of peace," he said. "He can only be truly destroyed by God's hand, and no matter how hateful he is, I don't think God is ready to do such a thing. So I imagine he has been waiting. Gathering his strength. Plotting his revenge while God doles out his punishment."

I shuddered.

"Have you known all along what would happen, Enoch? Back in the desert, did you know?"

The corners of his lips tightened. "I thought I knew. But I couldn't be certain. And in the end, it didn't matter what I knew. You two were the ones who needed to find the truth."

"But you understood what the words of the Prophecy meant, didn't you?" I pressed him.

He tilted his head in assent.

"And that's why you sent Arthur to my parents when I was a baby. It was you, wasn't it?"

He looked bemused. "Did Arthur tell you that?"

I shook my head, half-smiling as I remember how tortured Arthur had looked while Michael and I had grilled him. Over the years, we'd tried to pry it out of him, but all he'd ever say was that he'd been entrusted with a mission to make sure I came of age with both parents intact so that the Prophecy might be fulfilled. Try as we might, he wouldn't divulge who had sent him on this mission.

"No. But I don't think that many people really understood the Prophecy. I can't think of anybody but you."

He made a gruff noise in the back of his throat. "It doesn't really matter now, does it?"

I ignored his attempt to dodge the question and got to my real point. "Did you mean it, Enoch, when you said the Prophecy remained unfulfilled?"

He paused, choosing his words carefully. "I cannot be certain. But if the highest amongst the Fallen—those who were among the leaders of the rebellion—reject the sacrifice made on their behalf, then I worry we are left with unfinished business, Hope. Eventually, Lucas will be free again. We will need to reckon with him when that time comes."

I felt an unwelcome shadow cross my heart.

"Surely that'll be a long time from now," I said. "I can't imagine God would look lightly upon his attack and rebellion."

Enoch shrugged. "God's time—and God's methods—are not always discernible to humans. Or His angels, for that matter," he acknowledged, spreading his hands wide. "I hope for all of our sakes that you are right."

There was a gentle rap on my door. Elaine poked her head in. She eyed Enoch speculatively as she delivered her message.

"Just a reminder—five minutes until your next meeting. And Mr. Anderson asked me to remind you that he needs that amicus brief before seven tonight," she added, glancing over at the pile of files on my desk. "Will you be needing another consultation? Shall we set up a file for Mr. Angelus?"

I sighed. "No, I don't think that will be necessary."

Elaine pulled the door closed behind her as she slipped away.

"I suppose you have to go now," I said to Enoch.

He hoisted himself up from the table and waddled over to me. "Think about what I said, my dear," he admonished, placing his hand on my shoulder. He looked around my office one last time. "Think very carefully about just how important these stacks of papers, the polished marble and wood, are to you. And how important you are to them."

Then, with a twinkle in his eye, he was gone.

I looked around my office. Was he right? Were the mounds of files—cases pending, motions to be filed, precedents to be researched—really that meaningless in the scheme of things? I knew that if I chose to abandon it, the office would not skip a beat: my boss would simply shuffle another eager associate into my office, my caseload, and my spot in the queue for the DA's office. I would be forgotten within weeks.

But would *I* be the same if I left it all behind? And if I wouldn't be, did it really matter?

∿

My talk with Enoch had only deepened my worry. My mind was filled with warring thoughts about my relationship with Michael, the choices I had to make, and what I could expect when the eventual confrontation with Lucas came to pass—not to mention the intricacies of the Ike Washington case at work. I was so preoccupied that I barely noticed the abnormal quiet surrounding our traditional Sunday night family dinner. That is, until my mother started interrogating both Rorie and me.

"Something is clearly troubling you both. Neither one of you has touched a thing on your plates."

I quickly pushed my mashed potatoes around on my plate before answering her. "Just a tough case, Mom." I smiled.

"Rorie?"

Rorie was staring off into space.

"Aurora?" My mother insisted, her tone sharper. "Are you listening to me at all?"

"Yes, ma'am," Rorie answered, flushing a deep red. "I'm sorry. I was just thinking about school."

"I didn't know middle school algebra and Georgia history could be so fascinating," my mother retorted dryly. "If you're so preoccupied you can't even focus on your dinner, you may be excused."

That was all the encouragement Rorie needed. She chugged her glass of milk as she got up from the bench and dashed off, swiping the top of my mom's head with a kiss as she went by.

"I wonder what's eating her?" I asked. Rorie was normally sunny and outgoing. It wasn't like her to mope.

"Oh, I'm sure it's just normal teenage angst," my mother replied. "Nothing to worry about."

I hoped she was right. But I had my doubts. And of course, normal wasn't exactly a word I expected to hear people use to describe my family.

Surprised to find myself, rather than my mother, being the suspicious and careful one this time, I excused myself from the table to seek out my sister. I found her hunkered down on the porch swing, listlessly pushing it with one foot.

"What's up, buttercup?" I asked, tucking a strand of her loose blond hair behind her ear as I plopped down next to her. "You seem a little down. Something going on at school?"

She shrugged. "Nothing, really. It's just . . ."

I waited patiently, watching the shifting emotions flit across her face while she struggled to put her feelings into voice.

She looked down at her hands. "Girls can be so . . . so spiteful. So mean. Even I can be, sometimes. I don't mean to be, but it just happens. The words just come out, and then I feel so awful afterward. And I want to stop it, I want to stop all of it." Her hands twisted helplessly in her lap, the words spilling out without pause now. "But sometimes I can't. I see things happening that are wrong, and I try to stop them from happening, but sometimes my friends won't listen to me. And sometimes when I try to help somebody, it turns out worse because of me."

She turned in the seat, her eyes plaintive.

"Did that ever happen to you, Hope?"

I gripped her hand tightly in mine, my soul aching at the thought of the petty slings and arrows that I was certain littered her middle school life. I remembered how painful it was to learn the truth of unintended consequences—to learn that good intentions, no matter how heartfelt, could never make up for bad outcomes. Her world might seem small, the outrages she suffered and witnessed tiny in the scheme of things, but at her age her little group of friends was her entire universe, and the hurt would be deep, even if it was fleeting.

"Oh, yes," I said, squeezing her fingers in mine, pulling her in to sag into my shoulder, hoping she would draw some strength and comfort from me. "I know exactly what you mean."

seven

LUCAS

I love it when a good plan comes together.

At first, I had expected this to be a tad more challenging. I had thought that I might need to call upon some of my greater angelic powers by this stage. But not even the so-called security of a top-notch private school proved much of an issue—how could it, when we angels can change our guise at will? All I had to do was have one of my crew appear momentarily as Macey's foster mother—an uptight country club hoverer if there ever was one—and voila! Just like that, Macey's "cousin," Luke, received authorization to pick her up after school. I got a sticker for the window of my car and every-thing, gaining me free entry into the carpool.

Of course, I wouldn't be picking up Macey all the time—just every now and then. To help out. Because being a suburban mother, as we all know, is so dreadfully challenging and busy.

It didn't take much to get Macey to lie to her foster parents. We'd practiced it in the car, over and over, just like I wanted her to say it. How excited she was to get to work on the backstage crew for the fall musical. How she was making new friends. How sometimes, with it being theater and all, her schedule might get erratic, but she would always find a ride home so that she wouldn't inconvenience her uptight parents. How she begged them *please* to not to embarrass her by coming to watch the rehearsals—none of the other kids' parents did that; she would just *die* if they did that to her.

When she did it right, I showered her with praise and flashed her my brightest, most beaming smile. Awash in my attention, she was eager to lie to them, eager to let them hear what they wanted to hear.

Daddy and Mommy were nearly bursting at the seams with relief, I'm sure, when Macey told them her news. Messed-up little Macey was finally adapting. Was finally becoming normal. They would do anything to help her fit in—even if it meant holding their eager selves back and waiting, patiently, for the opening night of the musical, marked in a big red circle on the family calendar, when they could finally see just what Macey had been up to all this time.

They didn't stop to wonder just why they seemed to have avoided all of the pains of adjustment and rebellion—all the things that would be absolutely normal for a girl in Macey's situation—that the Social Services case worker had advised them to be mindful of. Why should they be surprised that she'd blossomed overnight? They'd been lucky all their lives, lucky and blessed. This was just another episode of perfection in their perfect Buckhead lives.

If they had questions—Who was in the show? What work was she doing on the set?—Macey was prepared, drilled by me with answers to hypothetical questions. We even made up cute stories of backstage intrigue and forgotten lines, understudies thrust into the limelight due to sore throats, the time the upper story of the set nearly collapsed during an early dress rehearsal when a main character's costume got stuck on a nail, the stranded child tugging so hard to get free and complete her blocking that the entire thing swayed, yet she never flubbed her lines as the crew watched in amazement. All of this, just to spin the fantasy of happy Macey for her foster parents. Macey did it willingly: after all, she loved me, and she wanted her foster parents to be happy.

Like I said, too easy.

I looked at the clock on my dashboard. It was time.

I turned my expectant gaze toward the steps of the school. Like clockwork, the big doors of the brick building opened and began to disgorge little khaki-and-plaid-clad drones. Some of the students dared to rebel against the required uniform, showing individuality with the meager options at their disposal—rioting socks, a more shocking haircut. But very few chose to stand out.

And that was why it was always so easy to spot my Macey in the crowd: Macey who never quite mastered her hair bow, so that her coarse hair always flopped into her face; Macey who still tugged at her ill-fitting skirt, uncomfortable and self-conscious; Macey who usually had some unsightly stain on her white polo shirt, which strained at the buttons; Macey who always trailed at the edge of some group, dragging her backpack on the ground behind her, not quite fitting in.

What was this?

I squinted to be sure. Then I leaned back in my seat, grinning.

Today, Macey was not alone.

I waited in the driver's seat, my fingers drumming a beat on the steering wheel. This was about to get more interesting.

Macey climbed into the front seat and pulled the door closed behind her. I looked her over. She was wearing the makeup I'd bought for her—a slash of red lipstick so bright it looked like her mouth was bleeding, heavy eyeliner and mascara, bright spots of pink on her cheeks. It made her look a little older than her twelve years, especially if one wanted to convince oneself that she was not just a little girl.

Macey looked at me anxiously, waiting.

I rewarded her with a smile. "Hello, beautiful."

She returned a shy smile. "Do you like my makeup? I did it just the way you said."

I took her hand in mine. "You did it perfectly. I knew you would. Thank you for doing it for me." I tilted my head toward the window. Through the tinted glass I could see Macey's friend, tapping her toe. "Is that Rorie waiting outside?"

Macey nodded. She fidgeted in her seat. It had been just a few weeks, but she was already aware of the rules. She already knew that I could get angry if she didn't follow them exactly.

"She asked to come with us. I told her that I didn't know, but that I would ask. Can she, Luke? Since I've been spending so much time with you, I haven't been able to see her for a while."

"You know I like to have you all to myself, Macey." Her face turned deep red. She was stung by my rebuke. But was it enough? I had hoped by this point she would be willingly leaving behind the few friends she did have, centering her whole life on me, like a flower turning its petals to the sun. I turned my face into a mask, testing how much control I had over her.

She darted a pleading look through her thick eyelashes. "Please?" So she was testing her own powers, as well.

Oh, little girl, I thought. You have no idea what you are playing at. But so be it.

"All right," I conceded, watching her bounce in the seat in delight. "Just this once. I had something special I wanted to show you, but I guess Rorie can come along, too."

The person behind me in carpool honked at me. I glared into the rear view mirror. "Hurry up, then, Macey. Get Rorie in here or we're leaving without her."

She flung herself across the front seat to hug me in gratitude, and then she scrambled out of the car to retrieve Rorie.

My body convulsed in agony as Hope's little sister climbed in the car. I gripped the wheel, breathing in and out, in and out, the steady rhythm helping me ride the crest of the torment inflicted upon me by God.

"Luke is taking us somewhere special," Macey burbled excitedly as Rorie settled herself into the backseat.

"Where?" Rorie demanded as I pulled away from the curb. She was looking back longingly at their school, as if she was already regretting her decision to come along.

"It's a surprise," I demurred, my lips turning up in a slight grin. "You wouldn't want to ruin it for Macey, would you, Rorie?"

"But I have to let my mom know where I am," she insisted. "So should you, Macey."

"Just tell her you're at my house," Macey countered. The lies were coming easily to her now.

I peered at Rorie in the backseat. Her arms were crossed, a slight pout settling on her lips. I raised an eyebrow.

"You don't trust me, Rorie?"

She flushed, embarrassed to be called out. "It's not that. I just—"

Macey interrupted her. "Don't ruin it for me, Rorie. Please. You always get your way. Let me get my way for once."

I watched as Rorie struggled with her conscience. Finally, she answered Macey. "Okay. I guess it won't hurt just this once."

I gave Macey's hand a squeeze. So far, so good.

The Atlanta traffic had slowed to a crawl. Why human beings would subject themselves to this kind of tedium was beyond me.

"Where are we going? What's my surprise?" Macey interrupted my thoughts.

"Patience. You'll see soon enough. Have a snack while you wait." I tossed her a bag of Oreos I'd stashed away. She hesitated, looked to Rorie in the backseat.

"I shouldn't. I've been trying to eat healthier like Rorie."

A flare of annoyance shot through me. Rorie, Rorie, Rorie. So meddlesome.

"Go ahead, you deserve it," I urged her. That was all it took for Macey to tear into the bag and begin stuffing her face with cookies.

"Where are we?" Rorie demanded from the backseat. Macey looked out the windows. We were almost to our destination, and it was clear from Rorie's reaction that she had never been to this part of the city. It was run down, the boarded windows and peeling paint of the surrounding buildings giving the whole neighborhood an air of abandonment. Chain-link fences sagged and flopped over. Everywhere one looked, graffiti tagged the walls, decrying the police and promising violence and hopelessness. Used needles jumbled and fought for supremacy with the mounds of trash that seemed to be overtaking every yard. *Warning: Pit Bull* had been carefully spray-painted over and over on one decrepit house, the words festooned around the walls and stairs.

"I recognize this place," Macey whispered, shrinking into her seat. "My mom used to come here."

"Your mom?" Rorie questioned, snapping her head around.

"My real mom."

"Oh."

I watched Macey out of the corner of my eye. The confidence that had started to blossom within her was snuffed out. She looked hunted now. Afraid.

Which was exactly how I wanted her.

"Why would you take us to a place like this?" Rorie demanded, her voice dripping with disgust. "I want to go home."

I ignored her outburst.

"Macey, honey. Remember the day we met? At the mall?"

She nodded, unsure.

"Remember what I told you about your voice? How I thought you probably sing like an angel?"

She nodded again.

"Well, I wasn't kidding when I told you my friends and I make music. I know it doesn't look like much, but this neighborhood is where my friends have their recording studio. They have mixers and even equipment for making videos. You'd like that, wouldn't you? To hear yourself singing on the radio? To see yourself on TV?"

Her eyes grew wide, unsure whether or not to believe me.

We had pulled up to a stop sign. A crowd of people was swarming on the corner, things passing quickly between hands. A few darted furtive glances at us, checking us out to be sure we weren't with the police. Others, sitting on stoops or on overturned milk crates, stared at us with dead eyes before returning their attention to the spoons and syringes in their hands.

"They're doing drugs," Rorie gasped from the backseat. "Look, Macey, look at them all. I think those people are selling drugs, too."

"I know," Macey answered with a flat voice.

"Those people won't hurt you," I soothed as I pulled away from the scene. "That's not why we're here, anyway. Right, Macey?"

She nodded silently, staring at her hands, which she now gripped in her lap.

"I don't care. We want to go home. Now." Rorie was leaning forward, hovering over Macey's seat. "Macey, let's go home."

"That's up to Macey," I said sharply, the warning note in my voice clear. "This is Macey's special day."

"Macey, please," she whined, not used to having her plans spoiled. "I don't like it here. Let's go home."

"Macey."

She looked up into my eyes. This was the part I loved. The part where I put her trust to the test. The part where she became mine, heart and soul.

"Macey, please stay. Do it for me." I reached out my hand, waiting for her response.

She blinked, hard. And after a long moment—exhaling a deep breath—she put her pudgy, sweaty hand in mine and smiled.

"For you," she said.

I beamed at her, giving her hand a squeeze. "Good girl." Looking over my shoulder, I gave Rorie a choice. "You can stay with us, or I can drop you at the commuter train station. It's up to you—here or MARTA. But Macey is staying with me."

Rorie squirmed in the backseat, struggling with her decision. Should she go home to mommy like a good little girl, leaving her friend in what she considered to be, at best, dubious circumstances? Should she stick around and try to protect her pet? She was a bit unpredictable—after all, she was Mona's daughter. Mona was no coward and could be prone to impulsive decisions. In fact, I had grown to appreciate Mona over the years. If it weren't for her steadfastly clinging to the safety of logic and science, who knew what comforts of religion Rorie might have embraced? That would have made my job that much harder. Even so, a daughter of Mona Carmichael would have a mind of her own—could be headstrong, even. What would Aurora do now as she grappled with her conscience?

Cowed, she dropped her eyes and looked out the window. "MARTA. I'll take MARTA."

The Vine City station was not that far away. I pulled up to the passenger drop and watched Rorie climb out of the backseat. She looked dejected—the queen bee, unsure of herself for once. She turned back, raising an unsure hand to Macey as we drove away. Macey's eyes remained glued to her friend, watching as she finally began the walk to the train.

It was the perfect opportunity to drive the wedge between them a little deeper.

"She's just jealous, Macey. Jealous that you are getting all the attention. Jealous that you have a boyfriend and she doesn't."

"She won't tell on me, will she?"

"Nah. If she told on you, she'd just embarrass herself. She'd have to admit she can't compete with you."

Macey turned. Her eyes glittered with pride, with love, with gratitude.

I smiled, indulgent. I knew I was lucky. I hadn't anticipated that her mother had been on heroin, and that Macey had been here before, to this neighborhood they called the Bluff. I hadn't anticipated the upwelling of caution that memories of this place had created. But Rorie's unexpected company had created the perfect foil. The meddling girl forced the issue much sooner than I would have preferred, but in the end, it worked to my advantage. Macey chose me over her friend. In doing so, Macey shook away the warnings of her troubled past, pushed underground any doubts she might have held.

We could go faster than I had planned. Now, each step she took sealed me in her trust. Any doubts would get harder and harder to confront. How could she back out now?

The searing pain that threatened to rip my body anew only confirmed my confidence. Rorie forgotten, Macey would walk into the lion's den willingly. No—eagerly.

eight

Three months later . . .

Macey stumbled into the school office during last period. As soon as she saw her, Rorie sighed. Luckily, she was there to intercept her friend—though, truth be told, she always made her own luck, putting herself in the places where she could trade upon her maturity and work ethic to gain the trust of adults and get access to freedoms that the rest of her classmates didn't enjoy.

Rorie pulled Macey into the hallway—the one where the counselors took harried parents who'd been called in for conferences—before any of the front desk ladies noticed her. It was about time she dealt with this.

"Macey," Rorie hissed through her teeth. "What are you doing here? Why aren't you in class?"

But as she took a closer look, dismayed, it became obvious why Macey wasn't in class. It had been happening over and over again, ever since the two of them had gone to that creepy neighborhood with Luke. Rorie knew because she'd been putting the teachers' complaints, including their requests that Macey receive detention and her parents be called in for a conference, through the shredder as soon as they landed in the discipline bin in the office. If Macey's foster parents knew about her problems, they might decline to foster her anymore; Macey had worried about that often in the early days of the girls' friendship. Rorie couldn't risk that: better if she trusted herself to help her friend.

Macey was asleep—or dead—on her feet. Her honey-gold skin was mottled, almost gray, and great dark circles sagged under her eyes, which themselves were barely slits.

"Is that a bruise?" Rorie reached up to gingerly touch Macey's temple. Macey flinched away.

"Don't. Don't touch me," she mumbled.

Rorie sighed and snatched the piece of paper from her friend's hand. The teacher had scribbled Macey's offense—sleeping in class. Well, duh. Rorie crumpled up the note.

"How many times is this, Macey? How many times have you been sent from class for falling asleep this week?"

She swayed on her feet. "I don't know. Just leave me alone, Rorie."

Rorie did the quick math in her head. This was already the third time, and it was only Wednesday. Last week there had been five notes, including an assigned in-school suspension for wearing her uniform too provocatively and a request that the school counselor speak to her about her hygiene. In the months since Macey had chosen to go with Luke to the Bluff, she'd quit trying to ingratiate her way into Rorie's circle of friends, preferring to spend all of her spare time with him. It was rare for her to spend any time with Rorie at all, now, and Rorie realized with a start that it had been weeks since they'd done anything together.

And all that time, the notes to the office had kept coming, a trickle at first, now a torrent. The two girls were just lucky, Rorie knew, that the teachers weren't talking to each other—at least, not yet. That the change of terms had disrupted their hawk-like surveillance of the class, and for now, the escalation of Macey's problems had escaped their eyes.

But Rorie wouldn't be able to shelter Macey much longer. The notes were coming too fast now. She examined her friend critically, wondering what exactly was going on, as Macey absentmindedly began scratching at her arms, pushing at her sleeves.

Rorie's eyes narrowed. "Macey, are you doing drugs?"

Macey snatched her arm away, hiding it behind her back. Before she could answer, the final bell rang. She twitched nervously. "Please, Rorie. Just let me go."

"Go where?" Rorie demanded. "To him? To Luke? No way. This is his fault."

"Then come with me. Please?" she whined, pulling Rorie into an awkward hug.

Rorie gagged, fighting back the impulse to push her away. Macey smelled like sweat and something else Rorie didn't recognize—the mixture of scents was worse than the miasma of teenage sweat and hormones that hung familiarly about the locker room. It was clear Macey hadn't washed for days. Or brushed her teeth.

"Luke really likes you. He wants you to come with me today. He told me. Please, Rorie?"

Rorie stepped away, unwrapping Macey's arms from around her neck and trying hard to not breathe in her sour breath. "Neither one of us should be going anywhere with him. Is he making you do this, Macey?"

A tear rolled down her face.

"I need him, Rorie. He's the only one who understands. He understands about my mom—my real mom—and everything."

Rorie snorted, disgusted. But then she thought of all Macey had been through—Macey's mom had endangered her, over and over again, with her drug use, Rorie realized—and she felt ashamed for being so judgmental. She sighed, forcing herself to remain patient with her friend.

"I know that must help, to be able to talk about her, not to have to pretend that everything is okay just because you're in a new foster home. But Macey, just because he understands doesn't mean he's good for you." Rorie reached out and touched her lank hair. "Your parents—I mean your foster parents—they still don't know about him. Do they?"

Macey hesitated, dropping her eyes to her shoes, before shaking her head.

"Don't you think you should tell them?"

Macey seemed to shrink into herself. "I'm afraid," she admitted, barely a whisper.

Rorie bit back the words that instantly sprang to her lips: *So am I.*

"Please don't get me in trouble, Rorie." Macey was begging. "You're my only other friend. They'll send me away if they find out I've been lying to them."

Rorie chewed on the corner of her bottom lip. There had to be a way to help without having to tell on Macey. There had to be.

"Macey, look at me."

Macey lifted her head, looking doubtfully at Rorie where she stood, arms crossed.

"Is he coming here today?" Rorie asked.

Macey nodded, sniffing back her tears and dragging her arm across her runny nose.

"Do you want me to make him go away?"

Macey shrugged, hesitating. Rorie looked at her hard and decided for her friend.

"You stay here," she said. "Don't move."

She pushed Macey out of the office into the hallway, warning her again to stay put, and made her way to the carpool line.

All the way she reasoned with herself. Luke wouldn't want to make a scene. He wouldn't want to risk drawing attention to himself. She could get him to leave Macey this afternoon, and then she could work on convincing Macey to tell her foster parents, herself. She could do this, she thought, squaring her shoulders as she burst from the brick building into the cold sunlight of the late afternoon. She was good at getting her way.

It was easy to spot his car.

Luke rolled down the window as she approached. "Hello, Rorie. Climb in."

"What are you doing to her?" Rorie demanded, ignoring the invitation and looking over her shoulder to make sure no one was paying any attention to them.

"Me? I'm just giving Macey the attention she deserves. Surely she's told you about her singing lessons. The recording sessions. The videos."

Rorie shook my head. "I don't believe you. But whatever it is you are doing, you're getting her in trouble at school."

"You think Macey's lying to you?" he asked.

Rorie's eyes narrowed. *Would Macey lie to me?* Rorie wouldn't put it past him to deliberately sow the seeds of discord between them. He was that manipulative, that controlling.

"Why would Macey do such a thing? I think you're just jealous of her. Look at her. Look at how she's blossoming." He pointed over Rorie's shoulder.

Rorie turned to see Macey making her way toward the car,

dragging a dirty backpack behind her. *No!* she thought. *You were supposed to stay inside. Now what am I supposed to do?* Wordlessly, with a rising sense of panic, she watched Macey climb into the backseat.

"What are you doing to her?" she repeated.

Rorie didn't wait for him to answer, turning to address Macey through the open window. "Can't you see that he's hurting you? Please, Macey, I know something is wrong. Just a few minutes ago you wanted me to get him to leave you alone. You don't have to do this. You don't. Please let me help you!"

Macey finally responded, lifting her head heavily to address Rorie.

"You're just jealous, Rorie. Luke told me."

"Why would you listen to Luke? I'm your friend."

"Luke loves me," Macey insisted. "You'll see. If you come with us you'll see." She patted the empty space beside her, absent-mindedly.

Frustrated, Rorie darted an angry look at Luke. He smiled smugly. It didn't matter to him, Rorie realized, that Macey was reciting the words like a zombie. As long as Macey kept telling herself that he loved her, as long as she was willing to tell Rorie the same, Luke had what he needed. He was in control.

"I'm not coming with you," Rorie shot back, not hesitating in the least. She leaned into the car, sticking her head in through the passenger side window, ignoring Luke and directing her words at Macey. "But what I am going to do is tell your foster mother. I know she doesn't realize what's going on. I don't think she'd want you to be spending all this time with Luke and his friends, Macey, in that horrible place. Please, just get out of the car and come with me, and we can talk to your mom. She'll know what to do."

Luke shifted in his seat and darted an anxious look at Macey.

For just an instant, Macey hesitated as she considered Rorie's proposition. A flicker of hope lit up her eyes.

But then Luke began to speak.

"She doesn't love you, Macey," he said. "Rorie doesn't understand. Your foster mother doesn't either—she doesn't know what you've gone through, so she doesn't understand what it's like to need a little something to get through the day. All she'll do is judge you. She'll punish you. Maybe even send you away."

Macey looked stricken. Just like that, he'd snuffed out her hope, playing to her greatest fear.

"Don't listen to him, Macey," Rorie urged. "The Jacksons *both* love you. They'll help you. They'll forgive you. I just know it."

A horrible silence settled around them.

"I'll tell the principal. I'll tell him you're not really Macey's cousin," Rorie blurted, her knuckles turning white as she gripped the edge of the window, leaning in even further to break the standoff. "I'll tell him where you've been taking her. I'll tell him how you've been lying about drama club, Macey. How you faked the note to get him carpool access. I'll tell him everything, Macey, unless you get out of the car and come with me now."

Before anything else could happen, Luke's hand darted out and grabbed Rorie by her shirt collar. She gasped and struggled, trying to breathe, but he just tightened his grip. Her neck startled turning a mottled red.

"Listen to me, queen bee," he whispered. "You're in over your head. I know where you live. I know everything there is to know about your family. I know your sister's license plate, and your mother's. I know where your sister goes to exercise class. I know where your mother throws her clay pots. I know their favorite coffee shops, and I know how they like their coffee."

Rorie clamped her hands on the car window, trying to pull away, but Luke yanked her back in.

"2260 AHJ DeKalb County," he said. "That's the license plate on your mother's Audi. Expiration in October, if I remember correctly. And she goes up to the Spruill Center, doesn't she? I think she likes their kiln."

The blood drained from Rorie's face as he continued to rattle off the facts of her family's life.

"She likes to get a matcha tea latte on the way home from the Center. Expensive tastes, your mother. Hope, though, she's fine with a plain black coffee, no sweetener. Am I right?"

He let the certainty of his knowledge, and what it meant for Rorie's family, settle around her.

"Don't think that pretty little Buckhead gate will keep you safe. You say a word about this to anybody, and I mean anybody, Rorie—including your mother or sister—and I will destroy your family. I will kill every last one of them. The next time I invite you to come with us, you keep that in mind."

He let Rorie go abruptly, leaving her to stumble back against the curb, catching her breath as it came in broken gasps. Luke rolled up the windows as he pulled away. Macey didn't even look back.

She *wanted* to be with him, Rorie realized.

Rorie's hands trailed up to her neck, fingering the tender spot where he'd choked her with her own shirt. For the first time in her life, she didn't know what to do. There was no one she could turn to.

No one.

nine

HOPE

"Honey, you're being awfully quiet. How is school going?"

Rorie fiddled with her silverware, not looking up from her plate. "Okay, I guess."

Something was not right. My mother saw it. I saw it. Tabby and Arthur, both of whom were having dinner with us, saw it. Our normally sunny girl was withdrawn and reserved. How long she'd been this way, I didn't know. I cursed myself for having been so preoccupied with my own problems that I hadn't been paying attention.

"What's up, buttercup?" I cajoled. "You're normally a chatterbox. Did you have a bad test today or something?"

She shrugged. "No."

"Bad basketball practice?"

"No."

My mother raised an eyebrow and looked at me over her glasses.

"Your friends haven't been around lately," she said to Rorie. "How are they doing?"

Another shrug. "Fine, I guess."

"You guess?" My mother was not one for vague answers. "Don't you know?"

"They're fine, Mom," Rorie mumbled, stabbing at her chicken breast. "They're all fine."

My mother and I looked at one another, puzzled by her recalcitrance.

"Well, I don't like all this moodiness lately," my mother added as gently as she could. "At least try to be pleasant at the dinner table, especially while we have guests."

Rorie rolled her eyes. "As if Tabby and Arthur are guests. They practically live here," she pronounced, drawing out the word "live" with dramatic flair.

Tabby and I hid our smiles in our napkins. Our own teen years weren't all that distant.

Arthur diplomatically tried another direction. "How is that friend of yours, Macey, adjusting to school? Do you still see much of her?"

At the mention of Macey's name, Rorie's head whipped up from her plate, fixing Arthur with a stare.

"Why are you asking about Macey?" she pressed.

Arthur looked bewildered. "I just haven't heard you talking about her lately. She used to be here all the time—you were virtually inseparable all summer. She seemed like a nice girl."

Rorie gulped hard. "I guess so."

Arthur continued. "Why aren't you spending as much time with her anymore?"

Rorie turned beet red, and then she looked down at her plate. "Macey has a boyfriend now," she answered curtly.

We looked around at each other, unsure what to make of this news. I felt a bit ashamed of my own reaction of disbelief that someone as mousy and plain as Macey could have a boyfriend while Rorie did not. Tabby had a completely different reaction, however.

"Rorie," she said sternly, fixing my sister with a hard look through her glasses, "you aren't jealous of Macey, are you? Please tell me you aren't fighting over a boy."

"No!" Rorie shouted back, her face turning a deeper shade of red. She jumped to her feet, throwing her napkin down on her plate. "I can't believe you would say that. You don't understand. None of you do!"

As she stomped off toward the staircase, Arthur caught her hand and tugged her back, pulling her up close to him where he could wrap a protective arm around her.

"Tell us then," he urged quietly. "Tell us what is going on."

Rorie's lips were quivering. I thought about the last real conversation I'd had with her—her frustration at trying to help a friend and having things go wrong. I had chalked it up to petty middle school mean girl behavior. But the way Rorie was acting, I could tell this was something bigger.

The buzzy feeling I'd reluctantly learned to accept as my own angelic intuition—the inadvertent transfer of Michael's powers to me—surged in my head, taking my breath away. I began to feel alarmed. Something was seriously wrong. Something to do with Macey. Pulse quickening, I peered closer at my sister, still and silent in Arthur's embrace.

"I can't," Rorie whispered, staring at her feet. "I can't tell you."

"Did you promise Macey you would keep a secret for her, Rorie?" I asked, struggling to keep my voice level.

Rorie shrugged, refusing to meet my eye.

"Honey, if it is bothering you, you should tell us," my mother coaxed. "Sometimes children are entrusted with secrets that are too big for them to handle. Sometimes the best thing you can do is tell an adult."

"I'm not a baby!" she protested, her head rising proudly. Her eyes were defiant, daring us to contradict her.

I looked at her, this girl caught on the edge between childhood and adolescence, and my heart caught. I wondered how any of us made it through when the world was sending so many mixed messages about who we were and what we were supposed to do. I thought of the piles of teen magazines Rorie voraciously read— their barrage of headlines about losing weight, having a "beach ready" body, and being sexy; articles about having the "right" clothes and the "right" hair, what was "in" and "out," and how to tell if you were popular—as if such things really mattered. And then there was the endless circling around the topic of boys—"Does He Like You? Take this Test and Find Out!" "How to Tell if He's Cheating On You!" The self-doubt the media could engender, even in a girl as strong as Rorie, could make anything seem like a crisis of epic proportions. My heart felt a pang of pity for what she was going through.

And now this. Whatever it was, it was clearly overwhelming her. I tried to banish the background noise in my brain so that I could focus on my sister. For now, I made myself stay back. It wouldn't help if all four of us jumped into the fray, making her feel like we were ganging up on her.

"Of course you're not a baby, Rorie," Arthur soothed, his low voice calming all of us. "Your mother was just offering you an alternative to keeping it bottled up inside. If Macey made you make a promise that you're uncomfortable with, you have a safe place—a safe set of people—with whom you can share it. We all need that— no matter what age we're at."

Rorie looked doubtful.

"Do you want to tell just one of us?" Tabby prompted, peering at Rorie over her glasses. I always found it disconcerting when she did that, as if she were somehow silently reprimanding me, but Rorie didn't seem to mind. She hesitated, as if unsure how to answer.

"Rorie," I said calmly. "Remember when we talked about how sometimes when we try to help, we inadvertently make things worse? Keeping promises that should never have been made can work the same way. If a promise puts someone you love in a bad position, you don't have to keep it."

"Really?"

"Really." I said it with as much certainty as I could muster.

"But what if by telling it, somebody else I care about gets hurt?" she asked.

My head was pounding so violently now that I thought I could hear my own blood, rushing through my veins.

"You can't worry about that. You can't know for certain that any of those things you fear will come to pass. You can only act on what you know for sure. To help the friend you know needs help," I offered, trying to draw her out.

"Even telling one of us might make you feel better, Aurora," Tabby said carefully.

Rorie hesitated, then nodded. "Just one of you."

"I can understand that." Tabby rose from the table. "It was time for me to go anyway. C'mon, Arthur, you can walk me out."

"No, wait!" Rorie cried. "I want you to stay."

"Me?" Tabby nearly squeaked. "You want to tell me?"

Rorie nodded quickly. "I need to tell you. I'm *only* going to tell you. But Hope can listen if she wants. I mean, it's okay if Hope overhears me telling you. But I'm only telling *you*, all right?"

Tabby shot me a look. It was a strange distinction she was

making, but it seemed important to her. I shrugged my shoulders. Whatever it was, we would just go with it.

"Okay, then," Tabby said, looking oddly pleased. "If that's what you want. Mona, Arthur—is this all okay with you?"

"Of course," my mother smiled wistfully. Try as she might, she always seemed to be the odd one out. But she, too, seemed to agree that the most important thing was getting Rorie to spit it out—no matter what it took. "Why don't you girls go out on the back porch? Arthur can help me clean up."

I took Rorie's hand and led her to the porch swing, pulling her down between Tabby and me. The winter air was crisp. In the dying light, I could see the last of the dead leaves clinging to bare branches, shades of gold and russet and crimson that danced as the sun's last rays glanced off their edges.

"Okay, Rorie. Tell us what's going on," I prompted.

"You won't judge me?" she pleaded.

"Of course not," I answered, startled that she would even think such a thing.

"Spit it out," Tabby pressed as she set the swing in motion with her foot. "Tell us—or, I mean, *only* me—everything."

Rorie settled into the cushions with a deep sigh, turning away from me and directing her speech to Tabby alone.

"So, remember how I said Macey has a boyfriend?"

Tabby nodded, spurring her on.

"We met him at the mall. He was with a big group of boys. Older boys. I don't even think they're in high school anymore. I don't know what they do, though. They hang out all the time, so I don't think they're in college, either."

Tabby shot me a concerned look over Rorie's head.

"The day we met him, he went straight for Macey. It was like nobody else existed. And, I don't mean this in a vicious way—you've got to believe me, 'cause I like Macey, I really do—but I was suspicious. I mean, out of all of us, why would he pick her? Especially an older boy like him? But I didn't want to hurt her feelings, so I didn't say anything to her. I just decided to keep an eye on things. And the more I watched them, the more it worried me."

"That was very insightful of you, Macey. But what made you so worried?" Tabby pressed.

"It was like the whole world centered around him," Rorie answered. "None of us even existed for her anymore. He wanted all of her spare time to be with him. He even arranged somehow to pick her up after school, with a carpool pass and everything. Macey started lying about being in drama club so that she could stay after school with him without having to tell her parents."

"You mean they didn't know about Macey and this boy?"

Rorie shook her head vehemently. "Not at all. See what I mean? Why would you hide it if it was okay?

"And she started acting different. When she was with him, he would make her change into these outfits he brought for her. Even at school, in her uniform, he made her wear all this makeup and do her hair funny. It was like he was trying to make her look grown up.

"At school she wouldn't talk to any of us. She never had her homework done."

Her tone was getting almost desperate now. I nodded at Tabby over my sister's head. She needed to keep drawing Rorie out.

"So as you were noticing all these things, what did you and your friends do?" Tabby asked, keeping her tone steady and calm.

Rorie shrugged. "Most of my friends hadn't really liked her anyway. They said it just proved them right, that she didn't belong. But I was really worried. So one day I asked if I could go with her after school."

Tabby gave the swing a push with her foot. "That was brave of you, Rorie. It takes a really good friend to do such a thing."

Rorie didn't answer at first. "I was scared," she admitted. "But I didn't trust Luke. I wanted to see what he was doing with her for myself."

I froze.

"Rorie, what did you say his name was?" I interrupted.

"Luke," she said, forgetting that she wasn't supposed to be telling *me* anything. "Why?"

Luke. Lucas. Luke. Lucas.

The two names, interchangeable, kept repeating on an endless loop through my brain.

I had been through too much to believe in coincidences any more. But how could it be? How could it be that Lucas was free, stalking the earth, stalking my family? I'd expected him to be jailed forever—at least as long as *my* forever. But he'd seemingly insinuated himself into the heart of my family—into my baby sister's very life—without me even knowing he was at large.

Tabby and I looked at each other. I knew we were worried about the same thing.

"Rorie," I said, forcing myself to remain calm, needing to get the full story from her while I let this new information sift through my mind. "When you went with them, where did you go?"

"He said he was taking Macey to a recording studio. But it was in a really scary part of town I'd never been to. It looked like a war zone, and everybody seemed like they were dazed. I should have stayed with Macey, but I was afraid. I made them take me to the MARTA station. And now I think he takes her there every day after school. Sometimes she doesn't even come to school any- more. When she does, she's not the same. She's always smelly and unwashed, and she's too tired to pay attention. She even sleeps during tests! I was trying to help her, but she wouldn't listen to me."

I tried to ignore the horrible images that were rushing through my mind, pressing themselves against my conscience, demanding attention. "Do you remember the name of the neighborhood?" I asked.

Rorie shook her head, shoulders slumping.

Tabitha had a glint in her eye. "Honey, could you see any big buildings from where you were? In the skyline? Think carefully."

Rorie paused, her forehead crumpling up in concentration. "There was a big dome. And I could see the Coca-Cola building."

"Was the MARTA station they took you to the Vine City MARTA?"

"Yes!" She turned to Tabby, excited and proud that she'd remembered. "Yes, that was it. How did you know?"

"My congregation volunteers in the Neighborhood Association Gardens there. There aren't that many parts of town that desolate." She shot me a cautionary look over Rorie's head. "They call it the Bluff. It's infamous. One of the most dangerous neighborhoods in America, with one of the biggest open-air heroin markets anywhere. It's been like that for decades—generations of people, lured into the drug trade and drug use, trapped in an endless cycle of poverty. Though now most of the customers are suburban rich kids driving in from the Perimeter."

She shifted in the swing to face Rorie, drawing my sister's hands into hers. "Rorie, is that the secret? That he is taking her to the Bluff? Did he tell you he was going to shoot videos or pictures of Macey? Did he try to get you to go, too?"

I felt nauseated, afraid to hear her answer. Rorie couldn't speak. She was sobbing, her wracked body shaking the chains of the swing. Tabby enfolded Rorie in her arms.

"There's no recording studio, is there?" Rorie asked, turning her tear-streaked face to mine.

There was no good answer—none that would soothe her broken heart.

"It will be okay, Rorie," said Tabby finally. "You did the right thing telling us. Now we can get the police."

"No!" Rorie shrieked, flailing wildly. "You can't go to the police. Tell her, Hope!" She turned and clung to me, begging. "You can't tell anybody. I promised! I promised! He made me promise not to tell anybody, especially not you and Mom!"

"Whoa, whoa, hold on, sweetie. Of course we need to go the police. They can help Macey. They can get her away from Luke." My tongue stumbled over his name, thick with fear.

"No!" she wailed, a long, mournful cry. "He said he'll kill you! He'll kill you all if he knows I told!"

A cold wave of shock went through me.

"Aurora," I said, a little too sharply. "Luke told you he'd kill us?"

She nodded, still sobbing. "He knows where we live, Hope. He knows everything about Mom. And you. He said he would kill us all. Please, please don't go to the police!" She draped her arms around my neck and pulled me close. I could feel her heart racing as I squeezed her hard.

"Go get my mother and Arthur," I told Tabby.

She shot off the swing in an instant. Rorie was shaking, quivering against me, her body wracked by heaving sobs. I held her close, rocking her gently, trying to get her to calm down.

"Shhhh. You did the right thing, Rorie. Nobody is going to hurt us. I promise you, nobody can touch us."

I hoped I'd be able to keep that promise.

~

Soon, Tabby came back, my mom and Arthur in tow.

"Tabby, can you take Rorie upstairs? See if you can get her to lie down for a while?"

"Sure thing," Tabby said, briskly.

"No! Don't make me go. I want to stay with you," my sister protested.

Tabby was all business. "No need for that. Let's take you upstairs and get you cleaned up. Come on, now," she tutted at Rorie, hustling her off the swing. "There's my girl." It was the same gentle firmness I'd seen her use on errant churchgoers: no nonsense, but kind. Rorie had no chance to protest before Tabby whisked her away, out of earshot.

I turned to Arthur and Mom.

"Did Tabby tell you what's going on?"

They shook their heads, confused. "Just that the big secret was something to do with Macey. What's going on, Hope?"

I let out a shaky breath.

"I think Macey's gotten herself into trouble. It sounds like she's taken up with an older boy, one who may be taking advantage of her. I hope I'm wrong, but I think he might be forcing her into child pornography—or worse. The way Rorie describes it, he may be trafficking her for sex."

Arthur sucked in his breath.

"Are you sure?" my mother demanded, her face full of concern.

"No, of course I'm not sure," I snapped, irritated. "But I'm worried enough about what Rorie said to take it seriously. You saw her—she's practically hysterical. This boy—if we can call him that—claims to know where we live. Apparently he threatened Rorie when she tried to intervene. He said he would kill us if she told anyone."

My mother gripped the long, billowy cascade of her sweater

about her, her shock subsumed by the systematic problem-solving that her mind had automatically kicked into.

"What do we know about the situation? Anything specific?"

I looked at Arthur carefully, hoping he could read the warning in my eyes. *Do not react. Do not react to what I am about to say.*

"We think he's been taking her to the Bluff," I said. "Rorie never actually went into whatever building they're using, thank God, so we aren't really sure where to look. But it's a small neighborhood, so I'm sure we can get somebody to talk." I paused, bracing myself to say the next words aloud. "And we know that the boy's name is Luke."

As I'd hoped, Arthur didn't flinch at the name. But then he looked at me, and I could see in his eyes what I was glad my mother couldn't: that he was as concerned as I was that this, finally, was how Lucas was making his return known to us.

My mother was already moving back to the kitchen to grab her phone. "We need to call the police. And Macey's parents. Immediately."

A part of me wanted to grab her arm, to stop her. I still remembered the last sight I'd had of Lucas, standing over Michael's body. If he really had returned, we were all in danger. Why should we do anything rash? Luke had been bringing Macey home every night, according to Rorie. She still showed up at school most of the time, albeit not in great shape. We could wait this out tonight, make sure Macey was safe at home before getting the police involved.

But then the lawyer in me spoke. What if this wasn't Lucas? What if it was just some trafficker who needed to be put away? If we didn't catch him in the act, even if we could hide Macey away so that he'd never find her again, the court wouldn't be likely to act before he went after some other little girl—maybe even ours—and do it all over again.

My brain was screaming. Didn't we all see? Maybe this was what he'd planned—to trap us! To punish me for the countless ways that opening Heaven's Gate failed to get him what he wanted. It was too dangerous to face him without knowing more about the situation.

And I could hear what my mother would say if I voiced these fears aloud.

One night more of abuse in his hands is too much for any girl, Hope. I would expect you, of all people, to realize that.

Of course I knew. Of course. There really was no choice except to act.

We had to take the fight to him now.

Just as Lucas expected me to—just as he expected all of us to—so that we played right into his hands.

I ran my fingers through my hair and started pacing. "Okay, then, what do we do? We can't go charge the Bluff by ourselves. And we can't take Rorie with us. Nor can we leave her here alone."

"Are you still in touch with that special agent? The one who handled Hope's disappearance?" Arthur asked, turning to my mother.

"Agent Hale?" she asked, startled. "Well, no, but he would be easy enough to find. I don't think he'd have retired quite yet. I may even still have his cell phone number in my contacts."

I stopped in my tracks. "That's brilliant, Arthur. Mom, try to call him. If we can get the GBI to raid the Bluff, we might be able to get Macey out and shut the whole thing down."

"I'll try him right now, Hope. Maybe he can tell us how to handle informing Macey's parents, too." My mother swept out of the room.

I waited until I knew she was out of earshot before I turned to Arthur.

"It's him. I just know it's him," I said. "But why would Lucas do this, Arthur? Why target Rorie's friend?"

He frowned. "She's not the target. You are. He's using her to ultimately get to you. You have to be very careful, Hope."

My forehead furrowed into pleats of worry. "Maybe you should go find Michael before things get out of hand," I said.

Arthur shook his head. "I'm not sure that's wise. It will leave you all unprotected. He'll come if he is supposed to. He—or Gabrielle—will sense that you need it, and if you do, he'll bring the entire brotherhood pledged to Aurora's defense."

"And if we don't need him, I don't want to distract him or Gabrielle from what he's supposed to be doing." I recognized the logic in Arthur's argument. "You're right. We'll be better off with you here. Just in case."

He smiled, a fleeting tenderness that showed the extent of his worry. "I've always been here to watch your back. Ever since you were a bitty baby. You know that, girl."

I reached over to squeeze his hand, thinking just how much we had needed his protection—then, and now.

"I know."

∾

My mother had been technically correct, but a little optimistic. Agent Hale was only one week shy of his retirement. But, as he and my mother reckoned, one week was plenty of time to stage a raid on the Bluff, and plenty of time to figure out exactly where Macey was being taken when she disappeared from school.

He still had a soft spot for my mother. I suppose it was because he felt sorry for her, the way he'd had to let her know about my father's death right in the middle of my missing persons case. But whatever the reason, he didn't hesitate to say yes when my mother suggested he let Tabby and me stand and watch the operation with him on the night it all went down. We had good reason to be there, of course—me to help any victims freed in the raid with their legal needs, Tabitha to provide expert psychological exit counseling. But I knew the ease with which we were integrated into the stakeout had a lot to do with his loyalty to my mother—as well as his need to move quickly.

In our navy GBI windbreakers, holding binoculars that we periodically scanned over abandoned buildings and flophouses, Tabby and I waited for something to happen while Hale directed the operation below. From our perch, we could see the desolation that heroin had wreaked upon the neighborhood. It was like a patchwork quilt—here, a square yard, its actual dimensions obscured by weeds that had grown higher than a car; there, the burned-out shell of a home razed by arson or accident, never cleared; opposite, a building that could only generously be called a shanty, shiftless people loitering about its perimeter, waiting for a dealer or maybe something even worse. Here and there, a tidy, manicured lawn interrupted the fabric of decay and neglect, evidence of a determined homeowner fighting against the tide that threatened to engulf the neighborhood.

No one strolled the crumbling asphalt streets. No neighbors leaned over neat picket fences. What fences stood were made of chain link and were more likely to hold back a vicious pit bull than anything else.

It was hard to believe we were less than a mile from downtown, some of Atlanta's greatest landmarks only a stone's throw away. It was like a war zone had been thrown down in the middle of suburbia and left, forgotten, for twenty years. I pulled back from the window and shivered—it was no wonder that with my sheltered upbringing, I'd never even heard of this place.

Arthur had stayed behind at home with my mother and Rorie

to make sure they were safe. Macey's foster parents were waiting at their home, too. They'd been shocked when the GBI contacted them, overwhelmed. Hale had handled them gently, informing them of their daughter's situation as delicately as he could, picking his way through the conversational land mines while Macey's foster mother averted her eyes, her cheeks staining red. His reminder that Macey would need to go to the ER immediately after the operation, before she could be released to them, washed over them without acknowledgment. I think they preferred to stay in a state of ignorance than to know the details of the horrible things that had undoubtedly been done to their foster daughter, things that were unspeakable in the manicured lawns of Buckhead. Hale had already taken their statements so that nothing would hold them up from taking their daughter when the time came.

He'd taken Rorie's statement, too. My hair had stood on end as she'd given her detailed description of Luke, and the police artist had rendered her interpretation of Rorie's words in charcoal: slowly, Lucas's visage had sprung from the page. He hadn't even cared enough to adopt another physical persona to hide himself. It was as if he was brazenly flaunting the fact that he was back, rubbing my face in my helplessness. It was then that I knew for sure his intention: he was coming for me. He would hurt me in whatever way he could, and he wanted me to know it.

But maybe I was wrong, after all. Maybe it was my own mind, projecting my memories onto an artist's sketch. After all, it couldn't be Lucas—for if it were really Lucas, wouldn't Michael have come back? Wouldn't he have invoked the oaths of the angels who'd pledged themselves to Aurora's safety, all those years ago?

But aside from Arthur, none of them had shown their faces.

So it couldn't be him.

I kept chasing the logic, endless circles in my head around the question that kept insinuating itself: *if this is Lucas, then where is Michael?*

Hale's voice crackled across the agent's walkie-talkie. "We're going in."

Tabby and I huddled at the window frame and peered outside through the binoculars. Several blocks away, a swarm of men wearing bulletproof vests and helmets had surrounded a ramshackle brick building. It was hard to tell, but from the boarded up doors off of the second-floor balcony, it looked like it used to be a motel.

Deep in the recesses of my memory, the images of the men who'd once rescued me as a little girl, when I'd been held hostage in another run-down motel, sprang too vividly to life. Shaking my head, I chased away the thought and turned back to the window.

The men regrouped, signaling at each other with their hands as they stealthily made their way up the staircase to surround the perimeter of the building. Then there was a flash of light, and smoke billowed around the building, obscuring the main door.

When the smoke cleared, the men had vanished into the building.

High-pitched shrieking suddenly shattered the quiet night. A few hollow pops—gunfire—split the air. Then, nothing.

I thought of Macey, somewhere inside the building. She was barely a teen—still a child, really, despite all that had happened to her in her short, desperate life. Would she have heard the boom of the flashbang grenades when they detonated? Would she have been caught in the showers of splintering glass as her would-be rescuers smashed in the windows? How many others were trapped inside with her? Would she get swept up in hysteria as the raid took place, caught in a stampede of terrified women and children, or would she manage to drag herself away to cower in a corner, huddling away from the noise and the bullets screaming across the room? Would she be coherent enough to welcome her rescue?

I expected to feel her danger, to relive it myself, even, but I felt nothing.

"What's happening?" Tabby demanded, pointing at the agent's walkie-talkie. "Why aren't they telling you what's going on?"

"Ma'am, they're a tad busy right now. They'll let us know when it's all over."

We all waited and watched.

Finally, the voice on the walkie-talkie spoke: "We're bringing them out."

Tabby and I crowded the window again. Several men and women filed out, their handcuffed arms pulled behind them. They were mostly defiant, not bothering to hide their faces, moving slowly as if to deliberately provoke the agents.

"We have the girls."

White uniformed EMTs ran against the current, trying to make their way through the crowd to the victims. And after what seemed like forever, a small klatch of girls—some of them too small even to be teenagers—shuffled out of a different door. They huddled together, hiding their faces as the officers shielded them from prying eyes.

And suddenly, darting over the street which was now crowded with onlookers, a murder of crows, raucous and noisy, swarmed and wheeled, blocking out the setting sun.

"Crows," I whispered, dropping the binoculars. A cold chill crept up my spine.

"Something's wrong," Tabby stated, confused.

"Let me see," I said, pushing her away from the window and drawing up my binoculars so I could get a better look. There was some kind of commotion—the EMTs and agents were arguing, separating the girls. I was so caught up in what I was watching that I didn't even notice that the agent had taken a phone call.

I put down the binoculars just in time to see him end the call.

"What's going on?" I asked, afraid of what he might say.

He ran a hand through his tousled hair. "That was Hale. It seems Macey isn't there. Nor was this Luke character your sister told us about. One of the witnesses claimed to have seen them both leaving together, that he was angry, yelling at her for getting him in trouble. The witness heard that Luke was taking Macey *home*."

"Home?" I swallowed hard.

"Home." The agent instinctively understood my fear. "Agent Hale suggests you call your mother, now, just to be sure she's safe."

My heart stopped. As quickly as I could, I punched in the number to the house into my phone, but no one picked up. I tried her cell phone, but it just rolled over to her voice mail.

Immediately, I turned to the agent. "Call Hale. Tell him to have your buddies meet me at the house."

"No way," he said, grabbing his jacket. "My car is faster. I'll drive you."

As I hurried after him, Tabby at my side, I couldn't help but wonder—*Michael, where are you?*

ten

LUCAS

"You're sick," Macey wailed through her tears, shaking from the force of them.

"I am," I acknowledged humbly. I paused, taking her in. I'd forced the poor thing to watch as I'd cut down her foster family—her just reward for even once thinking she could escape me. "I'm sick, but I love you, Macey." I dragged a bloody hand across her cheek, gently, wanting this to be the moment when I fused fear and love, rendering her incapable of ever, ever questioning me again. "I did it all for you, to free you from their judgment. And I'll do the same to you, if you ever try to leave me. You belong to me, now. So wait here, like a good girl."

She cried as I closed the car door on her and contemplated my next move.

Of all human pursuits, I always had a soft spot for the game of chess. Pitted against someone overmatched, one could theoretically achieve checkmate in four moves. Indeed, there is a name for such an outcome: the fool's mate.

But one is rarely put in such a superior position. And a good thing, for what would be the fun in that? No, the challenge, the delight of the game, is to envision all of it from the very start: the unrolling of move and counter-move in one's mind, probing your competitor's temperament and mind to find the soft underbelly of weakness—be it overconfidence or impulsiveness—that will let you lure him into your trap, start him on a path that has but one end.

It is a clash of intellect in which even a pawn, the lowliest of pieces, can be pivotal.

As the last of the sun ebbed away, the dusk cloaking us as we surrounded Mona's house, I could not stop the tiniest smirk from lifting the corner of my mouth.

"Queen's gambit," I murmured, relishing the moment.

Every move I had made had led us to this confrontation. Targeting Macey—whom I'd just left behind whimpering, terrified, in the back of the car being guarded at the curb—was easy. That pulled in Rorie, who was much too confident—a credit to her mother, I thought begrudgingly—to have fallen for more direct means. Like dominos falling, each piece moved into place, giving me exactly what I needed.

If I couldn't destroy Michael physically, I could destroy his world. What's more, by confronting him here tonight—him and all those who'd sworn to protect the girl, all those whom I and my fellow fighters would take by surprise, stealing her from them as they watched and tried vainly to stop it—I could make him feel he was to blame.

To blame for the murders—the blood of which Hope would also imagine, sticky and hot, on her own hands. To blame for Hope's sister's capture. To blame for the degradation Rorie would experience, which would be yet another failure Hope would count, over and over, in her calculus of all she'd done wrong. Their shared guilt over what was about to happen, the mistrust that would result from Michael's inability to protect Rorie in her hour of need, would tear Michael and Hope apart—and the sick love of angels for humans would be trampled in the dust, once and for all.

A question from one of my crew broke through my reverie. "Queen's gambit—what's that?"

I turned, extending my patience to the ignorance of the Fallen Angel next to me. I shouldn't expect him to follow the elegance of my plan, nor to understand my reference to human pastimes that, for the most part, we deemed beneath us. After all, he—like the rest of the Fallen surrounding me this night—was simply the muscle of this operation. An extra precaution, for surely the whole assembly of angels pledged to protect Rorie would be here tonight in this, her hour of greatest need.

"Never mind," I bade him indulgently. And waving an arm, I gave the signal to charge.

We burst through the door, our black armor glistening in the falsely cheerful lights of the Buckhead manse, fanning out to clear the rooms, cornering our prey.

It came like a series of snapshots, monochrome bursts of understanding thrust upon my searching mind.

Room after empty room, abandoned.

The dining room table, set for a dinner that had been pushed away, untouched.

The huddled figures at the end—only two—looking up from their whispered conferencing, startled.

I stared, nonplussed, as Mona scrambled away from the table, her face a mask of shock, Arthur pushing her back protectively as he rose. He glanced hastily around the room, counting us off, a sheen of sweat breaking out on his forehead.

"Where's Michael?" I growled, closing in on him while my crew spread around the table, trapping them both. I gripped and regripped the hilt of my sword as I moved closer, watchful, in case it was a trap. "Where's Hope? Where are the others who pledged their service to the girl?"

Arthur shoved away a chair, transforming in an instant, his majestic wings bursting forth as if he could shield Mona from the inevitable as he drew his sword in a spray of sparks.

"He's not here," Arthur said steadily. "None of them are. Except me."

My temples pulsed, disappointment and fury warring with one another. A cry of impotent rage escaped my lips. Convulsed with resentment at this unexpected disruption of my plans, I swept my sword in a broadside against the table, sending china and glassware careening around the room.

How was I supposed to humiliate Michael if he wouldn't even show up to honor his own oath?

Arthur braced himself. "He'll come. They all will, you'll see," he said, his Adam's apple bobbing in his throat. "In the meantime, you'll have to get through me," he pledged grimly, his sword poised above him for first strike.

My mind went blank with rage as I raised my sword and charged.

"No!"

The single word, a shriek of denial, cut me off. I wheeled to find Aurora—my dear sweet Aurora—standing in the doorway in her pajamas, her jaw slack with disbelief.

My rage cleared long enough for me to enjoy the shock of recognition on her face as she realized just who I was.

"Rorie, run!" Mona lunged as if to save her daughter, and I

kicked her hard in the stomach, laughing. She crumpled immediately, more quickly than I'd expected. Then I kicked her again, and again, and again. When she lay moaning on the floor, motionless, I drew myself up, my chest heaving from the effort, my rage spent, my mind clear and focused on what needed to be done.

"Take the girl to the car with Macey," I finally said dismissively to one of my crew, sending him barreling after Rorie where she stood, frozen. As he left, I wheeled back to Arthur, ignoring the sounds of Rorie's futile struggle and the grating distraction of Mona, hunched on the carpet and coughing up blood.

I graced Arthur with a mock bow. So unfortunate that he was the only one of my enemies to have the good manners to keep his promise. But so be it.

"After you," I offered politely, brandishing my sword with a flourish.

eleven

HOPE

We saw the smoke before we'd even gotten to my street. It was a black plume that stained the Buckhead sky. As we huddled in the backseat, pushing our feet against the floor of the car as if we could make it go faster, Tabby squeezed my hand.

"They'll be okay, Hope."

"You don't know that," I shot back, my words laced with fear and guilt.

"It would take a lot to get through that gate. Not to mention through Arthur."

"Not for him. Nor for one of the Fallen," I replied, under my breath. But I desperately hoped she was right.

When we pulled up, we found the gate completely crumpled in, smashed as if it had no more substance than a wad of tinfoil.

"Oh, no," Tabby whispered.

"Stay here," the GBI agent ordered as he appraised the situation.

"I can't have you wandering the property—not when it still may be an active crime scene. Stay put until I tell you it's okay to move."

He jumped out of the car, slamming the door behind him.

The black smoke was getting thicker now. From the curb, I couldn't tell what was burning, or how bad it was.

"Come on," I urged Tabby. "We have to go help them."

We slipped out of the car, careful that nobody saw us. The driveway was full of police, fire, and GBI personnel, all trying to sort out who was in charge and from where, exactly, they could pump water to douse the fire. I gestured to Tabby, pointing her toward the tree line that edged the perimeter of our property. Wordlessly, we ran the entire length of the yard to get to the house.

The whole back of the house was in flames.

I dashed across the yard, grabbing a thick fallen branch along the way. The dining room windows, blank and huge, offered the perfect point of entry.

"Give me your jacket," I ordered Tabby. She peeled it off and handed it to me. I wrapped it around my arm and picked the branch back up.

"Stand back," I cautioned, before approaching the window. I could feel the blistering heat. Wincing, I swung the branch into the glass. It shattered and gave, big chunks of glass falling into the dining room. With my wrapped arm, I knocked out the remaining pieces and motioned to Tabby.

"We can climb in here. Be careful."

I helped her climb over the low ledge and into the dining room, and then I pulled myself in after her.

Deeper in the house, I could hear the crackle and rumble of the fire. Though the dining room wasn't on fire, its walls and ceiling were marred by long scorch marks. Chairs were toppled all over the room, leaving it in disarray.

"What are those?" Tabby asked, pointing at the black trails that arced across the planes of the room.

I thought back thirteen years, to when I'd seen Michael and Lucas warring with each other in full angel regalia in the basement of the abandoned warehouse in Cabbagetown, and I felt the dawning of recognition.

"The angels have flaming swords," I answered. "There must have been a fight. Maybe that's how the fire started. We don't have much time. We need to find everybody."

"Should we split up?" Tabby asked.

I shook my head. "Too dangerous. Stay together."

We began cautiously picking our way through the room, stepping over the overturned chairs as we headed toward the front hallway and my mother's study.

We hadn't even gotten through the door when Tabby grabbed my arm.

"Do you hear that?" she asked. We paused, and I strained to hear whatever it was that had caught her attention.

"There, there it was again," she insisted.

I shook my head. "I don't hear anything."

"It's Ollie! Upstairs!"

We dashed out of the room and raced up the staircase, a wave of stifling heat descending upon us.

"I can hear him!" I shouted to Tabby, picking up my pace.

Around the corner we found him. He was hovering over my mother, guarding her and pulling at her clothing as she tried to pull herself across the floor.

"Mom!"

I rushed to her side and helped prop her up. Her face was bloody, although from what injury I couldn't tell. She looked up at me, and I saw her eyes were having trouble focusing. She was trying to speak. I leaned in closer to hear.

"You have to get out of here, Hope," she whispered. "It's not safe."

"Mom, we'll get you out of here. But you have to tell me—where are Arthur and Rorie? Concentrate, Mom. I need to get them out, too."

"Gone," she answered before a cough wracked her body. "Arthur tried to fight them off, but there were too many." Her eyes fluttered closed.

My heart sank. I shook her gently until she opened her eyes.

"And Rorie? Mom, what happened to Rorie?"

She shook her head. "They took her. I couldn't stop them."

She began to weaken, sagging in my arms. "Not human," she whispered as her eyes rolled back in her head. "Angels."

My heart sank. It was happening again. My family was being targeted, picked off one by one, all because of this damn Mark on my neck and everything that had come to pass because of it. I swallowed my tears, unbelieving that after all this time, after everything I'd done and learned, I was still unable to stop it.

Ollie barked, insistently. I looked up. The hallway was beginning to fill with smoke.

"Let's get her out of here," I shouted to Tabby.

We draped an arm each over our shoulders and began dragging my mother down the stairs, doing our best to cover our noses and mouths. The smoke was getting thick now, and I could hear the roar of the flames, could see them licking through the walls of the front hall. We didn't have much time.

"Hold on to her," I told Tabby when we got to the front door. Tabby held my mom like a sack of potatoes, all dead weight, while

I got the door open. I turned back, grabbing my mom's feet, and we hustled her out to the front lawn. We laid her down carefully, trying not to panic about the groans of pain that were the only sign she was still truly alive.

Behind me, I heard the frame of the house shudder and sigh. I turned to watch. Through the open doorway, I saw the staircase explode into flames and the chandelier crash to the ground. The roof was on fire, now, the flames glowing against the black night sky.

Ollie was missing.

"Ollie!" I shrieked, starting toward the door.

Tabby grabbed my hand. "You can't go back in there!" she yelled. "It's too late, Hope!"

"I can't leave him in there to die, Tabby!" I shook free of her restraining hand. "Ollie!" I shouted again, wondering if he could even hear me over the noise of the destruction that was engulfing our home.

The roof shuddered. I could see the waves of heat emanating from the house now, warping and distorting the night sky. My mouth fell open as I watched the roof collapse in on itself.

At the last second, Ollie darted through the door, leaping off the porch to run straight to us on the lawn.

Relief flooded through my system, and I knelt down to welcome him in my arms. "Good boy," I whispered, my voice catching. "Good boy." I kept petting him even as I dragged my sleeve across my face, wiping away my tears.

Emergency personnel descended upon the three of us, checking for smoke inhalation and other damage. I was reminded that I had no time to feel sorry for myself. Swatting away the EMT fiddling with an oxygen mask, I grabbed one of the firemen who were working to drag their heavy hoses closer to the house.

"Listen, there were two other people who were supposed to be here tonight. Before she passed out, my mother said they were gone, that they aren't in the house. Did you check the carriage house—is anyone there?"

He shook his head.

"Make sure your crew keeps an eye out for them, just in case. If you can get someone in now, before the whole thing collapses, then we can be sure they made it out safely."

He whipped out a walkie-talkie and began to confer with the rest of his department. I felt a hand on my arm and turned to see Tabby. Her face was covered with soot, her eyes sad.

"They're taking your mom to Piedmont Hospital," she said. "I'll take Ollie home with me. You should go with her."

I nodded. She squeezed my arm.

"We'll find them, Hope. I just know it. Now, hop in that ambulance before it takes off without you."

I looked back at the house as it burned. But I was certain my mother was right—they wouldn't find Arthur or Rorie in the ruins. Arthur was gone, vanquished by the Fallen—and Rorie was somewhere else.

The fluorescent lights of the hospital room seemed harsh and cold. My mother lay in the bed, a jumble of cords and wires surrounding her. She was tiny, her body barely a bump where the thin sheeting draped over her body. She'd been tubed through the nose for oxygen, the doctors having determined from her persistent coughing that she'd suffered from severe smoke inhalation before she managed to crawl away from the fire. Her arm had strayed from under the covers. It had a bluish tint to it that stood out against the starkness of the white sheet.

The whirr and buzz of the machines that monitored her every breath formed a steady hum in the background.

The doctors' words swarmed in my brain. *Edema. Bronchoscopy. Contusions. Concussion.* They couldn't operate on her internal injuries—probably the aftereffects of a severe beating—until her breathing stabilized. So all we could do was wait.

For the first few hours, the interviews with the investigative team kept me occupied. There was the arson squad, trying to determine cause and evidence of arson. I thought about answering, *Flaming sword and Fallen Angel doesn't work for you as a cause?* I'd smiled wistfully to myself, and then I'd given a straight answer, explaining very carefully the situation in which my little sister had found herself, handing over last year's school photo, preserved in my wallet, for the APB.

Then came Agent Hale. He was not there so much to question as to break further bad news.

"Our perp—or perps—unfortunately got to the Jacksons' home before our dispatcher could get a squad car deployed."

"The Jacksons?" I asked, confused.

"Macey's parents," he explained. "Or, I guess I should say, her foster parents." He rubbed his face, his eyes weary. "I should have just retired. I didn't need to see this on my way out, that's for sure." He sagged, defeated in the vinyl chair. "They're dead, Miss Carmichael. They're dead—one of the bloodiest crime scenes I've ever had. And Macey is gone, just like your sister. Searched the whole damn house, and there's not a sign of her." He eyed me speculatively. "How one family can go through so much tragedy as yours—especially so entangled with minor sex trafficking—is beyond me."

I let him wonder. There was nothing I could say that would make this seem any less strange.

All I knew was that Lucas had outsmarted us. We'd fallen victim to a divide and conquer strategy, allowing whatever Fallen Angels he'd amassed to overpower Arthur—who would now be the equivalent of benched until he was strong enough to return to the fight. And it appeared that Lucas was dragging my sister and her friend right back into the center of the filthy human trafficking trade.

And through it all, Michael was nowhere to be found.

I let the surge of anger wash over me. Yes, I was angry. How, exactly, had he failed to come to my side—to Aurora's side—when she was so obviously in danger?

I could feel my self-doubt and self-pity bubbling and swirling inside me, threatening to pull me down into a paralyzing spiral. But I squared my shoulders and pushed it away. I didn't have time for that. Not now.

Hale and I sat together and stared straight ahead at the cinderblock wall. The only noise was the loud ticking of a wall-mounted clock and the occasional ping of elevators as the devastated relatives of the intensive care unit patients came and went, their voices quiet murmurs.

"Arson told me they already took your statement. I'll just draft off of that, spare you the trouble," Hale said, breaking the quiet.

"Are you going to see it through?" I asked abruptly, focusing on one of the spots of faded cement between the cinderblocks.

"What?" he asked.

I turned in my chair to look at him. "If my mom were able, she'd be the one asking you. But she can't, so I will. Are you going to see my sister's case through, or are you going to hand it off to some rookie so you can skip out of here to the greener pastures of retirement?"

"Miss Carmichael," he began, but I cut him off.

"After all this time, the least you can do is call me Hope. Are you giving up on us now, Agent Hale? Are you leaving my sister in the hands of some stranger?"

"I don't know what to say," he mumbled.

"Say you'll help us with the case. If it's trafficking again, help us track these people down. Help me find her. Please, you've got to help me find her."

He gripped the arms of his chair and tilted his head back against the wall.

"You really know how to put the screws to a guy," he muttered. "You're making me feel really guilty."

"That's what you get with the best legal training money can buy," I quipped. "Hale, you can't hand this off. I know you're the best guy in the GBI on trafficking. You probably already have three suspects in your head. Nobody else can do what you do. Nobody has the experience."

Hale ignored my flattery. He simply laughed, a cynical, hollow sound. "I could give you a list as long as my arm. But when it comes to Atlanta, the same names always rise to the top. You'll have the Mexicans, who still operate here, of course. Given that this Luke character had Macey in the Bluff, you can't rule out one of the gangs. And then there's your old friends at Triad."

I sat up in my seat. "Triad is still in operation?" I hadn't thought about the Chinese crime syndicate that was presumably responsible for my father's death—nor Chen, the man at its head, with whom Michael and I had directly tangled—for a long time. Not since Chen had been thrown into prison over ten years ago.

He snorted. "You think a big drug, arms, and human smuggling operation like that goes down just because you locked up one of their majors? Nah. They just shoved another guy in place to keep things going while our old friend Chen rots in his cell. He probably still calls the shots from prison, though, filtering orders through his lawyer." He looked at me, visibly excited. "If your family is being targeted, which it looks like it is, it would make sense for it to be Chen and Triad."

"See?" I urged him. "You've got to keep on it, Hale. It would have taken a new guy days, or even weeks, to figure that out. Where is Chen? Maybe we should go see him."

He shook his head. "You'll never be able to get to him. He's in Florence ADX now."

"ADX?"

"Administrative Maximum Facility. The toughest super-max prison in the US. The most violent criminals—the ones the authorities think are still controlling their organizations from the inside, or the ones most likely to be broken out of prison by their cronies—are all sent there to serve out their sentences. It's full of baddies: foreign and domestic terrorists, drug cartel leaders, gang leaders. Real psychos. No visitors; not ever. The only way he'll get out of Colorado is in a pine box. And that's the only way you'll get to see him, too: when he's dead."

Another spasm of frustration gripped me. "Then how are we ever supposed to find Rorie and Macey? You know what they're up against, Hale. We don't have a lot of time."

He rubbed his tired eyes and stood up. "I know, Hope. We'll have to beat the bushes, walk the neighborhood, and see who we can get to talk. I'll stay on the case like you asked." He looked over his shoulder, back at my mother's room. "I know Mona would want me to."

With that, he stretched and yawned. "I'll see you tomorrow, kiddo. Keep me posted on your mom. I'll call you if I hear anything new."

I watched the elevator doors whoosh closed, whisking him away and leaving me alone.

Alone.

Where were the angels who were sworn to protect my sister? And most of all, where was Michael? I picked up my phone: no messages. I scanned the news sites for anything unusual, any breaking world crisis that would explain his absence, but there was nothing.

I didn't have time to wallow in dejection. I heaved myself up out of the chair and headed back in to check on my mom.

A nurse was holding a clipboard, writing notes of my mother's vital signs.

"How is she?" I ventured.

The nurse mustered a smile. "She's hanging in there. Stable, for now. We really need to get her in for surgery as soon as we can. If she manages to keep breathing through the night, the surgeon will most likely take her in first thing in the morning."

"And if she doesn't?" I braced myself for whatever bad news the nurse would deliver.

"If she can't keep breathing on her own, we'll intubate her. It will probably mean a day's delay, just to be certain." Her face darkened momentarily. "But if her other vitals worsen, we'll have to take our chances and take her in, regardless."

I slumped down in the chair, disheartened.

The nurse squeezed my shoulder. "The doctor will explain all your options when she comes by. For now, you should try to get some rest."

She gave one last look at the machine readouts and swept out of the room.

My eyelids were heavy, and I realized the nurse was right. I did my best to curl up in the chair, draping a thin blanket around my shoulders, until my exhaustion got the best of me and I fell into a fitful sleep.

In my dreams, I kept one ear listening for the steady beeping of the monitors.

~

"Hope, wake up."

A hand gripped my shoulder, startling me. I bolted upright, awake in an instant, peering into blue-gray eyes filled with concern.

"Michael!"

I resisted the urge to throw myself into his arms, the overwhelming desire to bury my face in his neck, letting his familiar waves of heat comfort me. But I couldn't stop myself, out of habit, from scanning his face for new cuts and bruises, making sure that he was whole. I gathered his hands in mine, turning them over to look for the stains and scrapes of battle I'd come to recognize so well.

There were no scars. No marks. Nothing out of the ordinary. Nothing at all to excuse his failure to show up when I needed him.

"Where were you?" My voice was cold, even to my own ears.

He pressed his lips into a grim line, and he dropped my hands, his own balling up into fists as he stood up. He was worked up—far more tense than I'd expected him to be. But before I could press him further, he turned to look at my mother.

"Your mother. What happened? How is she doing?"

"Not great," I said. "Stable, I guess. If she can keep breathing on her own, they'll operate on her tomorrow morning. They think she has a lot of internal injuries, Michael. She was pretty severely beaten." My voice cracked.

He nodded, taking in all the tubes and wires.

"It was Lucas, Michael. I'm sure of it. He was posing as a trafficker and lured Rorie's friend, Macey, by pretending to be her boyfriend. I'm not sure what he was planning after that, but he went after us when Rorie intervened and we got the GBI into the picture. I think his forces overwhelmed Arthur," I added, remembering the sooty slashes of swordplay that had marked our dining room walls. "He did this," I spat, gesturing to my mother where she lay motionless in bed. "He killed Macey's foster parents. And now he has Macey and Rorie."

He sucked in a sharp breath. "You're sure?"

"As sure as I can be," I answered, my face getting hot. "Michael, where were all the angels who were sworn to protect Rorie? Why weren't they there to help her? Why weren't *you* there? And what are we going to do?"

Michael began to pace, his stride taking him in circles inside the tiny room.

"Answer me," I said angrily.

He looked at me, his eyes full of misery. Confused, I began to speak, but I hadn't even managed to get a word out when I was interrupted by a noise from across the room.

"Michael?"

Startled, we both turned toward the bed. It was a faint, almost croaking sound, but there was no mistaking it in the quiet of the hospital room. My mother had awakened and called for Michael.

"Oh." The word slipped from Michael's lips, and I watched him sag, defeated. "Oh, no."

He swung back to me, his eyes grieving. "I didn't know, Hope. I'm so sorry."

"Sorry? Of course you should be sorry. You left us in a lurch, with no explanation—"

He shook his head, cutting me off. "You don't understand. I'm not here for you, Hope. I'm here for *her*."

He didn't give me a chance to ask what he meant, simply giving my shoulder a squeeze before moving swiftly to my mother's bedside.

"I'm here, Mona," he answered, gripping her hand in his. Her paleness stood out even more against his sun-worn skin. "I'm here."

Her eyes fluttered open at the sound of his voice.

"I'm so glad," she whispered.

Her gaze moved beyond him to me. "Hope," she began, before spluttering off into a hacking cough.

"Shhhh," I cautioned her as I moved next to her bed. "You've been through a lot. No sense wearing yourself out."

The coughing fit passed, and my mother let her eyes drift closed before speaking again with visible effort.

"Arthur tried to hold them off," she began. "But they were too much for him. He just seemed to melt into a flurry of sparks. And Rorie . . ." She strained at the sheets, pushing through the wires and tubes, trying to rise up as if to save them.

"Shhhh," Michael soothed, easing her back down onto the bed. "Arthur will be okay. He's just resting. And Rorie will be okay, too." A shadow of guilt crept across his face at having to lie, but it passed quickly, his attention focused on keeping my mother calm.

She closed her eyes, the relief on her face palpable. After a few moments, her breath ragged and labored, she opened her eyes wide.

"They were angels," she repeated, her head turning to focus on Michael. "Like you." She paused, panting for air.

I caught my breath, not believing what I was hearing. "What is she trying to say, Michael? How could she—?"

Michael simply shook his head.

When she'd gotten control of her breathing again, she continued. "I can see you now, Michael. The real you."

Michael wrapped his free hand around my mother's. Tears were forming in the corner of his eyes. I gasped, stunned, as the edges of his body began to blur and glow, a pixelated light swirling around him until his wings spread out behind him.

He was revealing himself to my mother. It was beautiful to watch, and heartbreaking, for I realized now what he'd meant when he'd said he was here for her.

He'd been sent to take her home—to escort her through death, another of his pre-ordained duties as one of God's archangels.

"I can see you," she repeated, smiling through her pain. "You're beautiful." She shifted, looking at the empty space at the end of the bed. "I see Don, too. Funny, isn't it? He was right all along. And now you are here for me. Both of you."

She turned her head so she could take in the both of us. "Take care of each other," she whispered in a hoarse voice. "You belong to each other."

With effort, she reached out with her other hand, gesturing toward me. I clasped her hand, and she drew it to Michael's, pressing our hands together.

The machines began a frantic beeping.

"No!" I screamed. I stabbed at the call button and then ran to the door, flinging it wide. "Somebody, get in here! My mother is crashing!"

Michael didn't move. He hung onto my mother's hand, a bittersweet smile on his face, as his image began to flicker in and out.

The alarms and beeps crescendoed as a rush of personnel swarmed the room, surrounding my mother.

"Clear!"

I heard the thump of their attempt to restart her failing heart.

"Clear!"

But in the next instant, everything stopped, and all the noises fell away except for the doctor's call for another charge.

"Clear!"

I stood by, helpless, as they tried again and again to draw my mother back from the edge of death. When they stepped away from her bedside, defeated, I shoved my knuckles against my teeth to stifle my cry.

My mother was gone.

And as I looked around the room, I realized that so was Michael.

twelve

LUCAS

The girls were huddled together in the backseat. I'd snatched Rorie away so quickly that she hadn't had time to change into street clothes. We'd been delayed by the presence of the angel, Arthur, and Rorie's mother—much more than I'd expected. I hadn't anticipated they could put up such a fight—not without the other angels to help them. That my sword sent Arthur to purgatory, to wait out his rebirth, was a gift—one fewer of Michael's goon squad to worry about. But Mona . . .

Mona I hadn't intended to hurt. She'd simply gotten in the way when she'd tried to intervene. The memory of how my own rage had gotten the best of me replayed itself in my brain, over and over, an itch that demanded to be scratched. It had been an unfortunate lapse. Perhaps she would survive her injuries, I told myself. I found myself rooting for her, hoping she would.

I shook my head, trying to rid my mind of the image of her crawling across the floor, trying to reach her daughter, to protect her.

Was I going soft?

No. Not soft. After all, the most delicious part of a kidnapping is the worried parent left behind, imagination run amok as she considers the torture and degradation being inflicted on the missing child. There was a part of me that wanted—no, needed—to know that Mona would be experiencing that anguish. She needed to be alive.

But there was another part of me, I admit—a begrudging part, but real—that respected how she never gave up. Even when confronted by something so obviously beyond the grasp of her feeble human understanding—the majesty of God's angels, flying in the face of her rigid adherence to science—she never wavered in her efforts to save her child, no matter the cost to herself.

No, it wasn't Mona's spirit that was flawed—just the imperfect flesh with which God saw fit to enrobe it.

She proved a stark contrast to Macey's foster parents, the Jacksons. Even as my Fallen and I faced them in our full regalia, they turned their horror of the situation on their child. "Oh, Macey, what have you done?" they'd asked, wringing their hands as we bore down on them. Their rejection of her was just what I needed: it wounded Macey, it proved to her that I'd been right all along, and at the same time it gave me an excuse to wipe them from the Earth.

As if I needed any further excuse.

I yawned, thinking of it, a great, exhausted gaping hole of a yawn, yet another proof of how inferior this frail-bodied race really was. But it served me, for the time being, to hide within this human shell. A slightly different human shell, of course: I had put away my angels' wings and dropped the guise of Luke temporarily, instead posing as a much older man, a mere go-between dispatched to deliver the girls to their ultimate destination. After endless muttering to herself, questioning what she'd really seen, Rorie seemed to have written off what she'd witnessed—the flaming swords, the armored angels—as a trick of her own mind, making it easy for her to accept me as what I appeared: a mere human, just a nameless link in the chain of hopelessness by which she was now bound. Both she and Macey assumed I didn't even know English, for that matter—and so they grew incautious, gifting me with a full window into their insipid teenage minds.

We'd driven all night from Atlanta and then stopped for a break at a cheap motel off the interstate. I'd cuffed the girls to the bed while I disappeared, just to make sure Rorie, in particular, didn't get the bright idea to escape. Now, after hours on the road, it was again beginning to get dark. When we'd started off, I'd thrown them in the backseat, one of my men ordering them to keep their heads covered with the thin blankets we'd tossed in after them. Disorientation and dislocation were all part of the plan.

Once we were safely out of Georgia, I grew lax, letting them poke their heads out of their blankets, even letting them begin to talk. It was probably a mistake to put them together, but it was too late to do anything about it now.

And in a way, letting them bond would serve my purposes later.

I smiled to myself, humming a little as we drove past the shorn, desolate cornfields of winter, headed toward Minneapolis.

Rorie wore what passed for pajamas these days: flannel bottoms and a T-shirt. Macey, on the other hand, was still decked out in the clothes I'd made her change into at the Bluff—a lacy camisole that draped suggestively over her bare shoulder, revealing a delicate cotton bra strap and tiny denim shorts. Neither had a jacket. That they were ill prepared for a northern climate was obvious and put them even more at my mercy.

"Where do you think we're going?" Rorie wondered aloud. She pressed her face to the window. "I don't recognize anything."

"It doesn't matter," Macey responded in a despondent tone. "As long as Luke is there when we get there."

Rorie snorted and turned back to her friend. "Wake up, Macey. Luke isn't going to be there. Luke wasn't your boyfriend. He was using you."

"Was not!" Macey shouted back, her face red. "He loves me. He told me so."

"If he loved you, would he have done this?" She turned over Macey's bare arm, revealing a trail of round burns from the cigarette I'd pressed into her flesh when she'd been particularly uncooperative. They were starting to heal, but the memory was fresh enough that Macey shuddered. She yanked her arm out of Rorie's reach.

"You're just jealous," Macey retorted, playing back one of the poisonous beliefs I'd planted in her feeble brain. "You don't like him because he picked me, not you."

Rorie rolled her eyes. "Yeah, that's it. I really wish I had a boyfriend that beat me up, got me hooked on heroin, and forced me to take nudie pictures." Her eyes narrowed. "What else did he make you do, Macey?"

Macey turned bright red before scooting across the seat, as far away from Rorie as she could get. "I don't know what you're talking about."

Rorie shot a look to me where I sat behind the steering wheel, as if making sure I was not listening. My face—a sliver of it visible in the rear view mirror—was a blank mask of indifference. She moved closer to Macey and put a hand on her shoulder.

"Macey. Listen to me. I don't know what he did to you. But you have to believe me. You deserve better. Someone who loves you would never hurt you. Not knowingly. Not in the way I think he was hurting you."

I frowned. This was not going in a helpful direction.

Macey leaned her head against the side of the car. "How do you know what I deserve?"

Before Rorie could answer, I swerved the car hard, horns blaring as I cut across three lanes of traffic to get onto the exit ramp.

The girls careened into each other and screamed.

So much for their little chat.

After a while, I spied a truck stop. We needed fuel. As I slowed to turn in, Rorie pushed herself back against the window, squinting into the headlights of the oncoming traffic while she scanned the collage of road signs.

"I don't recognize any of the roads," she whispered.

I pulled into the pumping station and got out, locking the doors behind me. I surveyed the area—no police. While the car refueled, I went inside and bought some chips and bottled water.

Back at the car, I unceremoniously tossed my purchases into the backseat. I pulled the car around to the parking tarmac and watched as the girls tore into the junk food like a pack of slavering dogs.

They were done within minutes. I watched, amused, as Macey looked longingly into the empty chip bag, tipping it upside down to be sure it was really empty before proceeding to lick the orange flavor coating off of her fingers.

"Time for you to earn your keep," I stated. The girls looked up at me, startled to realize that I'd been able to understand everything they'd been saying. It was the first time they had heard me speak in this body. I stepped out of the car and jerked open the rear door next to Macey. "Out. Now."

When she didn't immediately respond, I snaked an arm in and gripped her hard, pulling until I'd dumped her out on the asphalt.

Before Rorie could do anything, I slammed the door shut and locked it behind me. Rorie flung herself against the window, shouting and pounding on the glass.

I darted a glance around the lot, making sure nobody was around to intervene over Miss Queen Bee's fit. Satisfied, I turned my attention to Macey.

"Get up," I ordered.

Macey looked around. There was no one to help her, nobody to argue on her behalf. Slowly, she stumbled back to her feet.

"Walk." I gave her a little shove.

She began walking toward the parked trucks, trailing one last look over her bare shoulder to where Rorie continued to press herself up against the window. Defeated, Macey slumped her shoulders, tugging her camisole up and wrapping her arms around her waist for warmth before shuffling ahead, her eyes glued to the asphalt.

The trucks were lined up, engines still running. Dim lights shone from a few of the cabs. Most were dark. It was a little early for this, but I was sure I would find a taker.

I stood in front of Macey, frowning. I needed her to look the part. I pulled the camisole back down to reveal some skin and fluffed her hair.

"Now, Macey," I began, my tone stern. "Luke is in trouble because of you and what your parents did. He can't be here with you now, but he asked me to take care of you. To help him—to help yourself—you're going to have to do what I ask. Luke would want you to. You understand me, Macey?"

She didn't look up; she just nodded, once.

"Luke had you pretend with those men back in Atlanta, right? Had you act for them, for the videos?"

She nodded again.

"This time you're going to have to do it for real. There are men in these trucks. Men who are lonely. Men who could use the company of a pretty girl like you. You're going to do whatever they ask. You're going to let them do whatever they want to do to you. You just tell them it will cost them a hundred dollars, cash. Otherwise, you are not to talk to them under any circumstances. Just speak if you are spoken to. You got that, Macey?"

She whimpered, afraid.

I shook her hard. "They don't want a crybaby, Macey. Luke told me you were mature enough to handle this. That you loved him enough to be able to help him. That hundred dollars will help him a lot, Macey. Can Luke count on you?"

She dragged her arm across her face to wipe away the tears.

"No crying. Okay?"

"Okay," she whispered.

"Okay. Good girl. Because you're being a good girl for me, I'm going to give you a little something to help your nerves. Would you like that?"

She whimpered softly. "Please."

"Stand still."

I reached into my pocket and pulled out the syringe. She winced as I put it into the fleshy part of her upper arm and plunged the drug into her system.

"See?" I said, withdrawing the needle. "Luke asked me to take care of you, and I am. Nothing to it."

She rubbed the sore spot on her arm.

"Okay. Ready, now? I need you to walk, slowly, between the rows of trucks. I'll be standing over here, out of the way, but I'll tell you when to stop."

She began walking, a little wobbly, parading herself in front of the trucks with her eyes glued to the asphalt.

"Lift up your head, Macey," I coached from the shadows. "Look straight ahead—nobody wants a spoilsport."

She wound through the first row and moved back, walking to the next. My human senses were on full alert, knowing that I needed to get her into one of those trucks before the drugs completely sapped her strength.

Finally, one of the trucks flashed its headlights.

I had a buyer.

"Stop right there," I shouted across the lot. "See that truck? The one that flashed its lights? No, not that one. The red Peterbilt next to it."

She turned to face the truck.

"Go up and knock on the driver's side door. Let him tell you what he wants, and you tell him what it will cost. If he agrees, climb up on the passenger side. I'll be waiting right here for you."

She hesitated just a moment too long.

"Luke will be so proud of you, Macey. He will be so happy that you love him so much. He'll be with you at the end of our trip, you know. And then I can tell him how brave you were for him."

Hearing that, she squared her shoulders and walked over to the truck.

Funny how you could get a girl to go through hell just by promising her heaven on the other side. I watched her, feeling an almost parental sense of pride. I was pushing my baby out of the nest, and she, trusting or afraid—it really didn't matter which—was spreading her wings.

What she didn't know yet was that she would climb down from that truck and do it all over again. Over and over and over again, until I said she'd done enough for the night.

Shrieking pain whipped through my body as I watched the door close behind her. I turned on my heel, going back to move the car, and Rorie, to a less conspicuous space where I could keep watch. As I did, I wondered—had Hope and Michael figured out yet what was really going on? Did they realize that the hand moving behind the scenes, wreaking destruction upon Macey and their precious Rorie, was really me?

I certainly hoped so. I chuckled, embracing the pain even as it made my eyes roll back in my head, white and desperate in agony.

～

It was nearly dawn when Macey finally stumbled into the backseat of the car—our home away from home.

"Oh, sweetie," Rorie breathed as her friend collapsed on the seat.

One eye was swollen shut. Fingerprints—red, ugly welts—encircled her slender throat like a necklace. Her blouse was torn, and blood dripped down her leg. I could see Rorie shut her eyes in a vain attempt to try to shut out the reality of what had just happened to her friend.

And I could imagine what she was thinking: *when will it be my turn?*

I had been careful to park in the back of the lot, away from all the traffic, keeping us out of the way. From this isolated spot, I knew nobody would notice Rorie pounding against the glass and screaming until her voice gave out. Nobody along the route seemed to find it odd—two young girls, barely dressed, huddled in the backseat, driving cross-country in the company of an older man.

But even so, I knew Rorie was no fool and would be planning her escape. So I quickly slid behind the wheel and locked the doors before she had a chance to act.

She gave a tiny cry of frustration, pressing her face against the window as we pulled out of the truck stop, another chance lost.

Macey shifted on the seat next to her. "Rorie?"

"What is it, honey?" Rorie asked, smoothing the hair off of her forehead.

"I miss Luke," she mumbled through her stupor, pulling her legs in tight and curling on the seat in fetal position.

I smiled, imagining the flash of anger running through Rorie. But the girl buried whatever she must have been feeling, perhaps missing her own loved ones; instead, she took Macey's hand and stroked her hair, bidding her to sleep.

"I know, honey. I know."

I continued to drive.

thirteen

HOPE

My mother was dead.

I buried her, of course, in the tiny plot of red Georgia clay that held my father, in the forgotten cemetery that had the audacity to call itself New Hope. The one thing I could cling to was that in death, finally, they had been reunited.

Tabby paused, her voice catching as she read, her long black minister's robe fluttering in the wind.

> *For since we believe that Jesus died and rose again,*
> *even so, through Jesus, God will bring with Him those*
> *who have fallen asleep. For this we declare to you by*
> *a word from the Lord, that we who are alive, who*
> *are left until the coming of the Lord, will not precede*
> *those who have fallen asleep. For the Lord Himself*
> *will descend from heaven with a cry of command,*

with the voice of an archangel, and with the sound
of the trumpet of God. And the dead in Christ will
rise first. Then we who are alive, who are left, will be
caught up together with them in the clouds to meet
the Lord in the air, and so we will always be with
the Lord.

"First Thessalonians, chapter four, verses fourteen through seventeen," she concluded.

I pushed away the thoughts that sprang unbidden as she read the verse, forcing myself to focus on my best friend, who had stoically demanded that only she should be allowed to preside over my mother's funeral. She closed her Bible and pushed up her glasses to wipe away a tear. Wearily, she lifted up her head to look at the assembled crowd. "Let us return Mona now to ashes and dust, her soul finally reunited with the Lord."

As I stood before the gaping hole, waiting to throw the first handful of dirt upon my mother's casket, I thought of what my mother had said just before she died—how she'd claimed to see my father. How she'd looked at Michael and said that he and my father were there for her—to what? Escort her to the other side?

And why had Michael been sent to her aid, when he hadn't known to come to mine in the first place?

I looked up from the ground, seeking some reassurance in Michael's eyes. But he wasn't looking at me. He was looking hard across the cemetery.

I followed his gaze and saw them all lined up in the back of the gathered mourners, their faces sober. Gabrielle. Raph. Enoch. Arthur, who'd gone down trying to fight off the Fallen Angels who'd attacked my mother and sister, was the only one absent. My heart gave a tug at the thought that he, too, was a casualty of this war between angels—albeit, I hoped, a temporary one.

I looked more closely at the phalanx of angels, trying to discern what had captured Michael's attention, parsing their every movement and hoping to understand how this loss had ever come to pass. Enoch seemed truly grief-stricken, dabbing at his face with a ratty hankie and leaning heavily into his cane. Underneath his Army-surplus jacket, he had dressed up for the occasion, wearing a tuxedo T-shirt imprinted with a bow tie and lapels. His effort brought a wistful smile to my face. Raph, however, in typical fashion, stood still, his hands crossed impassively before him, his hooded eyes hiding whatever he may have felt. Gabrielle, on the other hand, seemed bored—her gaze wandering over the assembled crowd. For an instant, our eyes locked. She stared at me, her eyes frank, and I suddenly realized she wasn't sad or remorseful at all.

Frustrated, I squeezed Michael's hand. He finally dragged his eyes away to give me his attention. Now, more than ever, I yearned for his comforting presence; to feel his warmth ebbing and flowing through me; to hear his thoughts pulsing through my blood as I listened to the whispers of his heart. But I couldn't help feeling like even after all these years, I still couldn't fathom him—I was just as far from understanding him as I ever was.

When the attendants took up their shovels, I turned and began making my way through the assembled crowd, leaning heavily on Tabby's arm while Michael hung back. The mourners—some my own friends, some my mother's, and some Tabby's family—pressed their hands in mine and touched my shoulder quietly, not knowing what to say. In their eyes, I was alone now. Slowly, they broke away in small clusters, stepping carefully through the ruined graveyard back toward the parking lot, until Tabby, the angels, and I were the only ones remaining.

None of the mourners had said anything to me about Rorie's disappearance: it was already public knowledge, but too horrible and fresh for anyone to mention.

The wind rustled through the bare branches of the oak trees surrounding the cemetery, a lonely reminder of the changing of the seasons. I shivered, pulling my coat close.

"Raph." He bowed his head as I acknowledged him. "Gabrielle."

"Hope," she said, with a slight bow of her head. My eyes narrowed as I took her in—impeccable as always, still without a trace of grief marring her face. She gave a slight toss of her long, blond hair. "I am sorry for your loss."

"Are you?" I challenged.

Her eyes widened, startled, and she lifted her chin slightly.

"Of course I am. Why would I not be?"

Before I could answer, Michael came up behind me, placing a hand on my shoulder. I shrugged it off.

"I'll meet you all back at the carriage house," I said, my voice strangely flat to my own ears, and I walked away, pulling Tabby behind me.

It was disorienting to come home to the carriage house and see the burned-out shell of our own home up the driveway, the lingering smell of ash and soot ever present. The tiny kitchen was filled with gifted casseroles—sweet potatoes, gumbos, collard greens, grits done five ways—the bounty of the South, the way good people in my hometown expressed their sympathy and care. That I was the only one here to eat it was irrelevant. It was what one did when one was a good neighbor. Tabby and I piled them carefully in the refrigerator and freezer, setting aside the handwritten notes that had accompanied them, and settled down at the counter.

I looked at my watch. It was scarcely 2:00 p.m., and I was already exhausted. Ollie sidled up to me and whimpered, pushing at my free hand. Absentmindedly, I scratched him behind the ears.

"You did good, Tabby. Thank you. Though I think Mom would have been disappointed in your lack of 'flair.'" I forced a grin, remembering my mother's appreciation for Tabby's unique sense of style and penchant for drama. "You were practically sedate."

Tabby drew herself up in feigned offense, peering imperiously down at me where I sat huddled on the stool. "You underestimate me, sister. I just chose to pay homage to your mother in my own way. Not for show, but for real, so that only she'd know it. And now, you: look, and be amazed." She pushed her glasses over her head and unzipped her long black preacher's robe. With a flourish, she let it drop to the floor. "Ta da!"

I stared, confused. Her entire outfit seemed to be made out of newsprint.

"What are you wearing?"

"I got copies of every single scholarly or news article written by or about your mom and had them made into this." She swept an arm dramatically over her skirt and jacket. "A Chanel pattern, of course. It seemed only fitting."

My mouth dropped open in awe as she twirled.

"See down here?" She gestured toward the hem of the skirt. "This was the interview she gave to *The Economist*. And this?" She ran a finger down the length of her arm. "*Harvard Business Review*. They did a case on her, did you know that? Her own *HBR* case. This one here?" She patted her shoulder. "This is a picture of her ringing the bell on Wall Street. Come here, Hope, you've got to check it out. There were more than forty articles. And that's not counting the ones about your disappearance or your dad's death." She pulled me to my feet, dragging me close to her crazy newsprint outfit.

"Look at them all—*Business Week, Consulting Age, Forbes, Wall Street Journal.*" She was stabbing all over her dress now. "*Econometrica. The Financial Times. Journal of Management Studies.* Even the mind-numbingly boring-sounding *Journal of Financial Economics.* I used that one for the lining." She flashed me a view of the inside of her jacket. "Your mom was brilliant, girl. She was a trailblazer, and these articles prove it. But what she was most proud of was you and Rorie." She pulled me in for a tight hug. "I don't need to read any newspapers to know that."

A lonely tear squeezed out of my eye and dropped onto Tabby's shoulder, dissolving the print in a blurry smudge. I hugged her back, so hard that her lovingly made couture creation gave with a rip.

"Oh no! Your dress!"

She laughed. "Nobody expects a paper dress to last forever. I'm just glad it made it through the ceremony. That said, I am a little worried I'm going to dissolve into a sweaty, inky mess if I don't get out of this. You okay if I go change?"

I nodded, sniffing back a tear and a laugh. Only Tabby.

"When I come back, we're going to talk about what you're going to do about Rorie—and about Michael. Okay?"

I nodded, relieved to be able to unburden myself and grateful for Tabby's presence.

"There's nothing good about having to say a funeral service, Hope. I'm just glad to be the one to do it for you. She was like another mother to me, too, you know. Just like you're my sister—even if you are a little crazy sometimes." She let a mischievous smile steal across her face. "I'll be back faster than a Kardashian at a designer sidewalk sale."

When she returned, she'd stripped out of her official trappings and changed into a cozy sweater and jeans, a pair of leopard-spotted clogs adorning her feet. She perched herself on the stool next to me and peered at me through her cat-eye glasses. "Spill it. What are you thinking?"

I slumped in my seat. "Where do I even start?"

"Why don't you start with why Michael isn't here with you, hmm?" She skewered me with her most pointed look. There was no point in avoiding the conversation.

"I asked him to give me some time alone. I needed to think."

"About what?"

"About whether I can trust him. Whether, if it came to choosing sides between me and the other angels, he'd choose me."

Tabby let out a low whistle. "Why are you even asking yourself such a question, Hope?"

"How can I not?" I cried, nearly choking. I gripped the edge of the counter, my knuckles turning white. "He didn't even show up when I needed him the most, Tabby! None of them did. They didn't live up to their promise to protect Rorie," I said, the words twisting bitterly on my lips. "Not one of them, except for Arthur. They've offered no real explanation for it, either. All I know is that if they had been there when Rorie needed them, she'd never have fallen into Lucas's hands. And my mother would still be alive."

"You can't know that for sure," she said evenly.

"No. No, I can't. But I believe it in my heart. The only problem is—"

"—that you don't believe you can find Rorie and rescue her and Macey without them," Tabby said, finishing my thought. I sank into my chair, grateful to not have to explain my reasoning. "Agent Hale isn't giving you much hope, then?"

I shook my head. "Missing persons statistics put low odds on finding her now. Hale thinks she's moved outside his jurisdiction. GBI has done all they can, so it has to move to a higher level. But

nobody—no state nor federal body—is going to prioritize looking for two lost little girls. Not with everything else they have to
deal with."

"But Lucas—or Luke, whoever he is—he's wanted for murder,
isn't he? Not just for your mother, but for the Jacksons, too. Isn't
your office going to do something? Surely that demands some
attention? Some resources? Shouldn't the DA's office have to do
something?"

I was too tired, now, to let the outrage that fired Tabby's body
work its way on me. I simply stared at her fists, impotently balled
up on the counter, and shook my head.

"Apparently not. Not anything more than they'd do for any
case like this, anyway. The irony of it is that because of my family's
past history, the DA thinks it's a vendetta of some sort against my
mother. In other words, the risk Lucas poses to others is low. So it's
up to me and whatever urgency Social Services can muster up for
a missing foster child—which isn't, apparently, that much. As for
my office, well . . ."

I fought back the tears, remembering the frustration and helplessness I'd felt when Andrew had argued that it was out of his
jurisdiction. He wouldn't even promise to try to persuade the DA
on my behalf. He wouldn't do anything. Despite the flurry of media
and speculation that had surrounded the gruesome killings, it was
not his kind of case—not like asking me to prosecute a develop-
mentally disabled man like Ike Washington, for example.

"My boss forbade me to bring up the subject of my sister again
while I worked for him," I said. "So I quit. So working through the
DA's office is no longer an option."

I looked up to see Tabby pressing her lips into a thin, hard line.
"So we have to search for them ourselves."

"Not 'we.' Me. I can't drag you into this, too. But I need the angels if I'm going to pull it off. I just don't know if I can force them to help. They've already proven themselves to be untrustworthy."

"But surely Michael can get them to help you."

I shook my head again.

"He wasn't here either, Tabby. Besides—they made their vow to *him*. If that wasn't enough to command their allegiance, I don't know what sway he'll have now."

"So that's why you're having them come here? To confront them?"

I nodded. "I have an idea. I don't know if it will work, but it's the only thing I've come up with."

"Are you sure, sweetie? It's all happening so fast. The funeral was just a few hours ago. You could use a rest. Not to mention figuring things out with Michael." She put a protective hand on my arm. "You're hurting, and his involvement—or lack thereof—is still weighing on you. I can tell."

"We don't have time to wait," I answered, my heart constricting with fear as I thought of all the things that could be happening, even this very minute, to my sister and her friend.

The knock on the door was crisp, official sounding. Ollie's ears perked up, and I laughed. "Saved by the bell. Funny that the angels would suddenly become punctual, now."

Tabby, my new watchdog, eyed me with caution. She looked warily at the door. "I can send them away, Hope. Say the word and I'll do it."

I shook my head. "No. I need to get it over with. Let them in."

Tabby ushered the four of them into the cozy living room. They shuffled in together, lining themselves up as if they were shy middle schoolers hanging back at their first dance, half wanting and half dreading to be picked. They were larger than life, their dazzling beauty and presence—even in human form—overwhelming the little house. Wistfully, I wondered how Arthur had managed in such a small space.

I waited for Michael to come to my side. After an awkward silence, it became evident that he was staying with the other angels. I felt my face flush. Blinking back tears, I cleared my throat.

"I'm grateful that you came to my mother's burial today," I began. "I realize that for you, her death is probably nothing more than a transition to a state closer to God. For me, it is the loss of the last parent I had." I choked on the next words. "The fact that once again, my family has paid the price for my involvement in the Prophecy, for the enmity of Lucas and the Fallen Angels, makes my loss all that more difficult to bear."

Enoch leaned into his cane. "Now, Hope. The last thing you should be doing is blaming yourself for the tragedy that has come to pass. It was not your fault."

I didn't like what I was about to do, but I had to do it. I raised my head, trying to channel some of the steeliness that had been my mother's trademark.

"You're right, Enoch. I can't blame myself. I've done enough of that to last a lifetime. What I need to do now is focus on finding my sister. And to do that, I need to know how it came to be that despite the vows of four archangels, my sister was left to fend for herself against the Fallen."

Michael's head jerked back as if I had slapped him.

Raph's mouth dropped open in dismay. "You can't be serious? You blame us for her disappearance?"

"All four of you promised to protect her. Yet only Arthur was there when she needed him."

Michael began: "But, Hope, you can't honestly—"

"I never promised to be her 24/7 babysitter, Hope," Raph said, cutting him off. "None of us did. And I, for one, never thought that anything requiring me to fulfill that pledge would ever come to pass. In fact, I counted on it," he added cynically, his dark eyes glittering with outrage as he cast an angry glance at Michael.

"So you admit it?" I challenged back. "You never had any intention of helping her at all, did you?"

He shrugged, the casualness of his admission making me furious. "It's not like I had a choice. Your boyfriend over there coerced us all. Isn't that right, Gabrielle?"

I looked at Gabrielle. She was swathed in an elegant winter white cowl-necked dress that clung in all the right places, her face serene, completely unflustered by our heated debate. She tilted her head, clinically assessing the situation, before answering Raph.

"Michael can be very persuasive at getting what he wants. So yes, we took the oath he demanded of us. But what he forgets, sometimes, is that our first duty is to protect all of God's people. Not just his favorites."

Michael flinched at the implied shirking of his duties. "No one ever suffered because of my care for the Carmichaels!"

"That's your opinion," she countered tartly, one perfect brow arched in accusation as she turned on him. "We do not share it. Besides, it's irrelevant. Your regard for these humans is beneath you."

I darted a glance at Tabby, dismayed by what I was hearing. Trying to keep my emotions in check, I fell back on my lawyerly instincts.

"It doesn't matter whether you took the vow voluntarily," I said, "or whether you felt you had to do it to comply with Michael's request. The fact is, you all entered into a contract. Of which, as far as I can tell, you are all in breach."

"What?" Michael looked at me, perplexed. "A contract?"

"You've got to be joking," Raph said, his face splotchy.

Tabby grinned, crossing her arms and skewering Raph with her fiercest look. "You heard her, pretty boy," she said, pointing a finger at his massive chest. "You're in violation, and she's taking you to court."

"Court?" Gabrielle laughed haughtily. "There's no court on Earth that would recognize our vow as a contract. No court on Earth at which we would ever consent to appear," she added, drawing herself up to her full height to emphasize her point.

I looked at her calmly. "I'm perfectly prepared to argue my case before the court of Heaven. I understand from Enoch that you angels are fairly litigious, so I'm sure there will be no problem. There may even be a precedent, for all I know."

Enoch tilted his head, puzzled by the unexpected direction this was taking.

"May I have a word, Hope?"

I tried to guess what he was thinking behind the shiny lenses of his aviators, but to no avail. Curious at what he might have to say, I nodded and let him guide me back into the kitchen.

"Hope. You don't have to take them to court. They did their best. We're here to help now. What could you possibly win by seeking to adjudicate this?"

"They didn't do their best, Enoch," I said tersely, the words practically ripped from me. "The fact that Michael is just standing there, saying nothing—the fact that he still hasn't even tried to explain where he even was that night—proves to me that there is something going on, something I can't trust. But I still need them. So I need to change the terms of the contract. You see them: Raph and Gabrielle can barely tolerate me, or any human. If I don't change the terms of the contract, I'll never be able to get their help."

"That's not true," Enoch interjected. But I could tell from the expression on his face that my words were hitting home.

"They wouldn't have taken the pledge if Michael hadn't forced them to do it, and even so, they scarcely heeded it. If they won't follow through on a pledge, I need something stronger. If my plan has any hope of succeeding, I need to legally bind them to following my wishes."

"You have a plan?"

I paused. "I do. It's a long shot, but it's the only thing I can think of. And I can't pull it off without them."

He leaned into his cane, looking thoughtful.

"You're certain of this? You've thought through what this might do to your relationship with Michael? You've made the mistake of not trusting Michael before, Hope."

I swallowed back my first response—*if I can't trust him, what relationship really is there?*—and chose to nod, instead. "It's different this time, Enoch," I asserted and changed the subject. "You know your courts, given your own history. Will you help me?"

He scratched at his beard. "All right. I will help you, though it goes against my better judgment. I just hope you're prepared for all the consequences of your choice."

We rejoined the others. Raph stared at me stonily. Gabrielle disdained to even look at me. Michael shifted awkwardly, occasionally shooting me a pleading glance.

I cleared my throat. "I'm assuming that I can't physically bring my case to Heaven, so I'm expecting the case to be heard here. As the only angel present who was not party to the original contract, Enoch has agreed to help me with the logistics. The suit itself is simple—it's a breach of contract against the three of you. I am not seeking compensation. Instead, I'm requesting that the contract be shifted from an obligation to Michael, made at his behest, to an obligation to me, personally, so that I might—with your full cooperation—direct recovery efforts to save my sister."

"You're seeking to be in charge? Of us?" Raph pressed.

Gabrielle laughed. "You've got to be kidding. A human will never be acceptable to us—or to the courts."

"I'm deadly serious. If I thought I could trust you, I wouldn't have to resort to this. But I'm not sure, any longer, that I can."

I shot Michael a look that let him know my words were meant for him.

Michael clenched his jaw. I could see the telltale vein in his forehead throbbing—a sure sign that he was about to lose his temper. He stood in stony silence, his face turning successively deeper shades of purple as I stared him down. *If you'd just tell me what was going on, I wouldn't have to do this,* I thought, longingly, just as—without warning—he pivoted and stormed through the front door, abandoning our discussion. Raph and Gabrielle followed on his heels. The door slammed behind them, shaking the tiny carriage house to its foundations.

"Well, that went well," Tabby observed dryly, a hand resting on her hip.

"Let's just hope that the hearing goes better," Enoch added, his face a knot of worry.

～

Enoch successfully made the case that due to the nature of my sister's disappearance, time was of the essence, so we jumped to the head of the docket. The case was set to be heard later that night, right in the middle of the carriage house living room. Heralds—underlings of Gabrielle, the angel of messages, ironically enough—were sent out to inform Michael, Gabrielle, and Raph of the requirement of their attendance. There would be no legal representation—each angel, and I, would argue for ourselves.

At the appointed time, the angelic judge appeared, materializing in the middle of the room. I don't know what I was expecting, but the angel who was to decide the case was draped in a robe of glistening white, her massive wings—a riot of green, gold, and turquoise—folded tightly behind her. Her red hair, shot through with strands of white, cascaded down her shoulders in ringlets. She had the kind of sturdy plumpness that comes with content and success. Her face was kind, yet stern.

"You are the claimant?" she asked me pointedly. "An odd case you have brought. Interesting from the standpoint of jurisdiction. Interesting given the defendants' stature." She grinned conspiratorially and peered at me over her glasses. "Interesting for policy wonks concerning themselves with precedent setting, to be sure. I understand you are a lawyer yourself?"

I nodded, a bit in awe of her.

"Let's hope you're not in over your head. Where are the parties to this contract?"

As she spoke, the other angels appeared in a flash. They were dressed in their battle armor, standing shoulder to shoulder. They'd deliberately chosen to make a show of force.

"Need I remind you of the separation of powers in the heavenly realm?" the judge said sternly, staring at them over their glasses.

Raph, not impressed, scoffed at her. "We can dress as we wish, can we not, Chief Magistrate?"

She pressed her lips together. "Just be sure that's all it is—or your choice of costume will serve you ill, Raphael.

"Now, let's call this proceeding to order. Let all parties to this case be under warning that by agreeing to appear here today, they have acknowledged my authority, and they consent to receive whatever judgment I pass down. Plaintiff, please come forward."

The Chief Magistrate motioned for me to step in front of her.

"I have read your filing, as well as the amicus brief filed by Enoch, the Prophet, also known as the Librarian." The archangels looked startled by the revelation that Enoch had apparently taken sides. "Your contention is that the defendants willfully neglected their vows to protect your sister, one Aurora Carmichael. You claim that only one party to the pledge, the Archangel Arthur, fulfilled his promise and that, being left to his own devices, he fell in battle, leaving your mother vulnerable to the attack that caused her death and allowing the forcible abduction of your sister. Your allegation that the kidnappings and murders are the work of the Fallen makes these grave charges, indeed."

I gulped hard. Standing before this judge who'd arrayed herself in her full angel glory, I felt as if I was back in my first year of law school, struggling to defend myself before a professor eager to catch me in logical traps. I did what I had done then—saying nothing more than absolutely necessary.

She turned to the others.

"Would any of you like to explain your whereabouts the evening of the attack cited by Ms. Carmichael?"

Michael flushed. "It is not secret, your honor, that my . . . senses . . . are not what they used to be. I cannot unerringly intuit danger and humanity's needs any longer." He shot me an accusing glance. "I was elsewhere that evening, unaware of Ms. Carmichael's need."

"Did you not sense anything, then?" the judge pressed.

He looked at the floor. "I did."

"What was it that you sensed?"

"I did experience unease, I admit it. But I could not be sure whence it came, nor what it meant. That is frequently my lot."

"If this is a common occurrence, then, you must have a way of managing it. What do you typically do when you find yourself uneasy in this manner, but unable to pinpoint the source of it?"

He looked up again, a funny look on his face. "I confer with my colleague."

"You mean Gabrielle?" the judge confirmed. "Very well. Is that what you did in this case?"

He nodded.

"Let the record show that the defendant Michael has affirmed he conferred with the defendant Gabrielle on the occasion in question." For the first time, I noticed an angelic scribe, hunched over, scribbling furiously with a quill in a scroll, recording the proceedings. "Well, Michael, what was the outcome of your consultation with her?"

He paused. "She told me she felt nothing."

"Were those her exact words?"

Michael pressed his lips into a grim line. "I believe her exact words were, 'Our efforts are needed here, Michael. Ignore the vague impulses that flit in and out of you and focus on the task before you. Whatever is happening back in Atlanta can wait.'"

I winced. She'd downplayed the potential risk to my family, and she'd done so in a way that was calculated to remind Michael of his own weakness. It must have stung his pride—especially now, with the truth of what my mother and sister had faced that night so clear. I could hardly believe she'd be so callous.

Enoch tilted his head, peering at them both from behind his sunglasses. He looked very unhappy. I leaned over to whisper to him. "I don't understand. Did Gabrielle not sense that we were in trouble? Could Lucas have been preventing her intuition somehow?"

"Shhh," he warned, pointing to the judge. "Listen."

"Gabrielle," said the Chief Magistrate. "Do you agree with Michael's account of that evening's conference? Let me remind you that you remain under the jurisdiction of Heaven."

Gabrielle's mouth twisted into a small, tight smile.

"No," she said.

I felt like I'd been punched in the stomach. Michael wheeled on her, panic and disbelief in his eyes. "What?"

Raph eyed her speculatively.

"That is, I agree with his statement insofar as I told him there was nothing of consequence about which he should bother himself." She let her eyes settle on me, conveying with that one look just how insignificant I really was to her. "I asked him to stay with me that night, and he made a choice to do that."

She let the implication of her statement—the question of what exactly they were doing together—hover around us.

Raph didn't bother to hide his amusement. "Well, well. While the cat's away . . ."

I felt like all the air had been squeezed out of my lungs. Had the very thing I'd feared—the very thing Tabby had warned me about—actually come to pass? From across the room, I felt Gabrielle staring at me, mocking me. For a moment, though, I thought she looked unsteady on her feet, a strained grimace marring her perfect visage.

I looked at Enoch. "She can't lie—can she?" I whispered. "Isn't she supposed to be under oath or something?" I glanced at her again, wondering why she was wincing. Was God punishing her?

Enoch pressed his lips into a tight line, refusing to answer.

I turned back to Gabrielle. The unsteadiness I'd seen had clearly passed. She stood tall, defiant, and more beautiful than ever. One brow arching, she placed a possessive hand on Michael's arm. He angrily shrugged it off.

Michael's figure blurred as angry tears welled in my eyes. I dashed them away.

"How could you?" I demanded, my voice husky.

"Hope," he pleaded, reaching out a hand as he began to move toward me. "You've got to believe me, it's not what you—"

I flinched. "Don't come near me!"

He stopped, shocked.

"We were working," he emphasized. "We were working." He turned back to Gabrielle. "Gabrielle, tell her. Tell Hope the truth."

She tilted her head, weighing his request carefully, clearly enjoying the chaos she'd created with her words. I found myself holding my breath.

"Yes, we worked," she finally assented. "There was no romantic entanglement, you silly human. How very pedestrian of you."

"But then, why didn't you sense—"

She didn't let me finish.

"It was in the interest of the greatest good for me to keep Michael with me that evening, to suppress my knowledge—which, yes, I clearly sensed—of the risk posed to your family. I deliberately downplayed your family's needs." She continued, addressing her words to the judge, her voice full of conviction. "I freely admit my gratitude toward Miss Carmichael, and my appreciation for the role she played nearly thirteen years ago in freeing the Fallen from their burdens. But we must recall that it was Michael's sacrifice, not hers, that ultimately won their redemption. We angels owe her nothing. And her ongoing interest in Michael, and his in her, while quaint and understandable, is unseemly. I could not continue to pander to this unfortunate relationship."

Then she turned to Michael, and suddenly her voice had a hint of remorse. "I warned you," she said. "You should have listened to me."

I frowned. "When? When did you warn him?"

She shrugged. "Right before our last visit to your home. I told him then that his attachment to you posed a danger to the rest of us. To the world. That he needed to make you get on with your choice—ideally in a manner that severed your ties—so that he could be free to focus upon his duties."

His newfound insistence, the pressure for me to decide—it all made sense now.

"Your warning was unjustified!" Michael raged in response. "I fulfilled my obligations. I've never once failed in them."

"Did you?" she whispered, her eyes sad. "If I had told you the truth about the danger to Rorie—if you had left me that night to pursue Lucas and save her—what would have happened to the refugees whose boats succumbed to the violence of the Mediterranean?"

"You could have saved them by yourself. There were not so many," he countered, eyes flashing.

"There were ten boats, Michael. Ten boats crammed with women and children without life jackets. Nearly two hundred souls, seeking freedom from tyranny."

Doubt crept into his eyes. "Still, you could have saved them. It was within your powers to do so."

"And if I had heeded the pledge to protect Aurora, too? If I had abandoned them to follow you?"

She let the question dangle in the air. Michael's nostrils flared, chin raised, as he saw her point.

"I had to do it, Michael." She turned to me, hands outspread. "I'm sorry, Hope. But as you can see, my actions just helped him see the realities of the situation. He cannot cling to his foolish devotion to you and still serve as God's general. It is just not possible."

Michael and Gabrielle continued arguing, Raph now jumping into the fray. Enoch inserted himself into the tiny knot of angry angels, trying to soothe tempers, while I let the reality of the situation wash over me.

This revelation only confirmed my worst fears. Gabrielle had known. And she'd deliberately led Michael astray, letting my mother die, letting Rorie be taken. I couldn't trust them—none of them. Not without having greater control over them myself.

"Order!" the Chief Magistrate shouted, flapping her wings for emphasis as she cut him off. "I demand order during these proceedings. Michael—is what Gabrielle said true?"

He shot Gabrielle a venomous look before answering the judge. The cords of his neck stood out, straining as he nearly spat the words. "As you can see, Gabrielle misrepresented the situation to me."

The judge cut him off coldly. "It is a simple question, Michael: Did you, or did you not, actively choose to remain with Gabrielle the evening of Lucas's attack upon this family? I require a simple answer. A yes or no will do nicely."

He slumped his shoulders, letting his wings sag behind him. "Yes," he muttered, staring at the floor. "Yes, I decided to stay with her that night and tend to the refugees. She asked me to, and I did." He refused to look at me.

Gabrielle raised her chin, defiant.

"Despite your sense of danger?" the judge probed, driving home her point.

"Despite my sense of danger," he repeated, jaw clenched.

"And despite suspecting that your intuition, however imperfect, might have to do with some danger to the Carmichaels?"

He gritted his teeth. "Yes."

"I see," the judge intoned gravely. "This is an unfortunate finding. Though I am pleased we can at least now all agree on the facts of the matter. As for you, Raphael," she peered at him over the rims of her glasses, "I take it you were not aware of any need at all, and that you were reliant upon the two of them to alert you to any danger?"

"It wouldn't have mattered," he said, his face expressionless. "I have no love for humans. I admit, I might not have attended to them even if I had known. A forced oath does not an enforceable contract make," he said, looking at me slyly, "as my human friend, the lawyer, well knows."

"We are talking about heavenly law, now," she rebuked him sharply. "An oath given to the leader of God's army is, indeed, enforceable. Hence I find no other option but to find you all guilty of breach of contract, per the plaintiff's filing. I find her requested damages suitable to the injury. You will fulfill your contractual commitments by going after Aurora Carmichael now, at the direction of her elder sister—Hope."

My eyes stung with tears. I clung to her announcement—a Pyrrhic victory in my relationship with Michael, for sure, but necessary for me to save my sister. But I had one more request for the judge.

"Your honor," I began. "There is one amendment I would seek to your judgment."

She raised her brows. "Miss Carmichael. Let me warn you that we have accommodated you, and your request for speed, beyond what many in Heaven found reasonable. I have ruled in your favor—a precedent I may one day rue. Do not push your luck."

I gulped, but pressed on. "I understand. But the . . . revelations at this proceeding have made the continued involvement of the Archangel Gabrielle problematic at best. I seek to remove her from the contract, and I request that Enoch serve as her substitute. If he is willing, that is," I added hastily, not wanting him to think I was taking him for granted.

"Enoch is not a warrior," Raph protested. "That was the whole reason we didn't include him in the first place. With Arthur also gone, we cannot afford any dead weight. And he lacks the intuition to counterbalance Michael's deficit." He shot me a dirty look, reminding me of my own role in creating that lack.

"I note your argument, Raph," the judge said, clearly exasperated. "But how Enoch chooses to manifest is up to him. If Miss Carmichael finds his services to be of value, who am I to argue? And from what I understand, Miss Carmichael will be able to provide a useful complement to Michael's intuition on her own. Enoch, what say you?"

Enoch nodded, hobbling forward on his cane. "It would be an honor."

The Chief Magistrate drew herself up. "So be it. You have my decision. I suggest you vacate the premises forthwith, Gabrielle. You have brought naught but trouble upon this house. And, I might add, with your meddling, you have forced Michael into a proximity with Miss Carmichael that is the opposite of your intent."

Gabrielle sniffed at the rebuke. "I am aware that my plans have backfired, at least for the time being. But perhaps now, even if Hope has no sympathy for my point of view, she will realize the impossibility of her relationship with Michael. She will realize that for all our sakes, she must give it up. In the long run, their connection will do nothing but put others at needless risk."

She then turned her full attention to me.

"It is a fool's errand upon which you embark. For any human to attempt to fight against the Fallen is futile. And by insisting on entangling Michael in it, again distracting him from his duties, you render your mother's death in vain."

Her words stung, but I refused to dignify them with a response.

"Nonetheless, I wish you luck." She smiled sadly. "I truly wished you no ill, Hope. Everything I did, I did in the name of Heaven's order. While I don't expect you to understand, I had hoped others would," she whispered, letting her gaze linger on Michael. "I will tend to God's people while you are tied up in your fruitless searching. When you realize I am right, you know how to find me."

Then, in a flash of light, she vanished.

After a moment of awkward silence, the judge rose from her bench, the rustle of robes and gusting wings signaling her intent to depart as well.

"I will file my findings in the Library, Enoch," she said, smiling warmly at him. "And I will send your regards to your colleagues, whom I know miss you." She turned to me. "Good luck, Miss Carmichael. You have surrounded yourself with strange company, but whether they are willing or not, they will fulfill their duties to you or suffer God's pain as punishment. Godspeed."

Then she, too, along with her scribe, disappeared, only a twinkling trail of pixelated light trailing behind her.

I turned to the remaining angels. Raph was pained even to be in the same room as me, let alone forced onto a mission such as this. Enoch placidly unwrapped a granola bar, seemingly unperturbed by all that had just passed. Michael's face was blank, a cipher. Only the telltale vein throbbing in his forehead gave indication that he was feeling anything at all.

"You're in charge," Enoch said, chewing with his mouth open, letting little crumbles of oats fall into his scraggly beard. "Where are we going?"

"Colorado," I answered, steeling myself. "We're breaking in to the supermax prison to talk to Chen. We're going to find out where they took my sister."

fourteen

LUCAS

The roadblock as we'd headed into North Dakota had been their last hope. It had almost given me pleasure, watching the spark of life in their eyes when the girls had realized what was happening.

The police had blocked Highway 85, stopping every vehicle heading north—miles of pickup trucks, dump trucks, SUVs, campers, all being questioned individually. What they were looking for, I had no idea. But I needed to make sure that when it was our turn to be stopped, they didn't notice anything strange about two girls huddled in the backseat in skimpy clothing.

"Not a word," I warned from the front seat. "Let me do the talking."

I rolled down the window as the officer approached.

"License and registration," he demanded.

I fished in the glove compartment and smoothly handed them over.

While he called in the numbers, I watched Rorie in the rear

view mirror. Her face was strained with her silent hope—*notice me, ask me, talk to me, help me.* It was there in her eyes.

I knitted my brows together and shook my head slightly with a silent threat: Don't even think about it. That was all I'd needed—that, and the brandishing of the gun that was tucked under my seat, with a promise to kill us all if she made as much as a peep—to win her silence.

The officer thrust his hand through the window, offering me back my papers, not even bothering to spare a glance into the backseat.

"All checks out. Headed to Williston?"

"Yes, sir," I answered.

"Well, good luck then," he responded, pounding the side of the car as he backed away.

I closed the window, shutting out the cold night air and shutting down the girls' thoughts of rescue.

Now nothing stood between us and my object: the Bakken Oil Fields.

∾

"This is the end of the line for me, ladies," I said, giving them a mock salute as I swung the door open at our destination. "It's been a pleasure escorting you to your new home."

"You're leaving us?" Rorie blinked at the harsh parking lot lights, fast to pick up on the fact that the engine was still running.

No, I thought to myself. I'll be right here, destroying your friend before your eyes. Just in another human shell.

I didn't answer, just reached into the back of the car to haul Macey out. She was bruised from her night at the truck stop, her eyes still blurry with post-drug stupor. I made a mental note that I might have to drag things out a bit if she was to last for as long as I needed her. There was no need for mercy—who had showed me any, over the millennia of pain I experienced?

No one, I answered, with a grimace as the throbbing ache that was my constant companion spiked to fever pitch. *No one at all.*

A young boy, perhaps fifteen, approached our car. In the shadows, an older man who looked like a bouncer hovered, keeping a watchful eye on our transaction. The girls shivered in the night air, pulling the threadbare blankets around themselves, their breaths emerging in puffs.

"This it?" the boy asked gruffly. His face was wary, as if he'd already seen too much in his short life.

I nodded. He shoved a wad of cash into my hand, and I counted out the bills, making sure it was all there.

"All yours," I said, turning and climbing back into the car.

"Wait!" Macey called out. "Where are we? Is Luke here?"

"Luke's not coming for you, baby," I answered, enjoying the crushed look on her face as she took in my words. "Welcome to your new world."

With that, I slammed the door and put the car into drive, watching the girls standing, stupefied, as I wove through the junk that was strewn across the parking lot.

Funny how attached they'd become in such a short time.

Later, when I'd abandoned the car behind a motel, I pondered what to do next. Replace the fifteen-year-old boy? Take on the role of his mother, the former prostitute who'd come full circle to sell girls herself? Or pose as another victim, worming my way into Rorie and Macey's confidences?

There were so many choices. It was hard to decide, especially with the constant buzzing of pain in my head. But I smiled to myself, knowing that, really, there was no bad choice. I tossed the keys under the car and, whistling, started walking back to the warehouse where the girls were being kept.

I'd play the enforcer, the muscle. Such an important role, early in a girl's training. Lots of interaction.

This should be fun.

~

The girls were being kept in dog cages.

They were chained inside the wire crates, leaving them only one hand free and exposed to the cold concrete below. They'd been tossed in with their blankets and nothing else. The crates were small enough that the girls had to crouch low to avoid hitting their heads, forcing them into a position of submission from the very start.

It was brilliant, and sick. Just what I'd come to expect from humanity.

As I watched them, I felt a surge of delight, shot through with an arc of pain so exquisite it took my breath away.

Ah, the pain. The more it came now, the closer I knew I was to my aim. I embraced it. I let it wash over me and envelop me. I *was* pain, and pain was me. We were inseparable now.

They were in a separate room, a room that was set aside for new girls, apparently. There were a few empty crates around the perimeter of the room, abandoned clothes and blankets strewn in haphazard piles within them. Only one other girl was in the room, a dark-skinned girl with ebony hair that was matted and tangled behind her. She was curled up in the fetal position on the bottom of her crate, facing the wall, silent.

The vague smell of urine and vomit suffused the air, and I had to force myself not to gag. I silently cursed my frail human body with all its weaknesses.

I was trailing the boy, who was tossing cold Pop-Tarts and Fruit Roll-Ups into the crates, paying the girls less attention than one would a stray animal.

Through the thin corrugated steel walls, I could hear the barking and snarling of dogs, the shouts of a drunken crowd egging on the mangled animals, placing bets on which would emerge victorious. I felt a stab of outrage. Humans destroying one another with their craven depravity was one thing. Taking it out on defenseless creatures of God was another.

"You can clean the cages out," the boy ordered. "We're expecting another shipment tomorrow. Later on, you and I can mark them." I nodded to acknowledge the task and set to work, moving quietly so that I could listen to the whispers of the girls, looking over my shoulder every now and then to see what they were up to but hoping not to draw attention to myself. I didn't want them to notice me. Not yet, anyway.

"Macey, we have to get out of here." Rorie was pressed up against the crate, her fingers wrapped around the wire bars.

Macy huddled in the crate. "I'm waiting for Luke. He'll come for me. I know he will."

"Didn't you hear him, Macey? Luke's not coming for you. He's sold you."

"That's not true," Macey said. She pressed her hands to her ears, the chains jangling as she tried to block out Rorie's words. "He loves me, Rorie. He told me." She began rocking back and forth, trying to soothe herself.

Rorie persisted, her voice sharp. "Wake up, Macey! He took advantage of you. And nobody's coming to save us. We have to get out of here on our own."

She started shaking the bars of her cage, as if she could make the walls fall down by force of will.

"Shut up," the other girl croaked from her corner, not even stirring. "You're only going to make it worse."

"Worse? How could it get any worse?" Rorie challenged.

"Have you been taken out yet?"

"What do you mean?"

The girl sighed. "If you don't know what I mean, then you haven't. What about your friend?"

There was a long pause. "I think so. Last night, at a truck stop."

"Ah. So you do know what I mean. That's what they do here. This town is full of men working the oil rigs, men hauling water and gravel, men working construction sites. What your friend did last night is what we'll all be doing, every night. That's what's in store for me, and that's what's in store for both of you."

"How do you know?" Rorie whispered.

"They kept talking about it on the reservation," the girl answered. "The tribal council and the women. But we couldn't do anything. It just kept getting worse. And now I'm here. Trapped."

"We can get out," Rorie whispered, her voice faltering with doubt. I smiled to myself, moving to the next crate, and began picking through the pile of stinky clothes that the last girl had left behind.

"You won't. We're behind locked door after locked door, with guards all over the place. Nobody here cares. All they care about is the money."

There was a rattle, a jingling of chains and thump as Rorie sat back in her crate. Outside, the sounds of an angry fight crescendoed—men arguing over their winnings, accusing one another of cheating and who knows what else.

"What's your name?"

The Native American girl rustled at the bottom of her cage. "Waheenee. But my English name is Wanda. You can call me that."

I wiped down the crates, the noise from the dogfight dying down as the drunken men stumbled out, the betting done for the night. The only sound was the soft whimpering of Macey, crying herself to sleep.

"Wanda?" Rorie persisted.

"Yes?"

"What's going to happen next?"

I looked over my shoulder, pretending to be busy folding the blankets. Wanda sat up in her crate and turned so that Rorie could see her. She was dressed in a filthy T-shirt. She pulled up the sleeve and pressed her arm against the bars. In the dim light, an oozing sore glistened on her shoulder. It was a red, angry welt, full of pus.

Rorie gasped.

"They're going to brand you like a cow. Like this. So that none of the other pimps will steal you."

Wanda touched the infected spot on her shoulder and winced. She peered through the web of steel that enclosed her, her eyes full of pity.

"Rorie. That's your name, isn't it?" Rorie nodded, for once too stunned to speak. "Don't let them see you cry. Whatever you do, don't let them see you cry."

I felt a stab of pain, God striking me again for my audacity in challenging His will so directly. I leaned against the wall, my eyes rolling back as I battled my instinct to fight against it.

Outside, I heard the sudden whine of a dog. Angry now, pushed to the edge by excruciating pain, I threw open the door and stalked out.

The drunken handler was taunting one of the fighters—apparently the loser in the prior match, its ear torn, a trail of blood marking the place where it had wound its way around the concrete floor.

"Damn dog!" the man cried with slurred speech. "I lost two

hundred bucks because of you!" He pulled his leg back and kicked the dog in the ribs.

In an instant, I had him by the throat, backing him up against the cold corrugated-aluminum wall.

"Don't. You. Ever. Hurt. This. Animal. Again," I commanded, squeezing my fingers so hard that I could feel his windpipe. His face was turning purple, his eyes bulging as he stared at me, terrified. "Do you understand me?"

He shook his head, his eyes beginning to glaze over as he ran out of air, blood vessels popping.

"Good," I said, letting him go unceremoniously to fall into a gasping heap on the cold floor.

Humans.

～

I kept watch over the room with the cages into the night, assuming that eventually the girls would forget my presence. Once they did, maybe they would talk to one another. I hoped they would: I didn't want to miss a moment of it, the things they said to soothe one another, to pretend that none of this was happening to them. To get the full sense of what I would slowly, piece by piece, be destroying.

Sure enough, I got what I hoped for.

"Wanda?" Rorie asked, into the darkness.

There was no response. Nothing but the quiet blowing of the primitive furnace that rattled on and off periodically.

"Wanda? Are you awake?"

There was a soft rustle of fabric and a rattle of the wire cage as Wanda rolled over.

"You should get your sleep while you can," Wanda said in a

weary whisper. "Once they decide you're ready, you won't be able to get enough of it."

I could hear Rorie roll over; imagined the cold wire that must be poking into her spine.

"What makes them decide you're ready?" she asked. "Is there any way to never be ready?"

Wanda sighed. "Don't you ever shut up?"

"I'm sorry," Rorie said sheepishly. "I don't mean to bother you. You just seem to know what's going on."

"Yeah, I've got a whole two days' jump on you, kid. How old are you, anyway?"

"Thirteen."

"Your friend, too?"

"Yes, she is too."

"She looks even younger than you. More vulnerable."

Rorie was quiet for a while. "You're right. She is more vulnerable. She's had a tough life."

Wanda snorted. "Tell me about it."

When Rorie spoke again, she sounded embarrassed. "I didn't mean to sound so—"

"So what? Naïve? Privileged?"

"Yes. Both."

There was a slight pause. "It's okay. You don't have to apologize for having had a decent childhood. Just never figured I'd run into somebody like you in a place like this."

"Somebody like me, how?"

"You know. Somebody who's not already beaten down. Somebody who came from a family that loved her."

"You can tell that about me?"

"Yeah. I can tell."

"How?"

"I can just tell. You're smart enough to be afraid, but you're not defeated. Life hasn't gotten to you. You don't deserve to be in here."

"Wanda, nobody deserves to be in here."

She laughed, a low, throaty sound. "I guess you're right, kid. So how is it that you did wind up in a dog cage in the middle of the frozen North Dakota prairie? You clearly aren't from around here."

I smiled, standing watch, while Rorie remembered the past few days I had put her through.

"I was just trying to help my friend when she was in trouble. I guess I thought I could handle it, for the both of us. I was wrong. How about you?"

Wanda sighed. "I was stupid."

"What do you mean?" Rorie prompted.

"I got into an argument with my mom's boyfriend. He's such a jerk, always taking my mom's money and using it to get drunk. He came home in a stupor and started yelling at my mom for running out of money. It wasn't right—he doesn't even have a job. He just sucks off of her."

I could feel her sense of injustice, smoldering across the room.

"What did you do?" Rorie asked.

Wanda laughed. "I told him off. And then I threw the coffee pot at his head. It shattered all over the kitchen floor. It really pissed off my mom, but it caught his attention."

"So what happened?"

"I told my mom it was him or me. That she had to choose."

"And?"

"She chose him. So I left."

Rorie was silent. I thought of Mona living alone for all those years; I suppose Rorie found it hard to imagine her mother with any man, let alone choosing one over her and Hope.

Wanda picked up her story:

"After a few days of trying to get a job, I realized nobody was going to hire an underage runaway from the rez. I was getting desperate, wondering if I should just swallow my pride and go home. Finally some guy approached me at a bus station. Real nice, bought me McDonald's and everything. Said he felt sorry for me. Said he'd help me. I should have known better. I should have asked him how. Anyway, that's how I ended up here. At least I've got a warm place to sleep."

"Wanda."

"Yeah?"

"I'm sorry."

"It's okay. Shit like this happens to reservation kids all the time. I shouldn't have expected any better."

She yawned. I heard the rattling of the cage, the tug of the blanket, as she settled herself back in to sleep.

"Good night, kid."

After a while, rhythmic snoring emanated from Wanda's cage.

And then, after a long time, I heard Rorie whisper: "Maybe you shouldn't have expected it. But you deserved better."

It surprised me, that she would think that. Surely she should be worrying more about her own situation. I would be, if I were her.

fifteen

HOPE

The scenery in Florence, Colorado, was deadening: all scrubby brush and dust-choked gravel, stifling any majesty that the mountains, which loomed in the distance, could have lent. Guard towers dotted the perimeter of the facility, the sidewalk funneling us toward one entry. Our journey to get here had seemed endless: a flight to Denver, connecting to Colorado Springs, followed by nearly an hour's drive in our rented SUV. As we left the car and began to walk toward the razor-wire fences and twelve-foot walls, I felt just as uncertain as I had been when, as a fifteen-year-old girl, I'd gone walking into a casino, Michael at my side, playing a dangerous game of dress-up in Las Vegas.

Only this time we weren't pretending to be high rollers: we were posing as Chen's lawyers. And rather than a casino, we were about to infiltrate one of the toughest prisons anywhere in the world: ADX.

I threw my shoulders back, feigning confidence. I was swathed in my best navy suit, picking my way through the gravel in my highest heels. It was my uniform, the armor I put on before I headed to court, the costume that covered up any insecurity I might have. I felt a pang, knowing that this mental trick was one that my mother had taught me herself, right before my first job interview: good shoes and a chunky necklace for confidence. My head pounded, and I wasn't sure which was worse: worrying about Chen's reaction if he recognized me, or the hollow feeling I was carrying in the pit of my stomach, knowing Michael had betrayed me by choosing to stay with Gabrielle—a betrayal that had cost my mother her life.

I shook the thoughts away. I needed to focus, now more than ever. At least Michael had taken the guise of Chen's real lawyer; I could pretend, if only for a moment, that it wasn't him standing next to me.

I paused in front of the rubber pad before the door, unsure of what it was.

"Pressure pads," Michael muttered. "They'll be all over the place to detect footfalls in case anybody tries to escape." We stood for a moment, unsure of what to do.

I noticed wall-mounted cameras, training on us, and a slight whirring overhead coming from other devices perched high on the walls.

"Lasers," Michael noted. "Probably scanning the perimeter to be sure we weren't followed."

Without warning the doors slid open, admitting us through what I'd come to realize was just the first layer of security. Immediately inside, guard dogs on leashes patrolled the perimeter. The cement and brick walls of the main building loomed ahead of us, cold and institutional. I felt exposed, a sensation only worsened by the winter winds that tore down from the mountains, chilling me through.

I had to admit, though, that if I felt stripped bare, it was as much to do with the unfamiliarity of the situation I and the angels now found ourselves in. The easy banter of days past was gone. We'd spent the majority of our trip turned inward on our own thoughts, only occasionally making the effort to politely pick our way through the landmines of conversation by focusing on the mundane: directions, bathroom breaks, plans for our arrival. Only Enoch had dared to say more, seemingly oblivious to the chill that had settled around the rest of us, earning for himself everyone's irritation.

Once, while we walked between terminals, Michael had tried to engage me in a discussion of his innocence, but I'd cut him off:

"I don't want to hear it, Michael," I'd insisted. "You knew—deep down you *had* to have known—that something was wrong. You admitted it in the trial. But you ignored your instincts, and now we're here. The time for rehashing that is over. Just focus on our plan and make sure we get the information out of Chen that we need."

He didn't respond. I'd played the conversation over and over in my head since then, wondering if I was being too hard on him. But I couldn't let go of my anger. Not yet, anyway. It burned inside of me, pure and sweet, helping me concentrate on what I needed to do to get my sister back.

Michael cleared his throat, interrupting my thoughts as we walked toward the prison.

"You look like a sexy librarian," he joked.

I shot him an outraged look, daring him to say anything more. He flushed, ruffled by my response.

"Sorry," he mumbled. "I just meant . . . I mean, I usually only see you in T-shirt and jeans." He paused, turning an even deeper shade of red. "I didn't mean anything by it, Hope." Greeted by my stony silence, he sighed and then gestured ahead. "Very well, then.

After you." I nodded, pulling my suit jacket tighter around me and quickening my pace.

We checked in for visitation—a process that required the use of our newly minted fake IDs and extensive paperwork, including reading the twenty points of rules that covered attire, behavior, topics of conversation, length of visit, and the rights of the warden to keep all visitations under surveillance. The list of what I could bring in to our meeting was short. Luckily, I'd been forewarned and had left my purse in the car.

I noted that we were the only visitors on the premises this day—and I read, with a start, that Chen's only visitor had been his lawyer. It had been six months since the lawyer had last visited. A small flicker of pity welled up inside me, but I shoved it down. This man, for all I knew, had ordered the murder of my father. He deserved to be here, I reminded myself.

The check-in guard at the front desk looked over our paperwork and our prior petition for visitation.

"You just got added to the approved visitation list," she said, scanning a stack of forms. "New girl on the case, eh?" She looked me over with a hardened eye. "Here's the drill. I'll bring you into the booth first, the two of you. Guards will escort your client in after that. We'll be watching the whole time, but we won't listen in to your conversation. Any time you want out, you just push the button. Got that?"

I nodded.

"He's been in Range 13 for the last two weeks, so he may be a little screwed up."

Michael looked at me, confused. The guard continued. "Extra security measures. Locked down twenty-four hours a day. No contact with other prisoners, not even for exercise. Cameras on him 24/7."

"What did my client do to get himself placed there?" Michael prompted.

She shrugged. "I don't know what he did. Usually we place prisoners in the Range when they go on hunger strike, for medical monitoring and forced feeding. Real pain in the ass. Your guy doesn't seem like the type to go on strike, though. The only reason he's in the ADX at all is we caught him directing Triad operations out of prison—deemed him a national security threat. Maybe he'll tell you himself what he did that was bad enough to put him in the Range."

I snuck Michael a surreptitious look as the guard escorted us to another door. I hoped Chen would be in good enough condition to tell us what he knew.

The door slid open with a loud metallic thud. Two additional guards were waiting on the other side.

"One guard ahead of you, one behind. You'll have up to seven hours, which should be plenty of time for whatever business you have with your client. But if you leave, you're done for the day. Have fun," the guard said, gesturing for us to walk through the gap.

We stepped through, and the guards closed ranks around us. Behind me, the door clanged shut. A long hallway, sterile and quiet, stretched before me, turning every now and then at hard angles. One wall was a glass panel. The other was row after row of cells completely cut off from the hallway, just solid wall and metal door. As we walked, I noted the incongruity of the soft pastel peaches and mint-green paint that accented the trim and the doors. It didn't look like what I'd envisioned for a prison.

There were no noises. There were no people. None at all.

We approached another door. The guard punched in some numbers, and the solid metal door before us whisked open. The guard peered through a barred door, confirming that we were safe before opening that one, too, and passing through.

Nothing but hallway stretched before us.

We continued walking, the only sound our echoing footsteps and the reverberations of the door as it slammed shut behind us.

The eerie silence was unsettling. My palms were getting clammy from nerves. I itched to reach out and take Michael's hand.

"You'll be in this booth," the guard noted, gesturing to the small unit made entirely of glass. We passed through another door and sat down on the institutional metal chairs. We faced a clear glass barrier that ran all the way to the ceiling, bisecting a table that took up the width of the booth. There was a small opening near the tabletop, just big enough to pass through papers or files. That and miniscule perforations in the glass, framed in polished steel, were the only accommodations to real communication.

We sat down to wait. The awkwardness between us was palpable. I stared straight ahead of me, crossing my hands on the table, and focused on preparing myself to see Chen after all these years.

The door on the other side of the room opened.

We saw Chen before he saw us. He was dressed in a baggy khaki shirt and pants that loosely resembled scrubs. His hands were shackled and chained to a restraint around his waist; his ankles were shackled, too. He shuffled awkwardly, one guard in front of him, two behind. I remembered him as a proud man with presence. His twelve years in prison had clearly changed him: he seemed smaller, somehow, his face shrunken and wrinkled, his jet-black hair now a shock of white. Dark blue circles sagged under his eyes, which darted restlessly side to side.

The guards opened the door to his side of the booth and shoved him in.

"Remember, we're watching you, Chen," one warned, slamming the door behind him.

He sat down, the shackles and restraints forcing him into an ungainly position.

He leaned forward, his attention focused on Michael, whom he took to be his lawyer. If I had any doubts about the sharpness of his mind after his time in prison, they were dispelled as soon as he opened his mouth.

"What are you doing to get me out of this hellhole, Wang?" he demanded, his dark eyes snapping with frustration. "It's been months. I thought I made it clear the last time—my government, *our* government, will pay you handsomely if you are successful."

Michael leaned forward toward the barrier, keeping his voice low. "I've been working on a plan, and I think I have one. But you're going to have to cooperate with the Feds, do a little trading."

Chen arched a brow, suspicious. "Is that why she's here?" he asked, tilting his head toward me. "Who is she, anyway? My notice just said you were bringing another lawyer with you."

"She's working the Fed side of the bargain," Michael said quickly. "Her name is Michaelson. Hannah Michaelson."

Chen narrowed his eyes to inspect me.

"Michaelson, eh? That's an interesting name. Familiar, though. Like that bastard who blew my operation in Vegas—what was his name? Carmichael. Yes, Carmichael. Maybe not a coincidence?" With effort, he nearly climbed up on the table to get a better look. "No," he said, his mouth falling open in surprise as he looked me over.

I held my breath, beads of sweat trickling down the back of my neck as he inspected me. We'd chosen the alias deliberately, hoping it would jog his memory enough to get him to talk. That said, we knew the choice could backfire. Would he recognize me? I gripped the edge of the table, remembering that the last time I'd seen him, I'd been suffering from second-degree burns, forced to stand before him as he inspected my injuries—injuries he'd assumed Michael had inflicted on me to punish me for disobedience.

Nervous, my hand snaked to the back of my neck, touching my Mark as I waited him out.

Chen fell back into his chair, muttering to himself, looking around in confusion. "It is not possible. It must be a coincidence. She could never have recovered from those burns. Not without scars." He darted a glance, this time more cautious, back at me and then, confused, turned his attention back to Michael. "But the resemblance is remarkable."

"Are you done with your trip down memory lane?" Michael inquired with an edge to his voice. "I think you'll want to hear what she has to say."

Chen nodded, warily, and leaned closer to the glass. His hands were folded quietly in front of him. I looked closely: his once perfectly manicured nails were ragged and dirty. His hands shook with a slight tremor—whether nerves, drugs, or something else, I couldn't tell.

"You're going to have to cough up some good information for this to work," I began, feeling him out.

"Well?" Chen answered, the cynicism in his voice notable. "Spit it out then. What is it that the all-powerful United States government needs from its humble servant?"

You can do this, I thought to myself. He's just another client seeking legal advice.

"We have a situation," I said delicately. "The daughter of a prominent Republican party contributor has disappeared under suspicious circumstances. She was clearly taken against her will. She disappeared at the same time as a friend of hers—the foster daughter of another prominent family in Atlanta."

Chen's eyes were sparkling with interest now. "Go on," he urged.

"The evidence points to trafficking. There was some preliminary trafficking of at least one of the girls in Atlanta, we think. But now they've vanished. We need you to tell us where they might be."

"You are accusing Triad?" he asked pointedly.

Michael shook his head. "No. There are no accusations. The government is just asking you to suggest, based on what you know about the trade, where these girls may have been taken."

I offered what I hoped was the clincher. "We can get you out of the Range. Maybe even get you into the Step Down program so that you can get out of ADX for good."

He sucked his breath in.

"My government approves of this?" He looked questioningly at Michael.

Michael shrugged, noncommittal. "They see no harm in your helping with a case that does not directly affect Chinese interests."

Chen sat back in his chair. The opportunity being presented to him had recharged him. He was alert, eyes bright. I almost felt guilty to be lying to him in such a bald-faced way.

Almost. But not quite.

"I'd cough it up if I were you," Michael counseled. "I'm not sure how many chances like this you're going to get. And I don't know how long they're planning on keeping you in the Range."

"It's . . . how do you Americans call it? Trumped-up charges. I didn't do anything wrong. They are just singling me out." His face twisted into a bitter grimace.

Michael shook his head. "Don't waste our time, Chen. It doesn't matter whether you deserved it or not. The administration holds all the cards here. They can let you rot in that cell until the end of your sentence, and we won't be able to do a damn thing. Tell us what you know, or we're leaving."

Michael pushed back his chair and made as if to leave. Chen arched a brow and then held up one delicate finger.

"One moment. I may have heard a few things." He gestured toward the glass. "You'll have to come closer, though. I don't want to be heard." He looked over his shoulder. I followed his gaze to another booth: another prisoner had joined us, huddled close to the glass and consulting with his own visitors.

We squeezed as close to the table as we could. Chen looked around, confirming that the other prisoner wasn't listening.

"I have heard recently of some reverse migrations," he finally said. "American girls trafficked to India—Kolkata, specifically. Kolkata, of course, has a long history of selling its children."

He paused dramatically, checking to see if he had my attention.

"But then again, they could be in Brazil. The entire northeast coastal portion of the country is notorious for child sex tourism." He tapped a finger thoughtfully on the cold countertop. "Or could it be China? Russians, Ukrainians, Americans, other Asians . . . you can find almost anything you want in China. How to choose where to search?"

I threw an alarmed look at Michael. We couldn't possibly track them down if they could be in such far-flung places as these.

Chen leaned forward, enjoying my distress. "You seem concerned, young lady. Perhaps worried that you cannot find the girls you seek? You are right to be concerned. They will slip through your fingers, over and over—very difficult to find. Not important enough for foreign governments to care or come to your assistance."

He sat back then, a self-satisfied, smug look on his face. But I saw how his manacled hands were shaking. He couldn't hide them.

I leaned closer. "We can get you out of solitary confinement with one call. But this isn't good enough."

"I didn't realize how eager you were to help the American government." The corner of his mouth twitched a bit, twisting into a bitter smile. He would have enjoyed playing mind games with us, but we held all the cards, and he knew it.

"So," he sighed, spreading his hands as wide as the chains would let him, "you are in luck. They are probably in none of those places. There would be no need for them to be taken that far away—not when there is demand right here, in your own country."

I held my breath, forcing my face into a detached mask. He couldn't see that I cared. I couldn't let him exploit my emotions as a weakness.

He traced a pattern on the metal desk, dragging the chains of his restraint across the surface. "Where did you say these girls were taken from?"

"Atlanta," Michael said tersely. Out of the corner of my eye, I could see the vein throbbing in his forehead. He was losing patience. We needed to get whatever Chen knew, fast. I reached a cautionary hand under the table to rest on his knee. Startled, he shot me a confused look. I furrowed my brow and shook my head slightly, warning him not to erupt.

"Atlanta. I used to know that market well," Chen reminisced with a faint smile. "A very ambitious District Attorney, if I remember correctly. Also the Attorney General. But I digress. My colleagues learned that in Atlanta, when things heated up, so to speak, it was easy to move just over the border to Alabama, to Tennessee, and to wait for them to settle down. But if these girls had connections, that would not be far enough away. Also not the most lucrative place to take them."

Michael slammed his hand on the table. "Stop toying with us. Where are they?"

I placed my hand over his fist. His heat spiraled up my arm, familiar and strange at the same time. I realized that up until these moments, I hadn't touched him since the night of my mother's death.

Chen smiled. "Patience, my legal friend. I am getting to it. You know, I haven't had a good conversation like this in some time. Did you know that the most human interaction I get is when I am let out for one hour to 'exercise', as they call it? If I am lucky, there will be someone else in the adjacent cage. Though frankly, I am not sure I can call some of these men human. And the conversation leaves much to be desired."

He leaned back in his chair, enjoying Michael's embarrassment. "You really should come to see me more often," he chided Michael. "Then I wouldn't be so tempted to drag things out like this."

I squeezed Michael's hand, silently wishing for him to hold his temper. He pressed his lips together in a hard line, gathering his patience, before answering Chen. "I'll have to do that. I'm sure the loneliness is hard to bear."

Chen pursed his lips, deflecting the small kindness.

"It doesn't matter. Now, where was I? Oh, yes, the hot market for young girls. If I were you, I would be looking in North Dakota."

"North Dakota?" I repeated, dumbfounded. But even as my mind registered skepticism, a fleeting jolt of recognition shot through me. "Why would they be there?"

Chen shot me a dazzling smile. "Because it is the hottest market for sex trafficking in the entire United States. The oil boom has drawn tens of thousands of men: desperate men, men willing to take backbreaking work because they have run out of options, men who believe it is their chance to strike it rich.

"But—and here is the catch—it is almost only men. Men with

money to burn, stuffed into man camps to live alone in squalor and boredom."

I looked at him skeptically. "'Man camps?' Really?"

"Do not sneer down your nose. For them, it is a solution to lack of housing. But it is a breeding ground for stress. For tension. For loneliness. There is nothing to do there but drink away your wages, so it also becomes a breeding ground for violence and vice. It is the perfect place to take a young girl, if your object is to make a lot of money fast. Of course, the recent collapse of oil prices has made the men testy. The threat of unemployment tends to do that. The girls can prove to be handy scapegoats, a ready punching bag for the customers to take out their frustrations. So a foolproof invest-ment opportunity for the traffickers, regardless of the state of the oil markets."

He paused, looking carefully at me through the glass. "The color seems to have drained from your face, Miss Michaelson. You worry about the young ladies, do you? Tell me," he prompted. "How long have they been gone?"

I counted back. "A week."

He shook his head, adopting a sorrowful pose. "They will already have been used, then, I am afraid. You will not find them as they once were. But if you are to find them at all, that is where I would look if I were in your shoes."

He sat back in his chair with a self-satisfied smile. "I believe I have lived up to my end of the bargain. You will fulfill yours, now, won't you?"

I nodded mutely, trying to erase the horrible images that were running through my mind—images of Rorie and Macey that were coming, unbidden, because of what Chen had just told us.

"You have something for me to sign?"

I pulled a thin bit of paper we'd brought in, just in case we needed some way to make our visit look official, from where I'd set it on the table. With my fingertips, I slid it through the narrow opening in the glass barrier.

I watched, fascinated, as he struggled with the shackles and tried, for just an instant, to see if he could touch my hand. The slot was too narrow, and shackles too confining, though; all he managed was to brush his shaking fingertips up against mine. He let his hand linger there for just a moment; through the glass.

He looked up to find me staring at him with pity. Flustered, he pulled the papers back and scanned them.

"I don't have a pen," he mumbled, his discomfiture not yet passed.

Michael pressed the call button. "We need a pen for Mr. Chen to sign some papers. And then we'll be done," he added.

Two guards entered the room and then buzzed open the door to Chen's side of the booth. One hung back by the door while the other chained a pen into a specially made tether in the wall, in one swift move offering the ballpoint pen to Chen. Chen took it clumsily, testing the length of the short leash.

"Not like the old days," he tried to joke. He scanned the papers carefully and then awkwardly, like a five-year-old just learning his letters, signed his name at the bottom.

The guard withdrew the pen immediately, handing it over his shoulder to the other waiting guard. "Get up," he ordered, backing out of the cell, never taking his eyes off of Chen.

"Your escort will be here shortly," he added as Chen pushed up from his chair. His body seemed heavy now, weighted down with the knowledge that it might be another six months before he would get more than a fleeting glimpse of a human being; another six months of sensory deprivation and boredom.

"You won't forget?" he asked. It was plaintive. Needy. He locked eyes with me, ignoring Michael—his "real" attorney—and waited for me to answer.

I cleared my throat, looking away. "I won't," I answered.

When I lifted my eyes, he was gone.

~

"I say we split up. We can't rule out any of the places Chen mentioned. Better to cover all the bases," Raph argued, gesturing emphatically.

I glanced at my phone, the texts there from Tabby reinforcing what my intuition told me:

Chen right, but exaggerating.

Managed 2 get 2 Hale and charmed it out of him. He says American girls v unlikely 2 get trafficked overseas. 2 expensive & difficult.

My vote is Williston.

I squared my shoulders and prepared myself to counter Raph's forceful argument when Enoch surprised me by jumping in. "But Chen himself said that it was most likely the girls were in North Dakota. Why would we waste valuable time, traveling all over the world, when they might be right here?" he reasoned, scratching his beard.

"Old man, you should stay out of this. Don't you remember how you struggled to keep up the last time we went on a wild goose chase together? Oh, wait, I forgot," Raph sneered sarcastically. "That wasn't you, was it? That was your alter ego, Lucas, the one who got us into this mess, too."

Enoch shrugged, not bothered in the least by Raph's disdainful attack.

I looked at Michael, now transformed back into his normal human guise. He had put some careful space between us, treating me almost as if I were toxic. I could tell from the expression on his face that he was not going to jump in to resolve this dispute. He was going to leave it to me, since I had, after all, demanded that I be in charge.

I sighed, feeling like I was corralling a bunch of preschoolers.

"Guys, stop it. We won't get anywhere by arguing."

Raph rolled his eyes. "If you do as I suggest, we won't have to make a choice. India, China, Brazil, North Dakota. Michael, Enoch, me, you. It's the most logical way."

"Since when do we make decisions based on logic?" I shot back. I looked thoughtfully at Michael. "What are you sensing, Michael?"

He arched a brow. "To be honest, I'm not feeling a pull to any of the foreign countries. I'm feeling like they're much closer to us."

"Me too," I said, nodding. "And when Chen first mentioned North Dakota, I had the same feeling I had about Skellig Michael and Puy-en-Velay, when we were searching for the Key."

The corner of his mouth turned up slightly. "Then we know what to do."

"But where?" I asked. "North Dakota is a big state."

"A big, empty, boring state," Raph sniped.

Enoch whipped out a phone that he'd stashed away in his fanny pack and typed something in. "I'd say this looks right," he remarked, brandishing the screen so we could see. "Williston. Right near the Montana border." He drew back his phone and typed some more. "It looks like it's nearly a straight shot north from here. If we leave now, we can be there by tomorrow morning."

"Pack up the car," I said, not needing to hear anything further as my blood sang in response to his suggestion. "Let's go."

Raph fixed me with a dark stare. "Hope. Please don't take this the wrong way. But are you prepared for what you might find?"

"What do you mean?" I asked, tired of his constant sniping.

"Remember when we were in Istanbul? Remember that girl in the alley? The girl who had been trafficked? Do you remember what I said to you then, when you wanted to rescue her?"

I drew a blank.

He tilted his head, his dark eyes suddenly pooling with uncharacteristic kindness.

"You asked me if I could heal her," he said. "I told you then that sometimes people are too broken to be fixed, too broken to even want to be saved. Are you prepared to see whatever it is you will find when we locate your sister and her friend?"

I swallowed the lump that formed in my throat.

"Just pack up the car," I said brusquely, pushing past him so that I could be alone.

∿

We were halfway through the drive, in the middle of Wyoming and approaching midnight. We'd relegated Enoch and Raph, with all their snide bickering, to the backseat of the SUV where, after a stultifying meal of fast food, they'd succumbed to the natural rhythms of their human bodies and fallen asleep.

I snuck a peek at them in the rear view mirror.

"Are they curled up together?" I chuckled, not believing my eyes.

"Take a picture," Michael joked. "They'll deny it in the morning."

We laughed, a small break in the silence that had enveloped us for most of the ride.

I watched Michael's hands on the steering wheel—sure and steady—and thought of all the times we'd been together like this, him driving, me beside him in the passenger seat. The times in his beat-up but beloved Charger. The time he'd stolen me away to Las Vegas in my mom's Audi, after rescuing me from Lucas. The fancy car we rented in Vegas as we looked for Enoch and the Key, searching for my friend Ana at the same time.

So many times. But it wasn't the same.

At least that was what I kept telling my body, which felt the pull of him, so close to me, like the moon moving the tides.

The ring of a bell told me I'd received a text. I swiped the screen to see a note from Tabby.

Any news?

I frowned. With my thumbs I typed a quick response: *Headed to ND. Find out anything you can.* As an afterthought, I added, *Scratch Ollie's ears for me.*

The screen showed her busily typing a response.

What about U & Michael? Anything?

I sighed. In the course of the day, my feelings for him had swung from sheer rage to longing. There were moments where it had seemed just as it had been once we'd accepted our fates and set aside the lies—he and I, allies, standing against a common enemy. All I wanted to do right now was reach over and touch him. How to explain my conflicted feelings? I shoved the phone back in my purse, avoiding the topic.

As if reading my thoughts, he began to speak. "It was nice today. Working together like that. Like a team."

I nodded. "It was nice," I echoed, deliberately training my eyes on the inky Wyoming sky outside my window.

He waited for me to say more. When it became obvious that I wasn't going to, he cleared his throat.

"You know, Hope. That's the way it should be. That's the way it's meant to be. If you would just listen to me."

I closed my eyes.

"Not now, Michael."

"Then when?" he persisted.

"Not when Enoch and Raph are right behind us."

"They're sound asleep. A blizzard could blow through the car and they wouldn't budge."

I squirmed in my seat. God knows they'd been witness to enough awkward moments in the train wreck that had been Michael's and my relationship.

"You're not going to drop it, are you?" I asked.

Out of the corner of my eye, I saw him grin—the wicked, playful grin that always made my heart do flips.

"Nope."

"Fine," I conceded, throwing my hands up. "But there's nothing that you can say that will change what happened."

The strong line of his jaw tensed. I'd hit a nerve.

"Gabrielle told me that whatever was happening in Atlanta wasn't important enough for me to go back, Hope. There was no reason for me to doubt her."

"No reason but your instincts," I said, straining to keep my voice low. "You decided to believe her over them. Even though you knew how she felt about humans. You trusted her more than you took seriously your obligation to me. Either that, or you were so desperate to prove her wrong and show that you remained committed to your role as God's general that you simply ignored your better judgment. And because of that, my mom is dead and Rorie is missing."

He didn't say anything, his vein throbbing.

"And I know it's my fault," I said, wiping a hand at the hot, frustrated tears that had managed their way to the surface. "I wouldn't give you an answer. I kept you waiting too long. I couldn't decide. So you were caught in a bind—conflicted between your dueling responsibilities, Gabrielle manipulating you at every turn. But you didn't trust me enough to confide in me, to tell me that she was accusing you of shirking your duties—or, even worse, that you felt guilty because you *were* dropping the ball. Instead, you just put pressure on me, trying to deal with it on your own, trying to force a solution without having to admit that there was anything wrong."

I turned in my seat so that I could read his face. "Did you realize that I had honestly begun to think that you were cheating on me with Gabrielle?" A sputtering sound, half laugh, half sob, escaped my lips. "I know it makes no sense, but between her weird behavior and yours, I was so confused. If she hadn't confessed to what she had done at the trial, I might have gone on believing it. Why couldn't you trust me with the truth? Of all things, why would you keep that from me? Why didn't you just tell me?"

The slightest tightening of his jaw gave away his guilt. "I don't know."

"You don't know? You don't *know*?"

He didn't answer, letting the soft whir of the tires on the asphalt road below us fill in the silence.

"Well, that doesn't excuse it. And that doesn't mean you don't have a debt to Rorie now. You owe me that much."

"You know how much I care about Rorie, Hope," he admonished me, his voice breaking. "I didn't need you to sue me to go after her. I would have done it anyway. Nothing could have stopped me. Nothing."

I stole a glance at him. He'd fished something out of his pocket, letting it dangle from his free hand as he kept the other on the steering wheel. For a split second, it caught the dim light of a passing car, and I realized with a start that it was Rorie's agate pendant—the one he'd given her earlier this year.

"Where did you get that?"

"I fished it out of the rubble of the house. Can you believe it survived the heat? The cord is barely even scorched." His Adam's apple bobbed as he swallowed hard, enfolding the paper-thin slice of stone in his grip. "She'll be like that, Hope. Resilient. No matter what is happening, she'll make it. I know she will," he whispered. "We'll find her." He looked at me, his eyes almost desperately seeking confirmation. "We have to."

I refused to answer, training my eyes on the white lines of the interstate. The road whipped by, the occasional tumbleweed caught in our headlights.

"I guess we have nothing to talk about anymore," Michael finally said.

We drove the rest of the way without speaking.

sixteen

LUCAS

Where were they?

My impatience was acute. By now, Michael's every nerve ending should be shrieking, red hot with God's fire, demanding he fulfill his pledge and rescue Rorie—just like mine were screaming out for relief. It was exhausting. And it could be over so easily—if only they would show up and finish this thing, once and for all.

Surely his senses were not so dulled by his dalliance with Hope that he couldn't feel the pull of Rorie's presence in this hellish place? Surely the effects of their folly had faded with time? For my own pain scorched every sense, was all-consuming and unrelenting, annihilating everything but my will to lash out and punish those who had stood against me.

I'd waited long enough, I thought. Time for the next stage. Time to make the call to Michael loud enough to force him to respond.

Luckily, it was easy enough to manipulate the craven people who ran this operation. Their own minds were drug-addled and stunted from years of abuse as it was, barely able to pull together a plan. Barely able to think beyond the immediate situation before them.

That's where I came in.

I rattled the cage, jarring Macey. "Wakey, wakey," I cooed with false cheer. "Today you get to go out."

Macey rolled over in her crate, still clutching the raggedy blanket that had become her boon companion. A string of drool dripped from her lip. Her thighs and arms bore the crosshatch of the steel bars she'd lain against. Her eyes still had the drugged haze of confusion I'd come to recognize around this place.

She'd better be a little more energetic by show time, I thought. Customers wanted a little life, not a member of the walking dead. I passed her a bag of Oreos through the bars of the crate.

"Here," I said brusquely as she stared at them in my outstretched hand. "Luke told me that Oreos were your favorite."

Invoking Luke seemed to snap her out of her hesitation. She snatched the bag from my hand and fell upon the cookies, ravenous. I watched her, fascinated and a little disgusted.

"Come on, Macey. Be a good girl," I cooed as she finished up, wiping the crumbs on the back of her hand. I unlocked the padlock and swung open the door to the dog crate. "Come on out. Time to get dressed."

"Don't do it, Macey. Don't go. He's only going to hurt you," Rorie urged from her cage. She was huddled about as upright as she could get, watching us intently.

"You," I said, menacingly, glaring at the interfering little chit. "You shut up." I kicked Macey's cage. "I won't ask nice next time. Get out here."

Macey peered out between the bars. "He won't hurt me," she said. "He brought me cookies because Luke asked him to. And I know he'll give me my fix. Won't you?" Macey crawled out of the crate, standing up on wobbly legs. I sniffed at her. She was rank. I ignored her blatant plea for drugs.

"Come in here and clean her up," I called through the open door to one of the women. She took Macey away, leading her by the hand, speaking in low murmuring tones, trying to calm her for what lay ahead.

I knew she'd be coddled and fed, cleansed from head to toe. Her matted hair would be washed and dried, and then styled into the sort of ringlets that suggested innocence. With makeup, short skirts, and lingerie, she would arguably look older than her years; old enough for a buyer to tell himself she looked of age, old enough for a buyer to deceive himself that he didn't know, that it was all in good faith. That she did what she did willingly.

That she wanted it.

I laughed.

She would obey me because she saw no choice. She would obey because her childish brain reasoned that if she did it just this once, it would all go away. That she was doing it to help support Luke, the boy who still had not come back to claim her. She would do it because I promised her more drugs if she was a good girl. She would do it because she feared for her life. She would do it because by now, she thought this was all that she was worth, that there was no way out.

The stab of pain that shredded my body confirmed that I was on the right path.

It was quiet. Too early for dogfights. Too early for the steady stream of girls coming and going to their next appointments. It was so quiet that I could hear Rorie breathing as she sat, defiant, in her crate. The only sound was the hollow, tinny clang of her dragging her fingers back and forth against the cage. Back and forth, back and forth, grating in its impudence. Suddenly, I could not abide her temerity. I could not bear that her spirit was not yet broken.

I had to break her.

I gritted my teeth, forcing my mouth into a twisted smile, before I turned back to Rorie's cage.

"You'll be next," I taunted her.

She simply stared at me with hate-filled eyes, drawing her fingertips against the metal in a challenge, daring me to stop her.

"Yes, you're next, but you'll be more valuable," I continued. "You're not used up and damaged like your friend. People here will pay top dollar for you."

She flinched, but quickly composed herself. She didn't want me to see her fear, I thought. How cute.

"Macey's not damaged," she insisted, curling her fingers around the wires of the crate.

"You don't think so?" I answered, charmed by her naiveté. "Did you not see her yourself? She's dirty. Already, she probably harbors at least one disease within her weakened body. She has sores and injuries that will haunt her for the rest of her life, which will probably be, for her sake, mercifully short."

I circled closer to her crate.

"Most importantly, she has given up. Her spirit is broken. She will let me, let any man or woman, do anything they'd like to her now. She is beyond caring, Rorie. Can't you see that? If that is not the definition of damaged, I don't know what is."

She shook her head, not wanting to believe me, unwilling to see the obvious.

I came even closer. "But you? You are special. You are like a wild stallion, waiting to be broken and made to take the saddle. I've been drawing out the auction for you."

She looks up at me through the bars, surprised. This close, I could see the tracks of her tears in her dirty face.

"You didn't know that I was auctioning you? I put an ad for you on Backpage. 'Sweet girl, new in town.' It's catchy, don't you think? The ad will expire tomorrow, and that is when you, too, will go out and earn your keep."

She was shaken. I smiled again, enjoying my ability to inject hopelessness into her psyche. It almost made me feel sorry for her.

On a whim, I opened the door of the crate, reaching in to caress her face. She shrank back as far as she could, but there was nowhere to go. I trailed my hand over the soft skin of her cheek, imagining what it would be like for her when she met her first customer.

And then she moved, too quickly for me to stop her.

"Damn it!" I shrieked, yanking my hand away.

The child had bitten me. There, in the fleshy pad under my thumb, I could see her teeth marks. She'd even drawn blood.

I slammed the door shut, imprisoning her once again.

"You'll pay for this," I warned, leaning close to the bars. Her eyes were defiant. "Disobedience is the one thing I will not tolerate."

"There's nothing you can do to me to make me obey you, you monster," she countered. She spat in my face and drew back into the corner of her crate, proud that she had taken a stand.

I wiped away the saliva from my chin and pressed my shirt over my injury.

"We'll see about that," I promised her cryptically.

Just then, Macey's keeper entered the room, drawing Macey behind her. Just as I'd predicted, she was dressed and ready to go. To the unpracticed or self-deceptive eye, she looked like a sultry sixteen, or older. To me, however, she looked like a little girl who'd gotten into her mommy's makeup drawer.

"You can go," I said, dismissing the woman. I closed and locked the door behind her. I didn't want anyone interrupting me.

Macey stood still in the middle of the room, unsure of what to do. I began to circle her, enjoying her confusion. And when I spoke, I kept my voice low.

"You don't care for your own safety, Rorie? You think you can defy me and get away with it? That may very well be. But the person who will absorb your punishment on your behalf will be Macey."

Macey's eyes widened. "No!" Rorie shouted.

"Oh, yes. You think you're so strong. You think you're able to brave the worst. Well, now you're going to have to watch me beat your friend within an inch of her life because of your bad choices." I rolled up my shirtsleeves.

Rorie flung herself against the bars of the crate. "No! You can't hurt her because of me! Please, whatever you're doing, do it to me! Macey doesn't deserve this!"

I smiled, a taut, angry smile.

"You're right. Macey doesn't deserve this. Neither did your mother deserve the beating that she took." I stopped, enjoying her bewildered shock. "You didn't think I knew about that, but I do. Macey's boyfriend Luke told me all about it. And that was your fault, too, Rorie," I taunted. "You couldn't keep your nose out of other people's business then, and you're doing it again. You never seem to learn your lesson, do you? So now you're going to have to watch. Watch and learn."

I drew my arm back for the first swing.

"I'm sorry, sweetheart," I said with mock sincerity to Macey. "You're not going anywhere tonight. Tonight, you're all mine."

"No!"

I wheeled to look at Rorie, pressing herself up against the bars of her crate.

"Punish me! She didn't do anything. Don't hurt her. Hurt me! I deserve it."

Her face was shiny with tears. I couldn't help myself. I grinned.

"Very well," I said. "If you insist."

I walked to the wall and pulled the key off the hook. Slowly, deliberately, I approached the crate and crouched over it, twirling the keychain around my finger. She peered through the grates, chewing her lip.

I unlocked the crate and watched her scramble to her feet. Her T-shirt hung loosely about her pale, tiny body.

"Come with me. You stay here, Macey."

Macey nodded, keeping her eyes glued to the floor as Rorie walked just ahead. I guided her from the room, closing and locking the door behind me.

"Where are we going?" she demanded, a note of fear in her voice.

"We're just going to take a little walk. Just keep going that way."

I gave her a little nudge in the back and set her walking down the long hallway in bare feet. I watched, amused, as she pulled the shirt about her, tugging at it as she tried to cover her exposed body.

At the end of the corridor, we reached a door. She stopped, confused.

"Now what?"

"Allow me." I reached around and pushed the door. "Please."

We walked through into what could only be loosely called a garage, icy air blasting us in the face. It was dark, packed with detritus, reminding me of the warehouse where I'd revealed my real identity to Hope all those years ago. Rorie stopped short, shifting from foot to foot as she tried to avoid the cold slab of cement.

I pushed the wave of nostalgia back to answer Rorie. "I can't touch you. You're too valuable to hurt. Too valuable to be visibly damaged."

Swiftly, I snaked my hand around to grab her about the wrist. Before she realized what I was doing, I'd snapped one end of a pair of handcuffs around her birdlike bones. I clamped the other end around a piece of exposed pipe.

"Your punishment is to stand out here all night. Stand out here and suffer while you imagine what I'm going to do when I walk back in there and deal with your friend."

A heartbroken cry tore from her lips, accentuated by the puff of steamy breath that floated out into the freezing night with it. She lunged for me, but I just stepped back, barely out of range of her impotent, swinging fist.

"Oh, yes. Your little noble impulse is going to do you no good. Now you'll both be punished."

I watched, amused, as she slumped to the hard floor.

"Goodnight, Rorie," I whispered, moving to the door. I flicked the lights off, plunging her into darkness as I went back inside.

seventeen

HOPE

The angels and I pulled into Williston during rush hour and promptly got stuck in an hour's traffic jam.

Chen had called it a boomtown, but I hadn't realized what he meant, not truly, until we saw the towering rigs and construction sites emerge out of the flat prairie and rolling hills. We found ourselves trapped in long rows of dump trucks and tankers and semis, looking out at the sprawl of gravel pits and tanks beyond. It was a jarring scar against the vistas of grass, a wound upon the earth, a symbol—if Chen was right—of the festering rot that was taking over the town. In the dawning light, smokestacks belched writhing clouds of waste, and surges of flame rose from a few of the derricks, licking the sky as if trying to burn out the stars.

"Welcome to hell," Raph muttered from the backseat.

As we crawled along, I pressed my face to the window, taking it all in. Here and there, endless compounds of anonymous RVs and campers, packed in tight, crowded the road, alternating with whole fields of stark, modular housing: rows and rows of identical boxes, barracks-like, stretching as far as the eye could see: the man camps Chen had mentioned. Used condoms, liquor bottles, food wrappers, rags, clothing, and other human debris filled ditches and fouled fields, sometimes so deep they drifted like snow. Signs outside of cheap motels advertised rates of $200 per night. Decrepit apartment complexes—the few that showed vacancies—were listing two bedrooms at $4,000 per month. New York City rates, here in the middle of nowhere. And everywhere, the rumble of trucks hauling water, hauling gravel, hauling machinery and tools, hauling men to feed the endless extraction of oil from the earth.

Mother Nature had already dumped her first snowfall on the wretched town. Stubborn tufts of prairie grass poked their heads through, defying winter's onslaught. The snow was stained with exhaust from the steady stream of traffic and had mixed with dirt to cover the roads and sidewalks with gritty grime.

"We need to stop and get gas," Michael said, easing into a turn lane for a truck stop. The four of us tumbled out, stretching our bones after having been cramped on the overnight drive, and strode into the convenience store. Even though I'd changed out of my suit into clothes more suitable for traveling, my body ached.

It was a local business—not one of the big chains you could find anywhere—and you could tell. Folksy, hand-lettered signs— the kind you might find in a kindergarten classroom—were tacked up on a bulletin board right inside the door. The board was covered in paper, mostly advertisements seeking to rent a bed, to sell a vehicle, things like that. The notices were layered inches thick; nobody bothered to take down the old papers. I lifted up one and read the typed flyer: a warning about skyrocketing AIDS and chlamydia cases, offering walk-in clinic hours. One next to it offered the hours of the local domestic violence shelter; another advertised jobs at Walmart. My eyes popped at the wages: $17 an hour for a cashier, $19 for a lube tech. I let the papers fall back into place and walked on.

"We might as well get breakfast while we're here," Enoch suggested hopefully.

Michael shrugged. "Sure, why not?"

We walked past the rows of coolers, and I gaped at the prices. Eight dollars for a container of milk. The restaurant, one of those all-day-breakfast kind of places, was packed. We sidled up to the counter, snagging some stools, and looked at the menu.

Raph sniffed. "I guess if we want something fried, there are plenty of choices."

I shot him an annoyed look. "If you want to go wait in the SUV, be my guest."

The man down the counter from us commented: "You must be new here. I'd stay away from the liver and onions. Probably too early for it, anyhow. Can't go wrong with a stack of pancakes."

"Thank you." I smiled at him, appreciating his advice. "Right now, anything sounds great, so long as it comes with a whole pot of coffee."

"That they've got. But if you want the high-test stuff, the fancy stuff like a latte, you'll have to go to Boomtown Babe's. Just down the road here," he said, pointing outside. "You drive all night?" he asked, shrewdly taking in our rumpled clothes.

"Yes," Michael jumped in. "From Colorado."

The man nodded. "Thought so. You got a place lined up already?"

"A place?" I asked, confused.

"To stay. Even before a job, you got to have a place to stay." He looked us up and down again, puzzling over Enoch's hippie getup and cane, Raph's ascetic style, and the mishmash of clothes that

Michael and I had managed to pull together. "Though maybe I'm wrong. Maybe you aren't here for jobs."

I made an indistinct sound in the back of my throat, not sure how to answer his implied question, and let him continue.

"A lotta people just get fed up, jump in their trucks and drive like hell, thinking they'll figure it out when they get here. But there's not a lotta open spaces in Williston. That's how you end up with people living in shipping containers. Whole families living out of their cars. You look in the back of the parking lot outside. You'll see 'em. Some of 'em have been there for six months. They've got jobs, they've got money. They just can't find a place to live."

My heart fell. Of course, we hadn't thought through that part. I smiled weakly. "We didn't, really. But I think we'll only be here for a short while."

He shook his head. "That's what they all say. Then they get addicted to the money. A hundred thousand a year will do that to you. Me, I wasn't able to break in. Especially with the slowdown in the oil market, you need contacts, and it could take six months even to get a shot at a roustabout job on a rig. I've always been a trucker, so it didn't change much for me. Just bumped my pay up some. Who knew hauling water could be worth so much money? But then again, here I am assuming that's why you're here," he said, scanning us once more. "Maybe you're just passing through—for some reason."

"I didn't catch your name," Michael said, extending his hand in an attempt to divert his line of questioning. "I'm Michael Boyd." While he made the introductions all around, I surreptitiously texted Tabby: *Urgent. Need hotel room. Motel. Anything within 20 miles.*

"Clint Rogers," the man responded when it became his turn, clenching Michael's hand in his. Even from two stools away, I could see the stains on his hands, the dirt under his nails—signs of a true working man. "Pleased to meet you and your friends."

The waitress, coffee pot in hand, interrupted us. "You folks know what you want?"

After a hasty round of ordering and ample pours of coffee, she departed, leaving us to question Clint, who was enthusiastically stabbing at a plate full of pan-fried steak and eggs, sunny side up.

Michael lowered his voice. "Clint, this might seem like a strange question, but you sound like you've been here a while, know your way around. If I were looking for a runaway, a young girl who might have come here to Williston, where would I look?"

Clint sat back a little on his stool, emitting a low whistle. "Now that's unfortunate. This girl is someone you know?"

I nodded, mentally urging him to continue.

"How young?"

"Only twelve or thirteen," Enoch offered, eyeing Clint's plate of food.

Clint dragged his rough hands over his day old stubble.

"And from the looks of you, not used to this kind of rough and tumble environment, I'm guessing. That's tough. A runaway that age, real tough. Not a lot of options. If you'd said even sixteen, it'd be easy to find her. You'd just go to the strip clubs and the bars. Now, don't get me wrong," he added hastily, "I don't mean to imply anything. But unless this friend of yours had somebody to take care of her, that's most likely where she'd end up. Working the bars, trying to make a quick dollar. Heck, those strippers are probably clearing $160,000 a year. But girls that young . . ." I could see him considering carefully how much he wanted to say to us. "Well, they're hard to find out in public. The young ones won't be out in the bars; nobody here would risk hiring an underage girl and losing their license. So the young ones will end up with pimps. They'll be kept hidden. They're here, to be sure. But they get sold out in private transactions. Everything behind the scenes, using the Internet. Your best bet would be to watch the pimps and the johns in the bars, maybe scan the Internet ads, and see if you can track her down. Be careful, though. Those guys are nasty. Sure wouldn't want to get caught in a tussle with them unprepared."

"Couldn't she be in a shelter? Couldn't she have found a place to stay temporarily?" I asked, almost pleading with him to give me an alternative.

Clint looked at me sympathetically. "Honey, I hope she did. But the shelters here have been packed to the gills for two years. There's honestly nowhere for somebody to go. Why do you think those people are living out of their cars?" He shook his head. "It's a shame. It truly is. But as long as there are people willing to take advantage of these young girls, it's gonna happen. Nothing we can do about it."

"Should we go to the police?" I asked, hopeful.

Clint shrugged. "With all the other troubles they've got to deal with, I doubt you'd get their attention."

The waitress returned, rows of plates lined up on her out-stretched arms, which she spun out like a Vegas dealer, passing out cards for a hand of poker, to where we sat. I stared dispiritedly at my meal—a heap of greasy hash browns and scrambled eggs—and wondered what we should do next.

Clint waited for her to leave, and then pushed his plate away and stood up.

"Sorry to have been the bearer of bad news. I really do hope you find this girl, whoever she is." He slapped some money down on the counter. "Your breakfast is on me." He clapped Michael on the back as he left. "Welcome to Williston. Good luck."

Just then, Tabby texted me back.

Can't find a single room! Crazy!

BTW you picked a real vacation garden spot. Violent crime up 120%. 200% increase in domestic violence. Sex trafficking, heroin use, suicides. All up double to triple digits.

My gaze trailed Clint as the door swung closed behind him.

"We're gonna need that luck," I said.

eighteen

RORIE

I remember when I was little, and Michael and Hope took me to the beach. It was a makeshift beach that someone had constructed on the shore of the artificial lake created by a new dam. Hope spread out her blanket, basking in the hot sun, letting her body sink into the sand underneath. She didn't notice when I decided to wade out to Michael. He didn't, either. I'd wanted to go to him so badly that I didn't stop, not even when the bottom of the lake sank away and the water rose bit by bit over my head. I kept walking as best I could through the murky water until somehow he spotted me, and his strong arms gathered me up to his chest.

I sputtered against him, coughing and wheezing, while he scolded me and held me close. Hope hovered over me, anxious, until I blinked at them both and declared that I wanted to do it again. They laughed at my audaciousness, praising my courage.

What would they say now?

≈

It's cold.

No, that is stating the obvious. That is second-grade vocabulary, Aurora. You can do better than that, I chide myself, willing my brain to remain sharp.

It is arctic, benumbing, biting, bitter, bleak, brisk, chilled, crisp, cutting, frigid, glacial, hyperborean, nippy, piercing, polar, snowy, stinging, wintry. Every word carefully chosen, arrayed in alphabetical order.

I sag against my chains, biting the inside of my cheek, clinging to my vocabulary triumph as if it mattered. And it does. It matters.

I must not fall asleep in this cold.

I refuse to give him the satisfaction of dying.

I refuse to give him the satisfaction of anything.

I giggle, thinking of the absurdity of it all. He is going to shoot me up full of drugs, just like he did to Macey, and sell my body to the highest bidder.

Just like Macey, I must not care. But unlike Macey, I cannot let it crush me. I am more than my hymen.

"Hymen," I giggle, thinking of the *Our Bodies, Ourselves* book my mother had thrust upon me only a few short years ago. "A fold of mucous membrane partly enclosing the external orifice of the vagina of a virgin."

He is auctioning me off. He said that because I am a virgin, I am somehow more valuable.

I shrink against the chains and want to cry.

But I can't. I won't.

I strain against the cuffs, the metal chafing the tender skin of my wrists as I twist and turn, trying to reshape my hands into something that can slip through the bands that hold me. But there is no give. Frustrated, I sink to the ground, the chains scraping against the pipe in protest, the piercing sound of metal on metal echoing out into the empty shed.

I tuck my knees under me, trying to take up as little space as possible so that the filth and cold of the cement cannot touch me.

Hope and Michael didn't tell my mother what had happened that day at the lake. As if by solemn pact, we three kept that story from her, knowing that it would send her careening in fear for me. Even as a young child, I could sense her anxiety, even if I couldn't name it, even if I didn't know its source.

My knowledge of what had happened to Hope and my father in the years before I was born was sketchy, but somehow, I knew that I was the happy patch that covered up the old hurt so she could heal.

I was strong and happy so she could be strong and happy. Maybe that was my purpose, even. Sunny Rorie, the one who made it all better.

Out of instinct and habit, I reached for the agate pendant that usually hung from my neck, my arm heavy with the weight of the chains. My fingers closed on nothing as I felt the disappointment, again, of realizing that it was lost. I breathed out, a tremulous wisp that puffed into the darkness, forming a cloud that quickly dissipated into the frigid air.

I couldn't cry. I couldn't afford myself the luxury of self-pity.

How could I, when I had been surrounded all my life by people who loved me? Not just my mother, Hope, and Michael, but Tabby, who taught me how to whistle and how to sneak out of the house wearing a second outfit hidden under the clothes my mother had carefully inspected for propriety; who encouraged me to explore who I was, who told me that I could be anything and anyone I wanted to be and, in doing so, had taught me to see the people whom others could not see. Or Arthur, whose solid presence had been a comfort to me, kissing my skinned knees as he taught me to ride my bike, playing knights and dragons with me and allowing me to be the knight as he gamely put on a princess crown and cried out to be saved, telling bedtime stories about a brave girl who conquered the evil in the world before she went home for dinner.

Each of them taught me to be strong.

No, that's not quite right. Each of them taught me to find the strength in myself.

But Macey had nobody to teach her.

The unfairness of it all convulsed me, again, and I strained against the chains, determined. I forced myself to my feet, trying to ignore the stinging in my toes and the encroaching numbness as the night air sapped away my body heat.

I am strong. I will be strong. If not for them, if not for me, then for Macey.

I decided it was time for a rousing singalong on the theme of coldness. *Brace yourself. I'm gonna own this.*

nineteen

HOPE

I looked at the green awning over the windowless door. *Whispers*, it read in fanciful script. We stood in a small knot a few yards away from the entrance, watching men in work clothes or jeans go in and out of the building.

"This is what passes for classy in North Dakota?" Raph queried, disdain dripping from his voice. "What kinds of human trash are we going to have to wade through in this place?"

I sighed. Being here wasn't doing anything to elevate Raph's perception of mankind. But after hours of debate, Michael had convinced us all that our best bet was to do as Clint had suggested and stake out a strip club. We'd picked this one after reading reviews online. Its website had boasted of Russians and Ukrainians, Mexicans and Bolivians. While the presence of a large number of foreign women wasn't a sure sign of trafficking, it was our only lead.

"Are you sure you want to do this?" Michael asked, gripping my elbow. Even through the heavy fabric of my sweatshirt, I could feel his heat. I resisted the urge to melt against him, reminding myself that we were here for strictly business reasons: to track down my sister and her friend.

"I don't see a choice. Do you?"

"You don't have to go in there, Hope. In fact, I'm not sure you should. This is clearly a place for men. The only women in there are in there to work. If you insist on going in, you might ruin our cover and prevent us from finding anything at all."

I paused, searching his eyes. He had a point. But did he think I couldn't handle it? That I didn't have the stomach to do what I had to do to save my sister?

He leaned in close—close enough to whisper in my ear, low, so that only I could hear. "You don't need to prove yourself to anyone, least of all me or Raph. Please, let us do this for you. Don't let your stubbornness get in the way."

I closed my eyes. The sweetness of his scent and the feel of his breath against my hair were overwhelming my senses. He was too close—he was stirring up feelings I couldn't afford to feel any longer. Oblivious to my confusion, he continued.

"Sometimes, accepting help is the best thing you can do, Hope. Sometimes, taking help is the biggest proof of strength."

I shook my head, trying to chase away the old feelings I still harbored for him, and I thought about what he was saying. I opened my eyes to find him looking at me, his azure eyes intent.

"You're right," I said, clearing my voice. "Me being in there will only make your job harder. You two find out what you can without me. Enoch and I will wait in the car."

He took a deep sigh of relief. "Thank you," he breathed, just loud enough for me to hear.

"Great. We get stuck going into the human cesspool while

she gets a time out? Perfect," Raph said, stomping off toward the entrance to the club.

I rolled my eyes. Predictable Raph. Michael gave my elbow one last squeeze. "Keep your phone on in case we need you. I'll see you in a little while. Enoch," he said, winking, "keep an eye on things."

"Can do," Enoch said with a salute. "Come on, Hope, we'll listen to my Grateful Dead mixes while we wait, keep our mind off of things."

I called out one last time to Michael. "I expect you to tell me everything. Everything, Michael."

He nodded once, then disappeared with Raph into the club.

I let Enoch usher me back to the SUV. As he lectured me on the finer points of Grateful Dead lyrics and influences, my mind kept wandering back to the exchange I'd just had with Michael. Why was he being so nice to me? Especially when he'd turned so cold last night?

"Hope?" Enoch interrupted my thoughts. "Am I boring you?"

I flushed. "I'm sorry, Enoch. I'm just preoccupied, I guess."

He patted my hand. "That's understandable. I was hoping to distract you from your concern about your sister and her friend, but it may be a hopeless task."

"I wasn't actually thinking about them," I confessed. "I was thinking about Michael."

"Ah, yes. Of course, you would be. I couldn't help overhearing your conversation last night."

I flushed, glad that the darkness hid the embarrassment and confusion that was surely evident on my face.

"We haven't eaten since breakfast," Enoch noted, a tactful diversion I accepted gratefully. He patted down the pockets of his cargo vest. "It's hard to have any serious conversation on an empty stomach. I have some granola here that we could share. Homemade."

He fished a bag of it out of his pockets and dumped some into my outstretched palm. I popped it into my mouth, wondering vaguely from the staleness just how long it had been in his pocket, but I figured beggars couldn't be choosers and crunched away.

"I'm not really sure what there is to talk about," I began in between chewing. "I mean, you know everything. You were at the trial. You heard what Gabrielle admitted. You heard Michael acknowledge it. If I hadn't forced him here, I don't think he'd even be here right now, pledge or no pledge. What else can I say?"

Enoch looked through the window, giving me what space he could as we spoke.

"I heard Gabrielle say that Michael was with her," he finally said. "That he accepted her advice when he asked."

"She said it didn't matter what was happening," I argued, my anger feeling fresh.

"No, Hope. She said that it was not important enough to leave what they were doing. Did you never think to ask what they thought was so important?"

"The refugees. The rest of the world. Gabrielle said so herself during the trial. It just proves I was right all along—Michael would have never given up his role as guardian of God's people. And if I'd given up my life to join him, my family would be exposed, unprotected. Not that what I decide about him matters now," I added bitterly.

Enoch tilted his head and turned to me. "Are you sure?"

I felt a pang of sympathy for Michael, remembering how frustrated he'd always been by Enoch and his endless questions. I was in no mood to entertain them now, myself. I let his question sink like a stone to the bottom of a pool, swallowed up in the stillness that enveloped us.

"Hope," Enoch tried again, "do you remember what you said to me when we first re-encountered one another, after you'd found the key and after Michael had been reunited with you?"

I sighed. "Enoch, I don't want to think about that. Those memories are painful now. Please, will you just let it drop?"

"Humor me," he coaxed. "Humor this old angel in hippie's clothing. For old times' sake."

I threw up my hands. "Fine. Have it your way. We talked about lots of things, then, Enoch. To what, specifically, are you referring?"

"You told me your biggest regret, the two years while you waited for Michael, thinking he had truly died, was that you had not trusted him."

It was like a punch to my solar plexus.

It was not what I expected him to say.

But it was true.

I had ruminated on it for a long time, feeling guilty and regretful that I hadn't put my faith in the one person I loved more than anyone else in the world. That because I hadn't, I'd unwittingly betrayed him and led him to his death.

I swallowed, hard.

"You're telling me I'm wrong?"

Enoch picked up my hand and patted it. "My dear. You are professionally trained to follow the evidence. To be logical. But you have also been trained by painful experience to recognize that not everything is always as it seems. Talk to him. You may be surprised by what you learn."

"But what if I'm not?" I whispered, my eyes filling with tears.

He squeezed my hand. "Ah, but what if you are? Why are you so eager to give up your love? If, after you talk to him, you still find he betrayed your family and your trust, then you are no worse off than you are now. And even then," he added with grandfatherly sternness, "I would not be so loath to forgive him. After all, your whole journey together has been shaped by the very idea of for-giveness." He patted my hand once more. "Just think on it. Promise me that, at least."

I nodded mutely.

Just then, the door to the club swung open, and Raph and Michael came spilling out, tucking their hands under their arms for warmth.

"Don't say anything to him, Enoch," I asked.

"About what?" Enoch responded, winking. I smiled a tentative smile and wiped my face, trying to compose myself.

They piled into the car, blowing on their hands.

"You wouldn't believe it in there," Michael began, shaking his head. "One of the, um, dancers told me she makes over $2,000 a night. As packed as that place was, I guess it makes sense."

"Just more evidence of the depravity of your race," Raph sniffed.

"Now is not the time, Raph," Michael snapped.

"What did you find out? You must have learned something if you came out so quickly," I asked, eager to hear what they had learned.

"One of the bartenders filled me in on the prostitution that's going on. He was pretty nonchalant about it—except when it came to underage girls. I guess he's a dad and the whole idea of it makes him sick," Michael began.

"Once they turn eighteen, however, treating human beings like chattel is perfectly acceptable to him," Raph commented dryly. "How upstanding of him."

"Anyway," Michael continued, shooting Raph a poisonous look, "it turns out they had a major scene in the club a month ago when someone tried to put a young girl on the floor in there. He and another bartender got wind of it—didn't take much detective work, it sounds like; the poor kid was terrified and looked like she was playing dress-up in mommy's clothes—and they ended up kicking the pimp out. They also tried to get the girl out of it, but no dice; she left with the scumbag. The thing is, the whole incident upset one of their regulars—a newish guy, been working the rigs maybe six months. The guy tried to stop them from intervening on behalf of the girl, and he ended up storming out and didn't come back. Until tonight."

"What are you thinking?" Enoch asked. Michael looked gravely at us.

"The bartender said that if we were trying to find a young girl, we could do worse than to follow this guy when he leaves the bar tonight. I think he's right."

"That's assuming he has another girl lined up," I said, thinking it sounded like a long shot.

"I believe the odds are in your favor on this one," Raph sniped. "You couldn't swing a stick inside that club without hitting someone with a nasty habit. The question is whether we've picked out the human with the particular nasty habit we're looking for."

I felt dirty, like I needed a shower just from thinking about this.

"So we just wait?" I asked.

"We wait," Michael confirmed. "We wait, and we follow him wherever he goes."

Michael switched seats with Enoch, and we settled in, each of us preoccupied with our own thoughts, the low rumble of the engine the only sound. I wrapped my arms around myself, trying to huddle into myself for warmth and let the rolling engine lull me to sleep.

~

"Wake up," Michael whispered, jabbing me in the ribs. I bolted upright, wiping my bleary eyes, and I looked at the dashboard clock. It was just after three in the morning.

"That's our guy," Michael said. He nodded toward a young man, maybe twenty-five years of age and dressed in a leather bomber jacket and a baseball cap, as he wove his way across the parking lot toward a pickup truck. "Wake up, everybody. It's time."

We watched the young man climb into the cab of his truck and back out. Michael shifted into gear.

"Not too close," I cautioned. "We don't want him to realize he's being followed."

"Are you kidding?" Michael answered, his voice dripping with disgust. "Did you see him stumble across the parking lot? The guy's too drunk to notice anything. But I'll be careful, just in case."

We trailed him, staying a healthy distance behind him, across town to one of the older motels. It was a double decker with doors opening up right to the outside, the kind always associated with truckers. The lot was packed. The sign along the highway read *No Vacancy*.

We pulled in, parked a row away from him, and watched. He didn't go to the office to check in. He climbed up the stairs, heading straight for a room. Once there, though, he didn't take out his own key. He knocked and waited for someone to open up, disappearing into the room after darting a paranoid glance behind him.

After a few minutes, a muscle-bound man in a windbreaker emerged from the room. He leaned casually against the wall and lit a cigarette, waiting.

"Bingo," Michael whispered.

I felt a surge of anger. My hands were trembling with it, the adrenaline that coursed through my veins spurring me to action.

"Now what?" I asked, gripping my armrest to quell my hands.

"Now, we wait."

"Shouldn't we do something?"

Michael shook his head. "As much as I'd like to, we have to wait this out. We need to get as much information as possible, and we can't do that if we act too soon." He reached over, placing his hand over mine.

"Just a little while longer. I promise."

The idea of what was going on in that room filled up the car. As we sat, waiting, we saw more men coming and going in and out of the rooms, a constant pattern of traffic. Supply. Demand. Supply. Demand. A cold business, trading on the innocence and youth of girls who had no choice.

As I watched the ebb and flow of customers, I began to have doubts.

"Maybe we should go to the police," I ventured, staring out of the window into the dark.

"The police are just going to tell you they don't have enough manpower to search for girls who may or may not actually be here, Hope," Michael chided gently. "If we want to find your sister, it'll be faster if we do it ourselves."

I settled back in my seat, knowing Michael was right.

"There might be another way, though," he began, a note of excitement in his voice. "I can't believe I didn't think of this sooner. We keep hearing that people are posting these underage girls online. On that website—what did they call it?"

"Backpage," Raph answered from the back seat.

"That's it," Michael nodded, turning in his seat so he could see us all. "What if we monitored Backpage to see if we could find them? Or even pose as interested buyers?"

From the dark of the backseat, Raph spoke up. "It just might work."

I cringed in distaste, but I knew he was right. "Get on it, Raph," I urged. "Get on your phone and start scanning the ads while we wait."

On the second story, the door to the hotel room was opening. The man we'd been trailing stumbled out, closing the door behind him.

I glanced at Michael. His jaw tensed as he watched the man work his way down the stairs. His knuckles whitened as he gripped and regripped the steering wheel. I reached out and touched his knuckles lightly, raising my brows in question. He nodded quickly, no hesitation, in response.

"You guys keep looking," I spoke into the backseat, opening the car door to face the frozen night. "And keep an eye on that motel room. We'll be right back."

I slipped out of the car, Michael right behind me.

We tailed the man at a discreet distance as he strutted across the icy parking lot. At his truck, he fumbled around for his keys in his pocket.

"What's your hurry?" Michael demanded, wheeling in to stand behind him. The man jumped and backed into the side of his truck. He held up his hands.

"No, no hurry, man. Just a little cold, that's all," he said, giving a shaky laugh. He darted a glance around the parking lot and found himself alone. "But I'm good, man. Don't need anything."

"Maybe we do," I said, stepping in to block the other side. "Tell me. What were you doing up in that motel room?"

"Me?" he looked flustered. "Nothing. Nothing at all. Just. Um. Just having a rest."

"Not very long to be resting," Michael countered. "We've been watching you. You weren't even in there for two hours."

"You've . . . you've been watching me?" His breath was coming in fast, nervous gasps now, puffs of steam releasing into the frigid air. A sudden look of terror flashed across his face. "Are you guys cops?"

Michael's grim look exactly mirrored how I felt.

"We're much, much worse than police," he whispered. "You're going to tell us everything we want to know. Or you'll be wishing the police were here to save you."

The man gulped, hard, his Adam's apple bobbing in his skinny throat. He blinked and shook his head, as if he thought he was hallucinating and could simply will us away.

"I don't know what you're talking about," he said, laughing, his eyes darting around as he looked for an escape. Burrowing his hands deep into his pockets, he shrugged. "You got the wrong guy. I've got nothin' to say."

Michael's face darkened and he made a move toward the man.

"No." I reached out my hand and stopped him. "Let me."

Michael paused, looking at me thoughtfully, before stepping back.

The man visibly relaxed. "Okay, sweetheart. Do your worst."

In a flash, I darted in, trapping him against the side of his truck while I wrapped my elbow around his neck, putting him in a headlock.

"This isn't my worst," I said. "My worst is if I decide to break your neck. Which I can do, if I want to, in seconds. It's up to you whether or not I decide to do so." His face was turning red. I let up the pressure just a little and listened to him sputtering, trying to catch his breath. "Are you going to talk now?"

He nodded rapidly, blinking hard again.

"Good." I let go of him, letting him fall back against the cold metal of his truck. He bent over his knees, clutching at his throat as he gasped great, freezing breaths of air.

"Answer our questions and we'll let you go," I said, the steel in my voice a warning that I would do it again if I had to.

He nodded, wiping a hand over his face as he stood up, his

back rigidly straight. Michael didn't wait for him to finish catching his breath.

"You were with someone in the hotel room. Who?"

The young man looked down at his boots. "She called herself Sunny online." He kicked the snow. "Don't know why this matters so much to you."

"It didn't matter to you, you mean. Did you ever think about the fact that she's a real person?" Michael responded tersely.

The man jerked his head up. "Hey, man, I didn't make her do what she does."

"And just what does she do?" I challenged him. My voice was raw, and my hands were shaking with rage.

He shrugged. "She's a hooker. You know, a prostitute." He lifted his chin defiantly. "Out here, there aren't a lot of women. Everybody does it."

"Everybody abuses children? Is that right? Is that why you're skulking around, hoping nobody sees you?" Michael's voice was a low growl, his anger barely contained as he moved in closer.

The man shifted, nervous. "She's not . . . she wasn't . . ."

"She is! And you knew it!" I shouted, spittle flying from my mouth. I lunged for his collar and banged him against the truck. He raised his hands, defenseless, as he cringed back as far as he could.

"Honest. It said she was eighteen. It said she was eighteen. It said she was eighteen." He repeated it like a talisman, trying to convince himself that he really hadn't known.

"Did she look eighteen to you? When you wiped off the makeup, she looked like a baby, didn't she? But you did it anyway." Disgust dripped from my voice as I shoved him hard and stepped away, pressing my fingers to my temple. I couldn't let my contempt keep me from getting the information we really needed. I took a deep breath.

"Where did you find her—online?"

He nodded, once, quickly dropping his eyes to the ground. "Backpage. They get new ones every week. She just got here. Her and a friend. They were in a picture together."

My heart raced. It had to be them.

"You used her before?"

He nodded, refusing to lift his eyes.

I dreaded hearing his answer, but I had to know. "What about her friend?"

He shook his head side to side. "No. Just her."

Relief and panic warred within me.

"What was her name?" I whispered, praying silently that it wasn't either one of them.

His eyes darted away, trailing across the snow. "She told me her real name was Macey when she begged me not to hurt her. Not that I would," he added in a rush. "I would never do something like that. It just seems like that was what she was expecting."

Relief—that his victim was Macey and not my sister—surged through my body, quickly chased by guilt and rage.

"How often do they get used like this? How many times a night?" I managed to choke out my question, closing my eyes as I did so.

"All night. I don't know how many times. Probably eight or ten."

"Here? Do they always bring them here?"

"This girl, this pimp, yeah. Sometimes other places. They move around a lot. There are some other ones around town, too," he volunteered.

My stomach was roiling, and a lone tear trickled down my cheek. I wiped it away angrily. I'd heard enough. "Let's go," I muttered to Michael. "We got what we came for. We need to go get her."

"Not yet," he said softly. I trailed his gaze as he looked over his shoulder, scanning the parking lot. We were still alone. Slowly, he let his attention return to the pathetic man by his truck, fixing him with a stony stare.

In an instant, Michael's body pulsed with light, a throbbing ball of energy, particles like fire twinkling around him. I squinted, realizing immediately what he meant to do.

As the light receded, the particles fell in on themselves, a vortex at the center of Michael's body. As they collapsed, Michael was revealed in his angelic splendor—muscle-bound in armor, vast wings spreading threateningly behind him.

The man's jaw dropped. Michael took one step, then two, closing the distance between him and the man so that there was no more than an inch between them. I watched, bemused, as the man, terrified, seemed to shrink. A patch of dark wetness spread across his jeans.

"If you ever touch another child again, I will come back for you and send you to your grave," he said. "Do you understand me?"

The man sank to his knees in the dirty snow. "Please don't hurt me," he begged. "Please. I won't ever do it again. I promise. Please, I'll do anything you say." I felt the satisfaction in it—in this man being put into the same position he'd had Macey in, begging for his life, at Michael's mercy.

Michael's jaw tensed. "You disgust me. Don't forget your promise."

With that he turned, reaching his hand out to me. I clutched at it, my heart racing.

"Let's go get Macey."

He strode purposefully across the parking lot, his fury spurring him on, nearly dragging me as I struggled to keep up.

"Michael. Michael," I pleaded, trying to contain the note of excitement in my voice. "He said he wasn't with Rorie. He didn't hurt her."

He stopped dead in his tracks, turning to grip my shoulders.

"Hope," he whispered hoarsely, his voice breaking as he shook me a little. "Someone else could have hurt her. You know it as well as I."

I shook my head. "I can't think about that, Michael. We just have to find her."

He gripped my arms, harder now, insistent. "You have to be ready for whatever we find. You need to steel yourself, Hope. Raph was right—the girls . . ."

He stuttered on his own words, unable to bring himself to say out loud what we both feared.

I looked into his eyes, my vision blurry with tears. As I stood there, feeling the heat of him through my coat, I could almost forget about what had happened between us. All that seemed to matter was that he was here, now, standing by my side.

I trusted him. I couldn't do anything but.

A burst of icy wind whipped through the parking lot, swirling about us. A long strand of my hair fell into my face. Michael reached out, tucking it gently behind my ear. Carefully, he trailed his thumb across my cheekbone, wiping away a stray tear, before placing his hand back on my shoulder.

"We both have to be strong. For them."

I swallowed hard and nodded, dashing away the tears that threatened to spill over.

"Michael, I'm scared."

He nodded. "Me, too, Hope."

Silently, I wrapped my arms around him, armor and all, and pressed myself to his chest.

And as I held him, I thought about what I wanted. I wanted to press my hand to his heart. I wanted to finally ask him what had really happened between him and Gabrielle. I wanted to tell him I was sorry.

But most of all, I wanted to hear him tell me that everything would be okay.

"What's taking you so long?" Raph's impatient voice interrupted my thoughts. I peeked around Michael and saw Raph poking his head outside of the SUV, its lights on and motor running.

"They left the room—and it was definitely Macey," Raph continued. "Get in, we might still be able to catch them."

twenty

LUCAS

Macey was back from her work during the long, cold North Dakota night. She was worn, the poor thing. I tallied up her wounds.

Her lip was cut, a tiny smear of dried blood in the corner of her mouth.

It was hard to tell against the darkness of her skin, but bruises—fingerprints—were blooming on her upper arm. They would eventually deepen, then turn yellow, and finally fade from sight, but for days they would remind her of the person who shook her hard when she tried to resist.

There were other injuries, I was sure, but right now I was disgusted by the cruelty of mankind as I looked at this child, blinking under the harsh fluorescent lights, wobbling, dead on her feet.

I reached out a hand to wipe away the blood on her lip and she didn't flinch. She didn't react at all. "You've earned your sleep. No more crate for you. Come with me."

I reached out and took her hand to guide her, but when I did, what I saw startled me. She had managed to find a pen and had drawn a girlish heart in bright blue ink at the center of her palm. Under the heart, in the careful loopy script of childhood, she had entwined her and Luke's names. The ink was smeared from her sweat.

I felt a surprising pang of sympathy for her. Still so innocent.

I led her to another room. It was plain, with no windows, but there was a mattress with sheets and a pillow pushed up against the wall.

"Are you hungry?"

She shook her head. No, of course she wasn't.

"Then go ahead and lie down. No one will disturb you, I promise."

She looked longingly at the bed, and then she turned to me, her face plaintive, her eyes, despite it all, trusting.

"What about Rorie?"

Ah, yes. Miss Rorie, my bait, my treasure. I'd nearly forgotten about her. Wasn't that ironic? The whole reason I'd come out to this Godforsaken place, and I'd practically abandoned her out in that shed.

I chided myself for being drawn into Macey's troubles—now was not the time to get sentimental.

"I'll go get her. Don't you worry about it. I'll bring her here as soon as she's ready."

Grateful, Macey slumped down on the mattress and pulled the sheet about her as she turned to face the wall. I was halfway out the door when she posed her question.

"When will Luke get here?"

The poor thing still believed her precious Luke was coming.

"Soon, Macey," I said quietly. "He'll be here soon."

She pulled her knees up to her chest and hugged the sheet even closer.

The walk down the corridor seemed long. All the girls were sleeping now, locked away or, for many of them, simply left to be, the will so knocked out of them that there was no risk of them running, no risk that they'd call the police. This was their home now. It was all they knew, maybe all they would ever know in their mercifully short lives.

I found Rorie huddled against the pipe, clinging to it like a lifeboat, her teeth chattering. She'd tucked as much of her tiny body and legs into the drapey T-shirt as she could, but it wasn't enough to keep away the bitterness of the cold night. Her eyes were pressed closed, but I couldn't tell if she was asleep or not. She was muttering and humming to herself, rocking a bit as she tried to soothe away her fears.

I flicked on the lights. She didn't react, just kept rocking.

Annoyed, I looked around. Grabbing a flashlight, I shone it in her face. The delicate skin underneath her eyes was deeply shadowed; her lips purple with cold.

"Open your eyes, Aurora," I commanded.

Her eyes flew wide open as she stared blindly into the light.

"Am I dead?" she whispered. Her voice was hoarse.

I tossed away the flashlight, laughing.

"No."

Recognizing my voice, she shrank back as far as she could. Amused, I crouched down next to her.

"No, Aurora. You aren't dead," I whispered, leaning close. "In fact, you'll never die. I won't let you. I'm going to take really good care of you so that you can get used over and over and over again, just like Macey. But you're stronger than Macey. You won't break, like those other girls. No, your spirit is strong, isn't it?"

I grabbed her chin and forced her to look at me.

"For you, there will not be the blessed oblivion of drugs. I will never let you lose yourself like all those other girls. I want you to remain painfully aware of everything that happens, to have every horrific thing done to you burned into your mind so that you can never forget. You are too strong to die, Rorie. So you will live every day in this hellhole, trying to sleep but able to do nothing but relive these memories over and over again. There will be no escape. Nobody is coming for you."

She flinched, then, but she didn't cry.

"I don't believe you," she whispered, her chin trembling. "You're just saying those things to hurt me. You're going to have to try harder than that."

I raised a brow. Impressive. Bravery, strength, endurance. Even insight. So many of the gifts and blessings bestowed upon her as an infant on display, gifts that, twisted, were as good as any curse. So I dug deeper, each word calculated to wound, to isolate, to chip away at her resistance.

"Luke told me all about you, you know. And you know what else he told me? That your mother and sister aren't coming, Aurora. That your sister doesn't even care. She's too wrapped up in her own life. Why would she disrupt what she has with her boyfriend—Michael, isn't it?—to come chasing after you? Especially now that she knows what you've become."

She opened her mouth to argue but stopped herself. I felt the corner of my mouth lift, despite myself.

"Your sister won't come because she's ashamed. Ashamed of you, and ashamed of herself. For she is the reason this is happening to you. What is happening to you is all her fault. And she will never, ever, ever have the courage to face you and admit it."

She was staring now, confused and hurt. "I don't understand."

"And your mother? Your mother is embarrassed by you, too. How could she explain you to the country club set? You're worthless and useless, Aurora. Your mother knows it. Your sister knows it. Luke knows it. This is all you are good for, now. You might as well accept it."

I unlocked the handcuff and pulled her to her feet. Her stance was submissive, meek. Broken. When I let her go, she swayed, falling in on herself, her tiny body unable to bear her own weight after the night of cold.

Smiling to myself, I swept her up into my arms.

"As soon as you get some sleep," I told her, "you're going to start working—as early as tonight."

As I carried her back to Macey, I let my mind wander, relishing my impending victory. I could almost taste it, taste the salty tears that would mar Hope's face when she realized I'd destroyed her sister. An unforgiveable crime—and one, Hope would realize, that was all her fault.

But as I bore Rorie over the threshold, I heard her whisper with a note of triumph in her voice:

"If what you say is true, that means they're still alive."

twenty-one

HOPE

We'd been too late. By the time we'd gotten into the car, Macey's pimp—for that was what we'd concluded that beefy man who'd gone in and out of the motel room was—had driven away, losing us before we'd really even taken up the chase.

We had the same sensation, Michael and I—the buzzing of voices, the irresistible pull that took us closer and closer. To what, though, we could not determine. We were surrounded by rows of ugly trailers and hastily erected sheds, any one of which could have held two hapless girls. Raph drove us in circles as we hoped for something—anything—to draw us closer to Rorie and Macey so that we could rescue them, but it was fruitless. In frustration, we'd gone back to a diner to nurse bitter coffee and try to brace ourselves for the day ahead.

We were exhausted, but there was no hope of getting a hotel

room in this place. It was perhaps inevitable that the tension and stress set us all to arguing.

"What has happened to your vaunted skills now?" Raph taunted me. "And Michael's, too. Perhaps Michael was better off with Gabrielle; at least then he could find his way. The two of you together couldn't manage your way out of a paper bag."

"That's enough, Raphael," Michael warned. His neck was corded, his jaw tense as he shot Raph a black look across the table.

"You're right. It is enough. I have had enough of this desolate place. I have had enough of this weak human disguise. I will be elsewhere, waiting and restoring my strength in the glory I was meant for. I will await your command," he said snidely. He slid out of the booth to tower over our table, scowling. "Enoch, come on."

Enoch raised an eyebrow and looked to me.

I sighed and sank back against the vinyl banquette. "Go ahead. You might as well recharge your batteries while we think about our next move."

Enoch patted my hand. "You'll figure it out. The two of you, together." Then he slipped out and followed Raph out the door.

"How will they know if we need them?" I wondered aloud.

"They'll know," Michael stated flatly.

I wasn't so sure they would, and had my doubts about whether Raph would show up even if he did, but kept my thoughts to myself.

Instead, I text Tabby—*We're falling apart. I need you*—and focused on Michael, seated directly across from me. I fiddled with the little rectangular packets of grape jelly and butter, piling them in little walls, sliding the salt and pepper shakers around as if I were building a little fort.

A fort to keep my heart safe from him.

It had seemed so natural—really, too easy—to put myself in his arms last night. Even now, it was all I could do to stop myself from reaching out and grabbing his hand. I raised my head to look him in the eyes. He held my gaze, his eyes a stormy mix of gray and robin's-egg blue. There were so many memories, so many experiences, that only he and I had shared. How could it be that we had come to this place? How could we not be together?

I let a monster yawn escape me.

"Come on," Michael said, slapping some cash down on the table. "You need to get some rest."

"There's nowhere to go. And I won't go to one of those rooms where they're pimping the girls. I'm not that desperate."

He stood up. "We'll do like the locals. Come on," he repeated, reaching out a hand.

Confused, I let him pull me out of the booth.

"What do you mean?"

"You'll see."

The sun was just a dim promise on the horizon when we slipped out of the diner. The air was biting. I shivered involuntarily and Michael pulled me in, tight against his side.

Numbly, I walked along with him as he led me back to the SUV.

"Where are we going?" I asked.

"Nowhere. You're going to the backseat to stretch out and rest while I keep watch."

He opened the door for me. I peered in at the jumble of pillows, blankets, and granola bar wrappers that Enoch had left behind and sighed.

"I guess it's our only option."

I clambered in, wiping away the crumbs that had lodged themselves in the upholstery. Michael closed the door firmly and went to the driver's side, lodging himself in the front seat and turning on the ignition.

"Go ahead," he urged, darting a glance at me in the rear view mirror. "Stretch out. We have a nearly full tank of gas. It will warm up soon."

I hesitated. "Sleeping isn't going to solve our problems. We need to figure out where the girls are. Raph and Enoch never finished scanning Backpage. Maybe we should start there."

"Let me work on that while you get some rest." His voice was kindly but stern. I felt a twinge of guilt, knowing how draining he found it to be in a human body; how badly he, too, needed sleep— or, better yet, an escape to angelic form. But I didn't argue. Instead, I shook out the blankets and made myself a nest, stretching across the full breadth of the SUV as I nestled in, trying to get warm.

The bench seat was hard and narrow. I flipped around, trying to get comfortable. My body was crying out for rest, my brain too tired to fend off the thoughts that were racing through it: terror for my sister and her friend. Worry about the loyalty we could expect from Raph. Confusion over my own feelings for Michael and whether I would ever be able to trust him again. Over and over, I tried to chase the worries away. Over and over, I struggled to adjust my body to the hard contours of the SUV's seat.

Finally, frustrated and unable to chase away the chill, I pounded out a pillow and flopped over.

"Can't sleep?"

I sat up, Michael's question a convenient excuse to abandon my futile tossing and turning.

"I want to. I need to. But it's hopeless."

"I have an idea."

Leaving the engine running, he left the driver's seat and came around the opposite side, joining me in the back.

"Slide over."

I scooted across the bench, making room for him to join me. He pulled the door closed, giving a shiver himself.

"Here," he began, patting his legs. "Stretch out on my lap."

I stared at his thighs, his muscles tautly outlined against the worn denim of his jeans, and swallowed hard.

"I don't think that's such a good idea," I answered vaguely, shrinking back against the seat.

He pursed his lips together. "Don't be stupid, Carmichael. You need to warm up. And I'm a walking furnace, as you so frequently point out. You'll sleep in no time at all, I promise."

I eyed him warily. What he was saying made sense, after all.

"Come on," he reiterated, grabbing a pillow. "Spread out and let me warm you up."

The thought came to me: *old habits die hard.* Pushing it away, I tucked a blanket around my shoulders and stretched out, laying my head in Michael's lap. A surge of warmth enveloped me and, against my will, I let out a tiny sigh of relief, sinking into his body.

"Better?" Michael prompted, his voice a low growl that combined with the purr of the engine.

"Better," I confirmed, burrowing into my blankets.

My entire body relaxed, soothed by the heat and familiar scent of hay and honey that emanated from Michael's body. I didn't complain when he began stroking my hair, his fingers sending pulses of electricity to surge through my body. I let my eyes drift closed, basking in the comfort of his touch. But I still couldn't stop worrying enough to sleep.

"Did you find them on Backpage?" I finally asked.

His hand paused on the back of my neck.

"Yes."

My body tensed, and I started to push myself up, but he stopped me.

"There were so many of them, Hope. Just rows and rows of girls for sale. But I found them. There were pictures of them there, together. I tried to—" He paused, the words getting stuck in his throat. "Place an order," he said between gritted teeth. "But they're booked up for a few days. Both of them."

I pushed away his hands and sat up.

"We have to find them, Michael. We have to." I looked up at his face, pleading. There were shadows under his eyes, the lines around them deep. With a shock, I realized he was as afraid for them as I was.

I threw myself into his arms, burying my face in his chest, trying to chase away our fear. He kissed the top of my head, pulling me closer. "I wish I could sense them more strongly. But I can't."

Guilt now crowded in to join my other warring emotions. The invisible cord that linked me with Michael, the one that let us feel and think almost as one, was jumbled and knotted, the signals choked off by resentment and mistrust. Our unfinished business was impeding us from finding my sister.

I thought of what Enoch had told me earlier. *Just ask him*, he'd urged. Just ask him what had been so important that he'd stayed with Gabrielle the night my family was attacked. I sighed, pushing down the panic that surged from the depths at the thought of having Michael confirm what I'd already assumed was his betrayal.

"Michael," I began cautiously, keeping my eyes pressed tightly closed, listening to the steady beat of his heart.

He didn't answer me immediately. His hand had snuck under my shirt, his fingers absentmindedly trailing against my spine. It felt so natural, so right.

"I'm so afraid of failing you, Hope."

I started to protest, but the words stuck in my throat. Of course he felt that way. I'd made him feel that way. Over and over again, I'd forced him to prove himself. I focused on his heartbeat and chose my next words carefully.

"What were you really doing with Gabrielle the night Lucas attacked my family?" I asked. "If you knew something was wrong, why didn't you come?"

He stiffened, his hand suddenly stilled against my bare skin.

"It doesn't matter," he answered gruffly.

"It does," I insisted. "I want to know the truth."

He cleared his throat. "Hope . . ." His voice trailed off, uncertain.

"Just tell me," I urged, steeling myself.

He sighed. "Very well." There was a long pause. He started stroking my back again. "Yes, there was a group of refugees, as Gabrielle mentioned at the trial. But they were incidental. The only reason we were even there was that Gabrielle and I were looking for Lucas."

"What?" I flipped over to look him in the face. "What do you mean, you were looking for Lucas?"

He looked down at me in his lap. With a grim smile, he tucked a piece of stray hair behind my ear. "He'd been released from his sentence early. No one knew *why*, exactly, and very few of us knew about it at all. I only knew because I'd started to sense him again. The feelings were vague and undirected. But I'd grown concerned that he was about to make himself known. We'd followed a lead to Syria, trying to track him down."

I stared up at him, dumbfounded. "You never told me you knew Lucas had been released."

He shook his head. "I didn't want to worry you. And I wanted to believe that Gabrielle would do the right thing, that she wouldn't let her convictions about angelic superiority get in the way of her duty to me. To you."

I closed my eyes against the hot, angry tears that welled up.

He let a bitter laugh escape him. "So much for the infallibility and perfection we angels are supposedly blessed with. I can't seem to get anything right when it comes to you."

I sat up then. "That's not true," I whispered, wrapping my arms tightly around him.

He trailed a finger along my abdomen, feather light across my taut muscles. A yearning for him welled up, deep inside me, so strong that it shocked me. I took a deep breath.

He broke free of my embrace and brought his fingers to my chin, lifting my eyes to meet his. For once, he didn't bother to mask the centuries of pain he had witnessed as the protector of mankind. And he let me see into the depths of his soul—and how my rejection these past days, I realized with a shock, had wounded him more than anything else he had experienced.

"I love you, Carmichael. I swear to you that I will find your sister. But what happens beyond that is up to you, now."

He disentangled himself from me and pushed me aside.

I blinked hard, my body crying out from the suddenness of our separation. "What are you doing?"

"I'm going to walk the man camps to see if I can sense anything further. To see if anyone recognizes Rorie from her photo. I can't just sit here."

"What about me? Let me go with you."

He shook his head.

"I need to be alone, Carmichael. And I think you do, too."

He climbed out of the car, closing me in with a resounding slam of the door.

I sat, alone, stunned by the suddenness of his departure. The cold and silence pressed in on me, the longing of my body making me all too aware of the emptiness of my loss.

After a while, there was a tiny ping from my mobile.

It'll take me a day, but I'm coming. ND better get itself ready 'cause I'm gonna kick butt and take names.

I chuckled, wiping my runny nose and smiling.

Tabby was coming. I blew out a deep breath. My friend was coming. I could hold on for one more day. I could do that, nurse my broken heart, and more, find my sister.

twenty-two

LUCAS

I watched the girls lying on the mattress. They were puzzles to me, ciphers, confounding me at every turn, surprising me with their responses to the filth into which they had been thrust.

Rorie had been on calls for four days. Her innocence had been sold to the highest bidder: a man who claimed to be religious, from an oil town in Texas. Rorie had found this ironic, I suppose, and had said something to him. He'd told her his daughters never talked back to him that way.

She'd responded, immediately: "Are your daughters my age? Do you think there are creepy old men paying to have sex with your daughters tonight?"

He'd beat her, then, screaming at her to shut up; my bouncer had to break in to the room to protect my investment. We had to refund the man's money and give Rorie the night off. With a black eye and split lip, I couldn't allow her to go back out to work. She'd crowed about her insolence, recounting every word, every blow in their exchange—clinging to her victory, as tiny as it was.

The next night, fortunately, went much more smoothly.

So did the third, and the fourth.

Now she was here, lying listlessly on the dirty mattress next to Macey. Her whole body ached, no doubt. She bore welts and bruises and cuts. Her shoulder was dislocated by one man. Another pulled out her hair when she tried to fight. Again, both of them were too bruised to work, and my associates and I were the ones losing money because of it.

My eyes narrowed as I heard her giggle, an incongruous sound in this hellish place.

"Macey," she said, poking her friend in the ribs. "I did the math. We'd only have to work a whole year at Chick-Fil-A to pay him back the money we've lost today. A whole year! What do you say?"

She giggled again, and I remembered the gift bestowed upon her by that ridiculous excuse for an angel, Arthur. The gift of laughter. Humor, to tide her through dark times.

When Macey didn't respond, Rorie rolled over and scooched next to the wall, where she began digging her fingernails into the drywall. She was working out the math of the double shifts she would need to work to "pay back" her owner for her nights off. She set it up just like a middle school algebra equation, the dependent variable the number of men who would rape her.

Macey shivered under a sheet and groaned. Rorie sat up, abandoning her math problem to press the cool back of her hand against Macey's forehead.

"She's burning up," she stated, looking at me with accusing eyes.

I knew it was probably the onset of some sexually transmitted disease, but said nothing.

"Can't you get her a doctor?"

I laughed. "She's probably just faking it."

"You can't fake a fever. There's nothing here that she could use to spike her temperature."

Rorie narrowed her eyes, calculating. "If she gets worse, it's only going to lose you money."

I laughed, wondering at her ability to play into the game, her resilience and willingness to challenge me, despite it all.

"It doesn't matter," I stated baldly. "She's already given up. No doctor can save her now. I'll work her as hard as I can until she's done."

I left them then, Rorie fussing over Macey's feverish sleep, surely wondering what was taking Hope and Michael so long.

As was I.

I had planned everything so carefully. From the very beginning, I'd known the soft underbelly of Hope's confidence was the safety of her sister. The trap I'd sprung might have seemed convoluted to some, but it was the only way I could be sure that I not only physically destroyed Rorie, but that I systematically dismantled her psyche, as well.

That, I knew, was something Hope would never be able to bear. She would see it for what it was—her fault, her failure. And as a result, her damned love for Michael would taste like ashes in her mouth.

A searing jolt of anguish shook my body. Yes, I thought to myself, breathing deeply through the pain. Yes, the destruction of their love—the only thing that had made Michael's death a real sacrifice—was a just form of revenge. That its instrument was the abduction and violation of a child only underscored what I had asserted all along. It threw mankind's vileness in God's face. It forced Him to acknowledge and deal with His abomination.

Thus I would show Him what I'd always known: no human, no one, truly deserves the redemption He offers.

All I had to do now, I told myself, my frail human body quivering with fatigue and anticipation, was wait. There would be no others with me in my moment of glory. No flock of jet-black birds swarming around the site of their destruction. No armor-clad phalanx of the Fallen to back me.

Just me and them, as it should be.

twenty-three

HOPE

Cheered by Tabby's imminent arrival, I followed Michael and joined him in his search for any sign of the girls. But the man camps proved to be a dead end. Michael stalked the narrow lanes between the sterile metal boxes, crammed full of dirty and restless men, forcing every one he met to stare at the glossy eight-by-ten of Rorie that he bore before him like a cross. By sheer will, he forced them to look him in the eye and tell him whether they'd seen Rorie or anyone like her.

Every answer was the same: a disinterested shrug. It was as if she didn't exist.

I trailed after Michael as much to keep him from blowing up in frustration as to help in the search. We didn't give up until the sun had fallen beneath the horizon, the flames from the derricks providing an eerie glow. We did this for two days in a row, covering all the camps until, tense and cold, we decided there was no point. We needed to find a different way. As we walked back through the parking lot, I grappled through my mittens to read Tabby's message.

"I can't believe it!"

"What?" Michael responded, his interest piqued by the new note of spirit in my voice.

"She found us a place to stay."

"Who?"

"Tabby, of course. She's finally made it. And she sent me directions. C'mon."

Over rutted dirt and snow we drove, past the crowded strip malls and hastily raised shops, past the Walmart and onto a dirt road. A few blocks in we found it—a nondenominational church that had set up temporary headquarters in what had been a failed daycare.

"Mmmph," Michael mumbled as we pulled in. I didn't wait for him to turn off the ignition before I opened the door and ran to throw my arms around Tabby, who'd been waiting for us in the glass storefront.

"I can't believe you're here!" I said, squeezing her tight. I pulled back and looked at her, laughing. Her face was wiped clean of makeup, her hair pulled back into a tidy ponytail. She wore a very utilitarian stocking cap and a big, puffy coat. She'd traded in her signature cat-eyed frames for a sober pair of wire-rimmed glasses.

"What happened to you? You look almost . . ."

"Plain?" she half-laughed, her breath turning to steam in the cold. "That's the plan. I'm guessing I'm the only black person maybe in this entire zip code, if not the whole state. No need to call attention to myself. Besides, it's frigid up here! I needed to dress sensibly. My sense of style is just going to have to take a break in favor of frostbite prevention."

"Ollie?" I asked urgently, wondering what had happened to my faithful aging pet.

She smiled, patting my hand. "Perfectly fine. Past the smoke inhalation damage and enjoying himself at the doggie day spa. Let's get inside, out of the cold, so I can catch you up on things and you can fill me in on the search." She arched a brow as she looked behind me. "You too, lover boy. Let me show you around."

We tromped inside, shaking off the snow as best we could as she led us down a short hallway. Doors to either side opened into what looked like old classrooms, the windows now discreetly covered with curtains. After a short walk the hallway led into a near dead end with a handful of more utilitarian rooms bunched together. Tabby led us into the first one, an office. A filing cabinet, computer, and tiny desk were all crammed into the space of a closet, behind which sat a benign-looking young man in a Fair Isle sweater. The walls were overlapping with calendars, schedules, and directions of every possible sort, a veritable forest of paperwork.

"Reverend Krinke, meet my friends Hope and Michael," Tabby began, rubbing her hands together as she nodded toward us. "The ones I told you about."

The man reached out a hand, rising halfway from behind the desk. "Tabitha has told me a great deal about your efforts here. I am glad to be able to help you. Hopefully, it will give you at least some physical comfort while you search for the girls."

I turned to Tabby, confused. She grinned, obviously pleased with herself.

"I met Harlan at an ecumenical church conference last year. When I finally put two and two together and realized he was here, where you were, I gave him a call. His church is meeting here, temporarily, while they're building their new sanctuary. In the meantime, they've been hosting homeless families here during the week." She looked slyly at me. "He kindly offered to let us crash in the open space where they hold services for a few days."

I looked at Tabby. She grinned. I knew that the Reverend Krinke did not come up with that idea on his own.

Harlan shrugged. "We use the space for meetings and such during the day and weeknights, so normally we don't let families use it—with them staying here for a few months at a time, it wouldn't make sense. But as long as you don't mind packing up your things during the day, you're more than welcome to stay."

I thought of all the people we'd seen sleeping in cars and felt guilty. Tabby must have seen it in my face.

"A place to stretch out at night, Hope. And hot showers. Before it was a daycare, it was a women-only gym."

I could almost feel the knots unwinding in my neck and back at the thought.

"What can we do to repay you for this kindness, Reverend?" Michael said dutifully, our staying now a given.

Harlan shrugged. "If you're moved to donate before you leave, you are more than welcome." Then his chin lifted and his eyes flashed. "But the best thing would be for you to catch the criminals preying on those girls."

～

A quick tour of the facility took no more than thirty minutes, the residents darting in and out, shy, as we tried to stay out of their way. We'd missed the dinner hour, so we scrounged for ourselves in the utilitarian kitchen, making a meal out of the leftovers. As darkness fell, we cleared some space amid the folding chairs and old nap mats to spread out our blankets and pillows.

Michael was pounding his pillow as if trying to beat it into submission. I hid a smile of sympathy, imagining he was picturing the bland, blank faces of the rig workers he'd questioned earlier in the day.

"It will be nice to stretch out for a change," I offered gently, hoping to distract him. "Are the others coming?"

"No. They said that it's easier for them to recharge the angel way. They'll join us in the morning."

I hesitated. "You know, you don't need to stay. If you'd prefer to . . ."

"I know. I want to be here. I'm not going anywhere."

Tabby looked at me over her wire-rimmed glasses and mouthed: *Do you want me to find somewhere else to sleep?*

Blushing, I shook my head. *No,* I thought. *There's no need.* It's not as if Michael would find the aroma of crayons and spilled juice boxes on the ratty floor of a former kindergarten particularly romantic.

We all settled into our makeshift beds, and soon the air was filled with the rhythmic breathing of deep sleep. That is, Tabby and Michael's deep sleep: my body, feeling every little lump underneath the mélange of blankets, refused to relax, holding onto each ache and sore spot like a miser.

I flipped over and found myself staring at Michael's back. He was sleeping in an undershirt, the white cotton stretched taut over his broad shoulders, his skin gleaming impossibly golden in the faint moonlight that trickled in through the front windows.

I curled my knees up to my chin and watched him breathing, my own heart slowing to match his steady pace. Through the lingering smells of sweat and chalk dust his own scent of honey and hay, earthy and warm, drifted over to me.

It was all I could do to stop myself from reaching out to touch him. Instead, I slid out from the tangle of blankets and stealthily made my way to the back locker room, intent on a shower.

I pushed open the swinging door, flickering a glance at the posted men's and women's hours. Surely nobody would be up at this lonely hour—nobody but me, that is.

I blinked in the sudden, ghostly glow of the fluorescent light. The drab converted locker room was sparkling clean, the evidence of many hands deployed against the chore chart Harlan had showed us in the kitchen. I walked past the utilitarian sinks and toilet stalls, ignoring the bank of banged up metal lockers on the opposite wall until I reached one of two shower stalls and turned the water on, cranking the knob as far as it could go.

Droplets of water bounced off the tile, sprinkling me where I stood. Soon, a haze of steam rose from the floor. I let the water warm while I went back to the lockers, stripping down until my clothes were a neat pile on the scuffed wooden bench.

I snatched a scratchy towel out of a cubby and walked back to the shower. Hanging the towel on a plain hook, I pulled the vinyl curtain, its edges just beginning to discolor with mold, behind me and eased into the curling mist.

I sighed with relief, the pelting water sinking into my skin, washing away the weariness of the day. I stood motionless, letting the heat and the syncopation of the water echoing on the plain tiles echo around my head drown out any conscious thought of the dread that threatened to overwhelm me.

Soon the air around my head was a nimbus of steam. I eased the heat a little lower and let the water massage my hair, face, and body, my closed eyes shutting out everything but the delicious feeling.

I don't know how long I stood like that, engulfed in some primeval state of meditation. The air around me swirled, the currents of hot and cold warring with each other as reluctantly I forced myself to action, scrubbing away the grime of days' worth of hard living with the nub of soap I'd managed to scrounge. As my hands moved over calf and thigh, over taut stomach and back, I considered how long it had been since Michael had touched me: *really* touched me, skin on skin, with the rush of heat and pleasure that came along with his touch. I pushed the traitorous thought away and scrubbed harder, dropping my head to watch the suds whirl about the drain, circling until they succumbed inevitably to the dark vortex of plumbing.

I sighed again, knowing that the church's budget probably did not allow for hour-long showers, and I turned the knob until the stream of water dwindled to the *drip drip drip* of memory.

I threw the curtain open and stepped into the bracing air. Shaking, I wrapped the towel around my middle, the threadbare, patchy cotton almost translucent in places. I looked out at the rest of the locker room—it was nothing but steam. Guiltily, I wondered just how long I had lingered under the hot water. Shivering, I drew the towel tighter about me and made my way over the slick tile toward the sinks, a cautious hand stretched before me.

I finally hit cold porcelain. Reaching ahead through the steam, I swiped my hand over the mirror's surface.

Michael's face, hovering over my own reflection, stared back at me in the glass.

I whirled, clutching the towel before my chest.

"What are you doing here?" I whispered, the bare skin of my waist pressing up against the sink.

His azure eyes were clouded and troubled.

"I missed you," he said simply, staring at me intently.

I gaped back, feeling the rush of blood to my cheeks as I stood under his gaze.

"I didn't mean to scare you," he started again, taking a few quick steps to close the distance between us. "I just needed to be sure you were okay."

The familiar pull, low in my abdomen, was growing, threatening all my defenses.

"I'm fine," I finally managed to croak.

He smiled, the lopsided grin that always made my heart do flips. He reached out and caressed my cheek and then, ever so gently, trailed his thumb over my cheekbone to chase away an errant droplet of water, leaving a tiny wake of heat and steam in its wake.

"I'm glad," he said. He let his fingers drift down past my sopping hair to my neck, following the expanse of gooseflesh to my collarbone.

He stared into my eyes and I felt like a strange butterfly, stuck on a pin beneath his gaze.

"I just wanted you to know that I won't leave you—at least not until you tell me to. You told me once that some choices were only yours to make. So I'm leaving this one to you."

He backed away then, watching for my reaction. I could hear my heart, could feel it pounding frantically. I swallowed, trying to bring myself to speak, but my words had left me.

"I'll leave it to you. But don't you ever think that I don't want you. More than ever, Carmichael," he whispered as he disappeared into the cloud of steam. "More than ever. And for always."

I heard the clang of the swinging door as he left. My quivering knees betrayed me then and I collapsed to the floor, pulling the towel tighter, my tears mingling with the tiny rivulets of water that ran off my wet hair and skin.

~

For four more days and nights, then, we split up, circling the motel parking lots stained by dirty snow, haunting the places we thought Macey and Rorie might be, cursing the endless stream of men going in and out of the motel rooms as casually as if they were getting their hair cut or picking up a pizza. We watched and waited, Michael's and my senses seemingly stuck, unable to find our way out of the miasma of evil, hoping that we would see Macey or Rorie. We ignored the barbed comments flung our way by Raph. We ignored the inquisitive probing of Enoch, who wished to know exactly where Michael and I stood with one another. We ignored Tabby's arched, knowing eyebrows and her not-so-secretly mouthed comments—*just talk, you two!*—and sat it out.

Most of all, we ignored each other, focused on the task at hand, grateful that Tabby had arrived loaded down with hand wipes and carefully packed coolers of soul food to feed our hungry, homesick stomachs and keep our mouths occupied so that we didn't have to talk to one another. Even an angel used to manna couldn't deny the power of collard greens and corn bread.

The whole time, I concentrated on repairing my instincts, getting them back in order to help us find who we needed to find. But the insistent low buzzing in my head and the swirling impulse that chased through my body, leading nowhere, were constant reminders of how ineffectual my inherited angelic sense of direction had become.

I pulled the fleece blanket closer about my shoulders, my bones creaking in protest after hours of being cramped in the front seat of the car.

There was no trust left between us, I thought. Me and Michael. And it was standing in our way. Neither one of us was strong enough on our own, but our severed bond meant our signals were frustratingly weak. That was why we couldn't find Rorie and Macey now. And I knew that mending broken trust wasn't as simple as gluing back together a broken piece of pottery.

I didn't know how to forgive him—or I was too proud to do so. I didn't know if I could believe in the idea of us anymore. That thought went over and over in my head as I curled my legs up under me and pressed my face to the cold glass of the window.

"Hope."

I looked up and turned to face Michael. In the soft light of early dawn, his face was gray, shadowed by exhaustion.

"Look," he said softly, pointing ahead.

There, stumbling out of a motel room, was Macey.

I rubbed my eyes, holding my breath as I peered at her, picking her way across the slippery parking lot, an oafish goon watching her every step. She was shaky, as if the wind sweeping the parking lot would knock her over. She leaned into it, wincing, digging her hand into her pocket, fumbling around and mumbling something to herself over and over. Her flesh was ashen and dull, the remnants of the too-bright makeup smeared across her face highlighting her pallor.

"It's her," I breathed. "We have to get her." I reached for the door.

"No," Michael intoned, his heavy hand staying me. "We can't take her now. We need to follow her home. She'll lead us to Rorie. Can you drive, Hope? Can you tail them without being seen so I can get the others?"

I swallowed hard, nodding my head. He squeezed my arm reassuringly. "It won't take but a minute. I'll be back. Just don't be seen," he emphasized.

Then, in a flash of light, he disappeared, leaving a few twinkling pinpoints, like falling stars, in his wake.

I scrambled over to the driver's side and shifted into gear.

Don't screw this up, Carmichael, I thought sternly, trying to remain calm and focused. Every cell in my body was screaming with urgency now that we had spied our target. *This may be the only chance you get.*

I pulled out onto the street, keeping myself a safe distance back from the low-slung car into which Macey had been unceremoniously dumped. Each tick of the odometer was torture, each minute of careful driving stretching for an hour, every instinct urging me to go faster, to speed past the unseemly banks of snow scarred by exhaust, to ram the car and pluck Macey out, bringing her to safety.

But I couldn't. Not yet.

~

In the end, it wasn't that far away. We'd been hovering and circling about the spot for days, apparently, never finding it.

When the car turned into the industrial park, I kept going, my eyes never losing the car as it wound its way to the very back and parked next to a big warehouse.

There. There was where I would find my sister.

I parked and watched as Macey, dead on her feet, climbed out of the car and stumbled to the door. The man pushed her through unceremoniously and pulled the door closed behind him as they disappeared into the warehouse.

Michael had told me to wait. But I couldn't. Not when I was so close.

I slid out of the car and closed the door quietly behind me, the bracing chill of morning air snapping me to full alertness. Moving across the snow, I circled around the back of the warehouse to check it out. Beside the door into which Macey had disappeared, there seemed to be a dock for trucks on the back, huge garage doors lining up to break the great expanse of wall, a single door of normal size punctuating the row.

No other entrances. No windows. Just corrugated metal presenting an impenetrable wall of sameness. The outside was equally sterile, only the heaps of junk that dotted the parking lot there to break up the monotony.

The buzzing in my head was a full shriek, now, insistent, surging to a level that was painful. The building pulled on me, urging me closer, the pain nipping at me and punishing me for not moving faster to finish my task. I bit my lip, choking back the sob that threatened to be ripped from my throat.

How could they stand this? The thought came unbidden. How could the Fallen not go crazy, if this was what they dealt with every moment of their banishment from Heaven?

I shook the unwelcome thoughts away, trying to clear my head. Ignoring the throbbing in my brain, I dodged around the lights of the parking lot, still harsh and cold as the sun rose, and pressed myself into the shadows as I looped back around to the front door.

I wrapped my fingers around the knob and turned.

Locked. Of course.

When I went back to the dock side of the warehouse, I had better luck. The side door had been carelessly left open. Checking over my shoulder, I ducked inside and pulled the door tight behind me, plunging myself into darkness.

I shuddered as a feeling of recognition came over me. Suddenly, I was thrust back into my childhood, a fifteen-year-old girl once again picking her way through an abandoned warehouse full of junk, unwittingly walking into a trap laid by the Fallen.

But I wasn't fifteen anymore. This time, I was ready, I thought, for what lay ahead.

Slowly, I picked my way around the stacks of boxes and piles of junk that littered the floor, hands outstretched in the dark. There had to be a door to the interior on the other side of the building. There just had to be.

I made it to the far wall and groped about. A light switch.

I flicked it on and the blue tinge of fluorescent light flooded the room.

Blankets, chains, and handcuffs were strewn about the floor right nearby. I bent down to pick up the cuffs. The metal was heavy. I tried to imagine someone trapped out here, a tiny body bearing the weight of the cuffs in the frigid night, and frowned.

A hand clamped down on my shoulder.

I gasped, prying the fingers away as I jumped to my feet and whirled to face the intruder, fists raised, poised to strike.

"It's just me!" Michael whispered urgently, holding his hands up over his head in the universal sign of submission. He looked silly doing it—the mighty, muscle-bound angel, his armor molded to his body, magnificent wings outspread, each feather sparkling under the light, held off by tiny me.

A wave of relief swamped my adrenaline-laced body. I gave a great sigh, forcing myself to give up the instinct to fight, and smiled despite myself.

"Why didn't you wait for me?" he asked, accusing.

"I didn't know when you'd be back. I couldn't stop, not when I was so close." I bit my lip again, wrapping my arms about me. "The pain, Michael . . . it was too much. I had to keep going."

He nodded. "I feel it too." The sinews of his neck were heavy and corded with tension, the vein in his forehead throbbing. "We don't have much time."

I nodded, knowing instinctively that he was right. "Where are the others?"

"They're coming from the other side. If we can get the girls out without a fight, we will. But we aren't leaving without them," he said grimly. "Come on."

He led the way to the door and tested the knob. Unlocked. He paused, and then reached out to clutch my hand, pressing it to his chest.

"Whatever happens—" he began, but I cut him off, shaking my head.

"I know."

He squeezed my hand once more, sending a burst of fortifying warmth through my body before releasing it. Then he inched the door open and peered through.

A long hallway stretched away from us, a series of closed doors lining the way. A few bare bulbs studded the ceiling, leaving dim circles of light below.

Michael held out a hand, cautioning me to stay behind him. Impatient, I pushed him aside and plowed ahead.

The first door I came to was locked. So was the next, and the next. Frustrated, I rattled the doorknobs, the flimsy walls shaking.

"Stand back," Michael warned.

I pressed my back against the opposite wall and watched, amused, while he unsheathed his sword, raising it above his head. Writhing flames snaked up its silver blade, bouncing light down the dim hallway. With a smooth stroke, he separated the knob from the door, leaving it a molten blob on the floor. He reached through the gaping hole and unlatched the door from the inside.

He kicked it in, poised for a fight.

Empty.

"My turn," I said, squaring off to face the next locked door. I didn't wait for him to answer before I kicked it in. It splintered under the weight of my foot with a satisfying collapse.

"Hey! What the hell?"

I wheeled to see the goon who'd been escorting Macey to and from the motel bearing down on us, pistol raised and aimed at my head. I looked at the collapsed door. Frightened eyes suddenly appeared at the hole I'd made, peering out.

"Rorie! Macey!" I shouted. But the faces I could glimpse were unfamiliar. How many girls were in this place?

"Hope," Michael warned as the man closed in. "Don't do anything stupid."

The man grinned stupidly as he closed the distance between us, looming overhead.

I heard the rush of wings behind me. "No," I ordered Michael, raising a hand to stop his intervention. "I've got this."

The man pulled up short at the sight of Michael, confused. "Wha—"

I didn't give him a chance to finish. With one swift move, I wrapped my arms around his neck and chest, immobilizing his arm. He struggled against me, the gun going off aimlessly, taking out one of the light bulbs and showering us in a rain of shattered glass.

I brought a well-aimed knee into his gut and then aimed lower. His knees gave out and I let go, stripping away the handgun as I let him collapse, helpless, on the floor. He clutched at himself and writhed on the floor in pain.

"Are you done?" Michael asked from behind me as I stood, panting, over the man.

I shook my head, breathless. "Knock him out for me."

I stepped over him and turned to watch as Michael swung the blunt handle of his sword against the man's head, rendering him unconscious.

"Respect," Michael intoned, eyeing me thoughtfully as I bent over, hands on knees, and caught my breath.

I shrugged, pulling myself upright. "I learned how to take care of myself. Just in case. Come on, we need to keep going."

One by one, we got the doors unlocked. What we found sickened us. Women and children, cringing like animals inside cages meant for dogs. Chained to walls. Or left loose, but with crushed spirits and drugged bodies that rendered them incapable of escape, wallowing in filth and decay.

They cowered as we peered at them. Some wept. I looked at them carefully, knowing that any one of them might be Rorie or Macey. But none of them were.

We didn't have time to comfort them. We kept working our way down the hall, simply unchaining and unlocking and leaving them to wander, free, in our wake.

A few more oafish guards tried to stop us, but we dispatched them with ease and used the chains and shackles we found inside the rooms to immobilize them, unconscious, to keep them out of our way.

And finally, we came to the end of the hall. The last door.

The others converged on us at the same time. I don't know why I had expected Enoch to change himself into something more suitable for battle. He was just as roly-poly as ever, his rolls of fat on display in the costume of a sumo wrestler, massive wings flapping behind him for extra momentum as he waddled toward us, leaning heavily into his cane for support. Raph stalked behind him, breathing heavily, a sheen of sweat across his brow. He was magnificent in his armor, each panel articulating his muscles, their surfaces engraved with great battle scenes of history. A snowy white tunic and short leather skirt grazed his knees.

I did a double take. A trickle of blood ran down Raph's armor, congealing around the tiny figures where it had been trapped, splatters of it marring the ivory linen that swung gracefully below.

It was the only time I'd seem him appear even remotely ruffled.

"Disgusting human filth," he spat, shaking his head over what he'd just found. He drew his hand from behind him, tossing something on the floor at my feet.

I stared down, expecting to see his sword.

"Is that—?" My voice trailed off, shocked.

Raph nodded curtly. "A brand. Like those used on animals." He kicked it with his booted toe. "Even my hippie friend couldn't take it," he added, jerking his head roughly toward Enoch.

"I never said I was a pacifist," Enoch replied, brandishing his cane. "For once, Raph and I agreed on something. I have to say, I enjoyed meting out punishment more than I expected," he admitted, awkwardly adjusting his sumo belt as he leaned over on his knees, trying to catch his breath.

"Careful there!" Raph winced, shielding his eyes from the flash of bare skin to which Enoch had inadvertently exposed him. Enoch ignored him as he struggled upright, continuing his story.

"And those poor dogs. They were fighting dogs, too. Bloody business, that," he continued, rubbing a gnarled hand over his grizzled beard. "Though I think when it is all said and done, the dogs were treated better than the girls we found. Yes, if ever punishment was deserved, it was deserved by the men and women who run this operation."

I looked more closely at the knob on the top of his cane as he leaned into it for support. A thin smear of blood glistened under his fingers.

"Tabby," I said sharply, a stab of fear gripping my heart. I wheeled around, scanning the hallways for her. "Where's Tabby?"

"Relax," Raph said behind breaths. "We transported ourselves over, angel style; she had to drive. One of the more mundane limitations of being human. She'll be right behind us. We cleared out the whole front, so you have nothing to worry about. She'll be perfectly safe when she gets here."

I nodded, grateful that they'd thought it through. Still, my mouth was dry, parched with fear. I looked at Michael and then to the door before us, my stomach roiling.

The screaming of my nerve endings, the buzzing of my brain, now a steady insistent whining that would not stop, was all the confirmation I needed. This had to be it. Macey and Rorie had to be here.

We had seen horrible things, each of us, all the way to this moment—but this was going to be, by far, the worst.

What would we find behind this door?

I looked back up at Michael, searching his eyes. The stormy gray in them was resolute. He locked eyes with me and simply nodded. I walked up to the door, feeling the phalanx of angels close ranks protectively behind me.

Breathing heavily, I turned the knob. To our surprise, it turned easily beneath my hand, and the door swung open. We shuffled in, cautious, scanning the room.

I caught my breath.

In the corner, on a bare mattress, tangled in dirty sheets, my sister was cradling Macey's limp body. Blood was dripping from Macey's wrists, pooling underneath them and seeping into the thin mattress, her life draining away.

I stared in shock as I watched Rorie rock Macey back and forth, back and forth, her face glistening with tears. It took her a moment to notice us. When she did, her response was odd. She paid no notice to the fact that I came accompanied by angels dressed in armor. She didn't notice the wings or swords. I realized, with a start, that she had probably seen it once before—as a witness to our mother's beating. She ignored it all, accepting it as just as much of her new reality as the filthy mattress upon which she sat. Instead, she focused her attention on me.

"You came," she said, smiling tremulously through her tears. "He said you wouldn't, but I knew you would. I knew you and Mom wouldn't give up on me, Hope."

She still didn't know our mother was dead.

"Rorie—" But I broke off, unable to speak as I watched her cradling Macey.

"I tried to stop her, Hope," Rorie whispered, gazing down at her friend's face with a profound gentleness. She caressed Macey's cold cheek. "But I couldn't. She didn't believe me when I said it would get better. I couldn't save her, Hope. I couldn't save her."

"She smuggled a razor out of the motel room," a dark voice offered by way of explanation.

I turned, startled, to see a young man seated in the corner, watching the scene impassively. "I don't know how she managed to sneak it past Enrique, my bouncer," he added with a shrug. "But sooner or later something like this happens."

He rose from the chair, uncoiling his body like a serpent. When the outline of his body began to blur and melt, his form collapsing in on itself in a rush of twinkling light and stench of sulfur, I was not surprised. I had known all along that at the end of our journey, we would find Rorie with him. Always him, haunting and hurting my family.

"Lucas," I acknowledged as he emerged, his body reformed into that of a warrior, clad as ever in black armor.

"It took you long enough," he admonished with a shake of his jet wings, sending a rush of hot, sulfured air our way.

I felt the angels stiffen behind me. None of us moved as we watched him walk over to Rorie. He crouched down and slowly, reverently, began stroking her hair.

My skin crawled at the idea of his hands on her.

"Do you know how long I have waited?" he began, never lifting his eyes from Rorie's tear-stained face. "I was watching from the very beginning, you know. I was there when you blessed her. I was there when you gifted her with the things you thought would protect her. What you didn't realize, though, is that I gave her my own gift, too." He lifted his eyes to pin us with a look of bemusement, continuing to stroke her hair.

"I gave her the gift of endurance, knowing that one day, I would bring her to the brink of destruction. I would bring her so close to death, leaving her longing for it, but I would never, ever let her have that release." He let his hand rest on her bare shoulder. Only then did I realize Rorie was sitting in nothing but a thin tank top and underwear, the thin sheets the only barrier against cold.

"Look at her," he ordered, suddenly grabbing her lank hair and jerking her head around. "Really look at her."

I saw the dark circles under her eyes.

I saw the bruises, yellow and purple, that mottled her skin, a map of the abuse she had suffered. The indignity of the brand burned into her, still oozing from infection.

I counted the scratches and burns and cuts. I noted the swelling around her eye, the puffiness about her mouth, and I knew, then, that her wounds were much deeper than what the eye could see.

Rorie twisted her head away from his grip and cleared her throat.

"Nothing a little beauty sleep can't cure," she whispered, a brief flash of defiance disappearing from her eyes almost the instant I saw it.

"Shut up!" Lucas shouted, backhanding her across the face.

She pulled her body inward, being careful not to spill Macey from her lap, and she covered her mouth. But not before I saw a smile flutter across her face.

If she could provoke him, she could win. It was the simple calculus of a girl who had nothing but her wits, now; no other source of power. It was all that she had left, and she was wielding it as best she could.

Michael surged forward, his mighty hand already shaped into a fist, ready to strike, but I put out an arm and stopped him, shaking my head slightly. I could feel him trembling with anger, his fingers gripped tight in futility as he watched his girl nursing her cut lip. I felt a pang for him; he loved her as much as I did. But we couldn't move too soon—not until we were certain we could get Rorie away safely.

Lucas noticed none of this. He just continued his raging.

"This is your fault!" he screamed, pointing at me. "Your fault! If you hadn't interfered to begin with, this never would have happened. But you had to meddle in the things of Heaven—things that had nothing to do with you. You had no right!"

"That's not true," I asserted, struggling to keep my voice calm, taking a careful step forward, one eye on Lucas, the other trained on Rorie. "I was the Bearer. What happened to you, what happened to all of us—" I gestured about to the angels behind me—"it was meant to be, Lucas. It was as much my story as yours."

"No!" he shrieked, gripping his head, wild with pain. The pain he was suffering—how much worse it had to be than the pain I'd felt, just before, as God admonished me to hurry up.

As his eyes rolled back in his head, I felt a surprising emotion —pity.

"Lucas," I whispered, taking another step closer to the dirty mattress. "Lucas, it doesn't have to be this way."

He scrambled back into the corner, dragging my listless sister with him.

"You turned my army against me, you cleaved it in half with your offer of forgiveness!"

"It wasn't my offer. It was God's."

"It should never have been made!" he continued, his face contorting as he spoke. "Look at this!" he gestured wildly about him. "Look at the way you humans use one another. Look at the way you treat the gift of life and free will He has given you. How can you look at what has happened to your sister and believe that humanity deserves the place in the cosmos that God has granted it?

"Don't you see?" he pleaded, beseeching me to see things from his perspective. "Humans don't deserve His grace. And I cannot accept *His* grace—not if it is conditional upon my acceptance of your kind."

He watched, looking for any sign of doubt. Then he took a different tack.

"You know, you're not so different than me, Hope," he began with a silky voice. "The Devil's Advocate. Isn't that what your boss called you? It was just a job, wasn't it? A role he asked you to play so you could forget the truth about Ike Washington. You had a job to do, to whisper in the ear of the judge and convince her that Ike Washington was guilty. You had the evidence; you just had to ignore the surrounding circumstances so that you could live with yourself."

I winced, remembering all those records—the Social Services reports, the notes scrawled by concerned teachers in the margins of failing report cards, the detritus of a life ruined before it had even began. Yes, it had been my job to ignore all those things and make my case. And even now, it filled me with shame that I had done it.

Lucas continued, his voice winding about my guilty conscience like a sinewy snake.

"My job was—and is—the same. My job is to make God see things my way, whether He wants to see them or not." He smiled

indulgently as he watched his words hit their mark. "The only difference is," he whispered, "I believe in what I'm doing. How can you blame me for doing it, Hope, when it's what you've done, too?"

He searched my face, hoping for collapse or, at the very least, acquiescence. But I wouldn't let him burden me with this, too—not now. Not with so much at stake. His hopes dashed, Lucas scrambled wildly about him, pulling a dagger from the folds of linen under his breastplate.

"If I have to kill Rorie myself, I will get you to admit it," he said. "I will get you to admit that humanity deserves eradication."

"That won't do anything, Lucas," Michael interjected, his voice a low growl of warning.

"It will prove me right," Lucas snapped back. He held the tip of the dagger against Rorie's neck, pressing it so tightly against the carotid that I could see it moving with every pulse of blood, as if one with the vein.

"Don't you think there's been enough killing? Wasn't it enough to kill their mother?" Enoch interjected.

Lucas's head snapped back. "What do you mean?"

So he didn't realize, either. My tongue was thick, the grief coming afresh. It was Michael that answered.

"When you left Mona, you left her for dead. She didn't survive your beating."

For a moment, Lucas looked stunned. Quickly, though, his face hardened into a mask of hate.

"That's nothing to me. Collateral damage. And I'll kill again if it serves my purpose. If it hurts you," he hissed, pulling Rorie tighter against him.

I felt the bile rising in my throat. But then, amid my own warring feelings of panic and anger, I felt something else.

I raised my hand, warning off the angels behind me as I heard them stir. Then I stepped forward and crouched down, so close to the edge of the mattress that I could smell the urine and sweat that had penetrated it, could nearly taste the tangy iron of blood that even now seeped into it.

Lucas pulled my sister tight against his chest, the dagger barely pricking her neck, leaving a bead of blood to swell and drip against her white skin. He strained away from me, pressing himself against the walls. His wild eyes were nearly all white. He frothed, spittle spraying from his mouth as he spilled his words.

"Rorie, Macey—all of this. I planned it all. All to bring you down, to make you realize how wrong you have been. You took away my spot. You, the Shield? That was my role! My place in Heaven. Or did he not tell you that when he so generously offered it to you?" He sneered at Michael behind me. "Don't you hate me? Don't you hate yourself, that your mistakes brought your family to such ruin?"

I looked at Rorie, clutched against Lucas's chest. Her eyes were as defeated as Lucas's were wild. I thrust away the feelings of guilt and inadequacy that his words provoked. I couldn't change what had happened.

But there was one thing I could still do.

"I don't hate you," I whispered, tearing my gaze from Rorie to look Lucas full in the eye. "I can only imagine how you must feel— the centuries of hate and pain, eating away at you. I remember—I know what it's like," I added, crawling over the mattress and sitting before him. I reached out and placed my hand over his, where he held the dagger against my sister's throat. I felt the heat surging from him to me, heat that might have come from Raph or Enoch or even Michael. He eyed me warily.

"I couldn't understand Michael's reasoning, sometimes, back then in Istanbul while we looked for the Key," I said. "He would hurt me, if not physically, then with his words—maybe on purpose, maybe because he didn't know any better, couldn't find any way to handle it. He wasn't the same then. He wasn't himself, and I couldn't reach him. I felt so . . . small. So helpless. I was angry, then, angry with God for punishing Michael that way. I couldn't understand what good it would do to punish him that way. I was afraid it would only drive him further from God . . .

"Nobody could go through that unchanged, Lucas. I don't think anyone could understand what you have gone through. I won't pretend to accept what you have done to my family, but I understand how, in your pain-addled mind, you thought you were doing what you had to do."

I took a deep breath and picked up his free hand, clasping it between my two.

"I don't accept it, but I can feel sorry for you. Please. If you must take somebody, don't take Rorie. She has suffered enough. Take me. I'm the one you really want."

"No!" Rorie's strangled cry cut the silence. Lucas pulled her closer, eyeing me with suspicion. Quietly, I moved toward him. He scrambled away, wrapping his arm even more tightly around Rorie's neck.

"Don't get fresh now, mister," Rorie joked, sputtering with a choked voice. "Not on the first date."

I shook my head slightly. "Not now, Rorie."

I heard a commotion behind me. "What's going o—" Tabby's voice died out as she arrived and pushed her way through the angels. I heard her sharp intake of breath as she assessed the situation.

"Oh. Oh, Hope. No, no. You can't do this."

"Shhhh," I whispered. "It's the only way. Take me, Lucas. You know I'm the one you want. It's got to be me if you're going to end the Prophecy. If you're going to hurt Michael, it can't be Rorie. It's got to be me."

His eyes narrowed. "How do I know I can trust you?"

"Do you have a choice? To get what you want, you're going to have to. Fair exchange. My life for hers. Just let her go to Tabby. Tabby, come sit on the edge of the mattress."

Tabby sidled up next to me. I looked at her out of the corner of my eye and nodded, urging her on. Her hands shook as she held them out wide for Lucas to see she was unarmed and cleared her throat.

"Whenever you're ready, Lucas."

Rorie began thrashing wildly, kicking blindly at Tabby and bucking away from Lucas's body.

"No! Hope, you can't make me. I don't want you to! Michael, please! Don't let her do this, Michael! I'm begging you, please!"

Behind me, I could hear Raph make an angry sound deep in his throat. "Aren't you going to stop this? Put an end to this, Michael. We could take him if we charged now! Why aren't you giving the order?" he challenged.

I looked over my shoulder at Michael, hoping that he understood what I was trying to do. His face was an unnatural shade of gray, his lips twisted tight with fear. I felt a pang, knowing how much he loved Rorie. Impulsively, he reached out and made as if to rush past me, but he drew himself up short, closing his eyes and forcing himself to take one breath, two.

When he opened his eyes, he answered Raph with a preternatural calmness. "It's Hope's command. Until she gives the word, we stand down. It's got to be her way."

Raph swore in frustration.

"Thank you," I whispered, knowing just how difficult this was for Michael. But I could see no choice. I turned back to the hostage scene before me.

"Just give her over to Tabby, Lucas. Nice and easy."

"You first," he countered, struggling to contain Rorie as she fought against him. "You come to me first. Turn around and slide back here so I can hold on to you. Then I'll give up your sister."

It was surreal. I reflected briefly at the strangeness of the situation—me, negotiating with a prince of the Fallen Angels! But I did as he asked, sidling back to him, keeping my eyes trained on the tense faces of the angels, muscles tensed, their hands poised on the hilts of their swords, until I felt the cold press of sharp metal in my own back.

"Take her," Lucas said brusquely, shoving Rorie away from his body to wrap his other arm around me. "Take what's left of her, anyway."

One last cry, torn from Rorie's lips, broke the silence as Tabby gathered her into her arms, cooing and rocking her to soothe her tiny, broken body. Rorie, finally free from the need to be strong, dissolved into a heap of tears. My own tired frame sagged with relief. She was safe. At least for now, she was safe.

"You made a bad trade. She won't live for long," Lucas taunted.

I let his barb fly past. He couldn't hurt me. Not anymore.

"Tabby will keep her safe."

"Your friend can't protect her from me. After you're dead, I will just hunt her down all over again."

"Nobody's going to die here, unless it's you. I'm going to unleash a can of Southern minister whoop-ass on you if you don't shut your damn mouth," Tabby sniped, placing a protective hand over Rorie's ears as if shielding her from the conversation. "This child has been through enough without having to listen to you and your threats."

"You don't understand," Lucas sneered. I could feel his hot breath on my neck as he pulled me tightly against his armor, could feel the heat that suffused his skin—the fire of God, pulsing through his veins—and had to stifle the urge to vomit. It was the same golden warmth that surged through Michael's body, familiar and foreign at the same time.

I shook my head and reminded myself where the cold-hearted viciousness that permeated Lucas came from.

"Fear." I whispered it so softly, I thought nobody heard me. But Lucas's body stiffened.

"What did you say?"

I cleared my throat, conscious of the sharp knife blade against my skin.

"I said fear. Behind anger is fear. The reason you hate me so much—hate all of humanity—is you are afraid of us. You can't understand how something so flawed can be so loved by God, can you? And that frightens you. Especially you, whose whole role in Heaven was premised on order and logic."

He tightened his hold on me and a jolt of pain raced up my arm. "I'm not afraid of you. We'll wipe you off the face of the earth, eventually."

"Like a bug," I breathed. "Like a dirty cockroach or a snake. Because you're afraid. *Fear of man will prove to be a snare; but whoever trusts in the Lord will be safe.*"

As I spoke, I moved my hand over his fingers and loosened his grip so that I could turn and face him.

He didn't stop me.

I stared into his black eyes. The pupils were shrinking, the wild whites of his eyes betraying his desperation. I couldn't penetrate his thoughts, but the tension around his eyes seemed to be soften-ing. His pain was lessening; every extra moment he let me speak, every time he let my words touch his heart, he was moving closer to God. I plowed on, confident I was on the right path.

"Or maybe it's not mankind that you're afraid of. Maybe it's yourself. Maybe you're afraid that after all this time, after all the things you've done, God couldn't possibly forgive you. And you couldn't stand that rejection, could you? Not again. Not after all you've been through."

I was barely whispering now, focusing all of my attention on his face. Tiny beads of sweat had broken out on his brow; his breath was coming in heavy, labored bursts now. But he wasn't moving. Only the slightest twitch of his eye muscles and his fingers fidgeting on the handle of the knife he still pointed at my chest gave away that he was even listening to me.

"But don't you see, Lucas? Those things you did—they don't take away the fire of God within you. I can still feel it. I can." Impulsively, I reached out and placed my hand gently on his cheek. He pulled away, repulsed and confused. Undeterred, I pressed on.

"You feel it too, don't you? God's fire is still in you. Nothing will extinguish it, Lucas—nothing. *'Let all bitterness, wrath, and anger, and clamor, and evil speaking be put away from you, with all malice; and be ye kind, one to another, tenderhearted, forgiving one another...'"*

His lips twisted with nervous sarcasm. "Really. You need to find more interesting reading. Ephesians is so 60 AD."

I gulped hard, momentarily nonplussed by Lucas's attempt at humor, before continuing.

"All those things you did? You did them out of anger and out of fear. And from the depths of pain. I can see that now. But those actions aren't you."

He sat transfixed, now, my words washing over him.

"Someone once asked me if I thought humans were the only

ones of God's children to deserve forgiveness." I darted a look over my shoulder to where the angels watched, wondering if they would recognize the words as belonging to their missing comrade, Gabrielle. I turned back to Lucas and let my hands fall in front of me in my lap. "I didn't know how to answer then. But I do now. I understand, Lucas. And I still see the light of God within you. I can see it and I can feel it.

"I forgive you."

Lucas froze, his eyes full of shock, as I heard the angels behind me give a collective gasp.

As I said the words, my heart suddenly felt light, and I realized with a start that I truly meant it.

"I forgive you," I repeated with more conviction. "It doesn't have to be this way for you anymore, Lucas. You have a choice.

"I forgive you," I repeated, looking into Lucas's eyes, willing him to believe me.

He dropped the knife, his throat constricting over a choked sob.

"You can't forgive me," he whispered. "It's not possible."

I nodded, a fleeting smile on my lips. "But I do."

He clutched at his face, disbelieving.

"But . . . everything I have done." He looked over at Rorie, her broken body laid across Tabby's lap like a strange pietà, and choked back a strangled cry.

"It was wrong, but I understand why you did it. You couldn't help it. And I forgive you."

I sat back on my heels, watching him carefully as, hands shaking, he struggled away from Rorie. "No, no, no," he muttered to himself, scrambling back to the edge of the mattress, trying to get her as far away from him now as he could—this tiny girl now a threat as his worldview crumbled at its very foundations. I fought back the urge to move to her as she slumped, poised on the edge of consciousness, in Tabby's lap. Instead, I kept my focus on Lucas as he wrestled with his conscience, shaking his head and pulling at his hair as if wishing away my words.

He lifted his face, wet with tears, a mask of hate and confusion, and looked at me. The dark shadows under his eyes, the way the tendons in his neck stood out, ropey and twisted, the errant twitching of the muscles under his eye—I looked at him full in the face and gave a start of recognition. It was the same hunted look Michael had borne as we'd raced across Europe—a face etched in pain and anguish.

"You forgive me?"

I nodded again. "I look at you, and I see Michael," I added simply, knowing that I could never begin to describe the torrent of emotions that lay behind my explanation.

He wept, great, silent sobs that wracked his entire body, his jet wings shaking from his attempt at restraint. I looked away, shy now of intruding upon this moment, wanting him to have his privacy as he wrestled with the decision before him, keeping track of his progress through the tremors of the mattress on which we both sat. When the shaking stopped, I raised my eyes. His face was streaked with tears, but there was a new light in his eyes. He stared, wonderingly, at nothing at all. And as I watched, a funny, nearly stunned look crept across his face. The tense wrinkles at the corners of his eyes seemed to loosen just a little, and his eyes grew wide.

"What is it?" I asked.

"The pain," he whispered, his voice hoarse. "It's stopped."

He folded over into himself, chuckling low and then collapsing into outright laughter—laughter of disbelief, laughter of irony, laughter—at long last—of sweet release. His body began to twinkle, its edges blurring, this time no sulfur emanating from it as he shifted and whirled.

"A daughter of Eve, full of forgiveness," he said wonderingly as his form collapsed into a pulsing whorl of pixelated light. His disembodied voice called out from deep inside the light. "She forgives me! After all I have done, after the horrors to which I have subjected her, she forgives. Perhaps I was wrong. Perhaps there is hope for humanity after all. Who am I, then, to reject God's gift?"

The light grew and grew, swirling ever faster, the room growing as bright as the sun before the entire thing collapsed in upon itself. We stared, dumbfounded, at the empty space he'd left behind.

"He's gone home," Enoch whispered from behind me.

A gilded silver feather wafted down to land gently upon the soiled ticking of the mattress—all that was left of the Lucas who had hunted and haunted me for nearly all my life.

I stared at it, suddenly exhausted. I remembered what Enoch had said to me that day in my office: until the highest among the Fallen had accepted God's grace, the Prophecy would be unfulfilled.

"Is this what you meant, Enoch?" I whispered, barely able to speak.

"Yes," he responded, letting the gravity of what we'd just witnessed settle in, wrapping itself around our numbed emotions.

"But they won't all accept it, will they? Even now, the Fallen will resist. Some of them, at least. Evil will never leave the world, will it?"

He nodded. "I am afraid that is true."

Feeling as if my limbs were made of lead, I settled down on the mattress, holding my head. But I couldn't afford to rest yet. Wearily, I forced myself to rise and look to Rorie.

She'd fought her way out of Tabby's arms, overwhelmed by fatigue and confusion. My sister, once so full of life, slumped before me like an empty husk.

"No." The single word was ripped from my throat, unbidden. I couldn't accept that this was she. This hollowed-out shell was not my sister.

"Raph." I turned, beseeching him. "Can you . . . ?"

He strode over to my side, folding his wings behind him as he kneeled and wiped the corner of his eye. "It would be an honor."

I placed a hand on his arm. "In Istanbul, in that alley, you told me that the girl we found there could not be healed. That she didn't want to be." I let my unspoken question linger between us. He looked at me solemnly.

"I can heal her physical wounds, Hope. But the emotional ones . . . the only thing I can offer is to make her forget."

I didn't hesitate. "Do it."

He bent down over her. Fearful, she shrank back against the wall, pulling Macey's lifeless body even tighter against her own broken body.

"Shhh," Raph soothed, prying her fingers away from Macey. "We'll take care of Macey, sweetheart. But first let me help you."

Carefully, he lifted Macey's body away and held it to the side. Without speaking, Michael took her, cradling her in his arms.

"Take her outside," Raph directed. "For this to work, Rorie can't see her again."

I watched as Michael bore her out of the room, a bloody sheet draped over her. Such a waste, I thought, tears welling up again.

I turned back to Rorie. Raph was placing hands on her, just as once he'd done for me, bringing the seams of all her broken places together again through his angelic powers of healing. I watched, relieved, as the bruises faded; the scabs melted into perfect, smooth skin; the red welts and swelling shrank back into themselves, as if nothing had ever happened.

"There," I whispered, pointing to the ugly, oozing brand on her arm. My fingers trailed against the Mark on my own neck. As much of it was a part of me now, I remembered all those years as a child, when the Mark was a cipher, a reminder of the past I could not remember, a sinister thing that claimed me, for what I knew not: a brand that separated me from everyone else.

"Get rid of it," I said.

And so Raph did, the trafficker's claim upon Rorie's body melting into her skin, smoothed over like new. Rorie barely registered any of it, except to let a soft sigh of relief escape her lips as her body basked in the first freedom from pain she'd likely had in at least a week.

"Close your eyes, Rorie," Raph whispered.

She let them flutter closed, her long brown eyelashes resting against her cheek. Gently, he placed his hands on her head and began muttering under his breath.

I recognized his words as prayer, and silently joined him, wishing fervently that this would work, that my sister—my sister, who had been put in such danger because of me—would find peace and comfort under Raph's healing touch.

"Hope, are you sure about this?" Tabby whispered urgently, pulling at my shoulder. "Are you sure this is what you want for her?"

I pushed away her hand. "Of course it is," I answered brusquely. "I don't want her to have to live under the shadow of this."

But then, as I watched Raph at work, I began to remember.

I remembered what it was like, having my memory stolen away from me, leaving me to box with shadows in the dark. I remembered the pain of being a girl without a past, and wondering what it might mean for my future. I remembered my anger when the truth was revealed to me, bit by bit, and realizing that my whole life was being directed by influences I couldn't name, let alone remember; my whole life a lie.

My mind raced. If Rorie couldn't remember, how would I explain our mother's absence? And Arthur's or Macey's? I would have to lie to her, over and over again. Until the day she found out on her own. And then, she'd never trust me again.

I couldn't do that to her. I couldn't take away her past. She needed it to be whole, just like I had.

"Wait." I placed a hand over Raph's. "Don't. Don't make her forget."

Raph tilted his head, examining me quizzically. "You're certain?"

I nodded once. "I'm sure. Just . . . just maybe take the edge off of the worst parts, if you can."

He reached over and squeezed my hand. Then, his face the picture of concentration, he returned his attention to Rorie, lying in his arms. His mouth moving silently, he prayed: ancient words that might not make Rorie forget, but would at least make it easier for her to heal and deal with her pain. When he was finished, he watched her intently, letting his hands sit for just a moment longer on her lank hair. Gently, he eased her down to the mattress, stretching her tiny body out and tucking the clean parts of the sheets around her.

"She'll sleep more comfortably this way," he said, his voice gruff. Patting my arm awkwardly, as if to comfort me, too, he rose. "She'll probably sleep for a full day if you let her. Plenty of time to get her away from here. You can use the time to figure out what comes next. For all of you."

I stood up with him and turned. Enoch was wiping his face with a hanky, tucking the corners of the dirty rag under his aviators to dab at his tears. Michael had slipped back in while Raph had been at work, and now he slid away from where he leaned against the wall, his face contorted with confusion, frustration, and disbelief. He knelt beside me, next to Rorie, and he drew something out of his armor and pressed it into her hands.

It was her agate.

He closed her fingers around it and held her hands, struggling with his emotions.

"You forgave Lucas?" he asked, turning to search my face. "You couldn't forgive me, but you forgave him?"

I knew how he must have felt; how deeply my last decision must have wounded him. I reached up and placed my hands on his face, one on each side. His eyes were dark with hurt—almost black—the pain in them just as raw as it was when he'd been wracked by the fear that he would hurt me, all those years ago. I swallowed hard, knowing it was my fault, knowing there was nothing to do now but apologize for what I had done. I wrapped my hand around his and pulled him to his feet.

"There was nothing to forgive."

I stretched on my tiptoes and drew his head to mine. I breathed in the scent of hay and honey, letting his warmth suffuse me and calm my fraying nerves.

"I love you. I'm sorry I doubted you. And I hope you can forgive me."

I pressed my lips to his, searching. My lips parted, and I sighed as our kiss deepened, all barriers between us melting away. I wanted to lose myself in him, my yearning for his touch so great it threatened to overtake me. I arched against him, pressing myself closer, pretending for just one moment that we were alone, and that for once there was nothing standing between us.

Reluctantly, I pushed away from his chest, the sudden rush of coolness as our bodies separated almost painful. He raised a questioning brow, still not understanding.

Damn, I thought. *I wish he wasn't wearing his armor.* I looked longingly at the place near his heart, placing one hand there against his steely breastplate, wishing I could speak to his heart directly, through our touch.

I didn't want to say it out loud. His azure eyes glimmered with a spark of joy and relief. I could barely stand to take that away from him, but I had to. I put my hands on his shoulders and squared my own to face him and tell him the truth.

"I can't go with you, Michael. Not now. Not ever."

I felt him stiffen under my hands. I looked back at Rorie again, steeling my resolve.

"She's gone through too much. Our mother is gone. I cannot possibly leave her here on Earth by herself." My voice broke, each word catching on my shattered heart. I pushed on, each word rushing faster from my mouth, hurrying lest I lose my resolve. "I wish I could, but I can't. And you can't abandon your duties. I know you don't want to. And you shouldn't—even with Lucas redeemed, his master and the other Fallen remain. So I know you can't. And I don't want you to. I could never live with myself."

A silent sob wracked my body. He stood quiet, unmoving under my hands, only moving to bow his head low, knowing that I spoke the truth. A perfect teardrop trickled from his eye, dangling from his nose for a moment before it fell to the floor.

"I'll do it."

I turned to see Raph standing before me, sword unsheathed. The flames were restrained, tiny ghosts of blue and orange that barely rose above the surface of the shiny metal.

"Michael didn't believe he could trust me to protect humanity in his absence," he continued. "And until now, he would have been right.

"But after watching you today, after witnessing your grace in forgiving Lucas—seeing how your act spurred him to accept God's own grace and regain Heaven the way he was meant to do—peacefully, and lovingly . . ." He paused. "Let's just say that perhaps I learned a little bit about humanity today too."

Raph fell to his knees, offering up his sword to me on the tips of his fingers.

"It would be a privilege to defend it in God's name. And in your honor."

Confused, I whirled and turned into Michael's arms.

"Can he do that?"

Michael's stunned face split open into a grin. "He can."

epilogue

They'd left the window open, a gentle Georgia breeze rippling through the curtains.

This time, though, there was no need to worry about the safety of the baby sleeping in the crib. The baby's safety had been purchased with the blood of too many fallen innocents, years before, by his parents' renunciation of the heavenly gifts that could have been theirs, if they had made a different choice. By the painful experience of his aunt—now only nightmares and memories.

Just in case, his godfather, Enoch, had split aces and beat the house in Vegas the night of his parents' wedding, claiming it would guarantee any future offspring good luck in years to come. They'd chosen Vegas partly out of haste, partly in homage to the first place they'd truly expressed their love for one another. For Enoch, it was simply a convenient stop on the way back to his duties. His banishment to the dead zones between Heaven and Earth had been lifted in recognition of the role he'd played in winning redemption for the Fallen. He was eager, now, to get back to the routine of his Library, documenting and filing away other prophecies and stories of the angels for future generations.

The baby's godmother, Tabby, not to be undone, had unleashed the powers of her congregation's full choir, their soaring Hallelujahs and Amens descending upon the baby's head while he wailed and flailed, unimpressed by his baptismal service and his godmother's fancy sermon. But the congregation had noticed and appreciated her words. It was said that when she preached now, she seemed to glow at the pulpit, lit from within by some special knowledge of God that nobody dared ask her about, but that all could see as plain as the nose on your face. Her congregation swelled along with her fame as a preacher. Phalanxes of sober-suited recruiting committees kept showing up, offering her a bigger church with more money, but she preferred to stay where she was. It was her home.

"He's beautiful, isn't he?" Hope asked, leaning over the crib to inhale her offspring's sweet baby smell.

Michael took her hand, his thumb running over the soft fleshy mount of her thumb. "He looks like you."

She laughed; her dog, Ollie, lying guard at the foot of the crib, wearily lifted his head to inspect the scene. His snout was gray with age now, but despite being a little decrepit, he took his guard dog duties very seriously.

"He doesn't look like anybody," Hope countered. "He looks like himself. He is his own little self."

"Not you, then. Your father, perhaps."

She tilted her head in acknowledgment. "That would be nice." Her mother, Mona, would have thought so, too. Her heart tugged at the thought of her mother, grateful that by marrying, she and Michael had fulfilled one of her mother's last wishes.

He pulled her in close, wrapping a hand around her hip. She rested her head against his shoulder and, just for a moment, let her eyes drift closed. She thought of all he had given up, the look of respectful awe that had settled into Raph's normally stern face and the look of skepticism on Gabrielle's as she had witnessed his renunciation of his own powers, choosing to embrace the fragile shell of the human body they all disdained. But the angels had stood as their witnesses, honoring, in the end, the choice he had made with a promise to watch them from afar.

Michael had made it seem easy, slipping into the relatively sedate job of a beat cop working the streets of Atlanta, the best way he could think of to continue with his work of protecting the innocent. She worried about him daily, but knew it was a small price to pay in exchange for the chance for them to be together forever. He was the final bit of glue that had enabled her to put back together the pieces of her family, bringing Rorie back from the brink of destruction, his love and attention helping to heal her wounds.

As if reading her thoughts, he spoke. "Rorie will be back soon, won't she?"

Hope smiled, thinking of the work her sister did with rescue dogs. It was good therapy for her—a place to relearn trust, a place to witness that wounded creatures can heal, a place where she could learn to get out of her head, so crowded with painful memories, and focus on something else, allowing her to forget. It had helped that Raph's touch had softened many of her memories, leaving the images of armor-clad angels and remembered beatings fuzzy and distant—things that could be dismissed as nightmares. Yet some things were too deeply etched in her mind to be anything but painful. Deep down, Hope worried that Rorie was still trying to make up for the fact that she could not save Macey—might spend her whole life trying to compensate for something she wrongly felt was her failing.

"You need your sleep," Michael admonished, not waiting for her answer, planting a kiss on her forehead.

"No," she protested weakly.

"C'mon, let's go. He won't be up for another hour or so," he insisted, pulling her gently away. "Rorie will want to see him then."

Reluctantly, she followed him to the door. Over her shoulder, she left one lingering glance on her baby boy as they closed the door behind themselves.

They were lucky, she thought to herself. So very lucky.

"Good night, Gabriel Luke," she whispered, closing the door behind her.

ACKNOWLEDGMENTS

There are so many people to thank as I bring *The Archangel Prophecies* to their close.

Behind every author is a host of "beta readers"—and I am no exception. A special thank you to Kemal Cetin, Jake Houle, Lorraine Houle, and Beth Melendez for their willingness to read early and multiple drafts, struggling through plot holes and crimes of grammar to help me make *Dark Before Dawn* much, much better. An extra special thank you, again, to Dr. Shami Feinglass, for her overall reading and for also checking my medical facts and terminology so that Mona's death and the injuries sustained by Rorie and Macey could be presented as accurately as possible. Any errors, of course, remain my own.

To Errol Williams—thank you for forwarding me the verse from Peter. You have no idea how cool I found it that you were thinking about my story "in between" books, and I am grateful you took the time to send me your thoughts. As you can see, it was perfect for this chapter in Hope and Michael's tale!

Thank you to the wonderful volunteers at ECPAT-USA, Street Grace, Georgia Cares, and International Justice Mission, particularly Sarah Porter, Carol Smolenski, Cheryl DeLuca-Johnson, Lisa Clark, Andi Worley, and Stephen Cushman; Dr. Tamara Mattison, the volunteers at Brittany's Place, and the family of Brittany Clardy; and Linda Miller and Civil Society. You welcomed me with open arms into your fight to end human trafficking and domestic minor sex trafficking, helped me to understand it as an industry and business, and aided me every step of the way as I strove to represent it and its victims fairly, accurately, and with empathy. If I have succeeded at all, and if I have raised any awareness of this modern-day scourge, it is because of you.

Thank you, as always, to my friends and colleagues at the Coca-Cola Company and Tyson Foods for all of their support.

Thank you to all the book clubs and teachers that have invited me into homes and classrooms. I am so honored when you do, and so gratified to hear your love of my characters and the questions my stories provoke. I take my responsibility to raise awareness about human trafficking very seriously, so I am especially moved when you use my books to teach. If I have inspired any of you or other readers to get involved, then I am grateful. If I have done so while still entertaining you with a compelling story, then I am doubly so! A special thank you to Jane Gilles, Mary Graham, Linda Heinze, Bob McElrath, Bill and Jill Somrock, and Dorothy Sunne—you are my teacher heroes, and your support of my writing has meant a lot! Another special shout out to Amanda Leddy for her continued partnership in developing classroom-ready curricular aids so that more teachers can more easily teach about human trafficking—you have a special touch and I couldn't have done it without you!

To my team at Greenleaf: Jeanne Thornton, editor extraordinaire—what fun it was to work with you as we brought Hope's story to its close! I really felt privileged to work with someone who so clearly understood my vision and helped me sharpen it at every turn. Tyler LeBleu, Lindsey Clark, Katherine Kiger, Chelsea Richards—thank you for the attentiveness and creativity you brought to this, the last installment of *The Archangel Prophecies.*

To my children: to Trey—thank you for proving me wrong and making me proud by showing me that a teenage boy could love and learn just as much from *The Archangel Prophecies* as a teenage girl; to Reagan, who "pre-approved" my plots—thank you for giving me clear critiques from the vantage point of my target audience, putting up with the over-protective tendencies that have emerged as I've learned more about DMST, and, most importantly, for serving as the inspiration for a strong, female-driven series; to John, who became my cabin-writing buddy as I pushed to get *Dark Before Dawn* over the finish line—thank you for your patience with your mother when she was distracted by her writing. You all make me proud, every day, and I am grateful for your love and support. To my loyal Labradoodle, Jack, who faithfully kept me company on many an early morning and late night while I wrote and inspired me to bring back Ollie. Finally, to my husband, Tom—for so many reasons, I couldn't have done it without you. Thank you. I love you.

Finally, to all my readers—your response to this series, and your overwhelming embrace of the movement to end human trafficking, in particular DMST, has been immensely gratifying. Your interest, enthusiasm, and encouragement kept me going in the toughest stages of writing, editing, and spreading the word. Thank you for your support and thank you, in advance, for all you will do to keep spreading the word about DMST so that we can end this modern scourge once and for all.

ABOUT MONICA MCGURK

Monica McGurk loves nothing better than to craft thought-provoking, multilayered stories, showcasing strong girls and women overcoming big challenges. Already a fan favorite, she received the 2013 TwiFic Fandom Undiscovered Gem award for *Morning Star*, her alternate ending to the *Twilight* series, written before the release of *Breaking Dawn*. Her first novel in The Archangel Prophecies trilogy, *Dark Hope*, was published in 2014, and *Dark Rising*, the second novel in the series, was published in 2015.

Readers can learn more about Monica's work and passions on her website at www.monicamcgurk.com.

AUTHOR Q&A

Q: *What is the significance of Aurora's name and the blessing ceremony in which the angels gift her with laughter, insight, strength and bravery?*

A: Aurora is the name of the Roman goddess of the dawn. As such, it references new beginnings—each dawn bringing a fresh start to the world. I thought it an appropriate name for the child that brings about a completely new stage in Mona's life—even more so given the play on the word "dawn" (a homonym for Aurora's dead father, Don). Interestingly, the goddess Aurora is sometimes considered the mother of the morning star, Lucifer, suggesting an interesting connection to the Fallen Angels if linked back to Christian mythology. Aurora is also the name of Sleeping Beauty, best known through the retelling by Walt Disney. In Disney's version of this classic fairy tale, her fairy godmothers give her the gifts of beauty and song; when Maleficent interrupts the christening and curses Aurora, the third fairy's gift is used to change the curse from death to a sleep that will only be broken by true love's kiss. In *Dark Before Dawn*, there are no fairies, but the angel soldiers bless her with their own gifts, gifts I considered more suitable for a strong heroine who would need to fight and defend herself—not wait for Prince Charming to arrive upon the scene! Throughout the story, careful readers will see Rorie putting these gifts to work.

Q: Is there any significance to the title of the novel, Dark Before Dawn?

A: This common phrase is used, quite simply, to mean there is always hope, even and especially when things are at their most desperate. It is commonly attributed to the English theologian Thomas Fuller, dating to 1650. It seemed appropriate for this novel, as the characters find themselves with seemingly no way out—no way for Hope and Michael to be together, no way for Rorie to escape unscathed—but manage, in the end, to find their way. And, again, I liked the play on the word "dawn" and its oblique reference to Aurora.

Q: Many readers may find Hope's treatment of Michael in this novel frustrating. Why, after all they have been through, would Hope still not fully trust Michael?

A: It is frustrating, isn't it? But this is an example of the literary device of *hamartia*, or the hero's fatal flaw. Hope's downfall, over and over again, is that she does not trust. It compels much of the action and consequences we see throughout the three novels that comprise *The Archangel Prophecies*. It would be out of character for her to become all-trusting, but hopefully readers can see that she is a little more self-aware about this tendency (especially after prompting from her friend, Enoch) and ultimately takes responsibility for it by the end of *Dark Before Dawn*.

Q: What does it mean that Lucas used to be God's shield, the role that Michael says can be Hope's if she chooses to join him in heaven?

A: I wanted readers to see that Lucas and Hope actually have something in common. Essentially, as Lucas describes his role in Heaven before the Fall, he was a legal advisor—poking holes in the illogical, misguided attacks upon God's majesty, whatever their source. Hope, of course, is herself a lawyer and at several points in the story we see her putting her legal training to good use. And Hope's potential "replacing" of Lucas gives added dimension to his dislike of her—unthinkable that a mere human could usurp his role!

Q: Did Michael actually cheat with Gabrielle? And if not, why did she let Hope believe he did?

A: No, Michael did not cheat with Gabrielle. Gabrielle, as we can see even as early as her appearance in *Dark Rising*, wants the Prophecy to be fulfilled so the Fallen Angels can be forgiven, but still sees humans as beneath angels. Her main goal is to keep Michael focused on his heavenly duties and, hopefully, shake the unseemly infatuation he has for Hope. She takes advantage of the situation she sees unfolding before her to sow the seeds of doubt in Hope's mind, letting Hope think what she might about her relationship with Michael. Knowing that distrust is Hope's biggest character flaw—and having predicted that it would lead to Hope's betrayal of Michael in *Dark Rising*—she knew exactly how to lead Hope astray. And it worked.

Q: The device of the trial was very surprising. Just why did you have Hope pursue this route in dealing with the angels?

A: I wanted to position Hope as the leader of this expedition—less reliant on Michael or the other angels than she was in *Dark Rising*. This was one way to accomplish it. It also was a throwback to the character of Henri—readers might remember how litigious he was, threatening to bring Michael to angelic court for violating his rights as a Guardian Angel—and some of the references Enoch made as far back as in *Dark Hope*.

Q: Lucas seems to be dismayed when he learns of Mona's death, just as he seemed to have mixed feelings about Triad's murder of Don. Why is that?

A: Even Lucas has his good points. Remember, he is an angel, with a complex character! In reality, he respects Mona and Don—two of the only humans whom he does respect—and treats them as fallen adversaries, worthy of honor. And at various other points in the story, readers can catch glimpses into his feelings and motivations—his underlying sympathy for animals, for example, when he challenges the gamblers who are abusing the dogs at the dog fights, and his pangs of sympathy when he realizes that Macey is still holding out hope that Luke will come to her. It is God's punishing pain that has twisted his psyche to be so hateful—something Hope realizes and uses to her advantage at the book's climax.

Q: *Beyond Aurora, whose birth is previewed at the back of* Dark Rising, *you introduce us to two new significant characters in this novel—Macey and Wanda. Tell us a little bit about them.*

A: Well, Macey is clearly here to illuminate the risks of domestic minor sex trafficking (DMST) and to portray how easy it is for a young girl to fall prey to the "recruitment" tactics typically used by traffickers and pimps. Her psychological fragility, her possible history of being abused (shown when she flinches at Mona's dinner table, thinking she is going to be hit for spilling her milk), her history of being food insecure and hungry, her low self-esteem—all of these are common risk factors for being lured into DMST. So, too, is her status as a foster child—there is a very high coincidence of foster care with DMST victimization. Importantly, this is not causal—it simply reflects the fact that many children winding up in foster care have already experienced great instability and vulnerability in their lives. The tactics Luke/Lucas uses to trick her—using food to manipulate her, promising her stardom, drugging her into dependence, and telling her that if "she really loves him, she will do it for him"—all of these are very common tactics used by traffickers and pimps. The situations she finds herself in—particularly the scene set at the truck stop—are also very common for victims of DMST. (There is a wonderful organization, Truckers Against Trafficking, which has done much to tackle this problem and play a proactive role fighting DMST at truck stops—interested readers should check them out on social media to learn more.)

Wanda plays a similar but complementary role. She is a little wiser as to what is going on, but still falls prey to trafficking when she chooses to run away and finds herself stranded and hungry at a bus stop. I wanted to include Wanda's character, in particular,

due to the vulnerability of the Native American community to sex trafficking, especially around the fracking centers. I first became aware of the particular problem DMST poses to Native American populations when meeting with activists and social service groups in the Minneapolis-St. Paul area.

Q: *Some of the scenes depicting what happen to Rorie and Macey are very difficult to read. Why did you include them, and how did you approach writing them?*

A: They were tough, weren't they? As I drafted the storyline for this novel, I went back and forth on just how much to share and from what point of view to write those scenes. Ultimately, for the story to be real and for it to be of use in raising awareness, I felt I needed to share what I had learned from listening to survivors' stories and include the pieces that ultimately made it into the book. The fact that some readers of *Dark Hope* and *Dark Rising* had actually questioned me as to why I glossed over some of it gave me the confidence to put a little bit more out there. Sadly, everything that happens to Macey and Rorie in this book has been documented in real instances of DMST—even the entrapment of girls in dog cages. Importantly, there are a few scenes referring to or interacting with "johns"—the men who abuse the young girls featured in this book. As a culture, we so often blame the victims, or focus on the pimps, and overlook the fact that there would be no DMST if there were not customers for it. We write it off as a rite of passage or boys being boys. I thought it was important to point out some of these cultural conflicts in portraying the issue.

All in all, I tried to portray DMST realistically without overwhelming the reader. The device of differing points of view gave me a way to deal with it that felt a little more comfortable and non-salacious.

That said, I would strongly encourage parents to read this *with* their teen children, and *discuss* it with them, so that it can be a useful teaching tool and conversation prompt.

Q: If readers are motivated to take action against human trafficking or DMST after reading this book, what can they do?

A: I would be thrilled if any reader decided to get involved after reading *Dark Hope, Dark Rising,* or *Dark Before Dawn.* For ideas on how to get involved, or to link up with my charitable partners at Street Grace and ECPAT-USA, readers can check out my website, monicamcgurk.com.

Q: Can you tell us about the key themes in this novel? Or throughout The Archangel Prophecies *in total?*

A: Readers will see that the entire story arc draws together the themes that have been threaded throughout the trilogy—hope and forgiveness, of course, being at the forefront, but also the question of identity. Hope's struggle to make her choice—to join Michael in Heaven, or to have him join her on Earth—is just as much about her understanding of her own identity as it is her concern for her family's safety. The idea that you are not what happens to you—best expressed by Rorie as she defies Luke—the idea of resilience, was very important to me. From the very beginning of the series, I wanted to visit and revisit this theme, especially for adolescent readers who are figuring out their own identities, testing them and trying them on for "fit," as they grow and mature.

Q: *You killed off a lot of great characters throughout this series— why is that?*

A: I wanted the characters of my story to experience realistic consequences for their actions, and for Hope, in particular, to experience real loss. Sometimes that is missing from YA. The greatest YA books, in my opinion, deliver on that.

Q: *Your last novel,* Dark Rising, *took readers to some very far-flung locations: Turkey, Ireland, and France. This time you stayed closer to home—why?*

A: I considered going to more remote locations for this final installment of *The Archangel Prophecies*. I even give those alternative locations a shout out in the form of Chen's dialogue—Brazil, China, and India. But I wanted the story to highlight the problem of domestic minor sex trafficking in the United States, and having Rorie and Macey trafficked out of the country was not as realistic as moving them around inside the United States. It was just what the story and the characters called for.

Q: *Can you tell readers a little more about those rejected locations?*

A: Sure! India is reported to have the greatest number of people living in servitude in the entire world—not surprising, given its total population. Kolkata, specifically, has a long history of selling its children. There is a whole city of brothels, a vast industry if you will, which women typically escape only through death, leaving their children, who are born into slavery, to repeat the cycle. It is ironic, I have always found, that in August in Kolkata you can find whole families in the streets, celebrating the festival of

Raksha Bandhan—brothers and sisters tying Rakhi red threads onto the wrists of their siblings, symbolizing the ties that bind, the women implicitly asking their brothers' protection. Brazil's entire northeast coastal area is notorious for child sex tourism. There is a *trabalho escravo*, a blacklist, if you will, of traffickers and pimps, but the police frequently turn a blind eye to the problem, which becomes particularly acute around periods of great tourism such as carnival or sporting events. China has a large problem, as well, perhaps best exemplified by the city of Dongguan—a "sin city" of nearly 300,000 sex workers that draws tourists from all over Asia. Under pressure, the government conducted raids a few years ago, but many observers report the traffic just temporarily shifted.

Q: What about the locations you do highlight in Dark Before Dawn—*are they real?*

A: Yes. Williston, North Dakota, is a real place, with a real problem that has been very well documented. It is starting to improve with the growth in available housing, but the social services and policing infrastructure has not yet caught up with the problem of sex trafficking. The Bluff, in Atlanta, Georgia, is also real. Its huge drug problem, and the remarkable efforts of local residents, social service groups, and churches to combat it, turning it into a livable neighborhood, have also been well covered in news coverage and documentaries. And the ADX in Florence really does function as a repository for some of the most dangerous criminals convicted in the United States. Interested readers can learn more about these locations by checking out my Pinterest boards on each.

Q: *You typically do extensive research for each of your books. For* Dark Rising, *for example, you actually traveled to two of the settings featured in the story. What kind of research did you perform for* Dark Before Dawn?

A: I researched each of the settings featured in *Dark Before Dawn* quite extensively, but one of the more interesting—and disturbing—pieces of research I conducted was my participation in a call center-based effort intercepting "johns" that were attempting to buy young girls advertised on backpage.com. I have to say, it was a real eye-opener, and I found myself very shaken by what I observed. The details surrounding the selling of Rorie and Macey, including the use of ads on backpage.com, emerged directly from that experience.

Q: *Will there be more books in* The Archangel Prophecies *series?*

A: No. For now, anyway, Hope and Michael's story is done. I prefer to let readers imagine their own "happily ever after"! But readers may be excited to know I am working on my next book—something a little more lighthearted but just as action packed, with the same promise of strong female characters.

Q: *Does the end of* The Archangel Prophecies *mean the end of your involvement in anti-DMST efforts?*

A: No. I don't think I will ever end my involvement in the fight to end the sexual exploitation of children, and human trafficking in general. It has become too much a part of my life, and there is still so much to do. So as long as there are great organizations that could use and want my help, I'll stay involved.